IKONA

M.D. DIXON

IKONA by M.D. Dixon
Copyright © 2026 by Liminalia Press

All rights reserved. No part of this book may be reproduced, stored in a retrieval system, or transmitted in any form or by any means—electronic, mechanical, photocopying, recording, or otherwise—without the prior written permission of the author, except in the case of brief quotations used in reviews or critical articles.

This is a work of fiction. Names, characters, places, and incidents are either the product of the author's imagination or used fictitiously. Any resemblance to actual persons, living or dead, events, or locales is entirely coincidental.

Cover design by Reymadness. Instagram @reymadness
ISBN 978-1-7643451-4-9
First edition
Published in the United States and other countries

PRAISE FOR IKONA

Threads of religion, mysticism, meditation, and past lives are woven throughout the narrative, giving this story a soul-touching, deep vibe ... A compelling and mind-bending SF story.

— *KIRKUS REVIEWS*

IKONA is a profound transmission—one that speaks to the heart more than the mind. Through poetic and multidimensional storytelling, M.D. Dixon weaves the invisible threads that remind us our souls are infinite, time is fluid, and our choices ripple across every timeline when we follow the resonance of the heart.

These concepts may feel natural now, but the world wasn't always ready to hear them. *Now is the time.*

Reading this book stirred something deep within me. I felt energy move through my body and tears rise without explanation, as if my heart was remembering a truth beyond words.

IKONA is a story of remembrance and empowerment: an invitation to choose love, balance, and healing even amidst chaos, and to trust the unseen as we walk into the unknown.

This book will open readers to a new way of understanding themselves and the profound interconnectedness we all share. It asks us—gently and courageously—to *feel with the heart, not the mind.*

— *KIRSTEN SNOBECK, AKASHIC GUIDE,*
KIRSTENSNOBECK.COM

IKONA left me delighted and deeply satisfied ... [with] storytelling propelled by a magnetic flow of narrative which never falters or slows...Amidst challenges to individuals and humanity alike, *IKONA* inspires hope and brings comfort.

— PETER ZAWAL, GOODREADS REVIEW

Dixon crafts an absolute masterpiece. I read *IKONA* in three sittings. This hypnotic novel is layered with meaning, mythic depth, and curiosity about time, memory, and what might bring humanity to a new world.

This story hums with momentum, calling together the most unlikely constellation of characters — a mystic, a monk, a sex worker, a thief, a shaman — and the people they have lost, loved, or are willing to risk everything for. The narrative moves through multiple, liminal, mind-bending timelines held in perpetual suspense ...

A visionary novel that gestures toward a utopian potential rooted in connection, courage, and remembrance. I finished the final pages stunned with insights, eager to return, knowing there is more waiting within the pages.

— PRAJNA O'HARA, AUTHOR OF EDGE OF GRACE, FIERCE AWAKENINGS TO LOVE, HTTPS://PRAJNAOHARA.SUBSTACK.COM/

Dixon's debut novel *IKONA* reads like a culmination of one's well-earned life experiences. The epic story is filled with relatable, full-bodied characters and a page turning plotline motivated by courage and fulfilling one's destiny. Dixon has an exceptional ability to funnel heavy esoteric concepts through a medium of storytelling to produce an experience that not only helps you to understand universal truths but leaves you thinking deeply about your purpose in life. I saw an aspect of myself in each character and found myself constantly thinking about where their story would lead. I would highly recommend to anyone to give this book a chance!

— MICHELLE NOWLAND, INSTAGRAM
@MICHELLENOWLAND

IKONA is not a truth embedded in a story but rather a story woven through a truth. I felt something reading *IKONA* - something deep and inexplicable, like an awakening, and it only grew and intensified as the story unravelled and surfaced to its own awakening. I bawled my eyes out reading the last few chapters. I was overcome by a mixture of grief, love, relief, and something else I cannot put words to. Dixon's writing lands in your mind like poetry. I cannot choose a character I loved more than another. *IKONA* is brilliantly heartwarming, equally heartbreaking, and funny in all the right moments. It takes you to so many places in time, and so many places in yourself.

— *HANNAH, GOODREADS REVIEW*

Such an amazing book. I literally couldn't put it down! I don't usually read fiction, but the time-slip, action and humour kept me engaged whilst the spiritual message for our times embedded in the story moved me in a completely unexpected way, with 'The Bridge' becoming my favourite chapter.

— *RALPH YOUNG, GOODREADS REVIEW*

For those who remember.

*Each of us walks a timeline
shaped by the sound of our soul's note,
and within the song,
we are all dreaming
the same dream.*

PRELUDE

"I know who you are," he said to Finley, who at once felt a presence awaken within him.

And as he expanded into the space, a calmer, more determined energy emanated then, within which, unprompted, love announced itself, as if it were him.

He had the thought, "Who am I? What is this?"

But he was nothing if not practical, "I have already read the novel twice," he said.

Gutov laughed. "With your heart, or with your head?"

"I don't know," Finley replied, quite helpless.

"Let's sit here for a while on this rock then."

So they sat where the water lapped the shore, and allowed for Truth to be felt, at last.

– *Before the Bridge*

PART I

PROSTITUTE, MYSTIC, MONK, THIEF

I accept time absolutely.
   It alone is without flaw -
   it alone rounds and completes all;
   That mystic, baffling wonder I love,
   alone completes all.
   ~Walt Whitman, "Song of Myself"

And you?
   When will you begin that long
   journey into yourself?
   ~Rumi

1

FINLEY & THE SEA

MAY 2019

SYDNEY, AUSTRALIA

Finley Minor was by his own accounts an empty man, a listless man, spiritually and emotionally sparse. Blink a thousand times and his course in life would not have shifted an inch. He was motionless like a chameleon in the presence of a threat. But this was not fact, only fear, and that of a man who knew that he'd not lived at full throttle and had succumbed to the fate of it—a slow and shallow life. He ruminated on it. He judged himself for it. He laughed at his own expense, without thinking he might ever change a thing.

In the way one always has a beginning, a *great excuse*, this was Finley's: at the age of seven, in his native England, he sat on the beach as his stick wove tessellations in the sand (almost of its own accord, it seemed in retrospect), and he looked to the horizon towards France with the open, impressionable curiosity of his young age. He wondered at the sea's depth, its great distance, how one might (as many had) swim across the channel, what creatures might lurk there, what they might feel like against bare skin. He imagined something slimy and cold, fanged, and slithering. The waves seemed to roar at him, even though they descended in the rockpools with the gentleness of pooling cream.

He stood, determined to satisfy his curiosity. He took halting steps over the rocks and shells, straight ahead, then bearing left around a rock face that jutted into the sea. He sat on a big, flat rock and stared into the gray water. He heard his father calling out his name, but ignored him. The water rushed in again and again, and each time reached further and further, first sucking at his toes, then his heels, then his knees. His curiosity fled; he became afraid, and all sound was magnified, the dull ocean roar, the seagull squawking a few feet away, his heartbeat. He knew he had to go back to shore. He waved to his father, stood, and took a faltering step. There was a low murmur; the water fizzled once more in retreat from the rocky sand like the gasping breath of a dying man. He felt dizzy and fell to his knees. He crouched on all fours and steadied himself as the water swirled and grasped at him, and the sky looped and the clouds fell from the corner of his eyes. He felt his head winched back towards the horizon, and the sea reached for his throat. Blackness.

When he came to, dragged back to shore by his father, he announced that his aunt would never return from her Côte D'Azur holiday. He wagged his finger towards the surf and pulled a face, "Over there, there is smooching."

The official prognosis was that he'd had an epileptic fit, though none of the tests proved it. He must have passed out, in that case, the doctor pronounced, low blood sugar, a low-level virus, dehydration.

But Finley knew, only he knew.

The ocean had rent a hole in his soul, and let in the future.

HE MADE HIS SECOND PREDICTION, without preamble, at age twelve, as he fingered his Game & Watch and sucked on a liquorice. "Computers will get smaller and smaller and one day people will carry them around in their pockets and send secret messages to each other through the air like radio waves."

It was a year before the first smartphone, but years before anyone in his world owned one. No one responded to his prediction then or for years afterwards. It felt to Finley that he and his parents merely coexisted, on occasion bumping up against each other like marbles trapped in a jar.

He also said, weeks later, that Aunt Madge would finally move home from France, next week, five years after she left. At that his parents raised their eyebrows, a discernible reaction at least. But the next week, Madge was back, single again, crying over love, standing in their living room with a tattered suitcase and smudged mascara and a lasting disdain for truffles and Camembert. At which point Finley's father said, over dinner that night, after his aunt had retired to her room early, "Didn't you say something about little devices, sending messages...?"

"Just a thought, Dad."

"Like the one you had about Madge?"

Finley shrugged. He took note of his father's unshaven face, his calloused hands—proof of weekend gardening, tinkering in his garage, respite from office work. Sales. His father's world was the company. He thought in outcomes, measurable and saleable.

"You could be one of those people who predicts trends, you know. You could trade in the stock market."

"Sure."

"You would be very useful to the world in that way." His father spooned soup with one hand and read *The Times* with the other. His mother's fork clinked against the plate as she skewered gray broccoli with chunks of steak. She stared at her only child.

"That's rather spooky," she pronounced, a frisson of childlike delight lolling off her. Finley would eventually conclude that she was one of those middle class women who had cocktail parties over Ouija boards, or held séances. He never mentioned such things again, even when she gave him a quartz crystal on a leather band when he turned sixteen and told him to write down his dreams. He was having nightmares at the time, lines and whorls and sea urchins arrayed in mathematical formulas across the sand under the dark whining of an approaching cyclone. He often woke up in a cold sweat, in a damp patch; his father had a quiet word with him about wet dreams. No one mentioned his strange ability again.

Finley blamed his predicament on the ocean, for its roar that rent his soul, allowing in the future on its terms. He knew something he shouldn't know: that he had only partial control over his life. It was more like a multiple choice experience. Much was predetermined. He did not see all of the future because he mentally slammed the door—though he cracked it open sufficiently to catch glimpses now and again. A few things slipped through according to his stern will—he willed his vision be fastened to investments. He profited well.

But he was too afraid to throw the door wide open. He knew that his future was like a wavering line untangling into the distance. Whatever parts of it he couldn't see nevertheless existed. At seven years of age he'd foreseen his own demise as he gazed into a jar of 255 jelly beans at a fair, but had chosen to block out the memory. Fate awaited him, so nothing much mattered.

So NOW, this. This dull present, like any other day. The sun blinked behind a cloud as Finley turned onto Market Street, into a crowd of gray and black-clad pedestrians, into their clatter of high heels and shiny leather boots. Under cloud cover the city was washed of color, overbright in shades of gray and white. He loosened his paisley tie, the ridiculous, fat cravat pushed onto him by the David Jones assistant who had persuaded him to buy the more expensive suit. He tried motivating himself to waltz into his job with an aura of confidence. He had emigrated from London for this job. He had placed his hopes in the hands of this particular fate, a career analyzing and predicting market trends. He was good at it. It was satisfying. Yes, it was a combination of fate and foresight, that sliver of vision left open. So it was that he had millions invested and owned property, which accomplishment—and value—he dismissed. He had an innate drive to be normal which compelled him to continue in his profession, year after year. He also had little notion of what else he would do if he weren't working day after day.

As he turned the corner he saw Clare sitting at the café on the bottom floor of the building where both she and Finley worked. She sat at their favorite outdoor table, where they often met in the morning for a coffee. She waved when she saw him and smiled, all at a blurry, hopeful distance. He smiled, too. Then for a microsecond he detected in himself *certainty*—as in, "There she is! The love of my life!" But as he came closer, he saw that it was only Clare, his longtime girlfriend.

Clare. Sounds like *clair*, French for "clear," a sensible match for Finley, clear like Finley's dreamless mind, like Clare's innocent soul, like Finley's conscience (he reasoned that listless men rarely offend and thus he had no guilt). She was a good person, and clever. Her ambitions compensated for Finley's lack thereof, and she was supportive. He would go so far as to say she was faultless in any way which really counted—everyone had foibles, of course, irritating mannerisms, annoying habits, but her character was impeccable. He stood at the table, his heart ready to reach out to this emerald-eyed beauty, that her light might pull him to her, that they might journey into the future together. Then Finley saw that Clare's eyes were red, that her smile had vanished. He sat.

A brief, luminous ray of sunlight broke through the clouds, alighting on Clare's hair, irradiating strands of burgundy and orange and pale blond. Finley wanted to touch a strand of her hair.

"I've been transferred. To Melbourne."

Her mug was smudged with pink lipstick, her lips pale and taut. The sun clung stubbornly to flames of rigid curls at her neck. He waited for her to go on. The sky blackened and he felt a drop of rain. Now was not the time to speak, he realized. He wanted to take her hand from her lap, to feel her cool fingers, to kiss them—that was normal—but she pulled away as if in anticipation. He hadn't seen her for two days now, nor had they spoken on the phone, but that was not terribly unusual. He considered, for a moment, that he should have known she was being transferred.

"When did you find out?"

"I've known for some time. I'm sorry, Fin. I know it's not brilliant timing."

He watched her hair glow deep purple, then darken in the shade.

There were crumbs on the table. He wiped them off into his palm. He noticed, without looking closely, that her focus had shifted, her neck craned away. He knew: this was not about her transfer. She was dumping him.

Was this supposed to happen, he wondered, when there was nothing wrong with the two of them? He suddenly remembered how Clare had once said he was like a pre-modern man crashing through the jungle, aware only of his own primal needs.

"It's about me, isn't it," he stated.

She did not look at him and said, matter-of-fact, as if she'd been rehearsing it, "It's just not enough, what we have."

"Is it that I'm not ambitious enough for you? Do you think something is wrong with me?"

"No, you're just you. You're not a go-getter, Fin, that's okay. Melancholy is fine. It's how you operate, I understand."

He opened his mouth intending sarcasm, but caught himself on defensiveness. "Melancholic people *used* to be treasured, you know. In the 19th century melancholia had an aesthetic quality to which one aspired. Keats wrote a poem about it. My kind were considered special, Clare."

"Special." Her mouth was a straight line, a smudge of red jam near her lip. She licked her lips and pushed her hair back over one shoulder. She lay a hand on the newspaper on the table, and folded back the edge.

"Special. Because melancholy was seen as a state preceding Divine transformation. It was believed that to experience melancholia was symptomatic of a sort of 'dark night of the soul' that indicated a person was about to have a revelatory meeting with God."

"Or a melancholic person could, perhaps, take a turn for the worse."

"Yes, that, too. You never know." The waitress caught his eye and he shook his head no; he didn't want anything now.

"So it could go either way for you, Finley."

"I'm not looking to *go* anywhere, Clare. I'm not saying I'm in that category of melancholics. I'm just saying...it isn't always a bad thing to not be entirely normal."

Clare sighed.

"I hate it when you do that. It isn't communicating anything at all."

She shrugged. "Maybe you're just a realist, Fin. Let's face it. Life, by and large, for most people on the planet, sucks. So who am I to care if you lack jollity."

"True. Who needs to be jolly, you mean like Santa Claus? Like Anthony Robbins?"

A corner of her mouth turned up, but she didn't seem to want to say anything else, which was a relief to Finley. She cared, though, clearly she did care.

He watched her worried eyes unfocus, blur, shift into her depths. When she picked up the paper and started to read, he studied her intently. He took her hand from her lap and kissed it. She smiled, kept reading. He couldn't find what he was searching for. For an unsettled instant he saw her features melt together, a Salvador Dali pastiche. A mask, a mirror.

He should have known. He should have seen his own emptiness in her reflection and considered that no one would choose it.

He would not remember later if he said anything in response, in defense of them both, if he said anything at all. But he would never forget what Clare said next. She seemed to penetrate his mind, into its furthest reaches, to see into his deepest self and withdraw the sharpest object.

"Fin, I need to find my way to shore. We're like two little boats out to sea. And one of us is sinking."

She left him at the table. She went into their building and he sat across from her empty seat, hands mutely folded in his lap.

SHE MEANT HIM, of course. Clare would never sink. She was light. She held on in the most turbulent waters, and not just metaphorically. He knew; he had gone sailing with her. Just the weekend before last, two weeks ago. Clare could stand as the boat bumped and rocked. She was standing at his side and there he was, drinking a beer, sitting at the back as Phil—probably his only friend in Sydney—complained about his latest trying client. The wind picked up, the glassy harbor turned choppy, and suddenly the benign boats floating past all around were on a collision course with each other. Phil asked Finley to help redirect the sails, then a sudden current of air tilted the yacht at an angle. Finley lost his balance and saw the water gaping up towards him, saw its merciless volatility, and felt Phil's hand on his arm just as their sailboat collided with another. He was thrown into the water, knocked sideways by the cold, hard surface; saltwater poured into his mouth as he fought to surface, going numb.

Clare and Phil pulled him in. She held him as he vomited over the side. He registered, beneath the tang of brine, that she smelled of soap, that her skin was soft, and how her warm hand pressed between his shoulder blades. Her hair was pulled back and hidden beneath her wide-brimmed hat, which, he couldn't help but notice, had not shifted an inch. Finley swam in and out of consciousness for endless minutes before the pain in his head, the massive swollen lump, brought him searing to life.

"Close call," Clare said gently. She took a towel from Phil and draped it over his front.

Phil spoke. "Wind, mate. They were just kids, couldn't control themselves."

"I'm fine."

For the remainder of the outing, he sat on the bottom of the boat, wrapped in a woollen blanket, sipping Perrier.

The sea's indifferent, cold stare began to haunt him from that moment. Finley tried pretending the incident meant nothing—it was after all so minor, who should imagine it would affect him so? He hadn't rung Phil since. Every evening, when his mind and body relaxed, usually after dinner, or dozing at his desk at work, he could feel the wind sweep him into the sea, feel the impact of cold water and the crack as his head hit the side of the boat. Then his imagination took him deeper, on a slow, solemn descent to the ocean floor. In his mind his surrender was complete: nature always had the better of man and now it had shown Finley Minor his greatest weakness.

IN THE CAFÉ, now alone, even as it began to drizzle, his hand moved to the lump on the back of his head, concealed by his thick, brown hair. It still throbbed. Probably that wasn't normal. Anyway, what did Clare mean, how was he sinking? His thoughts turned to the dark, murky ocean depths and his toes instinctively curled to grip the solid earth. She meant his course in life. She was referring to his lack of direction, and the pathetic dead end that awaited him. Even now. Even with his glorious job waiting for him ten floors up. She saw right through his career to something more essential, to the unchanging pattern of his soul cast like a shadow to the ground.

An hour later, by which time he was forty-five minutes late for work, Clare appeared again. She emerged from the building with a crate full of office things: manila folders and papers half protruding, a clock, a photo frame. She gave him a wan smile.

"Finley," she said in a peculiar, haunted tone, as if speaking from an inaccessible past.

"I'm late." He stood up.

Maybe he would call her later, he suggested, to which she replied, "Don't"—she was getting on a plane that afternoon to stay with her sister in Melbourne until she found a place of her own.

Bewilderment gave way to emptiness—he did not feel sorrow, only a kind of meaninglessness, as if he'd lost his point of reference.

His mobile phone rang; he ignored it. It was his office. He quickly sent a text that he had a horrendous bout of gastro, and would be in the next day. Then he turned off his phone. He began to walk. The drizzle turned to downpour and as his pace quickened, all hope washed from him, pouring in torrents down the gutters. He went down Market Street and then Pitt Street, not bothering to cover his head or face. The urban throngs had dispersed for cover, but not he. He was consumed by the compulsion to keep walking. His hair dripped into his eyes so that he had to tilt his head down and could just barely see where he was going.

Quite abruptly, he stopped in front of a café and went in to order a latte. The barista made some comment about Finley's soggy state, whereupon he registered that everyone else was dry, all hovering in the doorway, crowded around the bar, watching the downpour. It gave Finley some small comfort to know that he, alone, had braved the storm. Whatever else one might say about his lack of initiative, Finley thought, at least he was no conformist.

He left in advance of the others in the café, while it rained still, and felt a thrill as he removed his sodden suit jacket and felt a touch of pleasure as the sun penetrated the clouds and heated his skin through his wet shirt. He walked towards Circular Quay, around the moored boats and the cafes spilling into the foreshore, up and around towards the white sails of the Opera House, where he sat on the steps and watched the ferries plowing the gray waters.

A week after the boating accident, he'd gone to sit on the beach at Manly, hoping that others' enjoyment of the ocean would be infectious. He walked up to the surf and stepped in, up to his ankles in warm, wet sand. The sound of the crashing waves resounded like cannon fire. His throat constricted and he stumbled back to his towel, his mouth like cotton wool.

Now he made his way home from the city by foot, through Hyde Park, down Oxford Street, into Woollahra, down towards the water and his apartment block. On his balcony, much later, dusk enveloping the grey-blue eucalypts, he surveyed the brilliant swath of blue visible over the treetops. He had bought this flat expressly for the view, to bear witness every day to his new life, and now it only made him think of drowning, and of Clare.

He needed to change. He had to—he would, he decided, look deep into his fear and conquer it. He would cease being so afraid of the future, how it came to him with its messages, without warning. He would live with *forward motion*. It was the best description to his mind; it conveyed something like *conviction*. Finley Minor sat where he always sat in his living room, looking at the unvarying, sparkling vista, and formulated his first plan for evolution in his entire life: tomorrow he would find help.

His initial twenty-four hour journey from London to Sydney was an airborne tracing of the British Empire's expansion East. He changed planes in Singapore, and then rising over the manicured Botanic Gardens, he left cultured colony for convict settlement, feeling unmoved by the deserted red center below, by the rushing white sands of shoreline. Sydney was unconstrained adolescence, addicted to espressos and trussed in business suits and black frocks. It was everything he was not and did not want to become, but within whose mirage a man of the Old World could walk invisible. Which suited him; he lived so as not to be seen.

Now he seemed to be avoiding *seeing*. The day after the breakup, he rode the wave of his previous conviction to find help even as he resisted. He called in sick to work but went into the city anyway, fumbling his way through the city streets trying not to notice every single sign, advertisement, or listing for all manner of therapy, self-help, or alternative medicine, though in fact, he noticed just that: acupuncture, Scientology, counseling, Chinese herbal medicine, aromatherapy, hydrotherapy, hypnotherapy. The hypnotherapy brochure he grabbed from the health clinic in Darlinghurst listed "conquering fears" on its therapeutic menu, so he went in and made an appointment for the next day before he had a chance to change his mind.

Still, the next day he attempted to find all manner of excuses not to go, and, as that had failed, to leave once in the waiting room. It took every fiber of his being to remain glued to his seat. He cast a cynical gaze over the gossip magazines with their skeletal glamor and neverending celebrity relationship crises. When Barbara, the middle-aged hypnotherapist with the 1950s style cat-eye glasses, called his name, he followed her obediently. He crossed his legs and sat in an armchair at one end of a Persian carpet, drinking water with nervous gusto, noticing her stockinged leg, crossed at the ankle, bob up and down.

"So you just ended a relationship. And you're afraid of drowning."

He nodded. He'd said as much on his booking form. Her glasses rose at the upper corners; it gave her a slightly evil look which was transformed by her indulgent, almost bored smile, at which his motivation for coming fizzled away like oil in a pan. He frowned. He felt sheepish, attempting to fathom what kind of fool he'd devolved into, to be visiting a hypnotherapist.

"Are they related, the event, and the fear, do you think?"

He drew breath sharply. There was a faint ache at his chest; discomfort, guilt—likely it was regret that he'd come.

"I've made that connection, yes. You think it's some kind of metaphor? That I'm afraid of intimacy? I don't think I am. I've had plenty of relationships."

"Mmm."

"Okay. I've had lots of relationships, none of which have lasted terribly long."

He tried to think of an appropriate joke, some sarcastic remark, perhaps even witty. In the face of her solemn frown, her summing up of his character, he felt water wash over him, and closed his eyes against the mortification. Fear, a certain social discomfort—two shades of gray, indeterminate, and they pulled him into black.

Barbara spoke. "Let's not jump the gun, Finley. You came for hypnotherapy. Let's take a look at the fear, which is your inner life, and the part of you I can work with. I can't help you with relationships."

She flashed him a row of white, a pink gum, mouth wryly upturned, eyes lifting in surprise.

"Does that sound okay?"

"Sure."

He was willing to try anything now, since he was there. He purposely did not inspect the environment, and only focused on her desk, and the outline of her form. He felt relieved, if that were possible, to agree to her terms. To let her take the reins from him.

"Your fear of water must have some origin, and as a hypnotherapist, that is what I can help you find, and release. So let's begin with relaxation."

"Just like that."

"Were you expecting more?"

"I had no expectations."

"This is hypnotherapy, not talk therapy."

"Okay. Let's carry on then."

She drew a hand across her hair, a blondish-gray bob, severely cut to align with her cheekbones, and crinkled her nose, then steadied her glasses. Finley noted the blond-brown grains of wood in the desk, the lacquer finish, the small group of items arrayed at her telephone: watch, photo frame, paper weight, pencil case. She cleared her throat and asked that he close his eyes and relax, told him that this would take time, and practice, and would begin now.

The air stirred, cool at his forearms; a window was open. He heard a car horn honk outside, and Barbara's suggestions to breathe deeply, to feel his feet relax, his legs, his groin, numbness moving up. As he focused on her words, he also reflected—how strange this was, how clichéd, in actual fact, to follow her suggestions so willingly, to allow himself to relax because she said so. Yet there was little resistance, and in some way, this felt natural, bending to guidance, going deeper and deeper, into *what* he didn't comprehend—and yet the feeling he had was of sinking, further and further down into some blank abyss. As if his thoughts were coalescing into a pinprick, and that pinprick, balanced so precariously on his worried, self-tortured thoughts, was descending through his brain with the single-minded smoothness of a needle through fabric, pulling the tattered immaterial clothing of himself down with him until he sat, in the calm of a dusk glow, alone and far from conscious life.

There was no sense of Barbara's voice, but his mind glided along as if tethered, pulled into a gathering storm of water. He registered with surprise his small, boyish hand, noted how normal it felt that he should be there again, fully present within a past long gone. And then, there was the sky descending, his hand scratching at the rock, his father calling for him, the acuteness of his terror as the clouds turned inside out and his soul was sucked through an aperture of time. He heard the laughter of wind pushing back against his fear, and he wound his way towards mist until he came upon the luring orange glow of sky.

Coming towards him was a black man in long, brown robes, and Finley could see into his mind as if it were his own. No sooner had the thought occurred than he experienced that he *was* that man, and all was perfectly normal, as if he'd never left, as if he'd always been him. Within the static of his thoughts, fuzzy but held aloft as if by sheer determination, hovered the image of an antique cross.

2

JIA LI: KNOWLEDGE NOT PROOF

MAY 2019

HONG KONG

Jia Li stood on the rocks and threw her chewing gum into the frothy ocean. The fog had swept down from the mountains and hid her from the world, so without inhibition she crept to the very edges.

The thought of ending it all mesmerized her. As her bare toes gripped the rock, she swayed, closed her eyes, and imagined the sensation of blissful surrender. Maybe it would be just like the seconds before orgasm, when nothing can stop the rush. Or like on a rollercoaster just as it begins to plummet from the steep climb, a surge of adrenaline before the fear catches up. She imagined that she'd be breathless for a moment, that maybe there would be a few seconds of fear or pain, but then the ocean's rhythm would soothe her; the current would pull and release and lull her to rest, like being rocked in a mother's arms. She imagined she would place her gold bikini on the rocks as testimony, and a single flower, along with her wooden placard, "Knowledge not proof."

Disappearing in any form was, in this instance, a meditative thought, so as she indulged it she closed her eyes and breathed into her belly. And since Jia Li was practiced at stilling her mind, she rapidly sank into herself, into the calm at the center of her despair, sinking to where her pink gum must lie covered in sand. Soon the ocean and the city did both disappear, and she was neither this nor that, here nor there. She just was, and in that final place life peeled itself back to its essence. She was a dreamer and an insomniac, a thief and a scientist, an introvert and a performance artist. Her English father had called her Jelly. Her signature was *Jia Li* written in both Chinese script and English on the programs for her shows when she stripped down to nearly nothing and stood on the stage, then suspended herself from the ceiling in Shibari. From her essence now she slipped into *I AM*, and became all of it and the part of her that was Jia Li simply rested, taken by an internal rhythm.

It never quite lasted long enough.

In this instance, Sam found her. It wasn't the first time. She heard the swishing of leaves and the crunching of branches as he pushed through from the track before he suddenly appeared through the treeline, sweating and shouting her name. She kept her back to him and continued her meditation—although clearly it was over. He took small steps down the rocks until he was beside her. He sat. Like a gorilla in a dress shirt. His muscles stretched his shirt so taut across his chest that the top buttons strained. He couldn't quite get his legs straight. It looked like his pants might burst at the seams.

"Here *again*? Baby? What are you doing? C'mon, Jia Li. We're late. Dinner, remember?"

He put a hand on her arm, gently, then an arm around her shoulder, and pulled her to him. Still, she ignored him.

"Why do you do this? It's kind of... morbid."

"It's peaceful, actually," she said. "I feel closer to him."

He cleared his throat and spat onto the rock. So ungraceful, Jia Li thought. But his hand remained on her shirtsleeve, light as wind, and his eyes softened. He kissed her shoulder.

"Babe?"

"Coming."

"I worry about you here all by yourself."

She kissed his hand. He was soft, her criminal lover.

"You just worry about yourself Sam Lai, missing me."

He grabbed her hand and pulled. "Not fair, but okay. C'mon. It's a dinner. No big deal, but it means a lot to me."

"I know you like me on your arm." She smiled.

She felt safe on his arm, there was that. And he accepted her, there was that, too.

"You make me look better, no question." He laughed.

They began walking back up the rocks and down the track together. Sam placed a hand on her back. "You are too accommodating, Jia Li. Life is a battle, so just fight it. Don't give up. Keep going. And I'll fight with you."

"I wasn't going to jump. And I'm not giving up."

"You say that, and I kinda believe you. But then you go missing every few weeks and I find you here. You can't let them win. You should let me help you."

She chided him. "I'm not here because I'm hiding, Sam. I'm here to find peace. And I can't let you help me because of my mother, you know that's why."

He took her hand to help her climb over a rock. She was barefoot and carrying high heels. "She won't be in danger, I promise!"

"No one is safe, Sam. Look what they did to your arm. You don't think you'd get worse if you interfered in my shit, too?"

He held up his arm and rolled up a sleeve to reveal the blood soaked bandage between his elbow and his wrist. "What, this?" He laughed. "It was just a test. If I do what they ask, it will be taken care of, fast. You can't even imagine what's going on."

"Some test. It needs stitches. It's deep, Sam. You need to get to a hospital."

"It will heal fast, believe me. You'll be amazed."

"That's a weird thing to say. It's still bloody. What, they're going to stitch it up for you? The Triads have their own doctors now?"

He kissed her cheek. "It will be taken care of soon. My point is, about your problem, there is nothing to risk. I can make them stop."

Ji Li sighed. "You can't, okay? You have no idea how deep and complex their network is. Nor do I. If they could do this to my father... Honestly, they'd threaten my mother next. Seriously, Sam. Think straight. Stalemate sucks but it's safer."

Their mutual attraction was underpinned by this particular negotiation. Secretly, she liked his readiness to fight for her, even if she assessed the inherent dangers and rejected it.

They trod the rest of the track in silence. It was a hot day, and a Tuesday, and not very busy. For the next twenty minutes they walked. Finally, as the path ended in concrete, Sam reached a hand into his pocket and pressed the button to unlock his Lexus.

"How long did it take you to walk here, anyway?" he asked Jia Li. "And how were you planning on getting home? You know you're crazy coming out here barefoot and in that dress."

Ah, her slip of a red dress. She'd forgotten she had it on. She'd come straight from her show, exhausted, sweaty, her face mascara-streaked from tears. She never planned to come here. Her mood just dragged her down after the performance high of her show and she found herself taking a taxi to Sai Kung, walking up the familiar path and then off the track to the spot.

The police had told her where to find it, only after she'd nagged them for GPS coordinates.

"It took as long as it took." She smiled wryly. "And there's a bus back, FYI."

He grinned and pulled her to his chest with his good arm. "You're crazy cute," he said.

Crazy he often called her. It was no joke. He did consider her to be a little unhinged. Jia Li found it amusing, since he found her supposed craziness so endearing. *Let him think I'm a bit nuts*, she thought. She didn't want him to fully appreciate the position she was in. It would only increase the risk of him taking matters into his own hands.

"Please, I'm sweaty, don't." She pushed against him as he bent down to her, nuzzling into her neck. Honestly, she just didn't like the smell of him right then, the cologne, the crisp dress shirt.

But he kissed her anyway as she pouted and pushed him away.

"Let's just go," she said and got into his car. Sam got in the driver's seat and started the engine, but he sat, letting the air con run, saying nothing for a few moments.

"What happened today, anyway? That made you come here? You seem more upset lately or something."

Upset or something. Jia Li didn't know if she was impressed he'd noticed, or annoyed that that's *all* he'd noticed. She sighed. He gently took her hand. She wished in that moment that she could feel more—more love, more *in love*, more connection.

"They were at my show today. The tall skinny white one, and the short Chinese one. They just stared at me like dead fish. And when it was over, when I was packing up, they said, 'Nice show, Jelly. Bet your mum's real proud of you.' It was a threat, Sam. They are threatening me. Fuck them."

Sam growled. He shook his head, as if angry, then let go of her hand and gripped the steering wheel so tightly his knuckles went white.

"It's okay. I'm used to it, I guess," she said.

"If I know you, you'll go do it again next week, because you're my brave girl. But if you want, I will send someone and..." He lifted a curled fist and grimaced. "Yeah, I know." He rolled his eyes. "Your mum."

"Thanks for the offer."

"Okay, babe. Let's get going. Let's be nice and have a good meal. Forget about it for the night." He reversed and put the radio on. He put a hand on her knee, a full stop to their conversation.

"Can you just drop me home so I can shower and change? You can wait in the car for me."

"Sure thing. That's a great idea."

They tore off into the pink and purple Hong Kong dusk, the softened edges of bright towers just visible in heavy smog. Their silence was comforting, until Jia Li's hopelessness began once more to simmer at her diaphragm. Week after week she breathed life in through this inner death as she sat in meditation by the rock where her father had leapt—at least that was the official report. Whoever had 'the proof,' it was not her, but somehow, just in living her life, she was defending it anyway. Her existence reduced to this nonelective act, coerced by her silence.

It was a lonely mission, but she had her people, at least—those who watched her perform. They saw what not even Sam could see. Within those ropes, she contained it all: the slow burn of despair that wrapped itself tightly around rage and bound itself to her grief.

Maybe she wasn't the easiest girlfriend to be around.

"Did your show go well today? Did they love you?" Sam asked, trying, it was so obvious to Jia Li, to make it all better, somehow.

"Yes. Same as always."

Only it wasn't the same. The two men who always watched her now seemed suddenly much more threatening. She struggled to justify her gut reaction since, by appearances, nothing had changed. Except something had. Their eyes accused her, and their bodies tensed as if they held an invisible knife at their side.

JIA LI RECALLED her father's last day, how she'd hesitated for a moment as she came through the front door into the living room, watching him at his desk, scribbling. Jimi Hendrix sang about the joker and the thief through her father's mini desk speakers and he occasionally stopped to bob his head gently in time as he wrote and she thought, *If only he knew I'd been the thief,* and *Now what am I?* Still sneaking around in the shadows, only she'd intended to reveal her secret to him that very day, a Saturday morning before her evening show.

She couldn't do it.

She tried to say the words, to say anything at all, but she just stared at him and sang along to the lyrics in her head, *all along the watchtower.* His glasses slid down his nose and he pushed them up again with his left index finger and when they slipped again his finger was ready, resting on his cheekbone. He did this for some time, writing and readjusting his glasses and occasionally nodding to the music.

Finally, he noticed her there. He stopped writing, and as his green eyes met hers, she lost courage entirely. He asked how her morning had been and said that he had to go out soon to meet someone, which she'd assumed was a friend, since it was not a workday.

"Have fun," was all she managed to say after all her anticipation, her fear of disapproval, the words caught somewhere between her heart and her throat.

The last glance she'd had of him was of his straight nose, his silver hair, and his expression—distracted, perhaps stressed, trying to work something out as he often did at his desk. It was his best thinking spot, he used to say, where he could get away from other humans and work meetings and rest in his creative mind.

Science was the ultimate act of creativity, he used to say.

He—Edward Macpherson—was a scientist, of course, and originally of Scottish descent. Even before Jia Li's birth he had been a long time denizen of Hong Kong. He'd built his career in medical research. He worked at a big lab and often led projects that resulted in breakthrough medications. His job was all consuming. All throughout Jia Li's childhood, as an act of concession in response to his wife's nagging, he would arrive at eight or nine p.m. with a bundle of papers shoved under the stained yellow armpits of his blue dress shirt. The house would fill almost immediately with the aroma of ginger and sesame oil, meat or fish, and like the perfect Cantonese wife, Mary would bring out plates filled with various dishes and a steaming pot of rice, then eat a second dinner just to be with him. Jia Li joined them if she were home, which was most evenings since she hardly went out. It was a strange family custom, a second meal with her mother prattling on about mundane matters while her father ate in silence, distracted by the pile of papers on his desk across the room.

By the time Jia Li was a sullen teenager secretly nursing her own dreams, she realized that her mother was unhappy. On more than one occasion she asked Mary what else she wanted to do with her time, other than shop and socialize.

Mary would not play the fool. "Daughter, what do *you* want to do with *your* time?"

Edward always smirked at their predictable interactions.

Jia Li said nothing. She wanted to be an artist, not a laboratory scientist. She did not see science as quite the form of self-expression her heart longed for. But that's not how life unfolded as it had, smoothly and logically, paved by intellect and family connections. She was good at science. Her dad got her a job. It was boring, but it paid the bills. By her late teens, she had begun to enliven her dull life with some petty shoplifting. Mostly makeup and jewelry. Minor acts of rebellion that at once soothed her fear that she could only ever be the bland good girl, and gave her a high she didn't get anywhere else. She told herself that she'd stop once she worked out how to get away with being herself, whatever that meant. She found it easy to get away with shoplifting. She knew where all the security cameras were; she planned her capers well. Anyway, even if someone saw something suspicious, they were unlikely to suspect her. She came across as so calm, detached. She meditated regularly. She knew how to breathe through chaotic thoughts, to project an air of tranquility.

When she found herself blissed out from being suspended half-naked from the ceiling at age 20, wound tight in ropes, she felt that she'd reached a state of being that answered all of life's questions, especially the very personal one of what she might do with her time. So Jia Li swapped one well-guarded secret for another. She ceased her soulless theft (or 90% of it barring emotional crisis). Instead, she shopped legitimately for g-strings and push up bras, plus dresses that could be unwrapped, torn off, or dropped to her feet in an instant as the red ropes fell from the ceiling.

On that fateful day nearly a year ago she almost *did* tell her father about her performances—she really had wanted to. He didn't always understand her, but he never attempted to change her. But she was vulnerable, newly single, her heart crushed, in fact, by a woman who said Jia Li's life was just too intense.

A woman she loved, who had left her. Everything felt emotionally exhausting. Maybe that's why she couldn't bring herself to speak to her father that day.

Of course the *what ifs* had plagued her ever since. Maybe it could have saved him had she told him. He might have been shocked. He might have asked a lot of questions. He might have suggested they go out to get a bite to eat together and then avoided conversation altogether, but it might have been bonding nonetheless.

Even his non-acceptance might have saved his life.

He wouldn't have met that person that day. He wouldn't have died.

But maybe not.

Of course, Jia Li often wondered what he had been working on at his desk that day, and whether his distraction, his meeting, had anything to do with his death.

ALL OF IT, her double life, her fear, her regret, her questions, her grief —it all hit her anew every time she walked through the front door of their apartment and saw her father's desk sitting empty and still, pencil in an upright cup.

But it hit especially hard today, nearly a year to the day he had left, when she'd just sat on those rocks and looked into the water that took him.

"Is that you Jia Li?" her mother's voice called out from the kitchen.

"Who else would it be?"

She took a deep breath and quickly traversed the room's emotional fog in a beeline towards her bedroom.

"I saved you dinner," Mary said.

"I'm going out with Sam. I'll eat with him and stay at his place tonight. Don't wait up for me, Mum."

"Okay then. As long as he feeds you. Otherwise you get too skinny."

Mary headed her off, just as she was about to disappear into her bedroom. She stopped short of hugging her. She wanted to. Jia Li saw it—with a single sidestep her mother danced past her need for contact.

Since Edward had died, her mother was so hungry for her. Hungry to know her. Hungry to understand her. She asked her so many questions, more like interrogations that had led to Jia Li's confessions about Shibari and performance art.

Oddly, blessedly, Mary responded with no more than a furrowed brow, and then eventually even more questions. She certainly had judgment; Jia Li knew her well enough to see her eyes flash and her jaw tighten lest she lecture her daughter to stay safe, to build a career, to find a husband, to create stability—not to rock the boat or bring shame to her family.

Those unverbalized words wouldn't have been hers anyway, Jia Li knew. Family patterns and cultural traditions die hard. She forgave her mother in advance, in case she slipped.

"You don't need to know everything," Jia Li told her.

"I just want to understand."

"You will never understand, Mum. You have no frame of reference."

"I have to try. I don't want to lose you too," she said. "Your father always listened to you. He asked a lot of questions."

True. And Mary had always admired her husband's restraint in matters of judgement. Maybe she was honoring his memory through emulation.

But then Mary went even further and attended Jia Li's show.

She commented afterwards, at home, to Jia Li's utter embarrassment, "I couldn't even tell you were naked under all those ropes."

"Mother! You didn't come watch!" Jia Li choked on her rice. She could barely speak above a whisper, so horrified was she. "I wasn't naked. I had on a bikini."

"What if they find out at work that you do that?"

"Doesn't matter. Lots of people have a hobby."

Then her mother observed, with an even tone of voice, "There were men following you. Watching you."

"I know, Mum."

"They are from HKK Pharma, aren't they? They think you have proof of something, don't they? Something Edward was working on. That's why you have that placard."

Jia Li sighed. "I guess."

In such instances, when Mary dropped the filter and spoke her mind, Jia Li wondered who this stranger was, this woman who had given birth to her twenty-seven years ago, who had packed all her school lunches and told her what a great idea it was to work for a medical laboratory. Where was that mother, now?

The lines around Mary's eyes had deepened suddenly over the past year; her hair had streaks of white coming out from her ears and hairline; she had lost weight. She was already so small, just 5'2, even shorter than Jia Li, and increasingly insubstantial, as if a strong wind or even the shock of her daughter's lifestyle might blow her away. So Jia Li had thought.

Yet it was evident that, on the contrary, the more she knew of Jia Li's life, the more solid she seemed to become—and the more skittish Jia Li became, so often was she cornered with questions like, Did Jia Li prefer having a girlfriend or a boyfriend? How had she known that she wanted to perform? And how had she found the courage to do it? How had she discovered ropes, and how did she learn something as esoteric as Shibari?

Jia Li faltered and did so often, half embarrassed and half unable, at a base level, to articulate what she herself had simply *lived*. She did eventually find words, even if halting, to explain the inexplicable. Sometimes Mary received her answers with grace. Sometimes with that raised eyebrow. On occasion, though, she let out a small gasp followed by a cough as her daughter spoke, as if she instinctively rushed into judgment just as quickly as she retreated back into acceptance.

It was the oddest dance, the most unexpected development, wonderful in some ways, just plain weird in others, and yet—*intense*.

Jia Li found it exhausting.

ON THIS EVENING, as was her habit, Mary hovered near Jia Li's bedroom door waiting for her to re-emerge. Jia Li knew she was there as she showered and changed and moved around the room, picking up clothes, opening and shutting her drawers.

She'd only moved back into her childhood bedroom a couple years ago when she went to work at her father's company, just until she could save enough money to live comfortably on her own. Now she couldn't possibly leave. She couldn't abandon her mother completely. But she hadn't felt such a need to hide out in her room since she was a teenager.

Mary remained near Jia Li's door on some pretext of tidying the living room, fussing around cushions. When Jia Li emerged, Mary took her in, her long, strappy red dress. A different red dress to the one she'd worn for her show. This one was more sophisticated—with thicker fabric, invisible stitching, and an hourglass shape with one bare shoulder. It was also much more difficult to put on and take off.

"Beautiful. So beautiful." She ran a hand through her daughter's long, dark brown hair. It was Edward's hair, so fine, with strands of red. She stroked her face. "Such white skin," she said, and did not move away. Jia Li was a couple inches taller, and her mother's face shone up at her.

Mary ran her hand through her own hair. It was straight, thick and black, chin-length.

"How was your show today?" she asked.

"Yeah. Good." Then quickly, "Mum, why don't you watch a movie? Here, I can put one on for you if you like?" She turned on the television.

Mary finally took a step back. "Yes, okay darling."

"Or invite a friend over?" Jia Li asked. "What about Marcy, that American friend? You love her. She's eccentric."

"She's on a cruise with her husband now," Mary said, and they both swallowed the silence that followed. She and Edward used to do that together, too.

"You can go on a cruise with me soon," Jia Li said.

"That would be nice." Mary smiled. She sat stiffly on the couch as Jia Li began to search for movies as the menu loaded onto the screen.

"You won't like me saying this, Mum, but I have been investigating local colleges and there are plenty that have art classes. Many have night classes with adult students. You might love it. You could make friends."

Mary looked tearful and fixed on her hands, wringing them in her lap.

"Mum, you used to create such beautiful paintings. C'mon. I'm trying to help you."

"I know. Maybe there are enough artists in the family."

"Never. Anyway, I'm not exactly an artist."

Her mother just gave her a look. Empty and indiscernible; it was an invitation for Jia Li to project her own insecurities.

What was *not exactly an artist,* anyway?

"Whatever, anyway, think outside the box, Mum. Outside this apartment, perhaps."

"Like my brave daughter?"

Mary smiled, returned her gaze to her clasped hands and became smaller in her corner of the couch.

Jia Li certainly didn't think of herself as brave.

In truth, Jia Li didn't know what she was. Exhibitionist. Performer. Activist. Rebel. (Recovering thief?) Okay yes, *mostly* she was an artist. But what use were labels? She was the canvas, the tool, the message, the whole thing. More art than artist. If only she could take the person out of it, remove the artist entirely, then

she wouldn't have to label herself,

or wonder over her identity, or her future, and

she wouldn't be watched by those pharma thugs.

Her phone buzzed. It was Sam.

"Sorry to do this to you, but that dinner is canceled. It's in two days time now. I don't know why. Someone couldn't make it."

"I have a show that afternoon, Sam. I don't finish until six."

"I can pick you up after, right from the club. Do you want to come over tonight anyway, or..."

"I think I'll just stay home with my mother and watch a movie. I'm pretty tired, babe. I'll see you right after my show in two days."

Jia Li squeezed her mother's hand. Mary leapt off the couch, beaming. "I'm going to make us dinner, really fast. You just wait here."

"Can't. I'm going to get my pajamas on, Mum."

Daughter. She was also a daughter.

3

FATHERS SERGASIN & YAKUNOV: GOOD VERSUS EVIL

LATE OCTOBER 1935

THE ASCENSION MONASTERY OF TUNGUSKA, SIBERIA

The peasant Pavlik called for Sava the priest at the entry to the church. He rapped against the wooden doors and shouted for his guardian, crying, "They are back for you, the Godless are back!"

A corner of his tattered coat hem hung brown with cow dung, as he had tripped on his run through the paddock from his hut in the settlement beyond to the monastery. He pulled his coat to him, his stench blessedly undetectable in the cold. A crunch of footsteps came from around the corner; a heavyset old man in a dark brown cassock dragged a log behind him.

"You forget, Pavlik, the ice already covers Sava," said Father Sergasin gently.

Pavlik shook his head. "No, no."

"But yes. He is dead now two months. What are you speaking of so urgently?"

The peasant fell to his knees.

"Oh, my saint, my emissary of God, it cannot be!"

The priest kneeled beside him and took him by the shoulder.

"What say you, poor soul? Why are you banging at the door? Have you need of food? Are you mad?"

He knew, of course, that the peasant was mad.

Pavlik banged at the ground, the patina of frost grinding to mud in the wake of his fists. He wept, dirt-smudged cheeks running in brown rivulets. His rank breath blown in white clouds, the peasant looked up at the priest and shuddered.

"It is too late, hear? They come again, Sava's murderers."

They were in the middle of nowhere. The carpet of snow and ice created a perfect echo chamber; nary a footstep escaped attention. The others were asleep. Father Sergasin became very still, like the peasant on the ground below. He heard it then: the woods growled with engines, there was a clamor of tires on ice, but before the vehicles came into sight, the priest leapt and ran back to the living quarters, his log forgotten. Pavlik was left in a heap, crying himself to a frozen death.

FATHERS SERGASIN AND YAKUNOV, having warned the few novices remaining in residence, stood at the altar lighting candles when two officers burst in. The men wore black leather trenchcoats, betraying their lesser rank. They made their summary announcement with vigor:

"This monastery will be converted for use of the state. It will now hold prisoners, of which you will be the first."

The tallest of the two men, with an adolescent's faint moustache and an odour of stale cheese, grabbed the elder, Sergasin, by the forearm and pushed him roughly towards the middle of the nave into one of a row of high wooden stacidia against the wall; his colleague, a stouter version with the same impish force, shoved black-haired Yakunov beside him. They held their .45 calibre pistols at their sides and formed a barrier before the priests, whilst other officers roared past them behind the altar towards the sacristy.

One spoke as he went by, "You are lucky, old men, you have been somewhat useful. You will only go to a labour camp."

Sergasin did not believe this pronouncement. He shuddered in memory of blood pouring into the earth from beneath Sava's head, and trembled at the thought of the outspoken novice priest Nikolai. He was, right now, with the few remaining others in their living quarters. There were only three buildings in the monastery complex. They would find him; it was inevitable. An officer emerged from behind the altar carrying manuscripts—liturgical texts, leather-bound, ancient.

Yakunov sent up a small prayer, fixing his eyes on the icon of Christ and the brocade cloth that fell from the altar to the floor. Their minders had shifted their attention to the commotion as another trenchcoat-clad man emerged with a larger icon, a mural on wood, glinting with gold filigree, the size of an opened book.

"Look at this!"

"Remove them all!" someone else shouted from the entrance. A wind wound its way down through the barren nave and curled around the feet of the two priests, before pulling back to force the wooden doors closed. The priests lowered their heads.

"Tell me what you think," said Father Yakunov to Father Sergasin in a subdued voice, quite sure no one else could hear. "If a blessed object, imbued with Christ's own powers to heal the sick, to bring man from the brink of death—if it fell into the hands of common man, what would become of it? Would it cause wars or heal the masses? Would its worldly trajectory swing wildly from causing good, to sowing the seeds of evil? Would its path mirror the progression of humanity, if indeed, humanity is on a path to salvation?"

"That depends on whether or not you have faith in man," said Father Sergasin. He pulled at his white beard. "I do not."

The commotion stilled. The church's wooden doors shook again, then there was only the sound of Sergasin's gruff breathing to disturb the sudden, all-consuming quiet. Yakunov and Sergasin looked out across the nave to the silent drift of first snow, bathed in orange through the stained glass. Then higher, beyond the painted dome, beyond the depictions of saints and sufferers and blessed virgins and babes, and far above the rustle of bared branches, there came the rush of wings, and a flash of long, white cranes in flight.

"It remains in the sacristy?" Father Sergasin asked. The voice of a young man echoed, in pleas, claiming righteousness. An explosion of gunshot. Then another. A tear ran down his face; he whispered, "Nikolai..."

Yakunov whispered back, "It is amongst others. Disguised by sameness." An officer appeared then, carrying a pile of icons in his arms. Five or six, small paintings, stacked, a glint of gold filigree that jarred with the coarseness of his hand, fingers like sausages. He dropped them to the floor in the corner, and called to his comrade, "More!"

A moment later, there was another pile, untidy, undifferentiated. Yet at the tip was a small red glare. Not an icon in the conventional style, painted on wood, a picture or a story; this was a cross. Bronze. Angels carved near the top crossbeam, Jesus hanging off it, all the normal features of an Orthodox crucifix. Hewn roughly, not even in surface, nor shiny, rather awkward in its fashion. It was simplistic and, perhaps for this reason, left unceremoniously in and amongst other items. The officer gave his latest collection barely a glance, then went outside, calling for help. The priests lowered their voices.

"But the time will come, and someone will discover it."

Yakunov nodded. "Indeed. Beyond our time. We might never know. So, I will take the opposite stance. I will place my faith in goodness and trust that the innocent will be healed."

4

WALLACE & THE INSTITUTE FOR PSYCHOCONSCIOUS DEVELOPMENT

MAY 2131 AD

KRASNOYARSK, EASTERN FEDERATION

Wallace sidestepped the fetid puddle with its cloud of mosquitoes and ducked into the alley between the bakery and the tech store. He recoiled against the tang of urine, even as the exotic aroma of warm yeast filled his nostrils. This new and no doubt fleeting fashion irritated him—bread baked fresh after a manner of ancient French traditions. Every other street corner now smelled of dough, suffusing the air with the entirely odd amalgam of urban decay and baguettes: potholes and rubble strewn with the first breadcrumbs in perhaps fifty years, since the fungal blight obliterated wheat across the Belt nations. He imagined black bread from the *Tale of Two Cities*, and realized that this fresh bread smell was as unfamiliar to him now as it would have been to those Parisian characters in ancient fiction. He had no benchmark for what lay beyond food security, and certainly no olfactory reference point for *bread*. He might, as he'd done for years in study, reimagine the past in various forms, but could not have conjured *bakeries*. Most of his senses were not primed for this level of detail.

Defaulting to vision, he gazed upwards. A flock of cranes formed a V formation overhead, giving the tall buildings a wide berth, sweeping down just below the top floors of Krasnoyarsk Towers, their reflection in blackened glass creating an illusion of parallel lines undulating across the giant complex. The dusty midday sky was beautiful, regardless of its cause—climate changes due to last century's pollution, combined with the fallout from the nuclear blast during the same era. He felt a certain childhood nostalgia for the dust storms, as he always did when rains were over, the air cooled, and the clouds swam in orange again. He turned abruptly into another alley, reflexively grasping the trail of his robe in his left hand and circumnavigating what was left of the puddles after weeks of sudden rains, and the ensuing heat. Most adepts from his monastery had permanently damp, mud-stained hems, but he was fastidious in this regard, the muscles in his forearms well-developed from holding the heavy ochre fabric at his waist throughout the winter and into spring. This subsection of the city (called, simply, "The Village") and all of its backstreets did not come under the jurisdiction of the Council and its urban refurbishment, obviously, falling to the less materially motivated auspices of spirituality.

He saw the plaque before he noticed the small door, inconspicuous amidst the disarray of overturned bins and overflowing rubbish. The Institute for PsychoConscious Development occupied the entire building in this back alley, he'd been told, but its main entrance was a five-foot high green door. Father Andrew had been correct in all his details, a small comfort as Wallace gave the door a shove and held it steady lest it fall from its hinges. He found himself in a dark corridor, rank, with a muddy floor. There was a stairwell before him, rendered in marble, dusty but perfect, a relic whose value was entirely lost to his era, but which he greatly appreciated.

Following his instructions, Wallace went up the stairwell to the first floor, turned left, and walked to the end of the corridor. He could barely make out the door at the end. He supposed that, funding inequities aside, discretion served a purpose. Like the full moon Vespers, a special event held monthly in the paddocks beyond the monastery—what was not seen or heard was also not questioned. Administrative minds could not wrap themselves around metaphysical anomalies or the tedium of lab work, and thus devolved into reflexive patterns of turning a blind eye whilst focusing on form. The world progressed in secret, and access to those secrets was guarded; this door did not even have a handle, for instance. He discerned, searching for one, a small crescent-shaped hole, releasing a sliver of dusty light. He tapped moderately three times, *tut tut-tut*, a habit instilled in him from a youth spent in boarding schools. The door shifted a centimeter, then flew open.

"Dr. Rinella," said the gentleman, extending his hand, "and you are Wallace."

Wallace took in the man's cropped white beard, his gray hair, and for a moment mistook his age—he had, of course, never met anyone truly ancient, what once was considered *elderly*. He recalled momentarily the ancient temple-keeper at the entrance to the river Ob, his wild hair, his brown, dirty robes, how the *ancien* had waved his staff angrily during a student excursion—to keep them out, Wallace had presumed. Then, before their eyes, the *ancien* suddenly collapsed. Heart attack. An old-fashioned death, so fast, relatively peaceful. It had made an impression on him, evoked a desire within him to know the kind of normalcy absent in his generation.

Dr. Rinella would be nearing sixty, like his advisor Father Andrew; they were peers, relatively old, but hardly ancient. In any case, this man had an air of robustness about him. He was straight, solid. When he beckoned Wallace inside and pushed the door closed behind him, it stuck, so he shoved himself against it. It closed with a raw thud that ended on a squeak.

"You're on time. No trouble finding me? Of course not. Andrew would have tested you beforehand on your comprehension of his instructions, I'm sure."

"Indeed."

"Well, sit. I will pour us some water and we will chat. You take the armchair, of course, it's the most forgiving. "

Wallace went to sit at one end of the room, in the plush armchair positioned against the wall—it fairly invited him to recline. There were three other chairs, white and hard-looking, lined up across from Dr. Rinella's desk. One side of the room was made entirely of glass, much like the residential buildings at the monastery. The other walls were a muted grey, so that the eye was drawn outdoors, and the room seemed to float in motley skies. A row of small pots lined the floor, sprouting various stems and leaves. Though it was warm outside, inside it was even warmer. Wallace noticed the climate regulator on the desk, and assumed Dr. Rinella had set the temperature high, perhaps for his plants. He wore a thin, short-sleeved white shift, the typical uniform of scientists, on top of long grey pants and slippers that made a 'swish' as he moved across the floor.

"My unofficial experiments," he spoke, noticing Wallace's attention. "Seedlings purchased on the black market, ancient manufactured breeds, some of them. Nonetheless, there are tomatoes, dill, basil. The rest, we shall see."

"That one is rocket, and that is cilantro." Wallace pointed. "We grow them at the monastery. They are good for chelating metals in the body."

"Indeed? Fascinating. You grow it with success?"

"With much effort, of an unusual type. Have you heard of the ancient Findhorn Community in Scotland?"

"Of course, yes, I am familiar with their lunar rituals, the meditation. Fantastic—ancient knowledge completely discredited now. It's that sort of thing which has motivated the founding of this institute. Possibly you and I are of like minds."

"Many of Father Andrew's initiatives would please you, in that case."

Dr. Rinella poured two glasses of water from a pitcher on his desk. He handed Wallace a glass and went to sit behind the desk. It was an old fashioned desk, constructed entirely of what must have been refashioned wood, a centerpiece cut out for the holographic technology housed within. With nature-first being the official paradigm, thus dictating both the use and presentation of the Interface, most were unaware of the Science Institutes' fanaticism for time-space distortion. That science was hidden to the masses, developed in isolated facilities, driven by this same Interface, the AI stream connecting all information. Interface-driven science also competed for funding with any and all other research, and usually won. Father Andrew had prepped Wallace well for the realities of life beyond the monasteries.

"He has spoken of his efforts. In particular, of his work with meditation," Dr. Rinella said.

Wallace nodded. He knew of their long association, despite differing philosophies. He would not be here were it not for Father Andrew's particular interest in meditation—his scientific approach was maligned by the bishops, yet he risked much for the sake of rigorous analysis.

"It has not been easy being his assistant in this, yet I have benefited, too," Wallace said.

"Oh yes? Do say how."

"Well, lucidity, for one thing. Awareness of the present moment. Clearer dreams. And of course, my memories from the past."

"You are from Africa? One of the last holdouts, I hear."

"My parents were from Sudan, but they moved us to Spain to be part of the Ibiza Experiment. They were passionate people, committed to non-violence. They believed in a future they could not see. They died in the Ibiza bombing. When they were killed, I was taken to the safest orphanage at the time, in Ukraine. My siblings also died."

Dr. Rinella nodded. "I'm sorry for your losses, Wallace. I have heard about the Ibiza Experiment. Quite a thing to commit to a nonviolent mission at a time when so many rebel groups defaulted into violence. I believe their experiment was too successful. They were self-sufficient, economically, too. The dying regime needed someone to use, as an example to others. No one was safe. Hmm, yes. Your name. Wallace Deng Moroz. Wallace is—I presume, not a family name? The Deng is Sudanese. I suppose your first experience of institutionalization accounts for your last name. *Moroz*."

"Yes. It means *frost*. Because I was brought there in winter. My parents gave me the name Wallace as they were inspired by Scottish freedom fighters, even though their methods were not the same. Although my family is of the Dinka tribe originally. But I transferred here as a teenager, when I decided to pursue monastic studies. It is considered the most progressive monastery. I have also had a long fascination with the history of the region."

Dr. Rinella sipped his water. "Indeed. Though since your... recent activities, I know you have not been treated with complete respect. There have been certain risks to your elevation in the ranks, as it were. Do you have ambition?"

"I feel only that I am content, at present. No, to answer your question. I have few desires, and the ones I have are not of a life-changing nature."

"And yet, what you bring to me could be, in fact, life-changing."

"Perhaps it hasn't sunk in." Wallace gave a short laugh, enough to cement an understanding between them, or even an affinity for one another.

There was a risk in being too honest these days, but Wallace felt instinctively safe.

"Regarding your memories of the past. One day, we will discuss at length what exactly constitutes the *past*. We at the Institute do not have a line about the transmigration of souls, you might know. If consciousness is at some level shared, which we know to be the case, and if time, as we currently understand it, is fluid in ways we cannot tangibly grasp, then it hardly matters on the whole whose past one accesses. Do you agree?"

"Yes. Although, at times, I feel that if a soul is one discrete unit, traveling through time, then at a personal level such memory as mine is relevant, indeed."

Wallace kept an even intonation, stifling a quiver of embarrassment. He did not like to think he promoted personal growth at the expense of science; this was precisely the fence he straddled at the peril of his monastic career.

"I can see why Father Andrew values you so highly. Your reflection is not incidental, Wallace. I am grateful you have agreed to help."

"Anything I can do, however unpopular, if it will have tangible benefits for anyone."

Just then the door shuddered as someone outside banged forcefully against it. Dr. Rinella stood slowly, with apparent exasperation, and ambled to the door even as the hysteria on the other side heightened. The noise reverberated across the walls.

"Hello, Ms. Potts," he said as a petite red-headed woman about Wallace's age, somewhere close to thirty, flew across the threshold. She cast a cursory glance at Wallace, a blush rising rapidly from her clavicle up her neck.

"I see you are feeling anxious," he said, then, "Wallace, allow me to introduce you to Justicia Potts. She heads the funding commission which gave the Institute its latest grant."

Now she looked at him long enough for him to notice her green eyes flashing. Their color perfectly matched the tight work dress she wore, which plunged into a V at her neck, stopping just short of her waist. Council personnel were the only ones freed from the strict uniform policies that science and religion put up with.

She swung towards Dr. Rinella. "What is going on, Lucio?"

"I should ask you. Your presence is a breach of ethics. You're clearly not here on official business." This was delivered in a flat voice, accompanied by a curious gaze.

She spoke at a constrained whisper now, fully crimson-faced, neck taut. "And yet it was *you* who informed me so obliquely as to the nature of your latest project. You want me here, do you not? Hence your unofficial letter informing me of your activities—sent to my *home*?" Here her eyes darted to Wallace and back to Dr. Rinella.

Now he smirked. "Justicia, what I will tell you is that this is real. What is happening in here is real, and it could help us. But, as always, it is your decision to attend my sessions."

She balled up a fist, holding it at her abdomen as if attempting to ground her fury as she hissed, "Rinaldo the Brazilian healer was *real*, Lucio. That witch doctor woman from, wherever it was, Bulgaria, Transylvania, whatever, she was *real*. They could heal people, certain people, under certain conditions, but that is the prerogative of the private market. We are dealing in mass. Universal application, for God's sake…"

"We have gone over and over this, I know. You are officially *not* here. However, should you need to procure funding for this project if it advances, then you will have context and, I hope, the conviction you need to fight for us..."

She sighed and spoke at a normal volume now, resigned. "Listen, I'm sorry, Lucio. I have the greatest respect for you. You know it was *I* who fought for you so hard in the past. That is why it is *my* reputation on the line here. Each time I procure funding for you and you fail, it's one step closer to me never working again. And being discredited in this political climate is no small thing."

"Then listen to me, Justicia, as a friend. A hopeful. As someone who has lost a loved one, listen with your heart, please."

Wallace's voice came quietly, as if from afar, though he was only feet away on the armchair. "Shall I wait outside, while you come to an agreement?" He stifled a smile. The bickering was somehow entertaining. He particularly enjoyed Justicia's fiery retorts.

"No," Dr. Rinella said, his forehead creased in puzzlement as he peered at Wallace carefully. "You find us amusing, don't you?" He smiled and continued, "Well, it's good to see an adept with a sense of humor, at least. I thought they zapped it out of you in the Monastery. In any case, this concerns you, Wallace. You must be more than a little curious as to why you are here."

"Father Andrew told me. At least, I think he did. He said you might help us—me—the work we are doing."

"Indeed. Did you know that I know Andrew from school? We boarded together."

That fact—boarding school—hung in the air for a frozen moment. So Dr. Rinella, like Father Andrew, was an intact child of cancered parents, and a boarding school orphan like himself. He felt he shouldn't know this about his spiritual advisor, that it was too personal, and he had always been told that the personal distracted from the universal. From the *real*.

"Don't let boarding school worry you. Being orphaned is the fate of many. We have a common goal, Andrew and myself. We visit, once, twice a year. He urges me to abandon this struggle for practical solutions, and to follow a path out of this world. As you have chosen,

Wallace. I press him for details on developments in the monastery. Adepts with particular insights. You see, I have not given up on spirit, Wallace, as I tell your advisor. Not in the least. I am open-minded. I only feel we—materialists—should work *with* you. That we might find a way to live in this imperfect world *and* remain spiritual."

Justicia now sat in one of the white chairs. She calmed, her jaw relaxed, freckles now appearing one by one as her pallor cooled to white. She stole glances at Wallace.

"Good that you're staying, Justicia. Now, listen, both of you, this is the interesting bit. Have you heard of the Russian science-fantasy author K.I. Gutov? No? I don't suppose you have. He was a sensation in the late 20th century. His work is considered classic. I have long been a fan. So has Andrew, I might add. We discovered him together, year eleven. Of course, Andrew being Andrew, he took from it all that was epiphanic, ecstatic, hopeful, whereas I was fascinated with the practical. You see, in Gutov's trilogy, our planet is dying, in that case, after an alien invasion which destroys most of the population and enslaves the rest. His hero discovers an icon which leads his people to a place called Shambhala. A new world, based on the mythology of a mystical place on Earth. There were theories, in the nineteenth century, that there was a magical place, another dimension, where people never aged, were always happy, etc. Some Tibetan Buddhists even claimed it was where their most spiritually advanced monks went prior to enlightenment, as masters on Earth. The icon, especially in his third book, *Ikona,* is described as a gold cross which conveyed by its glowing the location of this Shambhala.

"This book's story sparked a cult-like following. People believed Gutov really knew about a true Shambhala, that he was a mystic and not just a novelist. The author himself even claimed to have found this place in real life. Don't look at me like that, Justicia."

Wallace was at a loss for words. This wasn't going as he'd imagined, this talk of a science fantasy—the connection was the cross, of course.

"Oh, Lucio." Justicia sighed. "So much of your theorizing begins like this, in the fantastical. The rumors, the mystical emanations that electrify your imagination. It's not science. Perhaps you should consider *this* is why your Institute has had no results?"

Wallace, entertained and intrigued by both this talk of a novel and Justicia's annoyance, stifled his reaction lest he offend anyone. In his bid to quell his true feelings, he came to focus unwittingly on Justicia's small breasts, mostly flattened in her tight dress. He stirred, trying to figure out what about this woman was getting under his skin.

Her name was severe. Her parents would have been Adjudicators in the 2081 Revolution. So, she had been raised an ideologue. Wallace's entire vocation was a product of their antithetical reactions to the times of Chaos. The Adjudicators' lawsuits against the polluting corporate empires had brought down an entire world order and resulted in the Council and its New Administration policies, even as the Spiritualists attempted to fill the vacuum of meaning left in its wake, especially after the cancer epidemic began to decimate the global population from the 2090s.

Something about Justicia's indignation was put on, though, betraying the nature of her allegiance. Her eyes roamed outside, and her face slackened momentarily—until Dr. Rinella rounded on her again, and she came to attention as if by instinct. Glaring.

"But listen—not yet, no results *yet*. On one of our visits, Andrew told me that one of his adepts—" He nodded at Wallace. "—displayed unusual artistic talent which arose out of an altered state of consciousness. That this young man traveled into a past life, and in the liminal space of his present consciousness, he drew an icon which he called the Shambhala icon. Now, Andrew and I immediately recalled our fondness for Gutov's stories. Out of sheer curiosity I began to study his novel *Ikona*, in particular, and to study the events of that time which arose from the furore his books caused. Andrew found this greatly amusing, by the way. You'll appreciate that, Justicia. But, in the end, he saw the light."

Here Dr. Rinella giggled. "No pun intended!"

Wallace said, "You think my recollections are meaningful? That they relate to this icon? And how does this icon, from Gutov's stories, have anything to do with the epidemic? With healing?"

"Just a moment, Wallace. I will get to that. It has everything to do with it because in the decades after *Ikona* was written, at the turn of the 21st century, there was trafficking in precious icons by criminal syndicates, but it may be of just *one* icon in particular."

Dr. Rinella stopped to clear his throat.

Justicia leapt in. "Which led to the true Shambhala. And if we find it, we can lead humankind to a new world, of perfect health, longevity. This is your plan? Really?" Her shoulders slumped.

"Not my plan, Justicia. The rumors of the time do not link the icon to a mystical land. Rather, they recount an icon with spectacular healing properties. That is why it was so precious, why people killed for it. It had some effect on cellular renewal. It helped the body heal itself quickly. And *that* is why I have brought Wallace here. And, by extension, you Justicia. Because you need to see this young man in action so that you can assess the importance of this work, and ensure our funding continues in case we need to expand this project."

They both stared at Wallace as if he were a specimen. Somewhat discomfited, and simultaneously amused by their interaction, it took a moment for him to speak.

"My memories of the past do concern a cross that healed, that's true. And the memories do seem to be of the relevant time period. But I'm not sure how I might be of use. I understand, from what Father Andrew explained, that you think I might be able to locate this icon in my past life, or what seems to be my past life. And that I might confirm its properties, for present day purposes."

"Yes," Dr. Rinella said. "You see, spontaneous memory from the past is linked to evocative events which trigger an emotional reaction, which then finds an echo in historical expression. It is untamed, like lightning, its insight conveyed in feelings and images, without narrative coherence. Hypnotherapy is able to introduce control, to channel the past at will. In this way, we might be able to precisely determine where, when, and how you came across this icon in a past existence."

Wallace said, "And if, say, you locate this icon, what then? We pass it around to all of humankind?"

"We may find it, yes. But more important, we use the past to lead us to its *origins*, so that we might be able to re-create its effects ourselves."

Justicia practically spat. "This is preposterous. It doesn't even bear saying. You are using past-life regression to locate an object which *may* have magical healing properties, in order to either find it two centuries later, or re-create it in the present."

"Indeed."

A horrible tension filled the room. Both Dr. Rinella and Justicia appeared at once to recoil and restrain themselves from leaping towards confrontation, their faces pale and drawn taut. Wallace, not tempted to react, turned to the window. In fact, he smiled to himself. He had no idea what he was getting himself into, but it certainly seemed madness, which was increasingly amusing to him.

Suddenly, they both noticed him; he saw their eyes widen. Dr. Rinella smiled, but Justicia appeared furious.

"You think it's amusing?" she asked him.

He quickly frowned and shook his head no, but chose not to speak lest he betray the truth.

Dr. Rinella spoke. "Well, isn't it? Quite a labyrinthine path. Certainly it's better to be light-hearted. This is my last-ditch attempt. I have no other card to play. It's my only hope, unless you have a better idea. And you know, my dear, what is at stake. You know what others are doing and what will happen if they find a cure before we do."

She glowered. Dr. Rinella swung his chair around to face Wallace and rolled in so close that the younger man could see where the hairs of his beard were shaved lower on one side of his mouth than the other.

Wallace had not known that others were also looking for a cure, but then adepts were largely sheltered from politics and current events. He trusted Father Andrew. He also trusted the momentum from his own visions. After all, they had landed him exactly here, now, and he felt—for some unknown reason—that he had to trust the strange progression of this unexpected development in his own consciousness.

"How do we begin?" Wallace asked. "I am used to doing this on my own."

"We start at the beginning. We regress you to the first instance of recollection, of when you first learned about the cross. Are you committed, Wallace? Do you agree to this endeavor, which may require many sessions? And which may go on indefinitely? And with consequences for you, of course, which we cannot now imagine, should anyone at the Monastery discover our work?"

"I am already on this path. I see no other."

It was not defeat he admitted, nor fate; merely an adaptation to the present moment. He had no other plan for himself. Inner emptiness pulled him towards the past, to connection, if he were honest. He had no connections in his life quite so powerful as this character he became back *then*. Truthfully, he had no other plans for his life. He did not even know yet if he would survive; he had not yet reached the age past which survival was all but assumed.

Justicia crinkled her nose, which Wallace found, to his surprise, disarmingly charming. She squinted. She was thinking about what to say, he guessed.

"You really are sure about this, aren't you?" she asked Wallace. "Willing to risk professional destruction, or worse. That is most unusual."

He sensed her sudden respect, and he felt that respect morph into interest as her eyes fully took him in.

Indeed, Justicia took him into her sight greedily—he sensed it—as if her interest were an indulgence. She stood and pushed her white chair across the room to sit closer to him and watch the forthcoming drama unfold. She sat straight in her chair, one hand on her knee, blinking from Wallace to Dr. Rinella and back. Dr. Rinella took a sip of water and placed another of the white chairs directly across from Wallace. He sat and took a deep, grounding breath.

Wallace stared at Justicia. Her nipples were hard and her lips parted. She sighed, not breaking from their visual exchange, and he allowed himself to drift, to her breasts, to her flat abdomen, to the dress that enveloped her so intimately. He could see no further, but imagined her hard exterior betrayed succumbing softness. He closed his eyes and breathed the thought away.

Would this woman—his eyes blinked open to find her staring at him—be at every session, he wondered? If anything could change his mind about participating in this project at this late stage, it was her presence, he was suddenly sure of it. An internal *no* competed with his *yes*. He tried to reject the temptation. He pushed against his lack of focus. He closed his eyes as Dr. Rinella scooted in and put a hand on each of his knees. He wound his thoughts back to breath, only breath. The fabric of his monastic robes were sufficiently thick to conceal his erection. His attention went, with some effort, to Dr. Rinella, and he felt, faintly, the throbbing of his own heart and the retiring intensity of Justicia's probing eyes as his knees were tapped, rhythmically, and words spoken to lead him away from himself.

Slack, silent, eyes firmly shut, at last he gave himself to this project, to this hope. Following Dr. Rinella's words, he imagined the looming black of nothing as he opened the door from his mind into someplace else. Falling, falling, a pebble cast to the shore.

5

JIA LI & THE HEALING

MAY 2019

HONG KONG

Sam was silent all the way to dinner, which suited Jia Li just fine, since her mind was still mulling over the performance she'd finished not twenty minutes earlier. The memory of it lingered, a pleasurable buzz tinged with danger. The city at night was chaotic with floodlit streets and neon shopfronts bustling with pedestrians, but traffic was inconsistent. Between traffic jams, tidy roads stretched out lazily in front of them. Sam sped through the intermittent gaps and each time Jia Li threw her head back and let her nerves fire with fear and enthusiasm, a heady mix that took her right back to the stage.

Jelly Ropes.

Today she'd begun her performance in her thin, stretchy, long red dress. There was a diamond shape cut out in the center which revealed the bottom of her cleavage. She looked hot, which was the point, even though she felt she wasn't.

She didn't care either way.

She knew, without self-deprecation, that her form was more or less square. Boxy. Average looking, with an angular jaw and her mother's small, dark eyes. She had short legs and smallish breasts.

She was thin like a boy with no curves, yet somehow, all of this made her the perfect blank slate.

In the right dress, with a tight waist to give the appearance of hips, a very tight padded bikini top, and in heels that lengthened her legs, she was able to appear almost Barbie-like. Plus, she exaggerated her lips, her eyes, and her attitude. She wore confidence like armor, even as she stripped off items of clothing until she had on only her gold bikini. After which she wrapped and tied the soft red ropes over her arms and legs, pulling herself up so that she flipped upside down. Swinging around, limbs and neck extended, the longest she could extend herself, an almost-gazelle caught in a red knotted trap, bass thumping. Heavy metal pounding.

The crowd cheered, sometimes polite, sometimes lewd. She didn't care. From the ceiling a single giant bottle descended, like one containing pills, the label blacked out with heavy paint. Jia Li wound the rope expertly around her neck but tied it just above, and as she flipped she appeared to hang, but was caught safely in a chest harness, dangling for the audience to see. A wooden placard dropped from above.

Knowledge not proof.

At first she broadcast her words to let those who *did* have proof know that she did *not*. A kind of *fuck you*. A message to leave her the fuck alone. But over time these words came to release the pent up frustration of knowing that her silence defended secrets, no doubt evil ones.

Her father had been hiding something.

Only she was not privy to it.

It was 25 minutes of action in an unassuming nightclub, and as the reviews said, it looked like your average strip club with the same dark, seedy vibe, a smallish stage and middling impressive staging lights—but the audience was in for a treat. For those who had never witnessed live self-shabari, it was far beyond sexy, so the review went. "It is enticing and dangerous and somewhat mysterious, since no one really understands the performer's cryptic message."

This was her signature show, performed every month. Rumors

abounded as to the meaning of the words on the placard. Her words were not targeted at the punters, so she didn't get drawn into the debate. Silence was her bargain, after all.

Despite the mental and emotional pleasure of reliving her show, her body craved rest. She wished she could mull over it all alone, with a cup of herbal tea in the bath. She did not want to go to dinner with Sam and his colleagues—she couldn't bear to refer to them as *friends*. But she'd said she would two days ago. If she were less conflict avoidant, she'd make her own decisions, even knowing Sam would be cross with her. But she couldn't muster the energy. Such small battles were draining -

and maybe that's what her performance was, a battle waged on stage and in her heart.

Sam held onto her forearm and led her down the pavement to the restaurant from where he'd parked. It wasn't any kind of weird dominance. It was habit. When he was sixteen, his first girlfriend had arthritis and psoriasis and couldn't bear her hands being touched, so he'd taken to holding onto her forearm. Even now it amused Jia Li, how he pulled her along, and after six months together she'd fallen out of the habit of offering her hand. Just now, she appreciated his stabilizing grip as she tottled in her black stilettos. They had small chains dangling across the top and over the sides. She had chosen them because they looked a bit bad-ass. She liked to look the part of a gangster's girlfriend, or anyway, she found it helped her rouse herself to go out with him. That way, it was just another performance to get through.

"Hey." She stopped. There was a bit of blood that inked through his white dress shirt on the arm that held hers. "It's worse?"

"Don't worry about it. Please."

N ADYA SMILED from across the room and beckoned. Jia Li sighed with relief. One friendly face, at least. Jia Li rather liked this Russian woman. Beneath all her gaudy gold chains, her lash extensions, the layers of foundation, botox, and whatever else she did that Jia Li couldn't see behind—beneath all that lay a reassuring blend of warmth and grit. She was authentic, in her own way. Her husband had been killed in some kind of crime payback scenario—Jia Li never asked, and Sam never explained, although he probably knew. At least with Jia Li, Nadya had softened since learning that Jia Li's father had died suddenly, as if the silent undercurrent of their every interaction were shared grief.

"I want you to sit with me," Nadya whispered, "because this guy is really annoying." She indicated her date, a beast of a Russian man who strode towards the table. He was at least six foot four and built like a truck.

"Sergei." Nadya smiled, all charm now. "Jia Li, Sam's girlfriend."

He grunted hello. Jia Li smiled at Nadya sympathetically.

Jia Li hated this part—the fancy restaurant, choosing a meal, eating with perfect manners. Under the table, Sam kept a hand on her knee, which he squeezed occasionally, possessive and affectionate. He made every effort to include her in conversation, although she subtly demurred. When she was not onstage she was shy. Often overwhelmed by noise and crowds. Onstage, she knew exactly who she was and what she needed to do and the size of the audience didn't concern her in the least. She called the shots. Here, socially, in a public venue, it was all unpredictable—who she'd meet, what she'd say, what she was expected to say.

Another Russian couple joined them, and then a single Chinese man. There were so many new people that Jia Li could not focus on her food, or even Sam's hand on her knee, despite Nadya's sympathetic face across from her.

"You good, sweetie?" Nadya asked her at one point, between the first and second course.

"Sure," Jia Li said, and filled her mouth quickly with beef brisket, the house specialty.

Nadya seemed pretty bored herself. The other Russian woman seemed to be ignoring both of them completely, and no doubt on purpose—the social politics were way beyond Jia Li's comprehension. So were crime politics. She knew the Triads were collaborating with the Russian mafia over the past few months—that's how Nadya had appeared in hers and Sam's life socially—but she absolutely didn't want to know any more.

Jia Li asked Nadya, "How's your cat?" She remembered her mentioning an orange tabby who had by all accounts replaced her husband.

"He is my baby," Nadya said. "He is my divine little baby. He waits for me outside the bathroom. He meows if I'm on the phone. I love him so much." She placed a manicured hand on her heart, her long, soft pink nails tapping on her collarbone. "I show you photos later," she said.

"Wonderful," Jia Li said. "I'm glad you have some good company." She attempted not to throw a deprecating glance at Nadya's loud boyfriend.

Well, Jia Li thought, at least the mood had changed at their end of the table. At the other end, the men were smoking and the conversation had turned serious. Jia Li didn't understand why they were even out with these men—older men who now seemed rather ominous—but that wasn't her place. She watched them from an emotional distance. They leaned in, spoke in low voices.

Sam was young and naive, she thought. These men weren't good.

She didn't know much about his work, and she didn't care to—but she knew Sam was not important. He didn't do anything dangerous, as far as she understood. Petty drug crimes, moving products, that sort of thing. She never asked for clarification. Jia Li had enough on her mind with her own thugs.

Her personal opinion, however, was that he didn't quite fit into this crowd. He was shy and considerate, and wooed her with his above average EQ. That was their joke. He said he'd been raised well and that explained why—in his words—he wasn't barbaric.

"I would love to meet your cat one day," Jia Li said to Nadya, desperate to lighten the tone, or at least distract herself from it. "I love cats. But my mother is allergic, so we can't have one."

"You live with your mother?" Nadya asked, not in judgment at all, merely curious.

"I was planning to move out ages ago. But I don't want to leave her alone, since my father died," Jia Li said.

Sam heard her and squeezed her knee, then leaned over and kissed her cheek.

"Oh, yes, of course," Nadya said. "Well, you'll have to visit. Meet him. He is friendly."

Dessert arrived. Jia Li had a cramp in her leg from sitting, or from her show and then the hike. From all of it probably. She was losing sensation in her foot. She stifled a yawn.

"How is arm?" Sergei asked Sam in his heavy accent.

Jia Li perked up. His bloody arm.

"It's not bad," he said.

Yes it is, you bastards.

Sergei nodded, slurring, "You did your job, now you get reward. Also, it is test."

Sergei was clearly drunk. Nadya smiled blankly, straight ahead, well trained to ignore conversation that she really wasn't supposed to understand. Jia Li heard *reward*, and *test*, and inwardly cringed—he may not be barbaric, but this was.

Nadya left for the bathroom. The other Russian man waved a finger in the air in a circular motion. The waiter appeared with the bill. She felt Sam's hand squeeze her knee again.

"Baby, can you go wait for me outside, I have to do something upstairs. I'll just be ten minutes or so."

Internally she rolled her eyes, but the words that came out were, "I guess. But I'm tired."

He took her by the arm, kissed her cheek and whispered *baby, I won't be long*, and walked her out back. It wasn't an alley exactly. It was a bustling backstreet with nowhere to stand since everyone was passing through on their way to someplace else. She leaned against a wall and stared at the street. She practiced being invisible, still, being anywhere but there.

She heard Sam's voice a few minutes later, calling her.

She looked up. He was coming down the outside stairs from the restaurant's back door. Had it been mere minutes? Or twenty?

He was kind of glowing. All puffed up like he'd just been promoted. The other men patted him on the back. When he got to her, he kissed her on the lips, lingering there. She let him. He even smelled different.

As tired as she was, being inside Sam's apartment revived her somewhat, with the humming air conditioning and the emptiness. His sparse bachelor pad was tidy to the point of soulless, which was fine with her since she wanted nothing familiar that might tempt her into complicated thoughts, sad memories, reminders of obligations.

He started kissing her and her body quickened, defenseless.

Sam pulled away to take off his jacket and dress shirt and he pulled up the bloody sleeve. His arm was smooth and clean and there was no sign of the cut.

"See, I told you." He grinned.

"What, it's gone?" It took a moment for that fact to sink in. "I thought you'd been promoted or something. I was worried what your next job would be."

Even as she spoke those words, her eyes searched for signs of... something on his arm. *What, gone?* She blinked. It didn't make any sense. Her mind short-circuited. The cut had been deep. This was not possible.

"Well a promotion will happen too. Especially now."

"What do you mean, especially now?"

"I know what we've got. I was the test. So I guess I'm valuable."

He began kissing her neck.

"How is that possible, your arm? And what have you got?" she asked.

"I can't tell you baby." He nuzzled her neck. She let him but asked again, speaking into his neck.

"How, what do you mean? You don't want to tell me?"

"They pressed something against my arm tonight before we left the restaurant. Like they said, it was a test. They blindfolded me. So I don't know anything."

"But your wound is completely healed."

"I know. Crazy, right?"

But he said it like it wasn't crazy at all. His lips moved up her neck to her ear and he whispered into it, "I didn't even take off my shirt. Or the bandage."

"They just held something against your arm, that's all? What was it?"

He stopped nuzzling her, and smiled, indulgent. He pushed her onto his bed and climbed on top of her. He pinned her down by her arms, pressing into her, hardening into her groin. She caught her breath. He lifted his face for a moment to say, "Look I never told you anything, agreed? Anyway, as I said, I didn't *see* it. It was in a bag, all I saw was a white padded bag. They said that inside the bag it doesn't do anything. They blindfolded me before they took it out. I didn't even touch it, they laid it on my arm."

Now he kissed her chest through the thick fabric. He peeled her dress off her shoulders and brushed his lips against her skin, drawing a straight line down from her sternum.

"What can't it do inside the bag? Have magical powers?"

"Yeah, I guess so." His mouth had reached her nipple. She let out a moan. "Whatever it is can *heal*. Crazy, right?"

He peeled off his pants, underpants, pressing himself against her urgently, his erection hot on her stomach. *Blind heat.* She felt herself open. The intensity of his lust was persuasive; it reminded her body of what she stood to gain. Her mind went foggy.

"*Fuuuuuck*," she whispered.

Even as her body took him in, greedy, even though she mentally deferred the conversation until later, her heart posed its perpetual question. *Was this even right, this thing they had?*

Sam was insistent, whispering how hot she was, and other words she didn't take in, so crowded were her thoughts with the conundrum of their relationship,

and with objects that healed, and organized crime,

every thrust of his cock searching for her depths,

all of it,

lust vanquished it all.

She moaned, helpless.

She succumbed to Sam's passion, as she always did.

The relief of surrender. The full-bodied collapse of all intention, all thought.

He tried to draw her heart in, holding her head and pulling at her with his eyes, but she couldn't meet him. She threw her head back, offering her neck instead. He was always trying to *make love*. Whispering words of affection. *Love you.* She said it back sometimes, but it was her body that loved his passion and the pleasure he drew out of her. Her heart had no place in it, even when her orgasm shuddered through her, right up into her chest and opened her throat until she cried out.

Something was wrong with her, she thought a second later.

She never felt it in her heart. She couldn't love him the way he loved her. He was none the wiser though, and gathered her sweaty body into his arms, nuzzling into her face as he fell into sleep, his giant paws pressing onto her stomach, her legs sticking to his thighs.

She waited until he snored, then wriggled out. She lay there staring at his healed arm. There were little sticky gray bits where the bandage had adhered to his skin, and some pinkness around that. And a scar, long and white, but—had she misremembered? It looked faded even from an hour earlier. Jia Li thought, as she stared at his skin, that she could even see it fading more now.

She closed her eyes and came to her senses.

She quietly got up and went into his bathroom, locked the door, and started searching. Oil, oil, she needed mineral oil. And a razor. And a ziplock bag. This was crazy, totally crazy. But she had to try. She found some kind of face oil. A very old bottle. And a razor blade from a pack with his shaving kit.

But before she did anything else, she found his long sleeve dress shirt. Whatever they had pressed against him might contain residue of whatever it was. *Maybe.* She stuffed his shirt into her handbag, then found a ziplock bag from the kitchen. He had them because she'd bought them for him, along with other kitchen necessities like aluminum foil and napkins. Thank God she'd found what she needed.

She sat at Sam's side and waited until his breathing was slow and silent, then poured mineral oil onto his faded scar, and quickly, furtively, but forcefully, scraped his skin and the oil so deeply that his skin pinkened. As she slipped the oily razor into the waiting bag, she threw the blanket over his arm and pushed herself against him and cried out, "Oh no!" making as much noise and movement as she could. As he jerked awake and his eyes opened she mumbled, 'Bad dream, sorry babe,' and squeezed his arm at the same time, to distract him from whatever he may have felt there.

Groggy, he grunted and tried to pull his arm up, but she squeezed it, and cried out again, and instead he kissed her.

She wasn't a bad thief after all.

The next morning, inside a large paper bag, she delivered everything to Michael Lim at his apartment, where he had set up his own private lab. If anyone could find answers, he could. She had included lunch as a thank you, and explained what she could at the door. He knew her well enough to say, "Leave it with me. I'll be in touch."

SHE COULD NOT HAVE IMAGINED that life would get more complicated, or weirder, but given all that had happened last night and that morning already, no other possible reaction could overtake the quiet numbness which had suffused her senses,

so that when Jia Li returned home to hear her mother breathing before she even saw her or heard anything else, she didn't panic.

The lights were off and the blinds shut. The living room was dark and Mary panted and cried.

"Mum?" She switched on the front hall light and then she saw her there, lying on the couch. She stopped breathing and for a second could not move from the fear, as if a boulder had just landed on her chest. The scene before her seemed unreal. The room went opaque, as if a heavy mist had fallen around them. She blinked. In the next second, she moved fast to her mother.

"I'm okay," her mother cried, but she clearly wasn't.

"Mum, what happened?"

"They were here. The men from your show. They put something in me. They injected me with something. They told me I have three months. Four if I'm really healthy. They said they can fix me, but after three months it's too late. They said you have information they want and that you must give it to them and not share it with anyone *or else*."

Jia Li fell to her knees in front of her mother, pulling her blouse down below her clavicle.

That numbness. Impotence careening into acceptance. Okay, what now? Her mental faculties switched on and she searched her mother's skin for a puncture wound.

"Where did they do it? What did they do to you? How did they even get in?"

"Not there." Her mother pushed her hand away. "I let them in, darling. I didn't know any better. They said that you have information they need. From Edward. I said to leave you alone. Then they held me down and injected me. It was a needle, in my arm, here." She pulled up her sleeve over her left arm. "It is sore now, that's all." Her voice faded. "I'm scared."

Jia Li searched the room wildly for something—help, relief, a clue—until powerlessness descended; the numbness drained from her body and worry rushed into its place. She cried out, "This is so fucking unfair! I don't know anything! I mean I know something was up, but I have no proof."

She began to cry, too.

Mary said, "The worst part is that I was starting to think I'd be okay as a widow. You know, that I could go on a cruise and visit Italy. I've never been to Italy. And now—three months they said. I will be sick and there's no cure, they said. And I don't even know what Edward knew or what you know. I'm just caught up in the middle, aren't I? This isn't even my fight."

"It's my fault. Because they know you are all I have left, and they think I know something, so they're trying to force my hand. But I don't know anything."

"It's not your fault, Jia Li. We don't really know what's going on. I'm getting old anyway. You should just go away, and protect yourself. Somehow, I don't know."

"Oh, Mum, no. There is a way, I know how to help you. I can get help. It's crazy. It would sound crazy. And maybe it's dangerous, but there is something out there that might heal you. I know it sounds crazy, but... " Her voice faded.

Mary put a solemn, single hand on Jia Li's red face. She lifted up her chin and stared into her daughter's eyes.

"I always wondered what he knew. He knew *something* that troubled him deeply. He wouldn't talk to me. So probably he also didn't talk to you." She frowned.

"It's okay, Mum. He was protecting us. But listen, I can help you. There is this object, it can make you better. I think it can. I just have to get a hold of it. I have to ask Sam..."

"Listen, Jelly, you don't worry about me. Don't do anything stupid. I don't know what you're talking about but I have a feeling it's not safe. I don't want you involved in threats like this." She gulped and her eyes welled up. "I will not lose you too. It's too much. For myself, I don't care. But you, you need to go away. You need to go far away. Let their threats be empty. I am not afraid of death. But I am afraid for you. They've been watching you a while now. So Edward knew something, and they don't know that we don't know. So they'll be after you, next."

Jia Li wrapped her arms around her mother and cried.

No, she would not disappear.

She'd save her mum.

"They killed him, didn't they? My Edward. He never jumped off that cliff."

Jia Li lifted her tear-stained face. She sniffed.

No one had ever needed to say it out loud to make it true, but speaking it opened something in her. Jia Li nodded, solemn, and repeated the only words she had, words which would enlist her in the quest she knew was coming

"I just don't have the proof."

6

KATE & THE ICON
JUNE 2019
ATLANTA, GEORGIA

The seven-year old girl was all tender and listless in a heap on the rug. *Pajarita*, she was nicknamed in Spanish. Kate called her Little Bird, and she looked like one: all brown stick limbs and watchful eyes, quiet and busy with her hands from morning till dusk. She could make things out of anything you gave her: ribbons, paper, shopping bags, yarn. She made little people with paper skin, stuffed with cotton balls, and drew big eyes on them. She scribbled tiny bubble figures, and was working on her letters with Kate's help. Her English was hit and miss. She understood well enough but spoke just above a whisper, only a few words now and again, though she sometimes came out with a full sentence. She was only chatty at bedtime, if she and Kate happened to be together then, curled into the one pillow they shared.

Kate bent down and nudged the pink marker closer to the child's floppy hand. Little Bird looked up at her with doleful eyes. "Thank you, Tia." Kate felt so heavy with concern and at the same time, her heart still did somersaults whenever the girl called her *auntie*. She rested a hand on Little Bird's back and took a moment to sink into this small interaction.

The girl seemed unwell the last few weeks, and just terrible the past few days. She dragged the neon marker along a sheet of paper. Her shoulder length black hair pooled onto her drawing. Her bangs had grown down into her eyes and she didn't even push them away. Kate sat down on the floor next to her and removed a strand of hair from her nose. She pushed the little pink backpack out of the way and leaned in to kiss Little Bird's forehead. The little girl grabbed her finger and squeezed.

"I'm gonna tell Paula you're not feeling well. What's going on, honey?"

The girl didn't respond. Maybe it was shyness that accounted for her habitual quiet, or maybe it was grief pressed hard against her throat. Kate had some familiarity with the latter; the sudden waves of sadness, how they submerged you for a time, so she could imagine how much worse it would be for a child. When Hurricane Michael hit Florida, Little Bird's mother had disappeared, presumed dead. Her mother's cousin Paula had taken Little Bird back with her to Atlanta, but since she was the only one telling the story, who knew what had really happened. Paula was Kate's downstairs neighbor, but she seemed to be always out.

Paula presumably worked all the time and—probably given that the child had no ID at all—hadn't even put her in any form of school or care, although her official excuse was that the girl's family was coming from Mexico to bring her home any day. Whatever the case, Paula was cleaning rich peoples' houses by day and waitressing by night, so as it turned out, for the past six months, Kate had Little Bird two, sometimes three days a week. Often, the girl and Kate fell asleep together and Paula didn't even check on her. On occasion, Kate had to get her neighbor and best friend Victoria to take Little Bird when she had work at night.

"Do you want dinner then?" Kate asked the girl.

"No."

Kate put her hand on her back again.

"Rub?"

The girl's eyes filled with tears and her lower lip wobbled.

"Ow. Ow." She leaned her head down on Kate's leg and lay there motionless.

"What's wrong baby? We have to bring you back to Paula, now. Something's not right. You need the doctor."

Kate knew that Paula taking her to a doctor posed any number of problems—not the least of which was money. The girl could be removed from her care, and Paula could get in trouble.

"Paula gone," said the girl. "California. I stay *contigo*."

"Gone? California? She just left?"

Little Bird nodded. "She said that *mi tio* is coming."

Uncle.

"Your uncle is coming from Mexico—to take you home?"

The girl nodded again. She bit her lip and frowned.

That had always been Paula's line. He was coming for his niece. But he never came.

"*Shit!*" Kate exclaimed, and covered her mouth before the child noticed, as if that would help. How in the world was she meant to look after this child? And then she thought with a burst of anger, *That fool of a woman has left this little girl in a precarious situation, and sick to boot.* She wasn't one to be angry for long, though, and her mood quickly shifted as she considered the practicalities. She felt an urgency to protect the child and complete helplessness as to how.

"Oh my goodness, you poor thing. Baby, we will figure this out. But you need to go to Victoria soon. I have work, honey. *Trabajo*."

Little Bird nodded her head slowly, and a tear welled up.

"Okay Tia." She spoke in a compliant voice. "But I don't want to go to uncle," she said, and stared resolutely at the floor, as if she were being naughty even saying it.

"Oh, baby." Kate pulled her to her chest. "It's going to be okay."

KATE HAD JUST hours earlier gotten a booking from a new client. He was Russian, she knew the accent. He had made an appointment for ten p.m. The first thing she'd done was tell Victoria she had a new guy. Now she rang her neighbor again, and asked if Little Bird could come over, to sleep on her couch.

Victoria cooed, "Oh honey, Little Bird and I are *compadres*, of course—you just send her over."

To Kate's ears, Victoria's Southern accent was both luscious and magical. It had the power to calm her nervous system almost instantly. Combined with the small voice she used whenever Little Bird was around, whatever she actually said just sounded to Kate like an invitation for hot chocolate and movies and a soft pillow to curl up on. Kate was tempted to cancel the client and spend the evening on the sofa, too. But she couldn't. She needed rent money. She felt a bit weary, suddenly, but shook it off fast. It was only 90 minutes of her life, after all.

She definitely did not have the courage to explain to Victoria that this care scenario might be a permanent arrangement, that Paula had, by the sound of it, deserted her ward.

Victoria was more than a neighbour, she was Kate's only friend and her minder. Six months prior Victoria had been Kevin, and as Kevin, she had worked as a bouncer. This meant that Victoria was a pro at protective services. She didn't ask questions and followed the rule: *Just please make it safe for me by any means necessary*.

Kate's professional recommendation, if you happened to read it in one of several newspapers or magazines, was this: Vanessa, slender blonde, B cup, classy, discreet. Her website was simple, not tawdry, with tasteful but generic photos which emphasized qualities her clients wanted—the curve of cleavage, slightly parted lips, edited with a glowy filter like she was suffused in angel light, just ready to bless you with her presence.

In real life, she was pretty and slend*erish*, though definitely not skinny. She was not at all stunning, either. Straight nose, a little big. Thin lips. Blue eyes. Plain, she would say, and Victoria agreed in her own tactful way, frowning over the website images.

"That doesn't even look like you. In real life you look like the girl next door who is going to be a librarian in the 1950s. You should have your hair in a bun and prim dress, you know, strict. No one would guess what you do for a living, girl. Not that I care what you choose to do with your body parts. That is your choice."

"It's my fucking job," Kate retorted. "Pardon the language and no pun intended. I don't want the photos to look like the real me. I like my privacy."

"Girl, I think you're a nerd and you like your intellectual freedom. I know you like to read all day long."

"I like to keep myself to myself, on my terms."

And it was that, that certainty, that self-possession, which brought a glow to her cheeks. Her eyes flashed with a liveliness normally buried deep in her self-imposed anonymity and elective blandness.

Victoria smiled. "You do have a certain charm, Kate Davies, and clearly you know your own mind. But you're 30 now, and I think you're destined for more than this. Anyway, you live on your terms, it's the privilege of being human."

"Don't talk to me about destiny," Kate said, and smiled at her friend, enigmatic.

Not even Victoria really knew her. As for what she wanted, well, she sure knew what she didn't want, and that was to be known, not fully, not yet. Aside from her deepest embrace, Kate gave nothing of herself to her clients. Not an open gaze, not the truths in her heart, not a word spoken off-topic. She harboured the secrets of others, and kept her own secrets wound tight and deep where they could no longer make demands of her. The price was, maybe, a lack of vision for the future, but she didn't care about that.

After her mother died when Kate was just in her late teens, she lost any inkling of the set-in-stone path of her youth. It was a path her mother had forced on her, and one Kate had emphatically rejected. As it turned out, only death brought full closure. Later, after Kate dropped out of college midway, she fell into a timeless daze that continued now, and seemed to be her fate.

Kate considered herself content without ambition. Her interests were few. Nothing she learned at college had ever seemed relevant anyway. There was no *depth*. There was a lack of urgency. It was clear that no one cared about the world beyond their personal ambitions.

Friends sold out to corporate jobs they hated. Everyone had such narrow goals. Well, at least that was what her cynicism told her. Anyway, Kate didn't feel impassioned about anything, so why bother?

Kate figured if she couldn't find it in her to be passionate about a path in life, she at least wasn't going to do harm. Living your Truth, she concluded, was finding the right bargain with life, one that harmed no one and gave more than it took. So she reckoned she'd found it. She made the money she needed to live; she read novels and watched documentaries and speculated about the world behind the news. She sat at her favourite diner after midnight when she couldn't sleep, when she didn't have Little Bird to look after, and she people-watched. There was mystery in life. It was enough to bear witness to it.

And she did that well. She was attentive to innocuous, fleeting details in a way others weren't. She had the rare ability to touch Grace with thoughtless presence alone. She could find such immersive beauty in each moment, as if the whole of life's meaning existed in every single instance—from the stray hand gesture of a stranger eating hash browns at one AM, to the faint movement of the tree branch out her window, viewed each morning from her bed, to the hollow eyes of a latest client in that moment before orgasm. Sometimes, her attention fell into these moments as one might sink into a warm sea, the gentle tide carrying her into the next moment effortlessly. She could hardly imagine wanting more for herself. She was living truthfully.

She hadn't intended her lifestyle at all. It found her by accident. One guy at a bar and money on the table led to more. An ad, a website. But Victoria was the deciding factor and not just because she had been Kevin, the six foot four bouncer at that time, but also because behind a face that looked angry in repose, she was a carer through and through, and Kate knew she'd be safe in those strong hands. She had once been the guy—and was now the woman— who stopped to take animals off the side of the road when they'd been hit by a car. She'd kicked bullies out of clubs and tended to crying customers with hugs and, if need be, a taxi ride home. Now she looked after Kate. She made Kate herbal teas and chicken soup when she was sick and was on call when she worked. She occasionally suggested other paths Kate might take in life. But Victoria had never judged her for her work any more than Kate had judged her neighbor for having big breast implants. Or for her drunkenness. *There were reasons*, Victoria said in reference to her drinking. So that was their bargain: a slightly uncomfortable but nevertheless heartfelt acceptance.

Practically speaking, Victoria got fifteen percent of Kate's fee, and for that she was on call to rush across the hall with her sleek, black, 1970s vintage .357 magnum revolver. Kate had a spare phone expertly hidden, and Victoria on standby—if a call came through on that number, it meant intervention, immediately.

Victoria was also on "meet and greet duty" with new clients. The imposing female neighbor would say hello, grunt, and Kate would say, "I'll call if I need you."

Kate figured the look on Victoria's face, and her size, would keep most men in line even if the man in question had opinions about her gender or sexual orientation. A couple of clients had backed out at that stage.

The spare phone was stuck with blu tac behind the bed head, which had proven a handy location. Kate had only used her alarm system once, when some jerk tried to handcuff her to the bed saying, "it's just a bit of fun!" The drawback to him being thrown out of the building was that Victoria found Kate naked and half-cuffed to the bed. Not her best moment. Later they had beer and watched reruns of *Seinfeld* and an episode of *Housewives of New Jersey*. Their unspoken rule was sacrosanct. They made no reference to the incident then or after.

ON THIS NIGHT, Kate cuddled Little Bird to sleep and carried her over to Victoria's, where they tucked her into a corner of the sofa. Then it was meet and greet time for them both.

The man never told Kate his name. He didn't even blink when he met Victoria. Afterwards, they were quickly down to business. It was hot outside, hovering around ninety and humid: an Atlanta summer. The air con wasn't strong enough; they were both sweating, skin sliding against skin. Not much chit chat, which was pretty par for the course, only he did seem more nervous than most, which happened sometimes for any number of reasons that Kate didn't waste a minute considering. Not her problem. She was already thinking of a cold beer next door and microwave popcorn.

He did mumble a couple of times, "I'll be safe with you," which was a little odd. Kate was taken aback by the vulnerability of his tone, and assured him he was safe, though it felt strange saying it, unnecessarily maternal. She had a feeling he wasn't seeking emotional sanctuary, because some men did, and she tended to know the type.

Their time together was otherwise a blur, and before she knew it, he groaned, then rolled off her and closed his eyes. Only he kept groaning. He clutched at his stomach and rolled to his side. Kate began to wonder if he had, in fact, ejaculated, but she couldn't see the condom on him from his position, and all she could do was watch in a rising state of panic. She asked him if there was something she could do—he didn't respond. She got up and put on her bathrobe and brought him a glass of water, which he ignored. His groaning was louder now. Then, suddenly, he stopped. His eyes were squeezed shut, mouth drawn into a grimace, hands balled into fists at his abdomen. There was no movement; he stiffened.

Kate reached behind the bed head and rang Victoria next door. She dared not think, lest she entertain the worst case scenario. She pulled on a bra and her lace panties and a bathrobe.

A moment later Victoria burst into the room, gun pointed. Kate held up a hand to stop her.

"Something's wrong. He's passed out or something. I don't know what it is. I don't know what to do. Should we call 911? Is Little Bird still asleep?"

"Sleeping like a baby. And she ain't well. Pale as death."

The man was still; his body had not relaxed. His eyes were half open and dull.

Kate knew then that the man had not passed out. He was dead. She'd never seen a dead person before, but she knew it when she saw his eyes.

"I think he's dead," Kate said softly. Victoria's eyes bulged, but she didn't disagree.

Kate remained completely still and silent, containing the turmoil inside, despite the pounding of her heart and the sudden static in her ears. She bit her upper lip as her mind spun through the scenarios—*what must she do?* She'd never been in this situation before. She didn't even know this guy's name. What was she going to say to the police? She couldn't risk losing her only source of income right now if she got in some kind of trouble for it—or go to jail if things got out of hand! And she was not a good liar, so it was definitely possible. Victoria just stood there, weaving ever-so-slightly from side to side, from drink, or shock, or both.

There they were, the two of them, just staring at—they both seemed to have accepted it now—a dead body.

Victoria went over and felt for a pulse, shook him, put her head down against his chest, then shook him again, this time harder, as if she were trying to wake him up.

"Dead," she confirmed, stumbling back.

Kate ran into the other room and put on a t-shirt and sweatpants and her sneakers. She came back into the room and rushed around collecting his clothes, throwing all his things onto the floor in a pile.

"What are you doing, Kate, for Christ's sake! Don't touch anything! Shouldn't we call the cops?"

Victoria's voice shook but Kate grew calm. She was only thinking that she had to get rid of both the man and all his stuff, immediately.

"Cops Victoria? And say what? We need to get rid of him and not be involved in any way, shape or form."

"Just stop. Sit." Victoria's hushed voice was firm enough to break through her thoughts for a moment. Kate sat on the floor, well away from the bed and the naked dead guy in it, and she picked up his black pants, a white dress shirt, his red, plaid boxer shorts. *A dead man, in her bed.* She had to remind herself that she didn't sleep on this bed. This was the work bed. Her bed was in her bedroom through the door at the back of this living room. Her bed had clean pink sheets and an old teddy bear. Her sheets smelled of laundry detergent and the sandalwood incense that she burned in her room. She reviewed all the moments before as rationally as she could, and yielded only the man's nervousness. His comment about being safe with her.

"I think he knew he was in danger, somehow," she mumbled. "He was afraid."

Victoria hadn't moved an inch since checking for the man's heartbeat and leaping back up. "Well, that's none of your business, and it doesn't matter. It's not your fault what happened. Probably had a heart attack or a stroke. Just say you met him at a bar and went home together."

"Right. Except for the part that nobody would have seen us at any bar. They can easily find out what I do, and then I'll be on the radar. I can't lose this work." Her eyes searched Victoria's avoidant gaze, as she wondered for a moment what might happen to Little Bird if she and Victoria went to prison. Whatever it was, it wouldn't likely be good.

Just then Kate noticed the bulge in the trousers she was holding in her lap, and pulled out a wallet, and then a card from it. "His name is..." she said. "Oh, God."

"What?" Victoria seemed increasingly agitated, swaying from leg to leg as if she were about to make a run for it.

"Wife and kids." She held up the wallet for Victoria to see the photo of her smiling client alongside a brunette with bright red lipstick and eyes lined in kohl, and two blond, pony-tailed girls. "No driver's license. Credit card says Roman Ivanov. Wife and kids, Victoria!"

"Your point?"

"We can't let them find out he died here! That's not fair! It's devastating enough. They don't need this, too. Look at them!"

Victoria stared blankly across the room and continued her manic shuffling from foot to foot. Kate held the photo close. It was worn, by fingers, well-traveled. Probably it had been in more than one wallet over the years. Valued. Maybe it was a few years old; his wife had left him, and this was his memory.

Kate didn't want to take any chances, though.

Victoria took two vigorous steps towards Kate and towered above her. Her face drew back in a kind of despair mixed with fear. Her mouth quivered. "Get a grip on your sympathies. He was seeing a hooker. He wasn't a fucking saint. We've got to call the police."

Kate inhaled deeply. She did not like the word *hooker*. It was so demeaning. She was a sex worker. It was *work*. Anyway, now wasn't the time to quibble over labels.

"No way, Victoria. It's not just his wife, it's everything. We've got to get him out of here. I'm not messing with the police. Once they know who you are, there's no going back."

"You're crazy, Kate," Victoria hissed as she grew more agitated. "What do you think this is, some kind of Coen brothers film? We don't get involved in shit like this. We just don't."

Kate stood up and stroked Victoria's arm. It was like touching wet clay in the clammy heat of the room. "Shhh. It's going to be fine. We can do this together. We're a team, remember?"

That's when she took in Victoria's outfit. Oh *dear*. A reddish pink flowery dress, cleavage and a beer gut, and that smudge of pink eyeshadow and dark mascara. *Well, aren't we a pretty pair with a dead guy?* she thought.

"You were going out later? You finally took my advice?"

"Yeah. I mean, after you were done here. Then I was going to the Purple Parrot." Victoria shrugged, almost embarrassed. Her curly and usually unkempt hair fell to her jaw line, but today it was so glossy and clean that it sat just below her ears. Almost bouncy. She pushed a few strands of hair out of her face to behind her ear.

Victoria hardly ever went out, even though Kate kept encouraging her to meet some like minded people. She needed a *community*, she'd told her multiple times, not just a neighbor friend to watch TV with. And tonight of all nights, she was planning on going out.

"Well, good for you."

"Lot of fucking good it did me."

"I know," Kate said. "This sucks."

Victoria softened a bit, albeit still in a pose that resembled a pitbull about to charge.

"It's okay, Victoria. We'll do this together. Look, we just don't need to be involved in something like this. Besides," Kate showed her the photo again, the wife and kids.

"What exactly will we do together, Kate?" Victoria's eyes bulged, and the quiver was back, this time her entire face. She usually got wound up fast over 'problems.' Historically speaking, anxiety could erupt at any moment, even when she appeared calm, so for her this was a delayed response. Kate blamed her volatility on the hormone therapy, and sometimes the alcohol. Victoria insisted it was a long-standing anxiety disorder, so they agreed to disagree.

And there it was, Victoria had started pacing, sweating, breathing in a funny kind of pant.

"We don't know anything about this guy, Kate, anything about how he died. Who knows what he's involved in? What if there was foul play? What if this was murder? This could be a crime scene..."

"Don't go nuts on me, okay? Just breathe. We don't need to know anything. All we need to know is that he was having sex with me and he's got a wife and kids at home who don't deserve to find out what their dad was doing when he took his last breath."

She began to arrange his clothes on the bed, ready to dress him.

"C'mon! Help me out here, Victoria. We gotta move him."

Victoria paused at the foot of the bed, breathing fast. She started mumbling to herself, "Okay, okay, it's not a big deal."

"Had much to drink tonight?" Kate asked her, prying apart Roman's legs. She began pulling on the boxer shorts, which got stuck at his knees.

"Five or so beers."

That was normal, even babysitting at night. Certainly wasn't enough to worry about right now.

"You can still help carry him then. You finish dressing him. I'll move his car right downstairs, near the woods—it's a straight walk from the back door. No one else is coming home so late. We'll put him in his car and drive him away." Kate rifled around in his pockets for keys, and thankfully found them.

"Okay, when he's dressed, tip him over the side of the bed and roll him up in the rug."

"The what?"

"The rug." She pointed to the floor. "That's what they do in movies, right?"

Victoria just shook her head, fingers gripping her temple. "No, no, no. It would look like a rug concealing a dead body, because everyone's seen that."

"Please," Kate said. "We can't just walk out of here carrying a body! I'll be back in a few minutes." She left before Victoria could protest.

Kate ran down the outside stairs to the ground level and into the street. She pressed the button on Roman Ivanov's keys, and saw the lights of a black Saab flash to her left, a few cars down in front of her building. She made sure there was no one around and got in. She didn't change the seat position, or the mirrors, and sat with her bottom right at the edge of the driver's seat so that her foot could reach the pedal.

Praying no one would hear her start the engine and look out of their window to see her in the Saab (since some of her neighbors knew she drove a Ford Fiesta), she purposefully didn't turn on the headlights. She drove the car straight into the driveway of her apartment building, and around the back where the trash cans were lined up next to the remnants of forest, long ago razed for development. A few spindly pine trees and the needle-strewn ground was all that remained a good many yards behind a cul de sac of neighboring homes. Kate parked there so that the passenger side, where she'd have to put the body, was facing the trees and therefore would be hidden from view of anyone. Then she rushed upstairs and into her living room.

Victoria had moved Roman's clenched hands to his side and was now trying to pull his shirt over his head and down, all the while cursing under her breath as she fumbled with the buttons. She had already managed the pants and boxers.

"Did you take off his condom?" Kate asked.

"No fucking way!" Victoria exploded. "I'm not touching his *penis*."

"He needs *no* condom or someone will get suspicious." Kate's heart still raced from running down and back up the stairs and the words came out like a pant. It struck her again—she bit her lip. *Shit*, she had a dead body to get out of her apartment.

Victoria didn't budge. So Kate yanked down his boxers and pulled off the condom. *Empty*. He hadn't even had that small joy before dying. Victoria looked away, screwing up her face.

Kate quickly put on his socks and black dress shoes, and together they hauled him off the bed and onto the rug to avoid the *thwack*. The rug was too short to conceal him entirely, so they hid his face and wrapped a blanket around his feet.

"How do we keep this rug rolled up around him?" Victoria asked.

"Tape," Kate said. "I have that brown box tape."

She ran into the kitchen and came back with tape and scissors. Together they rolled the man up tightly in the rug and ran the tape around multiple times near each end to secure it.

"Just what the hell do we say this is, in case anyone asks?"

Victoria was now sweating profusely and her pretty flowered dress was obviously drenched.

"At midnight on a Monday, no one should be up to ask, but if they do, say... I don't know, that the rug got peed on by a cat and we can't get the smell out and it's keeping us awake. Let's just go."

"That's your solution? Cat pee? Just hope for the best? There are what, four floors in this building, and three or four apartments per floor? Isn't that a bit hopeful to think no one will hear, or be out to see us?" Victoria's accent was slurring, in her panic, into something far less melodic than usual. Stray curls stuck to her forehead with sweat, and her mascara was smudged beneath her eyes. There was no trace of the eyeshadow anymore.

"Look, just smile. We can explain better later, if we need to. C'mon! The car's waiting!"

"This is naive, Kate. People always get found out."

"Victoria, look at me. In the eyes."

Her friend did as requested. Kate's blue eyes were strangely clear and liquid, and steady, so steady; Kate felt her own certainty and her friend seemed to feel it too.

"We don't really have any control over the outcome. We just have to follow our instincts and do the best we can. We'll deal with anything else as it happens, okay? Take a deep breath now, and then three more, we're going to get this to the car."

Victoria took a breath, and then another. Kate knew Victoria would trust her. Their friendship was just about the most solid thing in her life, for which reason she tended to defer to Kate's opinions.

Lucky for them, no one was in the hall or the stairwell, (especially since Kate really did *not* want to betray that trust, ever). Roman Ivanov's body was so heavy they could only manage it to the stairwell door, and then had to slide him, inside the rug, down the stairs. She paused at the door and pushed it open by leaning on it with her shoulder. She poked her head out of the cool stairwell into the heavy heat and humidity and heard only the low hum of middle-distance traffic and no human sounds.

"Clear. Put him in the front passenger seat," Kate whispered as they lifted the rug and carried it ten feet to the far side of the car, setting the bundle down as gently as they could. "Here's his keys." She handed them to Victoria. "Drive him to Supreme Donuts. Follow me in my car."

"Why me? Why Supreme Donuts? Do you have something against doughnuts?" Victoria tittered, slightly hysterical, but mercifully quiet.

"It's a minute away and they're closed by now so no one will see us, and I'm not sure about the fast food places," she hissed impatiently. She ignored the *Why me*. She didn't have an answer to that.

"Fine. I'll do this for you, Kate, but fast."

Kate gave Victoria's arm a squeeze and they locked eyes. "I owe you so much, Vic."

Victoria responded with a subtle nod. "You do. Love you too."

They had to unwrap the body before shoving it into the car—that was the most harrowing part. They scanned the back of the building to make sure there were no lights on, no discernible onlookers. Then they unwrapped the carpet and rolled him onto the concrete. Anyone who saw him would have no doubt that he was dead. As Kate was the smaller of the two, she climbed into the passenger seat and put two arms underneath Roman's armpits and heaved him up as Victoria lifted his torso from his front. Somehow they managed to shove him into the car and prop him upright, then secure his seatbelt.

By now Kate's lower back was killing her, her head was throbbing, and she was standing in front of the car with a rug and the blanket they'd used to conceal his feet.

"I've got to bring this back upstairs!" Kate said.

"What if someone sees me?" Victoria asked. "*With him?*"

"Shit. I've got to go anyway," she realized aloud. "I don't have my car keys! Just get in the driver's seat. I'll be a second."

Fortunately the rug was reasonably light now that it was empty, so Kate managed to drag it back up the stairs to her apartment alone. She dropped it on her floor, threw the blanket on the work bed, and went to grab her car keys from the fruit bowl in the kitchen.

When she got back downstairs Victoria had turned on the engine. Kate went to her window and said, "Don't turn on your lights. Just follow me straight to the back of the building. There are a bunch of trees back there and it's always dark. I don't think they have security cameras."

"You don't *think*?"

"I mean, it's the suburbs, so probably not. It's in the middle of nowhere."

A few moments later they were driving down streetlight lit roads, past the nearby McDonalds and the local strip mall, and a minute later had pulled into the dark parking lot of Supreme Donuts. Kate wanted to pull him out and put him in the driver's seat, but she knew it was too risky, so she made sure he was well situated in the passenger seat, confirmed with Victoria the seat and mirrors were in their usual position, and used her shirt to wipe down everything they might have touched, including his wallet and the photo and cards inside.

Finally, even though she didn't believe in praying or in heaven, she said a small blessing in her head, that Roman might find peace if he made it to some kind of afterlife, and that his family might eventually find peace in his passing.

NOT SURPRISINGLY, Victoria decided against going out after all that. They went back to her place and had a beer and a packet of Oreo cookies and watched a documentary about lions while Little Bird slept restlessly in the corner of the couch, moaning every so often. Neither of them said a word about what had just transpired.

It was only the next morning as Kate lay in bed, Little Bird curled up beside her, that the previous night's events fully descended into her consciousness. Her chest suddenly contracted. She couldn't breathe. In a panic, she tried to review all the details, going over and over what she might have missed, what she might have done to leave a trail that would lead back to everything that mattered to her—and everyone. Details came in and out of focus, scrambled like a video on rewind, and then one fact Kate hadn't remembered until now roared to the forefront—that Roman Ivanov had left his coat hanging in her front hall closet: a grey, thigh-length overcoat, woolen, obviously of good quality. It hadn't occurred to her at the time how odd it was to wear it on a hot summer night. She'd only had the fleeting impression that he was dressed like a character from a 1940s musical, or old school mafia. Ah, how could she have forgotten such a strong first impression?

She cursed her oversight, and wiggled herself out from under Little Bird's heavy head on her arm.

She went to the closet and dragged out his coat. She opened it. It had pockets on the inside, one on each side. She reached into the first one. Nothing. Her hand delved into the second one, and landed on what felt like a padded envelope, but thicker. She pulled it out. Whatever the material was, it felt weighted, like it was filled with sand, so heavy.

She held it, heart thudding now. *Please let it not be some body part*, she thought, and shuddered at the gruesome thought, even as she unzipped it.

What she saw inside was definitely not anything she expected. She pulled out the cold, metallic object, and stared at what appeared to be an antique cross. The metal was a dull, unpolished brown. It was a bit longer than her ipad, with three horizontal beams across the vertical beam, the lowest one crooked. On the middle beam was the typical depiction of Jesus, and above and below were letters and other symbols. She caught her breath. She'd seen something like it before, hadn't she?

Little Bird's small voice spoke from behind. "*La cruz.*"

"Shhh," Kate said, hastily shoving the coat into a pile on the closet floor, and sliding the cross under it. She beckoned to Little Bird, and scooped her up into her arms. The girl was cold and clammy to the touch.

"Oh God. You're sick, honey. We have to figure that out first."

7

FATHER SERGASIN & THE TRAVELER
NOVEMBER 1925

THE ASCENSION MONASTERY
OF TUNGUSKA, SIBERIA

Nearly ten years before the purging of the Monastery, when such a travesty was yet unimaginable, when the hallowed ground was still a place of sanctuary, a traveler collapsed at the hermitage entrance, in devotion. Father Sergasin found him as the bells sang their morning song.

"What do you need, traveler?" Father Sergasin asked him. "You appear to be very weary. Why are you here?"

"I am those things, yes, but also I am filled with the love of God such as you cannot imagine."

He held his coat to his chest strangely, wrapping one side across the middle and beneath his left armpit.

"Have you got something there beneath your coat?" Father Sergasin asked.

"Yes, but please tell me. Are you Father Sergasin?"

"I am he, indeed. Do you need help?"

"Oh thank God! Can I beg of you a warm place to sit, and a quiet word, Father? I have asked widely who is the kindest, the most holy, the most loving of Christ's servants. I was told that he is the one who often rescues the likes of me, those who come to the monastery for help, and it is you who greets me, yourself! So to you, I must tell the holiest story, and entrust you with a miracle, for I have been very blessed and wish to return the miracle from whence it came."

Father Sergasin asked no more, despite the intrigue which beset him, and took the man straight through to an empty room, a meeting space that was heated. They sat at the table, and he asked a novice walking past to please bring the old man tea and porridge, which was brought shortly.

"You must eat and drink first, traveler. Then speak," Father Sergasin said.

"Thank you, I will," replied the man, and he did so, resting for a moment more before he spoke again.

"IT BEGAN when I was a young man. My wife and I were only just married a year. We had one son, and we lived simply in a village beyond Irkutsk. I am a merchant. A humble merchant, and God's servant.

"One day an *ofenya* came through town selling icons. He was different to the others, with a faraway look in his eyes, as if he had already joined with God, and was merely here in body. I approached him, although I was fearful, somewhat, because of the look in his eyes. I cannot tell you why, but perhaps it was a foreboding, that I, too, would be so changed as he was, and although I considered myself a pious man, I also knew my imperfection, my sins, and felt unprepared.

"On that fateful day, I purchased several icons for our iconostasis, for my missus prayed daily and her holy place was poor in relation to the richness of her devotion. I chose several icons in the traditional style, but I was drawn to a particular *ikona*—a solid crucifix, one to hold, with our savior and the angels and words of Grace.

"In all I purchased four icons, but the crucifix I held to me all the way home. Its weight was pleasing, and I cannot lie: Grace fell upon me as I traveled home. I was overcome by the feeling that God was so close, and the world all around me was bathed in light. That feeling, Father, it was emanating, I believe, from that cross which I held to my chest. I thought I was merely in a righteous fervor, and made not much of it at that time. I placed the cross, though, at the bottom row on the wall beneath the others, where one might easily reach it and touch it."

Father Sergasin sat forward, eager and nostalgic. "Forgive me for interrupting, but what year was it that you say you came across this particular icon?"

"It was...." The man thought for a moment. "It was 1909, I believe."

"Interesting!" Father Sergasin sat back, pensive. His eyes clouded with a dim memory. He wished to summon Father Yakunov, for he shared this memory, but he didn't want to delay this man's story, which was moving apace.

"So, where was I? Oh, yes, I brought the icons home. My wife was delighted with our additions and fell to her knees at once. She mentioned the particular beauty of the cross, but honestly, I thought no more of it. Then, many months later, during her difficult birthing of our second son, and forgive me for speaking of such matters—in the throes of birth she lost a great deal of blood. I was told by the midwife that she would not live. Our second son was blessedly alive. I came in at the last, and I did nearly faint at the blood which soaked the bedding, and pooled onto the floor. I knew in my heart that no mortal body could sustain this trauma, and I wept openly even as my dear wife asked for that icon, for the crucifix to shepherd her into her next life. So I ran to fetch it and lay it upon her chest. The babe lay whimpering beside her.

"I prayed, then, I prayed with her as she became completely still and as alabaster. She did not resemble the wife I knew and loved. Already, however, something was happening. I believed I was delusional or grief stricken, as the cold stone that was my beloved slowly gained color and softened before my very eyes. Her color returned over the next hour or so, and this despite the enormous loss of blood, and the certainty that she barely clung to life. Yet, by the Grace of God, by the next morning she was *fully* restored, and we prayed together over this *ikona*, this miracle, filled with the love of Christ, which we knew had healed her. We knew it then, it was special, it was a direct revelation from God. But that is not all. Not in the least."

The merchant took a deep breath. Father Sergasin tried to contain his excitement, for this tale was surely in reference to that icon about which he'd heard—as the man had said—in *1909*. Which he'd not seen with his own eyes at that time. This traveler must have this icon hidden in his cloak, he thought. That is why he held his hand to his armpit in such a strange manner.

"Years later, when our eldest son was six, he fell from a horse and broke his leg. The bone came through his skin. It was this tragedy which was the turning point, as we had not been in such desperation since his brother's birth, and it was this desperation which compelled us to take the cross from the wall, once more. What we witnessed next was unbelievable. After a few hours, our son felt an overwhelming energy surge through him and he leapt out of bed, and began to move his body as if possessed. We feared possession in fact. But he was calm, somehow, and radiating only peace. He moved, twisted, and bent over, writhing with his hips and then pushing, on his leg, and suddenly his bone slipped back inside his flesh. We watched as his wound healed. An hour later his flesh was perfect, with only a light scar, which too disappeared over the next few days. He never had a limp. It was as if nothing had happened."

Now Father Sergasin was so consumed by curiosity that he nearly exclaimed *show me* and went to thump both hands on the table, but to stop himself, instead brought a hand to his beard, which he stroked.

"That was our revelation," the man said. "And since that moment, every injury, every illness, caused us to rush to the icon and grasp it greedily in devotion. It never failed to disappoint us. The power and Grace of God, of the Holy Spirit, is truly limitless. From that day on, no one in our house ever suffered for more than an instant. And slowly, we found the courage to use it with others in our community, those close to us whom we could trust. Always, we gave credit to the Lord.

"Truly, our praise for the Holy Spirit never waned, and as our health and our physical bodies left nothing to doubt, our hearts, too, healed in proportion to that which we called a miracle. I cannot tell you the fullness of our hearts, and our devotion. It was as if we had a direct communication with Grace, which surely you know in your position as servants and representatives of God on earth."

The man paused to drink the last bit of his tea.

"I can imagine," Father Sergasin said, and swallowed his joy. It must really be true, what Visarrion had told him those many years past. He asked, "What happened next?"

"As our love grew, so did our generosity. My wife acquired a reputation as a traveling missionary of God, bringing the holy icon with her to tend to women and babies, to help the sick. And this was our life for many years. Even when our sons made their way into the world, we did so knowing that as long as we were devoted to the cross, all would be well."

Here he stopped and the long shadow of a frown darkened his face.

"But, as you know, there are dark forces in this world. Evil does exist, and perhaps it must, perhaps that temptation is there to make us stronger as servants of the Lord. These are not matters which are familiar to me, only unfortunately they became known to me through the contrast of God's greatest miracle in my life. Because, and I suppose it was inevitable, others began to whisper about this icon. And those whispers became a chorus, and suddenly there were those who came to us begging and desperate. My wife of course, being the pure soul that she was, wished only to help, and she did whenever she could, although she began to wonder aloud about when she might be left in peace rather than remaining an emissary of the Lord. Maybe, her prayers were heard, and such was the unfolding of our path."

He sighed. Father Sergasin waited with tense expectation. He prayed that the traveler would open his cloak, and reveal this icon soon.

"I suppose in retrospect, it is inevitable, is it not? That even those with impure hearts should want to have access to God's miracle. For their own nefarious purposes. And so it was that one day, after many years of sharing the icon, when my wife had grown quite weary from her daily ministrations to those in need, thieves arrived in the night."

"Oh no," Father Sergasin said, and he shook his head with pity.

"Indeed. And so it was that I was woken from my sleep by three thieves who began to threaten us if we did not hand over the crucifix. And, for my part, there was not a moment's hesitation. Like Saint Serafim, I renounced my strength and I chose the path of sacrifice."

Father Sergasin said a prayer to bless the noble act and this man who had performed it.

"The crucifix was now gone."

Now he had a tear in his eye.

Father Sergasin placed a hand on the merchant's arm, and said, "You show great devotion."

"That is not even the tragedy," spoke the merchant after a time. "For such goodness in the hands of evil not only deprives the good of Grace, but risks the holy becoming in service to the Devil."

"Say more," Father Sergasin said, resisting his growing impatience.

"I do not know exactly what happened, but there was a great deal of fighting afterwards. Rumors abounded. Woven amongst tales of bloodshed over control of some sacred object, there were tales of a miraculous cross that could heal. It seemed that the cross had fallen into the hands of those plagued by drunkenness. Then we heard that there were murders by other thieves, or some such unsavoury people. Next, I caught wind that that crucifix had found its way into the ranks of the Bolsheviks who possessed weaponry sufficient to foment a bloodbath far beyond that of petty thieves in dark alleys. My heart suffered, and my wife took to ever deeper acts of devotion.

"Then, as our good White Army suffered further defeats, I feared for this sacred object. Once we were defeated at Perekop, I knew that this icon would remain in the hands of the Bolsheviks, and what then? So I prayed fervently. I prayed with devotion I knew not until that time, prayed that I would find this icon once more, and that I could safely shepherd it to the Church, in hiding with good and holy men, where it belongs."

"Bless you," said Father Sergasin, trying not to stare at what must be that object, hidden in the man's coat.

"And that is when the miracles returned. The Red Army controlled Irkutsk, as you know. One day, two Bolshevik soldiers were conversing in my shop, and when they mentioned a cross, my ears pricked.

"They had heard that an officer in their corps had acquired a priceless icon known as the *healing ikona*. They are Godless, as you know, so they mocked its reputation, as if the rumors were absurd, as if it were a plot of the Church to trick good people into trading common sense for magic. They said that this certain officer was behaving strangely, and would not part with the cross, and his commanding officers were going to confiscate the *ikona* and send him packing because he was not a true Red Army officer if he held God above the State.

"They had all determined this officer to be insane, you see! But I knew the truth. I knew it. And I knew that I had to get to him. I had to find out who this officer was, and request a meeting. I followed these two soldiers. I followed them back to their headquarters.

"First, as I sat outside, I prayed. Then, I summoned the courage of God and requested a meeting with this officer.

"They laughed at me, but I told them that I had news he would very much want to hear, that could be important to their mission, and surely they would not want to be the men who refused to admit crucial sensitive intelligence. A ruse, of course, but effective. I was permitted to have an audience with him."

Father Sergasin said, "I cannot imagine what you said to him."

"The truth. That I had heard the rumors. That I knew what the crucifix was capable of, and that I also knew what his officers were saying about him. I told him that I would take this cross from him and return it to the church and would tell no one that I had done so. In return, I described to him the officers who had laughed at him. He was sufficiently scared, I think, of what might happen if word got out, although he was reluctant, too, as he was firmly attached to the miracle. I knew this feeling, and had to rise above it myself, because I knew that the correct course of action was to bring it here, tell you all this, and pray that you keep it safe from people, *for* people, for a day yet to come. The people are not ready for this miracle. Not the masses, Father. Their consciousness is low, and there are too many desperate ones who would choose survival over sanctity."

The traveler took a deep and sighing breath. He closed his eyes. He opened his coat, and from beneath the layers of clothing, he withdrew a bronze crucifix from that place nearest his heart.

Father Sergasin gasped, in relief, then in puzzlement. Its sameness was the most obvious characteristic. Many such icons were about in those days. By appearances, it was so unremarkable. He opened his palms on the table between them.

The traveler placed the crucifix in Father Sergasin's hand. He closed his eyes and said, "You will see for yourself, what it brings. And I pray that it finds sanctuary here, until the world is ready."

8

KATE & LITTLE BIRD

JUNE 2019

ATLANTA, GEORGIA

At Victoria's place, they all sat in a row on the couch watching Sesame Street at eight a.m., Little Bird squashed in the middle, a mini packet of potato chips on her lap. The girl had taken a single chip and had been sucking on it for well near a minute. Victoria put a hand on her forehead. "She's clammy." She gave Kate a look that just about summed up their chances of dealing with this situation.

"No help me," Little Bird sniffed. It was unclear if she was expressing her resignation or issuing them orders.

"You want help? Of course we can help you, honey," said Kate.

Victoria raised her eyebrows in Kate's direction but said to the girl, "We've got you."

"God helps," the girl pronounced. Victoria's eyes widened and Kate sighed. Again, her intention was open to interpretation.

They'd known it was bad before they even received the diagnosis. Kate wondered how anyone could not know the presence of something living inside you. Like the heart knows love, so too it knows sickness. Every time Kate looked into the girl's small eyes she felt it, a thief of life that gathered strength. The sweet, yeasty smell of the child lying against Kate's cheek at night was confirmation, not a clue, which was why they'd had to get her to the hospital. To save her.

Little Bird knew she was ill and that her life hung in the balance; how she might have understood the implications of that fact was another matter entirely. She was too clever and wise for so small a soul in some ways, and in other ways not, but one never knew which way she was trending at any given moment. She often saw through pretense and displayed pure generosity, and truly it was hard not to love her up when she offered you her last chip, or brought you a blanket, or gave you a kiss right when the weight of the world was about to spill out of your tear ducts. But still, she wasn't just *that* either. In fact, Kate and Victoria had checked their mothering fantasies early on, because Little Bird would periodically—and unexpectedly—fly into a rage over small, petty details. Macaroni and cheese without ketchup; a broken purple crayon; disrupted internet connection.

Now, made smaller and softer by illness, she offered only terse, unclear commentary, and dropped the bag of chips onto the floor like a toddler.

In better days, Victoria would have told her to pick up the bag and take it to the trash, but today she just kicked it away from the couch. This child no longer needed discipline, just healing, plus possibly a miracle intervention from her Mexican relatives to get her away from the clutches of social services, whose policies both Victoria and Kate feared, since they didn't understand them at all.

During her hospital visit the week before, Kate and Little Bird had waited for what seemed like days—though in fact it was six hours. No sooner had they been ushered into a room than the questions began. The young doctor, blond and unshaven and surely not more than twenty, looked tired and bored as he examined Little Bird, so Kate couldn't help volunteering information beyond what he specifically requested. She thought she should round out the impression he might have, the tentative legalities in particular, with the *humanity* of her ward.

Kate explained how the girl had been left at her doorstep by her neighbor who used to live downstairs. No, she had no papers. She spoke English all right, not bad considering she spent most of the time with her Mexican family until she ended up spending most of her time at Kate's. She watched videos on Kate's phone, childrens' shows, which Kate monitored closely, and she'd learned a bit of English that way. She loved macaroni and cheese and drew a lot with markers. She gave the young doctor lots of innocuous details, as if it mattered, but he seemed hardly distracted from the task at hand, until suddenly the tears started rolling down Kate's face, at which point he did a double take. Little Bird, meanwhile, had been so quiet and removed it was as if she wasn't even there; she only squeaked when they took blood. Otherwise she clung to Kate's arm and began crying softly when she saw Kate crying.

In his only admission of compassion, the doctor smiled—albeit strained—and said to the girl, "Well, you have been looked after well." An ominous statement in Kate's mind, being as it was in the past tense.

He disappeared and a short while later a redheaded nurse named Joleen came in. She was funny and kind and got Little Bird to smile. Joleen asked Kate, "Have you eaten today? Has she?"

Kate admitted she couldn't bring herself to leave the child's side even for a moment, not even for the bathroom. Joleen told her to go get food in the cafeteria downstairs and to go to the bathroom, that she'd stay with Little Bird— not to worry, nothing was happening today with social services. When Kate returned, Joleen patted her hand and said she could tell that she and the girl were very fond of each other.

When the tests came back a few hours later, Joleen explained that Little Bird was anaemic and had a high white blood cell count, and they needed to take a biopsy from her hip. It had already been booked for a few day's time. Little Bird had fallen asleep in the hospital bed by then, her hand clasped with Kate's. Joleen told her she should take the child home until everything was sorted, as they were too busy to manage her, social services wasn't coming that day and anyway, they had all Kate's details. Kate burst into fresh tears. She hadn't even told Victoria that she'd used a fake ID and a different number when she'd brought Little Bird in. She had a few SIM cards for work. For privacy. She gave the hospital one she'd never used before.

Joleen handed her tissues and patted her on the back. "Honey, I'm not saying it's not scary, but if it's what they suspect, it's curable. A long journey, but her chances are really good. She's lucky to have you."

"She won't have me. They'll take her."

"I'm really not an expert on how these things work. But if I were you I'd pray."

For the moment, Kate poured her hope into Joleen's reassuring smile like it was an insurance policy, until the hip biopsy two days later. Little Bird was once more floppy and drowsy and easy to manage. Again, Kate was on her own at the hospital battling worry and grief while Victoria went on a casserole and banana bread baking spree.

The diagnosis came fast after that. Leukemia. Now they had to go back to the hospital to be assessed for treatment. Urgently. Since Kate was paying, there weren't so many questions yet, but she was going to run out of money fast.

"Do you want to come with us to the hospital in the morning?" Kate asked Victoria, for the third time, glancing down at the frail child lying between them on the couch, watching TV.

Victoria's face fell and her eyes teared. She shook her head no.

"I know I should. But I hate being around sick people. Plus they probably won't let me in with you. Just a parent, and you're the closest thing."

The girl would be taken from them, of course, that's what Victoria was thinking, and so was Kate. Their little family-like unit wasn't enough, no matter how much love they had for each other.

They'd just had dinner. Well, not Little Bird, she had no appetite. Her body stretched across the length of the couch and at one end she snuggled into Kate's armpit. At the other, her legs were curled up under Victoria's bottom.

Victoria stared stoically ahead at the TV and muttered, almost to herself, "This should have been handled so much better."

"What could I have done differently?" Kate asked, directing her question in a rough voice towards Victoria's turned cheek.

Victoria took barely a breath. "We should have left town or something. What if they find out? What if they think we took her too?"

"Oh you mean handled *that* better," Kate snapped, realizing where Victoria's fears lay. "They don't know anything. It's fine." She looked down at Little Bird again and sighed. "She's not ours. They'll take her away."

Kate leaned over and kissed the child's head, her messy hair all knotted on top. It couldn't have been handled any other way as far as she was concerned. *All of it.* Sometimes life gave you so few choices you just had to leap in and tackle the most immediate thing, one after another. Like a small child sitting outside the door, all alone, those doleful eyes just blinking at you with pain and some silent invitation —until one day you brought her in and gave her a pen and paper, and one thing led to another.

"Honey, do you remember the name of the town your uncle is from?"

Paula had left a bit of paper with the uncle's name—*Jesús*—and number on it, but Kate couldn't understand the woman at the other end of the phone, other than "we come, we come." But when? How long do we have? Even if the uncle did come get her, then what? Her thoughts turned to rescue missions, to clean cancer wards in Mexico and an extended family to love the girl through it. None of it felt true, not even true enough for the relief of pretending.

She bit her upper lip. "Your town, honey? What is it called?"

"*No sé. El lago* and big sky."

"A lake and a big sky." Kate sighed. "Anyway, I called Jesús, *Pajarita*. And I spoke to your auntie. *Tia*. She said someone will come for you, from your family."

Little Bird just stared, as if she hadn't heard, or was blocking it out.

"I know you said you don't want to go, but he's family. He can help you get better."

"So we are waiting for Jesús," Victoria said, "and treatment in Mexico."

"Yeah. We are waiting for miracles." The room was silent for a moment, before Little Bird spoke.

"*Tio*—he's mean. He's not my family," Little Bird said, and snuggled in closer to Kate.

"Oh, darlin', that's alright, we are your family, too, now. May God protect you," said Victoria.

Little Bird shuddered a few moments later as she drifted into sleep, and Kate stroked her forehead. Victoria reached over to stroke the girl's hand, which was extended over her head. As the child went still, Kate sighed, heavy. "You're a gem, Vic."

"We're going to get through this, sweetie. You gotta pray, Kate, that's all there is to it. I'm going to make us tea."

Victoria extricated herself carefully from the sleeping child and made herself busy in the kitchen while Kate sat with the girl in her lap. Little Bird's hair stuck to the sides of her face. Maybe she hadn't bathed in a while, come to think of it. Kate would give her a bath as soon as she seemed up to it. She held the girl tight and tried not to stroke her face and wake her, though love sought some kind of expression and she had difficulty holding herself back. Finally Kate kissed her own finger and gently pressed it against Little Bird's forehead.

She asked Victoria, to distract herself, "Why do you pray so much anyway?"

Kate did not believe in any kind of conventional God. Consciousness, maybe. Goodness, perhaps. But without a god, to whom, exactly, did one pray?

Victoria emerged from the kitchen. "Girl, I've been praying since the day I realized nature got it wrong and made me a boy on the outside, and don't you underestimate the power of prayer. Sometimes it's all you can do. It might work some kind of magic, or it might just make you feel better."

"So religion for you is an insurance policy?"

"You make it sound like a transaction. Look, I don't believe in fire and brimstone and punishment. If God exists, God is pure love. And pure love would heal. It would heal anyone because that is the nature of healing. So I'm praying. I'm praying for my daddy too, and he disowned me."

"I'm not sure God is coming calling at this dark hour. He had plenty of opportunities before this. Even with your dad. He's got prostate cancer, right? Maybe that's karma, though, if he was an asshole to you."

"Ha. You're funny. Well, everyone deserves love. Maybe not being *liked*. Definitely not *approval*."

Kate smiled. "No, not everyone deserves to be liked, that's true. You're a good soul."

Victoria pushed a steaming mug of chamomile tea onto the coffee table in front of Kate.

"Too kind," Kate thanked her.

Victoria sat back down on the couch in the corner, squeezing in beyond the feet of the sleeping child. She balanced a bowl of instant noodles on her knees. Kate grimaced.

"Really? Don't you have something better to eat? Haven't you been baking casseroles?"

"We ate one and I froze two for the long days at the hospital. Besides, I'm not rolling in enough cash for Whole Foods these days. And you? You got some work coming, girl?"

"Not tonight. But I'd better. I have to pay a helluva credit card bill now."

"I'll help you pay for Little Bird, honey. I've got some saved up. I don't mind eating two minute noodles."

"Oh, Vic! The money for your surgery? You can't spend that! You've been saving for ages for your trip."

"Who do you think I am? Look at this child. Thailand can wait. It can wait."

By *it* she meant her vagina.

To give up the surgery was a sacrifice Kate never would have asked of Victoria. She didn't have the words or even the energy to express it. Instead she rested in the rare acceptance she felt in Victoria's company.

Yet, in truth, whilst she was probably Kate's closest friend—at the moment, her only friend—Victoria hardly even knew her. They had known each other for a couple of years and had that affection that builds between people who spend a lot of time together, but they didn't know each other's secrets—not until the most recent one, the one they shared and dared not mention. They didn't know much about one another's pasts. Victoria hadn't even been aware of Kate's last relationship, or how much it had broken her heart. Well maybe Victoria had seen something, and felt something, but it had been early on in their friendship and she'd never asked about it. And Kate didn't know why Victoria had been disowned, for example, not *really*, though she could imagine any number of reasons.

Kate let out a quiet *ha*, not quite a laugh, not even a chuckle, but she smiled with some effort. "Just look at us. We are kind of pathetic, aren't we? Oh, God," and she put her face in her hands, not sure if she was going to laugh or cry.

Victoria put her bowl of noodles down on the coffee table and took a gulp of tea, breathing out steam like she'd burned her tongue. She wagged a finger. "We are not pathetic, Kate. We're wise to the world. You and I know the underbelly. And if you don't know suffering you can't change a thing. I reckon we're the heroes of the story."

"Heroines."

Victoria returned a wry smile. "You got it."

"You can be deep when you're not drinking. It suits you. You need to give it up, for the sake of your deepness." Kate risked a glance at Victoria, but her face held only the wry smile. "Okay. I'm going to take this child to bed, and try praying. I'm going to borrow your conviction since I've got none of my own."

"You pray. You'd make a good mother one day, girl."

. . .

KATE KNEW she was not exactly Mary Poppins, but she reckoned she *got* Little Bird at a level that defied experience. Much of the time, Little Bird was self-contained and loving in the way of someone who's never been filled, hell bent on claiming whatever love was out there as her own—almost like she was gathering reserves just before an inevitable shortfall. Yet, any small imperfection in circumstances might trigger the child's enormous fear of loss, and the ensuing rage to either hold on or to push away. Given the kind of calamity that took her mother so dramatically, Kate forgave her all of it.

Even from early on in their relationship, Kate had always sensed the storm coming. Litter Bird's unwinding was on the clock. Her sadness just built and built until it reached a certain point, from which it couldn't shift without the release of rage. Silence was how the girl seemed to experience her sadness. Introspectively. Many of her little stick figure drawings were 'mama', and there were giant waves sometimes, and big, fat tears on little girl figures, and sometimes a man in the corner, probably her uncle in Mexico, and at times for ten or twenty minutes she could sit still and just stare, out the window or at her handiwork, just disappear into it like she was looking for something not of this world—like her mother, Kate speculated, or some kind of free floating salvation from so much hurt.

Then came a 20 minute meltdown because she couldn't find the right crayon, or because it was raining and they couldn't go to the playground, or they were out of ketchup. Kate just held steady, her own frustration grounded and still, in some kind of knowing that this was the process, the unraveling of pain, to be traveled through with steady guidance. She gave the girl space to scream and cry, and waited for cues to hold her, even if often she got it wrong and was kicked away.

Kate didn't really question why she accepted the girl, and the situation. She just felt a driving force to be a loving, soft place to land. Like she owed it to the Universe to nurture whatever required nurturing. Sometimes, it felt almost like a dare. Like "See if you can hold onto this broken girl, and help her be whole." The idea of a "higher power" directing her decisions was slightly problematic in

Kate's mind as she didn't really believe in the Universe, or God. As for fate, well she had a complicated relationship to it, but she reasoned that maybe, like Victoria, she did believe in healing, and that what was broken could be fixed with time and love. She knew without a shadow of doubt that for herself, she needed time to exist, from one day to the next, with a minimum of 'work', to read, and think and be—her own version of knitting oneself together again.

Then there were truths she couldn't articulate but which moved through her all the same. In the instinctive flow that existed between woman and child, there was a piece of Kate that was bound to Little Bird, which through her called to all the parts of herself that ached for love and acceptance.

Somehow, over time, she had realized—she was happily accustomed to the complications of life with a precious and illegal child whose wounds undid her. She tucked Little Bird into her own bed at night like she belonged there. The little girl slept right up against Kate. She didn't often stir, except for the occasional nightmare, but her leg wrapped around Kate's and in the morning she opened her eyes and smiled, just inches away.

"I love you, Tia!" she said every night before she slept, and she greeted her this way, every morning, too. Little Bird kissed her neck and nestled there with her hot breath. No one had shown Kate this kind of affection, ever. Especially not her last lover. She had to admit to herself that anyway she looked at it, she was thirsty for love just like Little Bird.

Surely that's what drew them together.

The girl's enthusiasm had gone with her health, though, and she was dead asleep even as Kate tucked her into bed. Kate wrapped the girl tighter in the blankets, swaddled her like a baby. Every cell in Kate's body was screaming *no*. She knew that leukemia in children could be treated, but it was no guarantee, and it was a long journey at that. How would the girl get through this alone with some foster carer? And what if her Uncle did come and take her away, and in Mexico they didn't have the means or medical help to treat her? Or she died on the way? Or what if there was no one willing to pay for it all, even here, not even a foster carer?

"God, we need to talk."

Kate felt that unfamiliar word get stuck in her throat like something swallowed the wrong way. She didn't much like the feeling, but it was the price you had to pay in moments like these.

Only she couldn't do it. She couldn't talk to God, since God had never talked to her, and she certainly wasn't counting her dreams, the so-called "prophecies" her mother had clung to. No, that was not God, that was indeterminate, not even science understood such phenomena. She had long ago tried to banish the memories of her mother bearing down on her, telling her she was special for things she didn't want to be special for, informing her that her life was not her choice, that it was meant to be in service to something else.

Kate extricated herself from the sleeping child and went to her closet. Back in the corner, in a box with her winter scarves, was that heavy padded envelope. The one from the dead guy's coat, which she'd since gotten rid of, or, more accurately, which Victoria had gotten rid of—she hadn't asked how. She pulled out the cross—the crucifix—that she hadn't even told Victoria she'd found, much less kept. Felt its weight in her hands, its coolness, and let her hand run lightly along the engravings. It was Russian. It felt so ancient. It was surely a relic, and no doubt illegal. It was probably bronze, so maybe it wasn't worth that much otherwise.

She closed her eyes and imagined its origin, and wondered who might have considered it holy. She pretended, or imagined (she was never certain about the difference), that she could feel something—a faint vibration, something spiritual. She opened her eyes and took a closer look. She had the same gut feeling she'd had the first time she saw it: something about it was familiar. The shape, the configuration of it with three crossbeams, the murmur of some unconscious information just there, nudging her. She held it to her chest, imagining that if God saw her clinging to a cross, she'd be in 'his' good books.

This is just desperation, she told herself, then grasped the cross harder. She held her intention fiercely to her heart, like faith. Wasn't that what faith was—belief without evidence? She carried the cross back to bed, believing for that moment that someone was watching, deeming her worthy of good things. She tucked it in between her and Little Bird, and she slept that way.

She felt as close to God as she'd ever been.

In her dreams, the cross was there, hovering and translucent in a smokey sky, and she followed it across cityscapes and undulating rural landscapes, barren plains and tundra. Kate slept fitfully, energy coursing through her body as if she'd had a strong coffee before bed, and in her night visions she pursued the cross, driven by some *meaning* just beyond her grasp.

Finally, as light broke through the blinds, she heard him.

Her mother's hero. The reason for everything that came before.

She startled as he called to her. She was awake now, the girl beside her, the rustle of leaves outside. It was no dream.

Konstantin Isakevich Gutov spoke, and she heard his voice as loud as if he were in the room with her.

Don't forget Shambhala, my dear Katya.

L<small>ITTLE</small> B<small>IRD</small> <small>WOKE</small> up with a huge smile. "I love you, Tia!"

She found the cross next to her immediately, and grinned as she pulled it out of the covers. "La cruz!" She buried it again between them like it was their secret.

The girl had color. She stretched like a cat and snuggled in closer.

"You are looking better, honey!" Kate said, not fully feeling the words. They hadn't landed yet, and Kate stared at her ward puzzled, because she was so changed.

Little Bird nodded. "I'm soooooooo hungry."

Kate lifted the cross from between the tangled sheets, and put a finger on her lips.

"Shhhh," she said. She climbed out of bed and went to the closet, stepping half inside to be sure the girl couldn't see where she was keeping it. With hardly a breath, she returned the cross to its padded bag and put it back into the scarf box in the corner.

What am I doing? she thought. *I need to get rid of this thing. Someone might come looking for it.* Even though she was back in bed, holding the girl to her chest, in her mind she still felt its coolness, the shape of it, and she could see all the small details. The angels bowing above the figure of Jesus. The flowery patterning on the back. *It's an icon*, she realized. *Oh no.* She felt her body leaden with fear, or anticipation, and then recognition.

It just couldn't be, but it sure seemed like it was.

It was Gutov's icon, the one from his novel. Or at least one very much like it. She saw her mother then, standing right over her, talking about fate and duty and how special she was. Kate shuddered. She had heard *his voice.* He had spoken to her just moments ago.

"No," she said out loud. "It is NOT my path."

Little Bird looked up at her, confused but quickly forgetting, and said once more, "I'm hungry."

LITTLE BIRD WAS CHEERFUL NOW, *lively.* A bit feisty, even, screaming out for more peanut butter on her toast like it was an emergency. *I need MORE, Tia!* It didn't make much sense, and Kate's heart was heavy with the expectation that the child could be removed from her now that she was meant to start treatment. She didn't really know, but it seemed likely, and her fears consumed her so much so that it was only in retrospect she noticed how entirely well Little Bird had seemed over breakfast.

Kate packed her into the car with her little pink backpack, crayons, markers, paper, and her favorite snacks. Little Bird sat in the front seat with an unusual composure, placid and bright-eyed and taking in the world as they drove. She crossed her legs and rested her hands in her lap, as if cupped for meditation. She blinked slowly and a light smile played at her lips.

"Red light. Green light." She called out the traffic lights as they drove. That was her game, one she'd not played in a while.

"You sure ate a lot this morning," Kate commented—the fact of it hadn't sunk in, though. She was searching for small talk, rather than confronting the matter at hand, the day they had, the life that might ensue.

"God fixed me." Little Bird pursed her lips and smiled smugly.

Kate was so lost in her thoughts that she nodded dumbly, and observed to herself, *Well, she does seem better today*. She thought it without making any meaning of it whatsoever.

They were driving to the hospital. Little Bird had leukemia. She needed treatment.

They pulled up to the hospital and parked, and went back to the same waiting area in the children's ward, but not before Kate got herself a cup of coffee and some hot chocolate for Little Bird, in anticipation of waiting. Little Bird drank it fast, chirping out observations as she slurped.

"That girl looks sick," and "Why is that baby crying?" and "Who is that old man?"

The same nurse, the redheaded Joleen, called them in. "You're nice," said Little Bird to her straight away. Joleen commented to Kate. "My, is this the same child?"

The pediatrician came in to have a chat, but it was Little Bird who asked more questions.

What's your name?

I'm seven.

Are you married?

And then she announced, "Doctor, I'm not sick. God fixed me. I want to go home with Tia."

The young doctor was flustered by all the commentary and questions, and while his reaction did amuse Kate, it did not prompt her to reflect on the girl's sudden change. Unlike before, when she was either quiet and tearful or crying out, today the doctor and nurse were met with smiles that sometimes turned into giggles.

Joleen furrowed her brow, but said nothing. Kate had long since relinquished any sense of agency in the current situation, and mutely watched, numbing the niggling feeling that something interesting was about to happen.

"Let's check a few things," the doctor said, and then asked Joleen to take blood.

So they took more blood, and this time Little Bird smiled faintly into the near distance as if it were mere amusement, only shuddering slightly as the needle penetrated her skin.

They were left again, waiting. Kate got out the coloring book and crayons. Time blurred. Joleen came in some time later and said that social services would be around soon, only this time the nurse was avoiding eye contact.

Suddenly Kate felt a burning in her chest and heard herself pleading as she leapt up from where she had been sitting at Little Bird's side. She touched Joleen's arm.

"Just let me take her one more night. They have all her details. What am I going to do, go on the run with a critically ill child? She'll be back to the hospital one way or another. She'll get treatment. I will make sure of it."

Joleen went very still. She nodded as if to say she'd get to it in a moment, and then turned all her attention on the girl. Little Bird was doodling now, a cross, an orange and brown cross, with a Jesus on it, and yellow light pouring out of it.

"What are you drawing?" the nurse asked.

The girl shrugged. "La cruz," she said.

Kate felt her cheeks burning.

"It healed me," the girl said.

"Is that so?" Joleen asked.

Kate felt a tear well up in her eye. She couldn't speak. It didn't make sense, nothing made sense. She seemed better, but maybe she wasn't. And the cross. No, not the cross. It couldn't be anything to do with *that* cross.

"Listen, I can see you love this child," Joleen spoke just above a whisper.

"I have no right. I know... I know she's got to go."

"I need to tell you something."

Joleen moved in close, on some pretense of making the bed, moving around the pillow, the sheet, pulling the curtain in.

She whispered, "I'm a mother. So as a mother, I have to trust you because love don't lie. So listen up. I shouldn't be telling you this yet, but they don't understand what's going on. It doesn't make sense. She does seem better, and I don't know the details, but they are afraid they got it wrong, so it could get complicated from here. They are going to come talk to you soon, but you have every right now to take her home, and I know you want to spend time with her before social services gets involved. But don't even worry about that. They don't have the resources to take a child from a carer. They're not doing anything fast."

"What do you mean it doesn't make sense?"

"It seems like whatever it was that was wrong is just gone. The pathologist is going over the blood results from today, and they can't figure out what happened. There is no sign of cancer anymore. She seems very healthy."

"She's... well?"

"It seems so, yes."

"No cancer?"

"Look, I'm not a doctor so I don't know what else they are going to check. But it seems like everything is normal. Her breathing is fine. The swelling around the joints is gone. She was anemic before, and she's not now. It's either a miracle, or a big fuck up. I can't say, because a few days ago, the results were clear. But in any case, you should go home, because they are going to be checking her again, and it just seems like there is no need. She's fine, and in the meantime, things are going to get complicated. So get her somewhere calm."

"But how did this happen? Why? Are you sure?"

"Miracles do happen. I have seen it before. One other time. And I don't mean cancer disappearing over months when a patient eats only green food and does yoga and meditates all day long. I mean *instant*. Gone. From one day to the next."

Kate thought of the cross, or rather, it was as if it thought of her— it hovered there, in her mind's eye, interposing itself between Joleen and herself. Little Bird hummed as she drew. Kate said, "What caused it, do you think, in the um... the other miracle you saw?"

"The patient was a Russian man, and he didn't speak English, so I don't know, unfortunately."

Kate's heart started to race.

"It was just—one day to the next, no more cancer, and *glowing* with health. That's what made it so strange. He was glowing. Like he could do anything. Like she is, right now." She looked at Little Bird.

"I see."

"It could only be God, I think. I am guessing you prayed? With a cross?"

Kate could feel the cross in her hands, its weight, not too heavy, like it was hollow, and the feel of it, cool and waxy, its bumpy surface with all those angel figures, the Cyrillic script, and Jesus. She recalled the words she'd reluctantly spoken to a God she was unsure even existed. *God, we need to talk. She hadn't even gotten to the begging and pleading part.*

"I mean, yes. Yes, of course."

Joleen nodded.

"Just be grateful honey. Not everyone gets this kind of free pass. Now you go."

Kate scrambled around in her purse for pen and paper, and tore off the blank part of an old receipt, scribbling her number, her *real* number on it. She pressed the scrap of paper into Joleen's hand and whispered. "Promise me you won't give this to anyone. Tell me when someone's coming to get her."

KATE DID NOT PROCESS—NOT fully—Little Bird's sudden health miracle until she was home hours later and Victoria knocked at the door. The need to communicate this development and the admissions that accompanied it shook Kate out of her shock, and right into the reality of it, including her guilt. With a pounding heart she opened the door, unable to meet her neighbor's eyes.

"I may have done something," Kate prefaced her reluctant explanation.

Victoria raised a single eyebrow as she stepped casually into

Kate's apartment. "What kind of something exactly?" To Little Bird, "Well, look at you, child. Looking so much better today."

"I'm not sick," the girl announced, and trotted off to the couch with her backpack.

"Yeah, that's part of it," Kate said. "I may have prayed. I maybe used something that I found... a certain person left something here that I didn't tell you about."

"Oh no." Victoria shook her head. "I don't want to be involved in any other shady bullshit. No." She wagged her finger. "You don't get me involved."

"It's okay," Kate whispered. "Inside that coat, *his* coat, there was a cross. And I prayed, okay? And anyway, she," she indicated the little girl with her chin. "She held it, the cross. And now she's not sick. I realize that sounds crazy. But *she's not sick*. The doctor confirmed it."

"Oh," Victoria paled. "*Oh*." Her eyes darted back and forth as she processed this admission.

"Well I'm gonna tell you off later for keeping this potentially very dangerous secret, but not now."

In the next breath Victoria and the girl were hugging on the couch so tight Kate was sure someone would end up bruised.

"Clever little bird," Victoria cooed, and kissed her face and her hands until she giggled. "God saved you, child."

"Maybe we have to take her to Mexico, Victoria. Find her family, make sure they are good people? Look after her. Maybe stay a while. I need a holiday."

"Where? Where are you taking her, sweetie? You don't even know her last name, or the town she's from."

"I have a phone number. We find someone to call her and translate for us, and we go. Soon, before social services find her."

"Just wait a minute, Kate. Maybe we will, maybe we won't. But just wait. Maybe you could be her foster mom or something, you don't know. It won't look good, just disappearing with a child when the police might still have you on their radar because of... other stuff. It might be dangerous."

"Okay, okay. For now, we'll stay."

Little Bird had pulled up a kitchen chair to sit next to the window and stared out and up, her small chin lifted high like she was following something specific with her eyes. There was a tuna casserole covered on the counter, ready for dinner, and banana bread in the oven, and to Kate the apartment smelled like family and love. She went to sit next to Little Bird. The motley clouds in gray and white and pink banded together in a brilliant, soft sunset. Little Bird just stared and stared out the window squinting upward, and Kate watched her in silence, feeling grateful as the room was suffused with evening light.

A MONTH LATER, when Kate woke up to the sound of rain lashing against the window, for a moment everything was right.

But then she turned to an empty pillow and remembered, as she had every day for two weeks: Little Bird was gone.

The girl's uncle, Jesús, a plain looking, short Hispanic man with a baseball cap, had come to take her home. He'd arrived pounding on the door so early that both Kate and Little Bird were barely awake enough to comprehend what was happening. Little Bird clearly knew him. And fair enough that she wasn't happy to leave, but in retrospect, Kate thought the girl's reaction odd. She immediately went mute, hunched her shoulders, and gathered her few belongings with dutiful efficiency.

Kate had done everything right—*she'd been responsible, hadn't she?* But she worried and second-guessed herself daily. She'd made Jesús scribble their address in Mexico on a piece of paper so she could write her, and she'd pushed Little Bird to memorize her phone number, one from a secret SIM card she kept in a secret, personal cellphone. She'd also written down her number and put it in Little Bird's little backpack, just in case.

Yet every day since Little Bird had left, a sickening feeling had been growing in Kate—that the girl was *scared* of her uncle. She'd once said he was *mean*, hadn't she?

The worry sat like a brick on her sternum, joined by intense grief, until she felt herself crack open into a painful inner fracture that only intensified day by day. She numbed her pain with sleep. An inordinate amount of sleep, at all hours except nighttime.

Then on some indeterminate day came a ferocious banging on the door. Kate's first thought was the police, something connected to Little Bird, and her heart stopped. *No, no,* she reassured herself, *don't panic, the girl is fine, just fine.* Then an image of her client's body came to mind and she froze. *Shit, it's only a matter of time,* she thought.

She didn't have a plan.

She didn't want a plan.

She wanted to go back to sleep and block out the world.

But Victoria screamed at her to open the door and Kate reluctantly let her in. It was noon. The blinds were drawn and Victoria said, "It's like you're dying in here. Get up. You've got mail."

"What?" Kate croaked.

"There was a package left for you that ended up in the wrong mailbox. It's been sitting outside your door for two days, but I got sick of waiting for you to act like you're actually alive."

"Open it then."

Victoria ripped it open. There was a note stuck to a small Spanish book. The note said, *I forgot to give you, Paula.*

Victoria opened the book, gasped, and showed Kate. It was Little Bird's Mexican passport. Her small face peered out at them, big round eyes and all that spirit freeze-framed in terrible lighting.

"Oh my God, Jesús didn't have any travel documents for her?" Kate said. Her heart began to race. "What was he going to do with her then? Could he get her across the border without it? What was he planning? He didn't even ask for it. I didn't even think about it!"

"Relax," Victoria said. "Maybe he crossed into Mexico somewhere where they don't check. Or maybe he had other documents for her. Maybe he didn't even know she had a passport. Don't jump to the worst conclusion, whatever it is that's going on right now in your mind."

Kate swallowed her fear. She didn't know what her worst conclusion was either. She pressed the passport into her chest.

"Okay, fine. You can go now."

"Okay girl but you need to start living or I'm going to make it my mission to bother you. Oh, God. Not that book again. That's not a good sign."

She pointed at the book on the couch.

Ikona, the novel. Worn, dog-eared.

Kate shrugged.

"You always read it when things get bad honey. I'm worried about you. You've got to get back to work. I can't lend you rent money forever. Get yourself together. I know you go sit at that diner every night reading and moping."

Kate couldn't explain anything to Victoria, how with every new loss she felt compelled to unearth old ones. Victoria was right about that book. Only she didn't know it was her past, or that her past was rising up to haunt her in the void Little Bird had left. She was even more sure as time wore on that the cross she'd found was eerily like the one in Gutov's novel. In his novel, Gutov's cross had a *meaning*. So might the one she'd found in the guy's coat. She reasoned that the meaning of this real life icon might banish the gathering storm clouds of meaninglessness that sat threateningly on her horizon. She might survive after all, if only she put her head down and filled her mind with something bigger, something greater, a mystery to solve, a path to follow.

Victoria left. Kate went back to bed, Gutov's book clutched at her chest. She thought of her mother, and how she'd insisted that *Ikona* had all the answers that anyone needed.

Maybe her mother was right, after all.

It was to Gutov that Kate spoke next, as she lay hoping for life to re-enter her.

"First the cross, then the passport. What does it all mean, Konstantin Isakevich? You would know, wouldn't you, you who always made meaning of things."

9

FINLEY & THE ALTER EGO
JUNE 2019
SYDNEY, AUSTRALIA

The room came into focus along with the woman sitting across from him. Her severe bob. Her pointy glasses. Her pale forehead creased in concern, cheeks slightly flushed. *Something was wrong.* Finley struggled to remember where he was, and who the woman was, and how long he'd been there. Then, in an instant, it all came back.

"Am I okay?" he found himself asking, as if her worried state were a reflection of whatever had happened to him.

"You tell me," she said.

"Barbara."

"Yes?"

"No, I'm just remembering. Your name is Barbara."

"Well done."

"How long... I mean... I came to you *today*, right?"

"Yes, it was a few hours ago now. I had to cancel the two appointments after you, as you were... well, it was... unexpected."

Finley lifted his hands from his lap and looked at them. He was Caucasian. He was... Finley.

"I was someone else."

"Yes."

Barbara suddenly jumped up and went to a table just inside the door where there was a water filter. She filled two cups.

"What was I thinking? Drink."

He drank it all in one gulp.

"And another."

He drank that one too. She returned to the water filter and poured herself two cups and also drank. Then she went to the window at the end of the room and pulled up the blinds. She sat back down.

"I had to get a colleague in here to sit with you so I could cancel my other appointments. You were deep. I wasn't entirely sure I could get you back."

She suddenly took a deep breath, as if to reassure herself that he was, actually, back.

"Could that happen?" he asked.

"I don't think so, no."

He looked around and took everything in for a second time—the light wooden desk. The photo frame, and clock, and... his attention wandered to the window, where the blinds had been closed before. There was a tree outside. And a building behind it.

"But you're not sure?"

"It was... unusual. Tell me what you remember."

"I went someplace. I was someone else... is that what really happened?"

"First, you went to a time in your childhood, near the ocean, and I thought we were getting to the root of your fear. Then something else happened."

Finley rubbed his eyes and took this *Barbara* in once again. Upon closer inspection, he saw that her once-neat bob was slightly disheveled—strands of hair stuck to her forehead, and her cheeks were actually *quite* flushed. She was perspiring. *Was she nervous? Uncertain?*

Was this experience of his so very unusual?

"Yes, I was Wallace. I *am* Wallace. Um..." He struggled to organize his disjointed memories as they tumbled out, one after the other. "Did I speak? Or was I just there?"

"It's been three hours since you sat down. The water should help. To answer your question—you did speak, yes. I asked you questions. Well, it wasn't exactly you, or... or the *other* you. Wallace? *You* were quite gone, so I had to speak to your Superconscious."

"My what?"

"The part of you that has the capacity to observe. I asked it to tell me what you were seeing, what was happening. Like a narrator."

"And... it told you? About Dr. Rinella, and Justicia and... Wallace."

Barbara composed herself with a sharp breath. "Yes, Finley."

"So, you know what was happening? They were—I was—being regressed, brought back in time, to me, now. And all in order to find some cross."

"Yes, that's right."

"It seems they need it for a cure." He hesitated for a moment. "I have the feeling that humanity is dying out."

"Yes, I gathered that, too."

"Why? How?"

She leaned forward.

"That part I'm not sure about. I guided you as best I could, Finley. In fact, it took me some time to figure out that we were not in *your* life at all, much less your personal past. It wasn't even a past life. And I do sometimes see that. You were in a *future* life."

"The future," he stated, as if that explained everything. "You mean, as in, a future incarnation."

"Yes. Finley, has this sort of thing happened to you before?"

He sighed. He had never told anyone about his experiences, not since childhood. He wasn't even sure how to begin. "Yes, it has, sort of."

Barbara nodded.

"I mean, I've always *seen* things in the future. I always have been able to *predict* things, but this was different. I was *there*. Inside it."

"I think you went into a future life. This might be beyond the realm of belief. It may be some unknown function of consciousness, even. I'm not claiming to understand it all at a metaphysical level. In my practice, I do sometimes see past lives, which suggests reincarnation. My clients sometimes remember being someone else in another era, in another body. But I have never taken them into future lives. Your experience feels significant, because of what you told me. Well, what Wallace told me, through your Superconscious. Do you remember the cross? This icon that you mentioned?"

Finley couldn't help but be slightly intrigued by Barbara's quick conclusion. Her manner suggested that she was slightly disconcerted by the intensity of their session, and yet she also appeared to have a conceptual container ready to make sense of it.

What is her agenda here? he wondered. *Or is this just professional curiosity?*

"Finley?" She prompted him. "The icon? And a reference to a book by someone called *Gutov*?"

"I remember it all, though I must say, it's starting to lose its edge. It feels more like a dream now than a minute ago. But when I was there, it seemed utterly real."

"Listen, I think you need to explore this further. And I don't think I'm the right person."

"What do you mean, *explore this further*?"

Finley contained his alarm, barely. "I came here because I wanted to get rid of my fears, that's all. I don't really want to go... voyaging in some trance state to the future."

Now, suddenly antsy, he wanted to stand, even to walk out. But his *head*. He was drained of energy, quite unable to rouse himself to standing, even. The entire situation was beginning to irritate him.

Why is she not the right person? Who is?

"Fair enough. But this is rare, and there seems to be some urgency. It seems like the future, at least, *this* future, wants something from you, from Finley. Again, it's not my area. My area is eliminating fears. However, I believe your fear of the ocean conceals a much larger fear, which took you far into the future, and which does seem to implicate all of humanity—not to pressure you—but, yes, I believe you *can* solve your fear of the ocean, if you address the larger issues. At least that seems to be what's on the table at this moment."

The more Barbara spoke, the more lucid Finley became. His previous irritation lingered, but now enlivened him.

"It sounds to me like you're saying I can stop being afraid of the ocean if some future aspect of myself stops being afraid that all of humankind might perish."

She smiled. Indulgent. "It's *your* mind, Finley. I'm just a witness. This *may* all be just your own internal... alter ego. A part, an alter personality. I'm not sure we really understand the mind sufficiently to interpret what took place here today. Nevertheless, whether it's all in your head or in some future reality, it does seem there's a lot at stake."

"My internal *alter ego*," Finley deadpanned. Then, drawing from a deep fear that was fast lifting to the surface the more he let his experience as Wallace settle, he admitted, "You think I'm some kind of savior? That I have a mission?"

"Would you like me to say that?"

"No! Absolutely not. I am not interested in that kind of responsibility."

He shivered, suddenly beset by the blatant emptiness of his life. A boring and self-validating career, the absence of love, his parents now deceased. No family, few friends. Means without an end. *Depressing.* He emerged somewhat from his self-pity a moment later, moved by curiosity.

"Well, in my normal sessions, the client who's sitting where you're sitting right now is the one doing the asking. In your case? It sort of seems like it's a future version of you who's the one doing the asking. So, I suppose you could say that whether it's saving the world or saving yourself, there's another part of you steering this ship, if you'll forgive the metaphor." She smiled wryly. "A part of you in the future, not here in this room—which means you must go back to learn more. Which is why I think you need to see my colleague in America, and not myself."

"Your colleague can help me?"

"She most certainly can. That's her speciality. Only she's in Atlanta. She specializes in the future—future lives, visions, visitations, timelines. You name it. She's written books about it. She's an expert on the modern mystic. She'd be the one to help you navigate this safely."

"First of all, *safely*? And second, can't I do this with a video call?"

Barabara smiled, but her eyes were serious. "I wouldn't recommend it. There are certain dangers. Someone needs to be in the room with you. To monitor you. Dr. Gloria is your best bet, but it's up to you. I understand it requires travel."

"Dangers. I must navigate it *safely*, as you said."

"There are always dangers."

"You think I *have* to explore it, don't you?"

"It's worth exploring, Finley. This phenomenon, this *opportunity* —it's rare."

"It would be a lot easier if you just told me that there was no other choice but to go."

"Is there?" Barbara asked, serious at first, but then she winked. "It's never just been about your fear of water, has it Finley?"

As uncertain as he was as to his mental state, as skeptical as he felt about Barbara's suggestion to go see someone—a hypnotherapist, a modern mystic expert, no less, and in another country—again and again his mind circled back around to Clare and the state of his life.

Here, there was emptiness and lack of meaning. A dead end. As a wind might blow through a desolate alley swirling up dust, so a force beyond himself blew through him; *he* was all that was left to be displaced.

He succumbed.

Finley submitted a letter of resignation that evening, effective immediately. It was a family emergency, he wrote, without offering any context whatsoever. The phone kept ringing but he ignored it— his boss, his colleagues. What could he possibly say to them? Deepen the lie or tell a most improbable truth. Best to remain elusive. Anyway, he fairly trembled with nerves about his upcoming journey as he packed, booked a plane ticket online for the following evening, then packed some more.

His head seemed to have settled into a dull and incessant ache. He didn't leave his apartment the next day. His bags were already packed and ready by the door so he had nothing else to do with his time. He'd never been one to lose himself in his devices, seeking distraction or amusement. He'd always found solace in the act of doing nothing, and thought it wrong that the world prized busyness, as thinking was itself a productive undertaking. So he sat on his couch most of the day and surveyed the skyline, staring into the distance to calculate emptiness. His, the world's.

With a mixture of dread and excitement, he also reviewed his dreamlike memory of another world, wondering what was in store for him. At last he had something to look forward to, yet simultaneously he feared that exact thing. He wondered if the secret to moving forward in life lay in reconciling those two polarities. This rumination occupied a good couple of hours of his time on the couch.

At six p.m. there was a knock at the door, just as he was considering defrosting some pasta bolognese for dinner, rather than let it sit in the freezer for who knows how long in his absence.

It was Clare.

His heart fluttered for a nanosecond, then went cold. He said nothing and stood in the doorway. She stared at him as if shocked by his inaction, or else just shocked to see him. He didn't know and didn't care. He didn't invite her in.

"I thought you'd left for Melbourne, to stay with your sister."

"She and her kids got gastro. So I delayed my flight a few days. I realized I left some of my things here, so I thought I'd come by and get them."

"Oh."

"I did text you, Finley. And I rang. But you never respond to messages. So I just came over."

"Okay. Well come in then I guess."

She stepped inside and saw his suitcases.

"You going someplace?"

"Yes. I quit my job. I'm going to America tonight."

"What? Why?" Furrowed brow. Lips pursed in concern, or bafflement, he couldn't tell.

"I felt like it."

"You're going to risk your career and go, just like that?"

Oooh, his heart thrilled. There was shock in her voice. He'd shocked her. She whom life never rocked, was shaken.

"Yes. Why not?"

She appraised him, silent, but he saw it—a flicker of respect.

"Well, I'll just get my things. I brought a bag. I don't have much." She showed him her zip up cooler shopping bag. He knew that she kept them in her car so as to be ready at any moment for eco-friendly shopping. She walked past him and disappeared into the bedroom.

Meanwhile, Finley defrosted his bolognese in the microwave and poured himself a glass of red wine. Clare reappeared after several minutes, taking in the steaming bowl that sat on the counter, and his wine. She stared at him with a mixture of reproach and betrayal, as if she'd just busted him with another woman.

"Is that the Shiraz we got in the Hunter?"

"Um, I believe so."

"Hmm."

"Got everything?" he asked.

"Yes."

"Good luck," he told her, getting cutlery from the drying rack near the sink. He opened the fridge and scoured it for parmesan. "In your new job, I mean."

She stood near the door now, hesitant. "Are you sure about going, Fin? Have you thought this through?"

"Not really."

She gawked. Clare, calm and clear Clare, was *not only* shocked, he surmised—she was also offended.

"You're absolutely starkers," she said. "It's not like you to leave your job, and just... go."

"Oh well, that's what's happened."

Her jaw slack, her eyes burning, she asked, "What happened to you?"

Finley shrugged. He took his bowl and his glass of wine to the table in the dining room, brushing past Clare as he went.

"So that's it. You've quit. You're going overseas."

He looked at her directly, taking her in—once his Clare, but no longer. She struck him as almost a stranger now. Bland, shallow. He smiled at her indulgently. Perhaps he *was* in denial. He did consider it—but as he faced the task ahead, any lingering hurt he felt over Clare was submerged far beneath nervousness and a faint tremor of excitement.

"Well, I may be a little ship out to sea, but I am certainly not going to sink. And anyway," he paused. "So what if I do?"

She pulled in her chin. "Well, you seem determined."

Finley said exactly nothing in reply, roused by the novelty of inner movement, and went to open the front door for her to leave.

10

WALLACE & THE COTTAGE
JUNE 2131 AD

KRASNOYARSK, EASTERN FEDERATION

The ocean of grasses in the Quarter Fields behind the monastery rolled and flattened and rose up again in the wind. Wallace reclined in the only clearing, in a wooden lounge chair at the pond, and watched a dragonfly zip across the water's surface, its tail a flash of blue. It rested on a cattail and flicked its black-threaded wings. The air was a haze of muted yellow, refracting sun through humidity. The dandelion and lavender beds were without company today, and the silence was profound. No buzz of insects, no stirring of undergrowth, no sign of life but for the creature on the cattail and its human observer.

"Content in repose, Wallace?" Father Andrew called in his booming voice. Wallace turned his head and saw only a blur of light and shadow coming from a distance. Red robes swished through cattails. He carried a large clay pot. Honeysuckle tea, if Wallace were to guess.

When Father Andrew arrived at Wallace's side, he took a long drink, then handed him the rough brown pot.

"You should take my chair." Wallace stood.

"No. I want to feel the earth beneath me. Shortly. Let me catch my breath." He wiped perspiration from his bald head and temples. "I was told you were gardening."

"I was." He sat back down. "I tested the soil. Now I'm observing."

"Very good. One must know the land, the soil, insects, and birdlife and so on and their habitats, in order to be attuned to the earth, in order to know what will grow. Are you attuned?"

The priest stood with a hand on his lower back, his belly jutting out proudly. He reached for the pot and took another long drink, then wiped his white beard with his sleeve. His skin was pink. Notoriously, he did not like the heat. He rather disliked the outdoors, in fact, so to Wallace, it was a little puzzling for him to be here, exposed to the elements, as it were—although rumor had it that in his youth he was quite the basketball player. This change in physique seemed to be something that happened to those in advanced age.

"I'm building a rapport," Wallace replied. He took the pot from Father Andrew and drank again. The men stared at the pond, but it was not nature with which Wallace was principally engaged on this day. It was with his own mind, pushing against the distracting memory of Justicia, questioning why this woman had gotten so deeply under his skin, and why he was so terrified of his attraction to her.

The priest burped, then excused himself.

He spoke. "Do you know, I once watched a film in school of a similar scene, only the pond in the film had frogs. They were wholly invisible, you could only hear croaking in rhythmic unison. At the end of the ten-minute documentary one emerged, leaping from one side of the pond to a lilypad, disturbing the cattail, from which a dragonfly disembarked. For some reason, it was very evocative. You didn't expect the frog to leap out, I suppose. It has stayed with me, to this day."

With some effort, Wallace held Justicia's image to his mind's periphery and scoured for a specific memory of frogs.

"I saw frogs in real life at a breeding program in Southeast Asia on a school science trip."

"What do you remember?"

"Not much, to be honest. Three froglets, rather quietly sitting beneath rocks."

"And did you *care*? Were you *moved*?"

Wallace had no choice but to fully let thoughts of Justicia go now, and apply himself to his mentor's questions. His libido steadied, and he traced his memory to primary school. *Froglets*. Both in the past and now, he was all too aware of his heart's wide and encompassing blankness.

"Emphatically *not*. I was meant to be, as were we all. We saw the frogs through glass. I often wondered if I'd touched one, if I'd smelled the dampness of their habitat, if that would have moved me. Anyway, the program failed. They released some, as I recall, and the chytrid fungus slowly ate into their populations again. The world is simply no longer safe for frogs."

"As I've always said, regarding these ridiculous re-education programmes that continue even today—no amount of propaganda, no matter how visually or aurally stunning, no matter how realistic the virtual tactile experience, none of it can tug the heart into caring when there is life to live in a hurry."

"Indeed," Wallace replied. "There is no time to care, for most."

"But for some there is time, and what do we do with it? People like me, we live past forty, and we slow down. We start to reflect on what's ahead, since we've clearly got lucky in the genealogical lottery. And when we consider the implications of a long life, which is likely if we've survived so far, barring some terrible accident—when we consider the years ahead of us, we then begin to think about the past. Or perhaps it's just me."

The older man held his robes up and with a swish, to and fro, splayed them out behind him and sat on the ground next to Wallace, a swift motion quite unexpected from someone of his girth. He was a Buddha in a sea of fabric. He straightened his back and wiped a palm across his bald head.

Wallace rested the clay pot on his knee, within easy reach for Father Andrew should he need it. "It's not just you, Father. I began thinking quite seriously about the past a good long while ago, and it led me back further than I anticipated."

"Ah. This Finley character."

They were by all accounts alone, a kilometer from the cloisters and other buildings, yet Father Andrew had lowered his voice considerably. He wiped his sweaty forehead once more and sighed, casting an odd glance at the adept, as if feeling him out.

"It has been quite a journey, hasn't it?" he asked Wallace.

"Have you notified the bishops?'

"I've told them I have an adept with exceptional meditative skills which we are studying. Dr. Rinella will not use your name in his separate reports. Though I'm guessing your concern is not of a personal nature."

"I'm beginning to understand that the implications of this project are great. The stakes are high. I just don't want this risk to be in vain."

The long grasses and cattails rolled flat and undulated out like a wave, stirred by the wind again. It was a picture perfect scene: the high, blue skies, clear today, the warmth of midday, untouched nature sprawling and messy. Yet, it was too quiet. Where were the birds? Wallace wondered. He felt nervous, as he did sometimes when something didn't quite add up.

"They won't shut us down. I've made sure of that. In fact, that is the reason I've joined you today."

Wallace regarded his elder with calm expectation. He knew this man well enough; no words wasted, no gesture without meaning, no time without purpose. Saying nothing, he returned his gaze to the pond until the priest spoke again.

"The Visioning Bill nearly went through, but was killed at the last minute. You know this, I presume?"

"Yes, of course, I've been following it. That is partly the basis of my concern. Why did those previously so enthusiastic suddenly have a change of heart? If Visionaries aren't allowed to work within the government, it doesn't bode well for us."

The elder man sighed; he wore a worried expression. "Not entirely. It means we must operate underground, yes—but that is good. The Visioning bill might have legitimized the contribution of the Visionaries to our understanding of the future consequences of present actions, yes. But what the bill would have also done is legislate *transparency*, and none of the parties involved desired that."

They sat in comfortable silence and shortly, though it must have been a good five minutes, there came movement and accompanying noise, a rush through the grasses, and then two men carrying a stretcher, one at the front, one at the back. On the stretcher was a female form lying perfectly still, all in white. Wallace was certain that he recognized her.

The monks carrying the stretcher nodded to Father Andrew as they passed. Both men stood as the men with the stretcher approached; Wallace peered at the recumbent woman as they passed.

"Do we have a new initiate?" Wallace asked.

Father Andrew sighed again, looked Heavenward, and wiped sweat from his brow.

"That was Eden Schopel."

Wallace tried to conceal his shock. He asked in a low voice, "The Cottage?"

Father Andrew nodded.

The younger man sat back down again, now with hurried thoughts. The stretchers *whooshed* through the cattails ever more quietly as the distance grew.

"Why is Schopel here? That is what you came to tell me, isn't it?"

Father Andrew was seated again, his legs crossed as if to meditate. He wiped his brow once more and sighed.

"Schopel would have driven the bill through—and there was nothing the Council could have done as she has that much influence. But in agreeing to step down, she forfeited that influence, and without it, her closest allies were persuaded to vote against the bill."

"But why?"

"Because most privately, in secret meetings, *we*, the most senior leadership of the Triumvirate as a whole—the Sciences Institutes, the Monasteries and the Council—we all came to an agreement: Schopel agreed to find God, and the Triumvirate agreed to look the other way if she carried on her esoteric efforts at the Monasteries.

"Thus, she has joined our Order, and so the government has lost its most powerful Visionary and the leader of the faction. The faction will cease to exist. Already, it has gone underground and lost access to the halls of power, as it were, and thus transparency is no longer an issue. Those Visioning factions can go rogue and do what they like. And of course then *we,* and now I refer to our project with you, Wallace, we have gained Schopel, and with her, the promise that her efforts here will have a degree of protection. Officially this project of ours will not be shut down. Not by the Triumvirate, anyway."

Wallace scowled. "She's been at the Cottage, then."

"It was her decision, in a manner of speaking. It's the normal procedure for initiates. The procedure has improved since you've done it. It will merely contextualize any trauma she might have suffered. Remove the pull of the psyche, which might otherwise distract her from her new path. Between you and me, though, she is more powerful than the Machine."

The pond rippled with a low breeze, and Wallace shuddered, the remains of the honeysuckle tea sloshing slightly inside the pot on his knee.

"I'm sorry to bring up bad memories for you, Wallace," Father Andrew said, reaching for the tea pot. "Suffice to say, the Council will not make a report on our activities this year, and that includes your project."

Wallace ran a hand through his hair, thick and damp with perspiration. He remembered how a nurse had grabbed his head in an effort to hold him down; electrodes studded his forehead and the base of his neck. Screaming. The currents of electricity, channeled through the past. How the memory burned like the fire itself, his heart searing. Ibiza reduced to rubble. His mother's arm with her small wristwatch protruding from a concrete wall that had killed her. His father, burnt to ash. Emotion now like fine dust smudged across the glass after the thickest layers of ash had been removed. Death. Father, mother, sister, brother. Screams. Now empty echoes.

Could emotion really be neutralized? Removed, as it were? He searched sometimes for the pain he used to feel, grieving it privately, though he never would have admitted to this. Such extreme emotions were thought to interrupt one's connection to the Divine. But Wallace felt empty with its absence, yearning for the equally powerful connection to his parents that was twinned with the pain of their loss. Perhaps there could not be one without the other. So he had secretly meditated on his empty memories, searching for the frequency of that which he must have felt as a boy, in Ibiza, during the government attack which had killed his parents and their peaceful rebel group.

For years, nothing.

Then suddenly, a feeling emerged from behind the neutral, void scenes—nameless dread, unattached to events, pure blackness. Panic, as if trapped, with no way out, buried alive in the darkness of his own mind. There was terror, but no love, and so intense was the feeling that every night, when it hijacked him, he leapt out of bed and stood at the window, grasping at the stars and clouds and vastness of the sky to reassure himself that there was spaciousness, immediate and vast, all around him.

And then, one day, in the crispness of dawn, the terror gave way to a vision of the cross, suspended in emotionless presence. A solid, and yet ephemeral thing right there before his eyes, and from the fact of that cross there emanated peace, wave upon wave of peace, such that he'd had to confess it all to Father Andrew.

He attempted now to gather his thoughts.

"It's true, as you say, my memories no longer carry the emotion, so they are not bad memories. However, there is something else now, as you know. Something I hardly grasp."

At this the older man stared straight ahead and spoke softly, with hesitation. "The experience for you, at the Cottage though. I read the report. It was not normal, Wallace. It was not meant to be painful. Your experience there must carry its own difficult memory, one which, alas, we were not able to clear for you."

"I never told anyone about it, Father. It worked, certainly. I understand now that the process is not painful for others. Understand, I do not judge you for accepting Schopel, though I don't understand why she wishes to be here. Such are the times we live in. Anyway, I understand that to take the emotion out of memory renders the past as a child's tale, more or less inaccessible. But for me, you see, it opened a Pandora's Box."

Father Andrew scooted his crossed legs around to face Wallace head on. Setting the tea pot on the ground, he put his hands on a knee each, as if preparing to meditate.

"You have never shared this with me, Wallace. Do you mean—is that when it began for you?"

"I never told anyone, because I hardly understood it myself, until recently. I think that it created a hole, Father. It burned a hole in my mind. That's what it felt like. I no longer felt the pain of my past, but it did something to my experience of time. At times, for reasons beyond my comprehension, I would go into that space, and travel far, and arrive at random moments, in random places. I lacked the discipline to direct it myself, of course, until my sessions with you, after I began painting the icon."

It had been—at first—like stumbling into a scene, foreign and indeterminate, without any context, then suddenly finding himself in another scene, utterly different, but equally obtuse. Different time periods, different people, in the middle of mundane activities. A thousand versions of himself playing out different roles. All quite meaningless to him—until the terror, and the cross.

Father Andrew watched him intently.

Wallace said, "I don't understand why the bishops allow this machine for initiates and yet we are so opposed to science otherwise."

"Ah, now that has to do with intent. The Monasteries are happy to adopt technologies which serve their mission of accepting the end of humankind and Ascension. But not if science hijacks our spirituality for other agendas—like saving us for a mere human existence. Hence why we keep this project of ours secret. I am sorry, Wallace, that this work implicates you. We are doing what we can to hide it."

"Yet our group at the Monastery is a powerful collaboration. It cannot remain secret forever."

He thought of Justicia, too, of course, and how Dr. Rinella had now involved her in their deception.

"Indeed. But we could speculate endlessly on the politics and be fearful of factions and conflict, or we could focus on the task ahead. I believe we—or at least *you*—should not worry about factors and interests beyond your control."

Now, from a far distance, a thin V appeared in the sky, and grew longer and larger within seconds. Wallace watched. Siberian cranes, necks stretched out ahead of them, passed overhead.

Wallace felt he'd witnessed a miracle, as he had assumed the species' extinction—he turned to ask Father Andrew about this but his elder was staring thoughtfully at the ground, rubbing his chin.

Before Wallace could direct him to look up, Father Andrew turned to him and asked, "Do you feel the pain of Finley's past, Wallace?"

Wallace did not reply immediately. He watched the birds disappear into the distance. His elder respectfully made no move to press him further, and the two rested in what would have appeared to be amicable silence. There was a faint smile at the edges of Wallace's mouth; but the sun was yet hot on his face, so it could have been a squint, or a grimace, that of a man lacking a sunhat, or umbrella. Finally, he answered.

"I feel everything, Father. In Finley's life, I feel everything, as if I am there. Inhabiting his mind. Merging, so that after a short time I *become* him. It is real. The past is finally real. No re-education programme could possibly achieve this. I think, to be frank, that those who spent so much time with the Visioning Bill, so much time refining their methodologies in meditation—that they've got it all wrong. They should forget the future, which is changeable with every choice. They should delve into the past. To know what we've lost, for that would inspire them to make the decisions which would ensure a better future."

"You may be correct."

"I am correct. I know this. There are senses we cannot engage, Father. Look around you. What do you see, what do you smell? Taste?"

Father Andrew remained still, but breathed in deeply. The air was vaguely damp near the pond, but the breeze which periodically stirred was arid, hot.

"If people remembered the smell of bread—real bread, not this modern equivalent. The taste of lamb. The sound of frogs, but not just the sound, which we have recorded: to be immersed in the sound of their croaking, to taste the humidity, to smell mud and wet grass. The full experience. That's what the propaganda misses. Full sensory immersion. When I inhabit Finley's mind, it is more than tangible. I *smell* the past, Father, and it is alive for me."

Father Andrew only frowned and lowered his chin. For a moment, Wallace wondered if he were overcome by emotion.

"Respectfully," Wallace said, "If I may ask. What of Schopel and her visioning work? She was a revolutionary. She's lost her work, her mission, her colleagues. Why did she agree to be pushed out? To come here? Was she threatened?"

Father Andrew looked uncomfortable.

"Well. Not entirely."

"Not... entirely?" Wallace repeated.

"I spoke with her. I told her about your project. She has long been passionate about finding a cure. She is a deeply spiritual individual, Wallace, with skills in consciousness far beyond what has officially been shared."

"She's interested in me?"

"She has a lot to offer us."

"But surely the Council is aware that she was motivated by something, which would raise questions..."

"In any case the Council are aware we are undertaking experiments, but they write us off as holy. Elevated. Impractical. They do not know what we've discovered. What you are discovering, because they could never imagine that we could have a mission *in* the world. Only beyond it."

"But Schopel does?"

"Yes. Enough to join us."

Bothered now, not knowing what pushed against him or what he was pushing against, Wallace scowled at the field, the pond, at the sky.

"I do not like this world," Wallace said. "It lacks coherence."

"Has it not always done so?"

"Why can we not cooperate? Why must we have different agendas when we are one humanity?"

"Ah," Father Andrew said. "That is where Schopel comes in."

"I do not understand. Visionaries journey to the future. We are concerned with the past."

"As is she. In her work, in her visioning, she began to investigate the very origins of the Visionaries. Her research yielded something quite valuable. She will communicate this to you soon, once she has recovered. Suffice to say, she will be a conduit of sorts, from the past, to the future. Facilitating the creation of a bridge, if you will."

After a long moment, Wallace gathered his robes and stood, collecting the tea pot from the ground.

"It's nearing supper. We should go. I have always respected your discernment, Father."

Father Andrew hoisted himself to his feet and brushed the dirt from his robes, gently taking the tea pot from Wallace.

"Wallace, I know it seems unclear and dangerous. But you have a gift, no matter the pain that was its origin. You have always had a mission to serve, from boyhood. It is not often an orphan arrives at the monastery with such clarity of path, and then this *aberration*, during your initiation... I must believe that you are meant to be on this path. You are a great hope. To me, now, and one day, for all people."

AFTER PARTING ways with Father Andrew, Wallace made his way through the narrow pathways and cultivated garden beds until he could see the enormous square residential building where he lived.

Surrounded by the fields, it sat like a grey, concrete sea creature in an ocean of green, a black, metallic tube at each corner descending tentacle-like from the top level to the ground—the emergency exits. He moved past the residential building towards the cement public areas outside the other monastery buildings—a worship hall where Vespers was normally held, the food hall, and several administrative buildings. He avoided the other adepts, who nodded in greeting. Their stares lingered as he strode past. Someone called out a greeting, but Wallace pretended not to hear. He wondered if there were rumors about his activities now, causing the stares. Secrecy carves a path to isolation, and his every step was heavy with this burden he carried.

Wallace went straight to Vespers, listening in silence, before making his way to his room. He submitted a request to eat in solitude, and sat near the glass wall which made up one side of his room, and which, like those of all the other monastery inhabitants, faced the fields, affording full privacy, along with the perception of full freedom. All the world was his, from this vantage point, miles of field and endless starry sky, the mountains beyond. He meditated here each morning and each evening, and now sat on the woven mat with his tray before him. He took each bite slowly, a habit which had been drilled into all children during the worst shortages. As he chewed, he considered the vast sky and what was projected onto it: fear, emptiness, the future, the past. It was only sky, however, which thought comforted him, somewhat. So much of life's unhappiness was failure to see things as they were.

When he had first confessed his visions to Father Andrew, he had faltered only at one crucial bit of information—how to communicate the full depth of the peace he felt with the cross. It was uncommunicable, though he had tried.

"It is peace, like that which surpasseth all understanding, as the precepts teach us."

"And which only saints experience," Father Andrew had added, quietly.

"Indeed, I realize it is controversial, seeing as Christianity and its icons are from past centuries, and no longer taken seriously."

"Well, I wouldn't say we've discarded the entirety of it, rather, integrated its precepts and abandoned the mythology around it. But yes, there is not much tolerance for idolatry. Still, it's the feeling you are experiencing which is intriguing. I say it's special, worthy of investigation. We should focus on this together, and you must allow yourself to go fully into the experience."

Focus.

Justicia's very existence distracted him. He took his mind elsewhere, but his heart beat too fast. The stars no longer called his attention. His plate was empty now, and he pushed it through the slat in his door to be collected later. Justicia would not leave him be. She had a grip on his mind. Her image pressed against his body like a weight. Without the distraction of hunger, and semi-drowsy now, he could think of nothing else.

He skipped nighttime communal meditation to quell the burning in his loins, drawing energy up from his base through each of his centers until it exploded through every part of him, blasting open his third eye, his entire body unwinding. His body turned to light. White, searing intensity enveloped him.

Then, just there, he saw the cross, and a female hand on it, fingers clasped across the hanging figure, and then another hand, and another, until the cross was submerged in hands, all grasping, a Hieronymus Bosch feast of flesh, and then,

Finley, peering through his eyes

My eyes

Pressure, pressure between the eyes, a wall that he, that *they*, pushed against as he dropped,

and then Dr. Gloria placed a cold, damp cloth on his forehead.

11

FINLEY & KATE: THE DINER
JUNE 2019
ATLANTA, GEORGIA

When next Finley experienced hypnosis, he was in Atlanta, and considerably more at ease than the previous time, despite the jet lag and the building anticipation. In fact, as he emerged from trance, and Dr. Gloria came into view with her encouraging smile, Finley believed for once that he was on the right path, and no matter how little it all made sense, at the level of experience it was right and good.

In this journey, he had sat outside his monastery as Wallace Deng Moroz, painting a cross on a canvas as orange-and-red skies lit the *Quarter Fields*. This time, the merging of their minds was a seamless caress. Pleasurable, even. Yes, there was a mission between them somehow, but the edge of calamity dulled and in its place arose a settled focus on uniting forces. If life were a series of boxes to tick, Finley felt that now he was at last ticking them, and returned to the present with a sigh of relief that verged on happiness.

"That was so lovely," he said, feeling like a weight had lifted from his chest. "More of that, please."

"This is why I suggested your mind go to a meditative, calming activity in Wallace's life," Dr. Gloria said. "Don't get too used to it though."

Finley was slightly taken aback by that pronouncement, but she reminded him of their initial conversation after she'd reviewed Barbara's notes with him. About how important it was first to cultivate a relationship with his own mind and with Wallace.

"You're building a relationship. You don't go rushing into a commitment of marriage on a first date. It's the same principle here. You're getting to know one another, even if at some level you're the same consciousness, and I never make pronouncements on such matters. We take what's presented as fact and work with what's before us. In any case, getting to know each other requires some sessions of simply being together, simply enjoying one another. We don't want you to wake up in someone else's crises all the time. So we need to be very clear with your Superconscious."

"It was certainly better. I feel much more at ease."

"Wonderful. Now onto the reality of the situation. As I warned you at our initial consultation, you will find that I don't mince my words, Finley."

Dr. Gloria was certainly more straightforward than her predecessor. This older black woman struck him as an expert who'd had her fair share of defending whatever she'd had to defend in order to establish a reputation as an 'expert on mystics.' He could only imagine the nightmare of having to explain her unique qualifications at dinner parties and professional associations.

Now Dr. Gloria smiled. He felt his gut clench. *Why did Americans have to smile so much?* he wondered. It was a deceitful way to wrap a shit sandwich.

"You're a mystic, and the sooner you accept that fact and just go with it, honey, the better off you'll be. It isn't an easy path. People aren't gonna believe you, but then you might not even believe yourself. Fighting it is never going to stop it. It will just lead to a helluva lot more hurting. Also, I believe you're having these experiences for a reason. You're experiencing that particular experience, that of Wallace, *for a reason*. It will sometimes be unpredictable and scary, but you have to accept that it's just your path."

"Um, understood," he said, rather wishing he didn't. He

attempted a smile and thought about his dingy motel room, a last minute booking made for its proximity to Dr. Gloria. He made a note to himself to find the nicest hotel he could in the city and just take a taxi to this random outer suburb from now on. At least he could live in comfort if he had to endure this unknown mind torture, and especially the prospect of having a *path*.

"Wonderful. It might surprise you to know that you're not the first person to sit in this chair and mention novels by Gutov or the icon. I did read Barbara's notes thoroughly, so I know all the details from your first progression."

Immediately it was as if a fire had been lit near him. Heat travelled up his spine. Sweat poured from his temples. So far, this entire journey had been a personal one, as if he were grappling with inner demons no matter the implications for humanity—and now she was saying that someone else may have had a similar experience. What might that mean?

His sarcastic interchange with Barbara about *saving the world* suddenly seemed not so tongue in cheek.

"I don't want to say more and break client confidentiality. But the truth is, I don't always play by the rules. Especially if it's in the best interests of the parties involved. There's someone you should meet. A young woman. A slender, blond white girl. She frequents a diner not far from here some nights, after 1 am. She would never pick up the phone from someone she doesn't know, and you cannot say I sent you as a conversation opener or she will leave. You have to run into her and tell her about your visions or travels or however you describe it, so that she knows you are legitimate. So that she trusts you *before* you ever mention my name. But trust me on this. She might have some insight for you. That's all I can say, but I urge you. Here—" She ripped off the corner of a piece of paper on her desk, and scribbled the name of the diner on it.

He took the paper. It was a relief when Dr. Gloria started scribbling notes in a giant notebook. She didn't look up again, so he mumbled *thank you* and left.

KATE WATCHED the man at the back of the diner, sitting alone, eating a plate of eggs, cornbread and grits. Eating like he hadn't eaten in a week. She was sure he'd been there before at this hour, because she didn't often see people eat eggs with ketchup, for one thing. She recognized the combination of fancy looking reading glasses with disheveled long hair and a fuzzy face. She imagined he was working on some conspiracy in his garage, was unable to sleep due to his obsession. By day he was an average professional, good income, but bored by ordinary life. Someone who liked ketchup with his eggs. Egg-ketchup man, she dubbed him.

Such was Kate's nighttime habit; she was accustomed to watching people, and the details she witnessed arranged themselves into a narrative every time. She'd never exchanged even a word with a stranger when she was out on her own, so she could never verify the stories her mind conjured, and yet sometimes she saw the same person again, at the diner, or grocery store, or 7-Eleven, and so on, and she'd still think of him or her as the character she'd created: the alcoholic single mother, the gambler whose father abused him, the crossword puzzle genius. Whatever he or she appeared to be, Kate embellished and ingrained it into her memory.

The fiftyish man in the back corner had a foreign air about him, for example. He had thin brown hair, clipped short and professional—despite its current disheveled state—and a small nose. Even from a few booths back she could tell he had thick eyelashes and she guessed he had dark brown eyes. He wasn't bad looking, although not conventionally handsome. He had a blank expression that gave nothing away, and a pale, stubbled face that suggested he'd not had time to shave. The foreignness was in his gestures. Somewhat effeminate, or maybe he just wasn't very macho. In any case, not what you saw in Atlanta, Georgia at a roadside diner at 3 AM. She figured he was European. As she watched him further, she updated his story: *A lawyer addicted to coke, and he's running from some romantic problems back home, and he came to the US for a conference, hoping to forget her.*

Finley noticed her watching him, the young woman in tracksuit pants with straight, shoulder-length blond hair drinking about her third cup of what he supposed passed for coffee in this country. Her stare (across the room into the middle-distance and sometimes at him) was laser sharp, with a critical eye; she was biting her upper lip. Attractive in a conventional way, kind of a typical blond American girl, he thought. Of indeterminate age, anywhere from 20 to 30. Young, in any case. *So let her look*, he thought.

He was sure he stuck out like a sore thumb, but he didn't care. His body clock was all turned around. He was starving at the oddest times, and the shitty little motor inn where he was staying near Dr. Gloria became claustrophobic at dark, not that it was conducive to relaxation at any other time. He'd finally secured a fancy room in the city—he had delayed it a bit to be near Dr. Gloria—but finally he could leave the next morning. In a few hours time to be precise, since it was now the middle of the night.

His mind raced with thoughts that didn't seem to be his own. And the grits were too salty. Nothing felt real; none of it was welcome. But he'd started what he'd started, so he may as well finish it.

The woman picked up a book, and balanced it just behind her plate. He still had a clear view of her face.

He accepted another top up of his coffee from the angry waitress —that's how she seemed, anyway, and he couldn't blame her, working here at 3 am. She'd not said a thing, but he could swear she emanated a low-level growl. And her scowl. *Geez.* He smiled at *her*—well, it was more like a grimace as he was exerting so much effort to convey an emotion he did not in any way feel, so that she wouldn't spit in his coffee.

He drank with half-closed eyes, felt the warmth of the liquid going down and just breathed slowly until he felt his body finally unwind. Ah, yes, he must become better at relaxing, he reflected, given that this was his life now. Stalking women at a diner.

When he opened his eyes again, he refocused across the diner to the woman and her book and took another sip. The title was clearly visible now. *Ikona.* He sputtered out the coffee. *It was that book, it definitely was.* He felt his palms go sweaty. He was going to have to talk to her, because finally, he knew it was *her.* He had no doubt.

It'd taken him three nights to identify someone who fit Dr. Gloria's description, and he wasn't going to let the possibility pass him by, even though he was typically the last person to strike up a conversation with a stranger, especially a conversation as intimate and vulnerable as the one he probably would end up having. *Ah well,* he thought. *Here goes nothing.*

"Sorry to disturb you," he said as he—with hesitation—sat across from her. "I just want to ask you about your book."

He'd brought his tepid coffee with him. It was refilled as soon as his bottom hit the booth and the waitress smirked, no doubt assuming he was hitting on the woman (it seemed to turn her in his favor at least). Now he was even more uncomfortable.

"I'm not interested," she said, "so you should go."

"Honestly, I'm not hitting on you, I promise. It's your book."

"You're hitting on my book?" she asked.

He caught a hint of an upturned lip.

"No, very funny. I came to ask you about your book."

"Where are you from?" she asked, without looking at him.

"It's that obvious? I've only said a few words."

"It's obvious."

Now they stared at one another.

Finley found her disarming, but cool. Her accent was bland and what he might refer to as *Middle American.* She looked like any other blond American girl he might imagine, only she seemed too pale and her eyes were red—from lack of sleep, he guessed. She returned her full attention to her book, pointedly.

"I'm English. But I'm from Australia. It's Gutov, right? About a mystical object and Shambhala."

Without removing her eyes from the book between them, she

responded, "Yeah. It's widely available. There's a library not far from here. I can draw you a map."

"No thanks."

"Okay then, honey. We've had a nice conversation. Welcome to the USA."

Finley took a distracted sip of his coffee. Her tone was not too off-putting, just a small hurdle to get past. Exasperating maybe. Truth be told, he was a bit too immersed in his own strange drama to fully appreciate what it would be like to be a woman, approached at a diner in the middle of the night by a foreign man. And he was only dimly tuned into the oddness of his opening gambit. He knew he must say more, but had not a clue what to say or how to begin again. His head began to ache. He brought a hand to his forehead, and squeezed his eyes shut.

"Migraine?"

"Huh? Oh, no."

"Sure? I've got some Advil."

"That's very kind of you, but no, it's just, I've been getting these headaches lately. Nothing really helps."

"Jetlag?"

"Not exactly. I mean, no. I had them before that."

"Okay then. Well I'm gonna get going in a sec."

"It's your book, I think." He had made that up, but it contained a partial or tangential truth at least. Maybe.

"My book?"

She laid it on the table.

"Yes, that's why I have a headache. Your book." Because the book was related to his experiences now, he justified to himself.

"My book is giving you a headache?"

"That sounds completely mad, doesn't it." He rubbed his temples, and squinted his eyes, even though it had never worked to relieve this particular kind of pain.

"Is that a question?" she asked.

He lifted his face and tried to unscrew it so as to look less crazy.

"No, that was definitely a statement. I realize it does sound completely mad. I just came across this book, you see, in a most bizarre context, and I have this strange sense that I should tell you about it. But that's also completely mad, because it's a popular book, isn't it? Anyone might have it."

He scrutinized her, waiting for her to tell him off. But then—he saw it—a flash of curiosity behind the smirk.

"Well then you might need to tell *anyone* about whatever it is you want to tell about it, and I just happen to be the person you met."

"Coincidence lately seems a trite concept. Life has taken a rather bizarre twist. And for some reason, I think it may all make sense to you?" He hadn't meant to end that sentence as if it were a question.

"Okay, then. Tell me why you're here quickly, because I'm beat, and this is kinda creepy."

"My name is Finley Minor."

"Kate."

"Right."

"Yes?"

"So. Okay I'll just say it, then. I've been having visions. Okay, not visions exactly, more like *journeys*. It began when I had a hypnotherapy session that was meant to cure me from a fear of the ocean, and the next thing I know I'm somebody else, a monk, living a hundred years into the future. And the future is not good, not good at all. It's quite dystopian, actually, and it's as if I'm *there*. Inside the mind of this man. And there's this icon. A cross. It's kinda bronze, brownish, with three horizontal cross things, and it has some kind of healing power, and there is something about this book by K.I. Gutov because I have just discovered that the same icon I see in my visions is in that book, only I've never read it. And here you are reading it." He noticed Kate had gone still, mouth terse. " Are you... all right?"

His head began to ache even more. He rubbed his temples.

She seemed almost... frightened. But why? Well, so was he, in fact. Who was she, anyway? It was mad, *utterly mad*, that he should find himself in Atlanta, in a diner after midnight, talking to this stranger on the obtuse advice of a hypnotherapist. No wonder he didn't feel able to get any sense of this young woman beyond her apparent vulnerability, and her, well, obvious intelligence.

"Please don't worry. I just wanted to share because I thought, maybe, you could give me some insight, or..." He couldn't finish that sentence, because the word he wanted to use was 'help' and they both knew it. Help. *He needed help.* That was precisely what seemed to disconcert her so much.

"I should go," she said. "I'm tired. That's quite a story."

She stood and grabbed the book and a handbag which had been sitting on her lap and looked as if she were about to speak, but couldn't get the words out.

Finley started, "Did I say something to upset you? I mean, of course I did. I sound crazy. I'm not. Well, it's all a matter of definition in the end. But I'm certainly not dangerous. In fact, I'm quite sincere. I'd really like to talk to you about this more."

She swayed ever so subtly. Finley noticed that her knuckles were white, her hands taut on the black leather strap of her handbag.

"I don't know who you are, or why you're here. But I'm just fine without knowing about your visions. So I should go. Nice to meet you. Okay then. Bye now."

Kate put some dollar bills on the table. She walked out in a hurry, and Finley watched, baffled and a bit concerned that he'd lost her. He couldn't lose her! He dashed out after her into the quiet dark. There were hardly any cars in this suburban diner parking lot at this hour, and none on the roads either.

"Kate! Wait!" His voice echoed in the emptiness even though they were just about twenty feet apart.

She fumbled at the door to her car and he ran up to her.

"I'm sorry if that all sounded weird, about an icon and all that. I'm still trying to work it all out myself. I didn't mean to frighten you."

"Shh. Keep your voice down. Anyone could hear us."

"Is that a problem?"

"It could be."

"Anyway, there's not even anyone around right now," he pointed out.

She glared at him. *Shit.* He didn't want to piss her off even more.

"Sorry. I know that there is a lot of crime in the US. I wasn't thinking."

She rounded on him. "For goodness sake. Are you serious? I'm not worried about some random mugging. Who are you? You're talking about visions, and an icon. I don't want to get involved in anything..." she spat, "that *you're* involved in."

It took a lot for Finley to raise his voice, and even more to lower it once he had decided the matter was urgent enough to raise it. It had always been a sticking point between him and Clare. She'd liked a good row, at top volume, but she fizzled out almost as fast as it took him to get fired up, and he usually only caught up to her when she was done. But he raised his voice now. Anyway, there was no one around to hear them.

"Please. Hear me out. I'm not exactly involved in anything. I'm... I'm just a normal person who suddenly started having these weird experiences, okay. I'm a market analyst, in fact. I don't know anything about icons and I only just found out about Gutov's novel. That's why when I saw what you were reading I just felt compelled to say something. It's been a strange twist in my life. I certainly didn't ask for it."

For a second, comprehension dawned in her eyes, which then softened towards him.

"Why are you in Atlanta? In the US?"

"My hypnotherapist in Sydney told me to come to see someone in Atlanta called Dr. Gloria. She specializes in past and future lives and trance states, apparently. I had to get some help, or advice or something to make sense of it... to... to... *manage* it. And she..." He spoke so quickly that he was stumbling on his words, afraid if he didn't get them out, Kate would turn and leave.

"She told me that if I went to this diner late at night, or rather, early in the morning, I would find a blond woman who may be able to give me some insight. And I need it. I think I might need some help."

Finley pulled Dr. Gloria's business card out of his pocket and showed it to Kate.

Kate blanched. But she took it, read it, and handed it back.

She sighed.

"Dr. Gloria. Was it—your name's Finley? And you didn't think to tell me she was the reason you were here?"

"She told me not to, okay? She said you wouldn't ever pick up the phone so I had to run into you here, and that I should mention the visions first, before I said her name and scared you off."

Kate rolled her eyes, and then suddenly, like a light turning on, she smiled.

"She knows me well."

"I'm sorry to bother you, but I really am... lost at sea, and I could use some... I don't know. Any insight whatsoever, really. I've been having visions of that same cross, from the future, and it seems important, and you seem to know about it. So."

He swayed, hands in his pockets. Completely unthreatening, he hoped. He realized that there he was — *drifting aimlessly in the sea again*, and silently winced.

"And you're really not part of any... group?" She asked.

"No, I'm afraid it's just me."

"Fine. Well, I need to go now. So just meet me here tomorrow, only a little earlier, around 1 AM. It'll be empty then. In the diner. Give me time to think about all this, decide what I can tell you."

"Done. Thank you." He bowed his head.

Kate unlocked her car and got in. Finley didn't know quite what to do, and was still charged from their interaction, so he stood frozen as she began to drive off. Finally he turned and walked head on into a parked car, nearly falling, just as its owner opened the door.

"So sorry," Finley bumbled, wiping a smudged sweaty hand print from the car with his sleeve as he desperately searched the parking lot for his own rental car. It took him much too long to remember what his rental car looked like given that there were only about three cars in the parking lot anyway.

The long-haired man with glasses smiled just enough to communicate that he was amused by Finley's clumsiness, rather than irritated, which was fortunate so late at night in America, Finley thought, where everyone had a gun and many used them.

He was on edge, to say the least. He imagined his nervous system had been permanently thrown into fight or flight. Normally the certainty of numbers and company statements reassured him, but now certainty and calm had vanished, perhaps for good. In this new life, his head ached with a single-minded desire to understand the improbable, to discern his role in it. He drove the few blocks to his motor inn, and collapsed into the overly soft bed, knowing full well he'd hardly sleep, again, but not caring at all. He was no longer alone with the mystery.

DR. GLORIA BEGAN their session at eleven a.m. sharp, without so much as a *how are you, did you sleep, how are you feeling*. He had thought Southerners were into their chit chat, but not so in her case. She smiled, though. That was her preamble. *Oh how her smile grated on him.*

"How about we start again at the Quarter Fields, and see where it goes this time?" she asked.

He did not, in any case, feel like he had a say in the matter. So he nodded and mumbled, "Okay."

"Lovely."

She began her counting, bringing his attention to his body, suggesting he fall, fall. Finley disappeared, second by second, minute by minute, until stillness entered and time itself disappeared.

He was drawn again into a pinprick in his mind, and pushed through, which felt somewhat like a sword piercing his head. He cried out as a force beyond him pulled him through. He landed, now painless, in Wallace, with the dazzling, empty sky and the wind, the fields and the smell of dry earth.

PART II
THE QUEST

Don't get lost in your pain,
 know that one day your pain
 will become your cure.
 ~Rumi

For life is a journey, and in that journey
 you take many roads, and they all
 lead to the same destination—
 to the beginning of another journey.
 ~Khalil Gibran, The Madman

12

FINLEY, KATE & VICTORIA
JUNE 2019
ATLANTA, GEORGIA

"My head is hurting, oh my God. It's like a knife went through it," Finley said, grasping at his temples. "It's burning, like a fire behind my eyes. I felt it as I went into Wallace, and then as I returned."

"Okay, honey. Just hang on."

Dr. Gloria jumped up and left the room. She returned quickly with a cold, damp cloth, and told him to lie down on the couch. She lay it across his head and said nothing.

"I think they are trying to close the door, the portal, the—whatever it is that allows us to connect, me and Wallace."

"Oh? Who is trying to close it?"

"No idea."

"You've felt this before?"

"No. I mean, I felt pain in the first session, a scene from my childhood and the ocean. I don't recall *this* pain, though."

"We can explore this next time, but for now, I think you need to take some time to rest. Between now and our next session, please do this: Notice when the headache appears and what makes it worse. What are you doing or thinking about when it comes on? Where is it in your head? And so on. Rest here a little while."

He pressed his thumb into the soft spot on the side of his forehead, as if it would bring some kind of relief.

Dr. Gloria disappeared again, and returned with a cup of warm tea with milk, just as he liked it. *Bless her.* He was starting to like her.

"I had this headache a bit when I met Kate," he confessed.

Her curled upper lip betrayed the faintest smile. "I knew you'd meet her."

KATE FELT the transformation stirring in her in the hours since she'd met the English Australian man the night before. For too many weeks she'd been fighting off a creeping depression after Little Bird left. The mystery of the icon and Gutov had done nothing to lessen her anguish, and yet it grew alongside her grief as a vine might speed across a trellis and obstruct an unfortunate view. Now suddenly, she was not alone with the mystery. For the first time in as long as she could remember, certainly since she'd attempted to describe her childhood to her last lover and been met with disbelief and derision—

she felt an opening in her heart.

She guarded that opening tenderly. She had arrived at the diner early and had drunk one coffee already in order that she not hold back the moment she saw Finley. Now, as the waitress approached, she readied herself.

Finley entered the diner with a backpack dangling off one shoulder. Maybe he wasn't the cocaine-addicted lawyer she'd written him as. In fact, he seemed *helplessly* honest, and also just a tad helpless in general. In over his head.

"Look," Kate said, from the second Finley sat down. "I spoke to Dr. Gloria. So I know you're legit. A client of hers. But that's all I know."

As soon as the waitress left the table, Kate continued. "For the record, Dr. Gloria told me that she suggested you might connect with me because we have certain things in common. Very specific things, she said. But she told me nothing. She's all about client confidentiality, of course." She rolled her eyes, given that two 'confidential' clients were sitting across from each other in a diner a few blocks away from Dr. Gloria's office, at her bidding.

"Of course. And, yes, she told me exactly that. Specific things in common. And so here we are."

Kate sipped her coffee. A memory of her mother intruded, faded, intruded again. Her mother. The one who'd taken her to Dr. Gloria so many years ago, with hopes that her daughter would *change the world. Be Somebody*. Until she didn't. Kate pushed the thought away.

"Dr. Gloria used to come here in the middle of the night sometimes, after I stopped seeing her as a client. She was clearly checking in on me. She's sent me other people before too, and it's gone all wrong. That's why she didn't want you to start with mentioning her name, because she didn't want me to dismiss you. She's just trying to help me, I get it. So I can meet other weirdos or something, I don't know, so I'm not so alone."

"I'm sorry that you're so alone."

"Don't be."

She meant it. She didn't want any kind of pity. "I'm not alone in a bad way necessarily."

His coffee arrived, and Finley grimaced when he tasted it, but he took a couple of sips.

Kate's caution vanished at the sight of his discomfiture, and his ensuing, thoroughly earnest effort at nonchalance. She leaned in and chuckled. "I was a special case, you might say."

"I gather I am, too."

"You mentioned visions last night. Tell me more."

"Jumping in at the deep end, I guess," he said. He added, "I suppose it's best that I tell you everything."

Kate nodded.

He took another sip of coffee.

"So, um, I've had this weird ability, you might say, since I was a child, to know things about the future."

He rambled as he shared his rejection of that ability so far; he explained how he permitted himself only a narrow inner window to investment opportunities as a reluctant compromise, and admitted to his fear of drowning. He shared how, after Clare dumped him, he decided to find help and at least cure his fear of the ocean—but instead, landed in Wallace's life.

Kate felt him relax as he spoke.

"It felt like I fell through a hole, like a black hole, and my head was searing with pain and then suddenly I was *him*. I was somebody called Wallace. In the future."

He took a large gulp from his mug and grimaced. He looked at Kate tentatively, as if asking permission.

"That's—I don't know what to say," she offered.

He drank again. "Ugh. I forgot it was coffee."

Kate laughed. "It's *barely* coffee."

So he *had* had relationship troubles. That much she'd intuited at first glance. Or had guessed correctly.

"So... then what happened? I need more."

"Well, you know it's difficult to explain, because as I told you last night, I *became* him. I *am* him. In the future. Like more than a hundred years into the future, I believe. I'm a black man, a monk, and I go into some strange meditative state in that life and we're connected. He's me, even now, and I'm him. But, I don't come back to my present life with a memory of everything. I come back like... like I'm waking up from a dream. And like with a dream, there are a few details that I remember, sometimes more than others."

"Like the cross. You said you saw the cross."

"Yes. I'm being told to find it, or Wallace is being told, and it's like he's telling me that it's important. I'm meant to find it, or more specifically, to find out how it was made, its *origin*. And I remember a few other things... like there's a crisis, people are dying, and the cross is vital somehow to helping them, in the future."

Kate, stoic and unblinking, hung on every word.

"I first heard about Gutov's book *Ikona* when I was Wallace. Then Dr. Gloria told me that she'd had other clients mention it. And that was when she suggested I meet you. I actually bought the book today."

He winced, then rubbed his temples.

"You okay?" Kate asked.

"Yes."

"Well of course it's about *Ikona*." She pursed her lips and her eyes shifted from side to side as if she were calculating.

"Of course?"

"Yes, it's always that novel. I have a long history with it, you could say."

"Is that why you trust me? Because of Dr. Gloria, or the connection to the novel?" he asked.

"In part Dr. Gloria's recommendation. She's never sent me anyone dangerous, no matter how weird things got with them. But I also trust you because I'm a good judge of character, because I spent my childhood with people who manipulated me. So I'm—you might say—sensitive." She took a breath. "As for the novel."

Finley pushed away his empty mug. "Yes?"

"Let me read you something."

She pulled a notebook out from her purse and opened it to a dog eared page. She read:

THE ICON WOULD LEAD *the followers to its origin in the deepest reach of mystical Shambhala. That this Kingdom of Heaven exists amongst us is undeniable. It shall be reached only when the destined explorer awakens from his dreams of fantasy, to don the cloak of truth. He will enter pure of heart, his mind freed from all doubts...*

"THAT WAS from *The Planet's Relapse*, Gutov's second book in his trilogy. It was the mantra of my childhood." She checked that she hadn't lost him. He leaned into his elbows, as if riveted, so she continued.

"When I was a little girl, my mother was part of a community of

Gutov fans. I call them *followers*. It was like a cult. They believed that Gutuv knew the secret to saving humanity from itself. Via a mass ascension into paradise, otherwise known as Shambhala—like I just read to you. When I was five or six, I told my mother I'd had a dream that in his next book Gutov would reveal the location of Shambhala and how to reach it. He'd announced by then that he was retired, you see. He'd publicly refused to write any more books after *The Planet's Relapse*. So after my dream, that group, the cult, used me as a poster child to lobby Gutov to write a third book and reveal everything."

"They took your dream that seriously?"

"Yes. Because I'd had other dreams, small ones, that apparently were accurate about what was happening. Always things happening right then that no one could have known. Weather events, or famous films being produced. I can't remember, actually. I was that young.

"Anyway, so my mother took me to Russia and I met Gutov in person. I was still only about six. Basically, I had been prepped to *pressure* him to write this third book in his series, what would be *Ikona*. But he and I had—it was some kind of connection. He got into my head. It was like he could see what my mother was doing to me before I even understood it. Anyhow, he did finally write *Ikona* and in it he *did* suggest how to reach Shambhala, which was all exactly what I'd dreamt, only the actual story in his novel was clearly coded. I mean, it probably wasn't even literal, but my mother's group believed it was. Fans have been trying to decode *Ikona* ever since. After he wrote it, he disappeared and people thought he did actually go to Shambhala. That's when my life changed. I started having dreams about him *all* the time, and in my dreams he would tell me things about the future, some of which I told my mother, and lots of it came true. So then my mother decided that my destiny was to find Shambhala. I would decode the book, she said. I would be the one to find the cross, like the one in the novel, and use it to lead people to Shambhala. It's literally insane. Except now you're here talking about a cross and the saga continues. Apparently."

Kate, relieved of holding this particular burden alone for so long, felt a profound unwinding and sank into the booth.

"All when you were a child. This is exactly why I didn't want my visions when they came to me either. Everyone wants something, and as a child, you can't say *no*."

"I know." She laughed. "I couldn't do it. By the time I was a teenager, I wanted my own life. I didn't have any more psychic dreams and I didn't want any. My mother sent me to Dr. Gloria because she thought that if she hypnotized me, I'd have visions or dreams again, but it didn't work. Instead, Dr. Gloria very gently helped me understand that I was in a cult, and she helped me find the strength to leave it. When I was fourteen, I rejected Gutov and I rejected my mother. I mean, *totally*. My mother sent me to live with my aunt in Georgia, and told me that I had not fulfilled my destiny and that if I didn't return to it one day, I could never be happy.

"When I finally left my aunty's home I cut off all ties to those relatives, and, eventually, my mother died of cancer. To be honest, I felt like finally I was free. After that, out of the blue, when I was 19, I had a dream again, for the first time in years. In my dream, Gutov told me that he had in fact hidden the information I needed in his novel *Ikona*, but that my Shambhala was my own, and when I was ready I would find it."

"Oh, that's... it's so..."

"Crazy, I know. Again. I realize this."

"I was going to say *intense*. It's intense. I'm sorry you were put under so much pressure. I felt something similar, when I was a child, though nothing like that. That's... really horrible. And what about your father? I mean, did you have a father?"

"Well obviously *someone* contributed to my creation. My mother told me he was a non-believer and we should never speak of him again. I think he was a member of the group and maybe he left. I've never looked for him though."

"I'm sorry, Kate."

She sensed that he did actually care, but she also *only just* tolerated his caring. Whoever found out about her past inevitably felt sorry for her and said so. Which is why she tried to never tell anyone. Pity, or compassion—whatever it was—only made things feel worse.

"I didn't want any more dreams or communications or premonitions. And I didn't have any again until just recently, not long ago actually, just in time for your appearance."

"Lucky me."

"The thing is, as you now know, I'm not the only one who has had visions involving a cross that leads us to a future utopia. Every so often, Dr. Gloria sends me others, like you."

"Who've had similar visions? About the cross, or in general?"

"In general. Visions about the future. Or those who also grew up in a cult." Kate chuckled wryly.

"That's kind of her."

"Yes, only most of them haven't really had visions. I can tell. It's more like, they want to have visions, but something's missing when they talk about it, so I know it's not really legit."

"Missing?"

"Fear. They're not afraid. It's terrifying, seeing something others can't see, the reality of it. You get used to it, sure. But it rocks you. It throws you into a metaphysical confusion. It can't *not* unsettle you. That's how I knew you were the real deal."

He smiled at her and Kate smiled back, just faintly, but it was warm.

"Yes, it is actually *terrifying*."

"I know you *know*. Honestly, I'm not sure what's even real. Truth exists in... in a web of complexity. There's always at least one really true thing, a truth with a capital T. And that Truth is easily adopted by the masses, but then it gets warped, so much that the original truth is difficult to truly see anymore, and then the new Truth is completely compromised. And IT becomes a pawn in someone's power games. A commodity, a means to an end, and no longer works as it should."

Finley nodded as she spoke.

In that moment, for the first time in a long time, Kate felt *seen*. And, as if the narrative had collapsed, stillness ensued. The silence felt anchoring.

FINLEY INDEED SAW her truly now, and he knew there was something brilliant in Kate, in her perspective and thinking. He admitted, "I have no idea how these things work. Could you please explain something to me—what exactly *is* Shambhala?"

"It's a kind of mystical utopia. A place of freedom, and love. It's been known by many names throughout history, but it's always the same concept. It's about getting away from suffering, if you ask me. Suffering in life. Really, it's about getting away from the enemy within. That's why every culture has its utopia, whether it's Heaven, or Shambhala, or anything else."

Finley nodded. He knew *the enemy within*.

"And you say you've had a vision recently?" he asked. "Was it about the cross?"

She looked around, conspicuously. "I actually saw it."

"Are you saying that the cross exists?" he probed.

She nodded.

He knew his face was drawn, betraying his shock. He couldn't help it. He suddenly saw things differently. His vision was becoming something else now—it was real, a physically tangible cross.

"Hang on, did you have a vision of seeing it, or did you actually see the real thing?"

"The real thing." She avoided eye contact.

He started to say something, then thought better of it.

"And yes, it heals. Listen, it *healed*. It healed the little girl I looked after, my neighbor's niece."

She lowered her voice and leaned forward. "She had leukemia, and then, after a night with the cross, it was gone. Completely gone. Vanished."

"It *healed*? You had the cross, and it *healed*?"

She nodded, and looked away.

"The one from the novel, the one that looks like this—" He pulled the book out of the backpack he'd lain across his lap beneath the table, and there it was, on the cover, book three of the trilogy. *Ikona*.

She nodded again.

"The same one I am being shown a hundred years in the future. But for real? You... saw it?"

"Yes, I had it, and it healed Little Bird." She sniffed and her eyes watered. She hastily wiped her face with a napkin.

"Little Bird?"

"The girl I looked after. She's gone. Her uncle took her back to her family in Mexico. She's not mine. Just my old neighbor's niece. Anyway."

Kate faded like someone had switched the channel and she was the static between stations. Finley wanted clarity though.

"Kate. You still have the cross then?"

She didn't respond.

"First things first." She put up a hand. "Given your visions of the future or whatever. What is your mission, actually, and why?"

"I literally have no idea. Wallace is looking for the origin of the cross through me, I guess. And here I am, talking to you, and you have it. Or had it. Pretty weird."

She tapped the table with her fingertips and bit her upper lip. Finley rushed to explain, painfully aware of his chronic inability to drive his life forward in any meaningful way.

"I guess I feel an obligation to find the cross, but to tell you the truth, I've got no idea what I'm doing. I don't even know how my *travels* work, how I become Wallace."

Almost as if to herself, Kate spoke, staring blankly somewhere in the middle distance, "I didn't want to accept any of the truth my mother filled my head with, or her community, Gutov's followers. And yet, there it is. The cross. My dream, and then, *you* appear."

She met his eyes, stubborn. "There's no victory in this quest, Finley. Believe me. I've been waiting for it."

Then she deflated like a small child denied ice cream after eating all her vegetables. Finley actually felt sorry for her. Momentarily, at least.

"I guess we're both part of something whether we want to be or not," he said.

Her eyes glazed over. She was far away. She bit her upper lip. Finley wanted to reassure her, but was unsure what the etiquette was—if he should pat her arm or say something encouraging. He didn't want to leave the wrong impression. He didn't want her to think that he saw her as unequal to the task or that he fancied himself *paternal*.

She affected him in a way he didn't quite understand. He wanted to protect her, not exactly like a father, but perhaps slightly so. She was obviously much younger than him, at a guess, twenty years at least. And at the same time, he knew instinctively that she didn't need his protection (and might well be offended by it). Then there was the obvious alliance: they both inhabited the in-between, flung together into a reality that could not make sense of people like them.

They needed each other. He felt it to the depths of his soul.

He'd never needed *anyone* before.

"But you have it, right?" he whispered.

She went rigid, putting her finger to her lips in a subtle *shush*. Her expression changed abruptly, and she leaned forward again. "I just saw someone I've seen here before, egg-ketchup guy. We might be being watched. I just don't know anymore. I feel on edge, and don't tell me that not everything means something."

"I wasn't going to," Finley protested. "Egg-ketchup guy?"

"Nevermind. Anyway, let's continue the conversation at my place tomorrow, maybe 11 am, okay? We need a plan, but we can't be out like this anymore, just in case everything *does* mean something. Follow me home now, so you know where to go. Tomorrow, you just meet me on the second floor. Take the outside door and just go up the stairs."

As it turned out, the police also arrived at 11 am the next day. Finley had just made it to the second floor landing when two officers came down the hall from the opposite end.

Finley didn't particularly like authorities in any form, whether it be bosses or tax agents, police officers or doctors; he went out of his way to avoid them. He didn't like to be around those for whom (as he saw such people) identifying what was *wrong* wasn't just temperament, but professional duty. In reality, he'd not had a bad encounter with authorities since some aggressive high school teachers found weed in his backpack. In this circumstance, however, in which there were already serious matters at play, like a magical cross, mystical experiences, and possibly something else disturbing which Kate seemed to be withholding from him, the two male police officers evoked a kind of panic that felt more premonitory than regressive. His heart raced and his palms sweat.

Finley pretended to fumble for his keys in his pocket and then retreated to the stairwell, closing the door, but he stayed there, breathing fast. After a few seconds, he cracked open the door and strained to hear. The men knocked at an apartment about three or four doors down. He heard the door open, and a voice—Kate's—say, "Yes?"

"Miss Davies. We have some questions about Roman Ivanov."

Finley couldn't hear her reply, just the slightly exasperated response of the officer that followed. "Look, we know you're a sex worker, Miss, but we're not interested in that. We know he booked with you. He died that same night. So you can help us out or not, but it's only going to get complicated if you don't."

At that point there was silence, followed by the sound of the door shutting.

In the corridor, Finley let the stairwell door close silently behind him before running back down the stairs. He got into his car, gripped the steering wheel and told himself sternly that none of this was really any of his business anyway.

Sex worker. Dead man.

But he wasn't having much luck with not panicking. His knuckles were white. He let go of the wheel. *Stop the thoughts,* he told himself. *It's all okay—she will be fine, and you're not involved in any way.*

He waited. He pretended to be busy on his phone, and as soon as he saw the police leave the building, maybe 20 minutes later—and *without* Kate—he pretended to be speaking to someone. His heart pounded in his chest as he watched them get into their car, just a few steps away. Finally, only after the policemen had driven off and were completely out of sight, he ventured back upstairs and directly to the door he now knew, without doubt, led to Kate's apartment.

"I saw," he said, when she opened the door. "And I heard. A bit."

She rolled her eyes when she saw him. "I'm guessing you heard enough. Come in."

"What's going on?" he burst out as she shut the door behind him. "You're a prostitute? Why would a nice girl like you..."

"Please." She put up her hand to stop him. "Spare me your judgment. This way." She led him around a corner to a small-ish kitchen with a circular table and four chairs. She raised an eyebrow but not her voice. "And about two hours of my day, a few days a week I sell myself. How many hours a week do you sell yourself, on average, would you say?"

"I don't sell myself."

"You said you were a market analyst. Who do you work for?"

"I *worked* for an investment bank." He was indignant.

"How many hours a week?"

"Fifty-ish give or take."

"So who's *selling* themselves? I'm just a part-time whore. You?" Now she glared, defiant.

"Okay." He threw up his hands in protest, but at the same time, he was beginning to feel sheepish. "I get it. I'm not judging you."

"No, of course not." She half rolled her eyes. He found himself containing a bemused smile at this feisty and self-assured young woman who apparently let strangers fuck her.

"Ok, I *am* judging you, but it doesn't change anything, except for making me an ass, just to be clear."

"Well done, Finley. Anyway, just so you know, Roman never showed up for his appointment, in case it ever comes up."

"Right, but... he did?"

She ignored him. She pointed to the table and chairs, and indicated he should sit.

"Want anything?"

He shook his head no, so she poured herself a glass of water from the tap, drank it down, and went to sit with him.

He took in what he could see of her apartment. Quite clean, modern, simple. Grey couch. Potted plants everywhere. A burgundy rug sort of wall hanging. It was cheerful. He wondered where her bedroom was. Where she took her clients.

"Finley. Come back to Earth."

"Sorry."

"I also didn't know his name until just then, by the way. I had a booking from a Russian man. I guessed the accent, but he didn't give me a name on the phone. And then this Roman Ivanov was found dead in his car, and I didn't know that the man who booked was that same man because, again, *he never showed up for his booking*. Got it? Anyway. They found my website because it was saved as a bookmark on his computer—*idiot*—and it had been visited loads of times until his death, and he'd texted me on my number which is on my site. That's the last of it as far as I'm concerned. He was involved in organized crime, so it's really nothing to do with me."

"But... what happened? How did he... you know."

"Well, apparently he was *poisoned*. They think it's mafia related. That's what the police said. I don't think they even suspect me, anyway. Female sex workers don't tend to be the ones doing the killing, if you know what I mean. They just wanted to know if I knew anything else about him, like if he'd seen me before. And I hadn't. He'd only texted me once, ever. And that's the truth. The police would know that anyway. But all that was weeks ago, and now you're here and we have more pressing things to discuss."

"So," he stuttered. "So... I'm guessing that's how you got the cross, that it came from him, and he was Russian, and if he was involved in organized crime, that means the cross was probably being trafficked by the Russian mafia, right? That's why they poisoned him? They mustn't have expected him to end up at your place. So they might be looking for you, or... *it*. Can... can I see it?"

"Hold on, cowboy. Yes, it's probably something like that. That all makes sense. Maybe they *are* looking for me." She looked surprised by that revelation, a little freaked out in fact. "Anyway, I don't have it anymore."

"You don't?"

"It's being kept safe."

There was a knock at the door, three raps—da da-da. Then the same, again.

"It's Victoria," Kate said. "My neighbor. Just please try to stay calm."

Kate had no sooner opened the door than Victoria launched right through it, her face awash in concern.

"Honey, are you okay?" A thick, Southern accent coated every syllable like treacle. "What was that all about? I saw the police." It took her a moment to notice Finley at the table, and when she did, she did a double-take. "Who the fuck are you?"

Finley took in the rather tall woman. At least, he thought she was a she. In any case, Victoria was rather *imposing*.

"I'm Finley Minor. Nice to meet you." He stood and extended his hand.

Victoria sneered at the proffered hand.

"Finley *Minor*?"

Kate snapped. "Behave. He's a friend. A new friend."

"I see."

Finley withdrew his hand and sat back down. Kate returned to the table to sit with him.

"The cops were looking for a Russian guy. I handled it. And it's okay. Finley knows."

Victoria raised her eyebrows in alarm, and pursed her lips. "What does he know, exactly?"

"He knows what he needs to know, okay? We don't need to talk about it. Just trust me."

Finley squirmed in his chair, weighing up the pros and cons of volunteering to substantiate claims of his trustworthiness.

Victoria shook a finger at Kate. "They'll be back, hon. The police. It's becoming a big investigation. There's organized crime involved, so you can expect this investigation to be a *thing*."

"That's worrying," Finley said, unable to stop himself. "You should be careful, Kate."

Damn, he chastised himself. He hadn't meant to sound like she needed protecting.

Victoria's jaw dropped. "You think? Kate, it's a good thing you have Finley here to help."

"Cut it out, Victoria. Please. Anyway the police told me the dead guy was poisoned. He was found poisoned in his car, so they don't even suspect me. I have more to worry about from the Russian mafia. He was involved, apparently. Possibly trafficking something *valuable*. We can't know for sure." She stole a glance at her friend.

"Oh. *Shit*." Victoria went white. "I did suspect as much. That is *not* good."

"I think I'm being followed. Maybe it's the Russians. I'm not sure. There was a guy in the diner I saw the night before, and then I'm sure I saw him following me last night, too."

"Last night? At your diner?" Victoria asked.

"Yes, and please don't look at me like that."

"You've been through a lot. I'm worried for you."

"Anyway, is it safe, Victoria? You know, the..."

Victoria glanced at Finley then evidently decided she wasn't bothered by him anymore.

"Don't worry. It's safe. Nobody's gonna find it."

Kate bit her lip and stared into the cheap laminate kitchen floor.

"In *Ikona*, the cross led to Shambhala. It was like a magical key that opened an invisible door to another dimension. It glowed. It didn't heal, it *led* people. But here, this cross heals. So will it even lead somewhere?"

"Oh, hon," Victoria spoke softly. Patronising, to Finley's ears. "Kate, maybe you've just been reading too much. You do live half your life inside novels, and it's not real. The cross is safe. *You're* safe."

Kate still couldn't meet her friend's eyes.

Finley broke the silence. "I need to understand this cross better, too."

Victoria took a step back towards the door as if about to leave.

"Look," she spoke to Kate. "All I can say is honey, you be careful who you trust. You've been through a lot, and you need to just look after yourself now."

"I need to help Finley, Victoria, that's all. I'm the only one who can. I wish I could explain it better."

Victoria looked back and forth between Kate and Finley, as if failing to see any obvious connection. Finley knew there was a lot between those two, said and unsaid. And he knew to stay quiet.

"Let me be honest here, Kate. I know you're hurting. We're both hurting with Little Bird gone. But she's healthy, and she's with family, and we need to get on with our lives, not go chasing something that doesn't make sense, something that dangerous people are after. If you get caught up in this business with the cross, I'm worried I won't be able to protect you."

"It's my mystery to solve. I wish it weren't. And I don't expect you to protect me. Don't worry, Victoria. I'll be okay."

Victoria opened the door to go. Finley saw the tears in her eyes so he knew Kate did, too.

"It's all rather complicated, isn't it?" Finley said as the door closed.

Kate stared down at her hands, now on the table. "It wasn't the productive discussion I'd hoped to have today. I'm a little tired now. Maybe we should continue tomorrow if that's okay?"

"Of course. What's the next step then? I take it we're assuming it's the same cross, that Gutov based his book on the real one?" Finley asked.

"That's the best explanation for all the weird synchronicities," she sighed. "So I'm going to finish going through the book. Take some notes. Glean what I can from Gutov's depictions of the cross in the novel, and then I'll get back to you. He obviously knew something specific about a magical cross that he embedded in the narrative. We just have to find out what he knew."

"I'll do the same."

A momentary sunshine warmed his soul, a shining few moments as he imagined applying himself to logic, which tended to yield tangible outcomes, and generally kept him safe.

"Okay then," Kate said. "It's a plan. It's a start, anyway."

She ran her fingers through her blond hair. For a second, she radiated absolute certainty and calm, and Finley didn't miss the look of clarity which passed over her face. She seemed to come into sharp focus.

Together maybe they actually could make sense of the senseless.

Finley realized that he'd underestimated the extent to which he'd been carrying this burden on his own so far. Maybe, he thought, he hoped, *she* was the key to everything, and from now on, they could steer this ship together.

13

WALLACE & LOVE'S ARRIVAL

JUNE 2131 AD

KRASNOYARSK, EASTERN FEDERATION

Wallace stared at the small paper folded in a perfect square on the floor of his room, pushed in beneath his door. His first name was written out in block capitals, so he knew it was a note. But as he had never received a note beneath his door before, he had no clear presentiment whatsoever. It was an anomaly, since messages were normally sent via the Interface. In each room discrete panels were embedded into the wall near the doors. Personal messages were announced with the sound of rushing water. Vespers was announced with a single, resonant bell, and meals with the twinkle of wind chimes. The panel lit up in a soft, blue glow when any form of communication arrived with its corresponding sound.

This note, however, was silent and colorless, and also somehow intrusive, sitting there on his floor like something discarded. Perhaps for that reason, Wallace left it where it lay until he had eaten his breakfast and dressed in his robes, and only then retrieved it. He sat at the edge of his single bed and unfolded it. The writing was messy, as if written by a child with a shaky hand.

. . .

There are those who know what you're attempting even in the past and some who will attempt to sabotage you from that timeline, although you also have allies there. Please understand that allies are helping you even now, and that all of time might turn in your favor should you continue in this endeavor with the correct resonance. You must find the secret room, and you must go there. Destroy this note.

He re-folded the note, and, not quite ready to part with it yet, tucked it into the inner fold of his undergarment. He sat with many questions fighting for dominance over his morning meditation, as he stared out the window at the Quarter Fields. *What does the correct resonance mean? A secret room? Who would know about their project, from inside and out, and thus know of enemies and allies far and wide?* His meditation labored beneath the weight of this development, which at least kept him from thinking of Justicia in advance of their meeting that day. After an hour of monumental struggle, Wallace admitted defeat, and prepared to go to Dr. Rinella's. He put his key necklace around his neck, watered his plant, and placed his breakfast tray through the slot near his door. When he opened the door, Alex stood there, stoic and stiff.

"You were not at breakfast this morning," Alex stated, the barest hint of a question in his tone. A gentle breeze from the open-air walkway behind him ruffled his short brown hair.

"Since when are you bothered by my absence?" Wallace asked. They were old friends, both adepts, but hardly friendly these days. They hadn't even dined together in years, though Alex sometimes joined him on contemplative walks through the Quarter Fields.

Alex, still stony-faced and immovable, seemed to be waiting expectantly—though it was unclear for what. Wallace squeezed past him and locked his door, and only then did Alex budge, walking alongside him. But it wasn't until they had moved from the level landing outside the rooms, and down toward the spiral walkway that led to the ground level, that Alex spoke again.

"There are whispers that you're up to something."

Alex's face remained impassive, as was characteristic of most adepts after undergoing the procedure at the Cottage during their pubescent years. In contrast, Wallace knew himself to be considerably livelier than most. He knew some in the monastery believed he was *aberrant*, and thus further from his Divine potential. Other, more lenient members of the monastery, however, simply considered him a smart-arse. Few knew the depth of his gifts.

Wallace and Alex continued side by side, robes brushing as they entered the spiral descent. The walkway was designed to be a walking meditation, leading, eventually, to a small natural courtyard in the center of the building. Exits on three sides led from that inner, sheltered space to the outside world, and to the path that took adepts to the rest of the Monastery grounds.

Giant mandalas made from living grasses and moss drew Wallace's eye at intervals along the stone walls. Each piece of artwork featured a spiral pattern that collapsed to a stillpoint, yet at other angles, seemed to widen into the infinite. Most adepts, becoming entrained to the visual effect as they walked, fell into an internal rhythm of peace, and ultimately bliss—the design's intended result. Adepts who required more *support*, as it were, were placed on the highest floors, to receive maximum benefit.

Wallace, restless now, only felt impatience.

"So you've heard whispers." Wallace stated the obvious, waiting for more information.

"Yes."

Alex was too still, too bland, even for an adept— something about his manner unsettled Wallace.

"You've heard that I'm up to something?" Wallace continued to probe. He watched Alex from the corner of his eye.

Alex nodded. "With Father Andrew. A mission of God." That was all he offered before falling silent again.

"And if I am?" Wallace asked.

Alex blinked too quickly. "It would be unprecedented. And thus it would be important."

Alex's tone still revealed no hint as to his feelings, or motive, and

Wallace felt a shudder of annoyance run through him. He suppressed it quickly and smiled instead at the sight of the cafeteria girl standing near the tunnel door. She was empty handed—she had either missed his breakfast tray or was having a bit of fun first. She cast a furtive look their way before disappearing behind the door; then came the audible *swoosh* of her descent down the tunnel.

The tunnels were essentially giant slides, one positioned at each corner of the building. They'd been built as emergency exits, to bypass the time consuming spiral walkways, though they'd also been a stroke of quiet genius in the early days of mass orphanages, helping children forget, if only for a moment, some of their worst memories of pain and loss. On drill days it was a sight to see, ochre robes spilling en masse from the slide outlets into the green fields below. Now, these tunnels were reserved for drills and emergencies only, though young children often used them for entertainment. Until the procedure, of course, which seemed just as effective at removing natural childish frivolity, as it was at numbing emotional expression.

Wallace let the silence stretch as they circled down further and further, fast approaching the lowest level, then said lightly, "You don't wonder what it might be about?"

"No. I suppose it must be about a cure, if such a thing exists. That's what most research is for." Alex's tone was still flat, almost rehearsed, but his jaw tightened. Wallace noticed. For all his conformity, something in Alex strained against the script. *Had someone sent him? If so, who?* Wallace's thoughts went again to the morning's strange note, which he could feel pressing against his upper thigh.

Moving through the inner courtyard and out the south exit door, Wallace relented. "All I can say is that I am doing something secret."

Alex, with uncharacteristic intensity, said, "Stay safe, Wallace."

Safe? Perhaps Alex was just the emissary for someone else's agenda, or maybe he *was* actually curious all of a sudden. Still, this sudden interest, this note beneath the door, it was all unsettling.

As Alex turned and began walking in the opposite direction, Wallace caught a glimpse of fiery red hair from the corner of his eyes.

It was Justicia, of all people; she rushed past from somewhere on the Monastery grounds, headed toward town. She hadn't noticed him.

Justicia was most likely on her way to see Dr. Rinella, as was Wallace, so he followed her at a distance, taking a slow pace, so that she could not see him, at least until he got his heartbeat and breathing in order once again.

THE MONASTERY'S district was the most fertile natural haven in the Krasnoyarsk region, and had been selected by the bishops for its rewilding potential: to be close to nature was to be closer to God. Despite the raging intensity of the long ago blast, and the immense destruction that poured out over the surrounding area, the relatively short half-lives of the radionuclides that spilled out meant the radioactive effect had been blessedly short-lived. Already, only fifty years since, in the Quarter Fields immediately surrounding the blast site, there reigned a veritable wilderness which suggested the gradual return of biodiversity.

In the midst of this verdant landscape, the Village with its alleyways and dilapidated buildings felt deeply incongruous. Wallace did not enjoy leaving the wild fields for the invasive concrete and putrid smells, especially today. And now his heart raced at the thought of running into Justicia without the buffer of Dr. Rinella's presence, so he elected to pause in an alleyway and then walk past the ten or so shops on the high street, pretending to be searching for... *something*. Food. Warm socks. A snack at one of the two cafes.

There was not much on offer. The Monastery District, which included both the wild grounds of the Monastery itself as well as the Village proper, unfortunately encompassed the poorest part of the Krasnoyarsk urban region. Because the Monastery did not have the same funding to put towards refurbishment as did the Science Institutes or the Council, there seemed little hope of a proper shopping district any time soon. Yet, the Village *did* have a certain charm—or so Wallace assured himself as he lingered outside the grocer. It had the light fountain in the main square, for example, a dazzling display of technology that was at odds with its surroundings.

Before the nuclear incident, this street was 'millionaire row,' where capitalists had constructed their ostentatious homes along with a small array of exclusive shops and cafes. Since his first visit to the Institute of PsychoConscious Development, Wallace had discovered that its building was once a regal manor for an AI developer, hence the marble staircase. As for why Dr. Rinella chose to work in their district, it turned out to be pure prejudice against the kind of science Dr. Rinella was willing to explore, or so Father Andrew had informed Wallace. The Science Institutes *official* premises in their own district were always conveniently 'at capacity.' So Dr. Rinella traveled, daily, from the Science village center on the other side the Monastery grounds, at the outskirts of the once-Krasnoyarsk-city, to what was considered a backwater.

Wallace still stood awkwardly in front of the small grocer. There were no shoppers to be seen—typical for a weekday. After a few idle moments, Wallace made his way to the old building and its short green door.

This time Justicia was polite and self-effacing when she greeted Wallace, but she was still irritable with Dr. Rinella. When Wallace arrived, it seemed they were already deep in disagreement.

"Wallace here might have more insight," she announced.

Wallace had only just sat in the armchair, mentally preparing himself for regression. He blinked, confused as Justicia swung towards him. She wore a long, loose wrap that fell below her knees; it was difficult to see her slight form within it. He did try, but then looked away, willing himself not to stare.

"I was invited to a Bishops meeting today, as a representative of the Council Funding Committee," she began. "There was a *suspicion* mentioned, that certain *forces* are covertly being funded to carry out unorthodox research to find a cure. They asked me directly what I knew. They were trying to make a case for more funding for the

Monasteries and complaining that monies were being unfairly directed elsewhere. Their suspicions put me far too much in the spotlight, which endangers us all. Don't you agree?"

Her gaze penetrated.

"I suppose," Wallace replied.

"You *suppose*?" She grabbed a hem of her wrap and swished back to face Dr. Rinella.

Dr. Rinella reassured her. "First of all, there are some at the highest levels who are aware of Schopel's involvement in Visionary research and keeping quiet about it. Hence her joining the Monasteries, as you know. But as for the particulars of this project, and the fact that it involves Wallace, I don't think they know anything at all. We have been extremely careful. Moreover, no one can possibly know what Wallace sees in the past, the icon and its potential. But this suspicion, this atmosphere of distrust and rogue forces pervasive throughout the Triumvirate, *that* is a larger problem, as I was saying before Wallace arrived. Your focus is wrong, Justicia."

Dr. Rinella now directed his rebuttal to Wallace. "It's true that we are not the only ones doing covert research. The Council, by controlling the pursestrings, has far too much power over the direction of research, and thus is creating this situation in which money is being siphoned off covertly for separate agendas—not ours, however. This is a direct result of the Visioning bill being quashed, which forced divergent groups with different agendas underground. Each of those groups has a representative in the Triumvirate, and each is getting a piece of the pie. My point," he glared at Justicia, "is that it's all collectively destabilising the Triumvirate."

"I know you lack faith in the Triumvirate, Lucio! But there are still procedures, committees, access to legitimate funding—which we risk losing in this atmosphere of suspicion. I don't pretend to have the answers, but I feel we need to find a middle ground. Some degree of honesty to leave a door open to funding, should we need it. Should *you* need it. And I'm not claiming I know how to do this." Justicia's face purpled. She drew her fingers through her wavy red hair, pulling it away from her forehead.

"Why must you defend the Triumvirate so patriotically?" Dr. Rinella hesitated for a moment, before reconsidering. "I forget. You came from a Revolutionary family. No doubt in your girlhood you were made to memorize the rise and fall of industrialization and Market Capitalism. And what did you learn? Did you learn to trust one power absolutely over another? Even the Triumvirate is not beyond reproach."

"My parents were *healers* long before they were Adjudicators. By the time I finished school, they'd given their lives to the Revolution. Our home was a commune for political refugees." Her color paled as her voice became softer. "The Triumvirate reflects a more balanced approach. We hold each arm of government in equal esteem. Or that is our aim at least. We are doing our best. *I* am doing my best... but..." and here she looked at Wallace. "Lucio is right. There are other forces in the mix, and there is suspicion. I don't know how long I can be part of this if I am to continue to conceal my involvement, both for the sake of my career and for the sake of this project." Her voice quietened even more.

There was a sober silence. Dr. Rinella poured himself a glass of water and drank. Wallace, ever watchful, gave away no clear opinion. Father Andrew and Dr. Rinella had not shared everything. Other factions. Doing what though? He didn't need to know more. He steered clear of politics. His parents were killed for their politics—that fact was a sufficient deterrent.

Suddenly, Dr. Rinella sighed.

"I'm sorry, Justicia. Forgive my temper. You have a right to defend the Triumvirate. However, I am justifiably concerned that the Council has too much power over funding, so we need you on our side—and yes, let's brainstorm a middle ground, as you said. I feel that we have a great opportunity here, better than most. I suppose I want to ensure that you represent us well to the Council in case—in case we need funding the most, through conventional channels, in case this project requires expeditions beyond the mind."

"I am here with an open mind, Lucio."

Wallace now felt moved to interrupt. He spoke with a quiet voice.

"Isn't a cure bigger than politics? If there is a cure to be found—would that not unite all factions?"

Justicia nodded. "This is my deepest hope, Wallace. " She pulled up a chair and sat near him.

Dr. Rinella spoke. "You've named our next challenge. If there is a cure for the cancered, then who controls it? Who might we trust to control it? The Council with their visioning agenda, which is no secret? The Monasteries, who believe that life in body is a distraction? The Science Institutes? We need leadership that is benevolent, united, open to collaboration."

Justicia opened her mouth to speak when an abrupt knock came at the door.

"Eden Schopel," Dr. Rinella announced, suddenly looking more pleased than he had thus far. "I forgot to tell you we have a visitor today."

IT WAS AS IF, along with Eden Schopel, a strong wind had blown through the door, cleansing the air of all prior content. Justicia paled to her habitual white pallor. Dr. Rinella's fervor dampened as he performed what appeared to be a mini bow of greeting. Only Wallace remained unchanged at the far end of the room.

"Welcome," Dr. Rinella finally spoke, and grabbed another of the white chairs from near his desk, ushering her immediately to where the others sat. Wallace jumped up to give her his plush armchair, but she shook her head.

Schopel was tall, full-figured, brown-skinned, with a flat nose and large, penetrating brown eyes. Somewhere in her early forties, she had only recently been declared safe from illness—a memorable event due to her public renown. Despite all the recent scandals and whatever experience she might have undergone at the Cottage, she still had the aura of a *declared survivor*, the telltale glow of a second life, a genomic gift granted randomly and suddenly, just when certain death loomed.

She was too tall for the small white chair, but managed to arrange herself on it gracefully, hands folded in her lap. She neither smiled, nor frowned, and with studied neutrality began to speak quietly.

"Thank you for having me. Thank you for your trust. I will not abuse it nor take it for granted. Lucio, Miss Potts," she looked at them directly. "I hate to burst in so abruptly, but we have little time, given recent developments. You both know the circumstances of my presence, but Wallace, it's to you that I now owe an explanation." She turned to face him as she spoke, binding him with her dark eyes.

Wallace nodded in response, utterly taken aback by this woman's self-assurance and urgent tone. The procedure at the Cottage had evidently not dimmed her passions. Wallace wondered if it were her age, or if she, like him, was an anomaly.

"Good, I shan't take long and then Lucio must perform the regression."

The room seemed to warp for a moment, and the others, to Wallace's eye, receded into the background. Schopel, somehow—despite her size, made herself small and the room seemed to collapse into her stillpoint. The respect which her presence demanded did not take up any psychic space. *How is she doing this?* Wallace wondered, as he felt himself lulled into complacency. It was almost hypnotic, in fact, how her eyes zeroed in on his so directly, how her voice, sonorous yet reassuring, poured into the room like warm caramel.

"Young man, you are how old?"

"Thirty."

"And you have been an adept for many years now?"

"It will be one decade in a month's time."

"Yes," she replied, as if she knew the answer already and had been merely testing him. She continued, "The Visionaries, as a faction, came into being about the same time that you were initiated onto your path. Coincidence? Seemingly unconnected, and yet I have found, through my work, that much more is connected than we understand from surface events only. There are events in consciousness, throughout time and space, which have relationships beyond the Veil, as I call it. The Veil being a sort of ethereal wall that separates inner worlds."

Wallace pushed his line of sight toward the seemingly far off figure of Justicia, and saw she was also deeply entranced.

"I, too, am able to travel through time, Wallace, or at least my consciousness does. Officially, I acquired this skill through vigorous training, all orchestrated by the Council. I was the star pupil, you might say. Unofficially, there was a predisposition. A family history, you might say. Once we found a methodology that worked, and once I disclosed to the committee overseeing this work the exact nature of my discoveries, I began to train others. The rest, as they say, is history."

No one spoke, as indeed Schopel's words did not invite response.

She continued, "The Visionaries have been controversial yet highly valued since our inception, because of course we are able to see possible futures, and identify the most likely one we will arrive at, given our present circumstances. Yet in our travels, we have also forayed into the past, which not many people realize. In fact, there are a few of us who have known, for some time, that we must cast our vision toward the past, rather than the future.

"The origin of the Visionaries is, indeed, the past. We, the few who look back, know our own origins, in lives past, though our past selves hardly grasp how their roles will evolve across lifetimes. Still, as we've discovered, our past selves are helping our cause *now*. We have worked out that to communicate with the past, we must send our fervent thoughts, like prayers, back through our very souls."

Dr. Rinella spoke, ever the clear-minded scientist. "Your work then confirms the transmigration of souls, from one human body to the next through time?"

"Yes, but Wallace knows why we cannot speak of this openly, correct?"

Wallace nodded. "It seems that the transmigration of souls has been proven many times experientially in centuries past—and even in our time. There are others in my year group who have been able to reach their past selves through meditation. But such experiences have been dismissed as irrelevant to earthly life. I've been told by Father Andrew, in confidence, that all references to reincarnation have been destroyed. *Centuries* of proof. It's considered a distraction from the present attempt to awaken our consciousness, and accept our fate."

Schopel nodded once, sharply. "Yes. I can tell you that through the work of the Visionaries, now we understand that there is a thread of spirit working through the flesh—contributing to a joint endeavour as it were, the evolution of humankind. Not entirely separate but, rather, intimately entwined."

Justicia spoke, "It's only a matter of time before the official line changes, in this case."

"Indeed. Who we *were* is sometimes not only relevant, but vital for who we are *becoming*, as Wallace's experiences are showing you here, with this project. Thank you, Lucio, for the briefing papers you shared on the work to date with yourself and Father Andrew." She took a deep breath. "As to why I am here with you today. Wallace—"

She addressed him intimately now, tempering her tone. It seemed as if she were suddenly closer to him, as if she'd scooted in. But she hadn't, or at least he hadn't seen her move at all. She leaned down towards him conspiratorially, though, resting her elbows on her knees. Her energy, her every gesture conveyed that she was about to make a deeply personal admission.

"Wallace, in a past life, I knew your past self, Finley, in those critical times. I knew Finley's friends as well, and crucially, I knew about the power of the icon. My visioning skills were weak then, yet I clearly grasped an apocalyptic future. I was the first Seer of that era, and gathered around me others who would form a faction, at the time quite outside the halls of power. Eccentrics, you might have called us, society's fringes, meeting in secret, and sharing our discoveries on hidden technologies, on scientific advancements. We met on an interweb cloaked in darkness.

"There is a direct lineage, as I have discovered, from those Visionaries of the past, to our faction today. It was because my past self followed Finley and his friends. My network from that past life knew I was doing something critical for humanity's survival. They didn't know about the icon because I have, as Eden Schopel, made sure of it via my... forays into the past. It is our greatest advantage. However, there are factions then, as now, who are trying to find out what we know. They are attempting to do so in waking life through politics and espionage, and in consciousness by attempting to block you.

"So here I am in this timeline, offering my support, to ensure your safe passage. I have seen, from my travels in consciousness, that there are forces interfering with your communication. So I will journey with you, in spirit, an unseen ally, to protect what you and Finley both know."

All present seemed to be holding their collective breaths. Wallace looked around. No one was speaking. *Am I the only one who didn't know this?*

Justicia said with uncharacteristic restraint, "Lucio, I'm sure you were going to tell me about these past life *factions* soon enough."

For the first time, Wallace felt nervous about going into his familiar trance state. Which was better, he dared admit to himself, than being distracted by the sexual charge of Justicia sitting so close by. Still, the revelation that there were interfering forces at work in his regressions activated his nerves. But hadn't he known it already, without actually drawing that conclusion consciously? There was that pressure, a wall being pushed against. He'd felt it both in his own meditations, and in trance with Dr. Rinella. What did this mean, then, and was it safe?

It was as if Schopel had read his mind.

"I am here to protect you, remember?"

Dr. Rinella asked, "Do you need anything from us, Eden? Or a moment to prepare yourself?"

"No, I am quite ready now."

With that, she closed her eyes, took a deep breath, and within seconds her head dropped down.

"In that case," Dr. Rinella said, "we will begin. Wallace, ready yourself."

Wallace closed his eyes and breathed deeply into his heart-space.

It was buzzing rather than empty as it should have been, as it might have been without so many distractions. *Just breathe*, he told himself. Dr. Rinella lowered his tone an octave and instructed him to follow his voice, tapping on his knee.

"Follow me down," he said calmly, "into the room of your mind where all might still, your comfortable yet solitary confinement, a most familiar resting place, where you will find a door,

and so Wallace dropped down, down

and it began.

SCHOPEL CAME out of her trance first. Her nostrils flared. She gripped her knees.

"Those who are attempting to intervene are growing stronger," she announced.

Wallace slowly came to. He had the sensation of falling upwards, slotting back into his body from the ground up. Justicia's eyes met his as something in him clicked into place.

She brought him a glass of water. There was a sweet fragrance around her, of flowers, like perfume; he could smell her as she leaned in. She whispered, "Are you okay, Wallace?"

He nodded yes, breathing in her smell. She paused, just a second, and seemed to linger there willingly, then abruptly moved away. He blinked the room clear.

"What do you mean?" Dr. Rinella addressed Schopel. "Wallace? What did you sense?"

He drank the water Justicia had given him, his gaze following her for a moment.

Finally, he spoke. "Yes, there was some kind of pressure. It feels a bit like I'm being squeezed."

"They cannot succeed, as I am also there, pushing back against them," Schopel said.

"What does this mean, Eden?" Justicia asked. "Are you sure others from the past are not seeking this icon?"

"In the present day no one knows of the icon but all of us, here, and Father Andrew. Even Wallace's paintings of the icon were destroyed once this project began, not that anyone had any idea what they represented. Today's Visionaries don't know about the icon, so they cannot send the information to their past counterparts—it's simply not in their field of consciousness. I am constantly travelling in time to ensure this remains true, and it is true, for now. However, both in the past and in the present, there are forces that know Wallace is onto something that could disrupt their plans, and they want to stop him. They are tracking me now, as they did then. There is always a *chance* that someone will discover the truth about the icon. But so far I have stopped it."

Wallace suddenly remembered the note left beneath his door that morning. He debated with himself for a moment, but decided it was senseless to conceal anything now.

"I nearly forgot. I received a piece of paper beneath my door this morning. It was a message. Written very crudely, as if by someone who is illiterate. It spoke of others being aware of what we are doing, both now and in the past. And that there are those who wish to stop us, but also those in the past who are assisting us. And something else, I don't remember."

Justicia took a sharp intake of breath.

"I think we have more than ample proof that all of that is true," Schopel said. "All the more reason to push on. We must be the first ones to find the information we are seeking and keep it secret as long as possible. Long enough to find a cure."

Justicia interrupted. "Forgive me, Eden. I feel swept away by your self-assurance, yet I must ask nonetheless, how are we meant to trust you? There are so many competing interests."

Eden turned to Justicia, her voice soft but firm. "I do understand completely, and you would be foolish not to ask such questions. Yet, I can no more reassure you than you might reassure yourself. What I mean to say is that it is not my role to convince anyone of anything. There are some eras in which you can only trust your gut, Miss Potts. There is no other barometer of trustworthiness. You either know that we are on the same side, or not. So I suggest you meditate on it tonight. Now, I must go. I know some of the players involved in the past, and their present selves. I may be able to assist in real time as it were, but I need to act quickly. Thank you for having me, Lucio."

With that, she stood and went straight to the door. Dr. Rinella jumped up to follow her, and closed the door behind her with a thud. Justicia took the opportunity to lean forward in her chair and whisper to Wallace, "Meet me at dusk at the Square, please, a private matter."

Wallace held himself in check at her nearness, though his heart thumped absurdly, until he stood, excusing himself as Eden had done, and left the room.

WALLACE WENT DIRECTLY to Father Andrew, and when he arrived, sat in his office, waiting for many minutes as the priest tended to some immersive task, moving images around on the projector table with a furrowed brow.

"I hate bureaucracy," he apologized to Wallace. "So I am reluctantly relying on the Interface to help me with some tasks. I will not keep you waiting for long."

Finally, the older man swiveled his chair around and across the polished concrete floor to face his adept.

"Something troubles you. Was it today's session?" Father Andrew had known him since boyhood, and was familiar with all of his expressions, as Wallace knew well.

"In a manner of speaking," Wallace offered.

"Is it Schopel?" Father Andrew asked. "Does her presence disturb you?"

"No. Although the situation does seem unfathomable and complex beyond what I initially thought. At some level it also seems entirely logical. And I understand her value."

"Do you trust her?" asked Father Andrew.

"Are you asking me for your sake or for mine?"

"Both, I suppose," said Father Andrew. "I believe myself to be a good judge of character, but these present circumstances have tested my faith in this regard."

"I understand," said Wallace. "For what it's worth, my feeling with Schopel is that her presence is entirely benign, if not somehow reassuring. I could feel her mind joining me in my travels, and I can feel myself aware of her presence in the past. Forgive me, Father. I am assuming that she has already told you her theory about her connection to all of this?"

"She has."

"There are, without doubt, forces which wish to stop me. I can feel the pressure, as if the door is being pushed against me the moment I open it and the moment I return back through it."

"Oh." Father Andrew sighed. "This does not surprise me, although of course it saddens me. I'm glad Schopel is helping you. But is that what's troubling you?" he asked Wallace with a gentle tone, as a father to a son.

"No, I wish it were. I am afraid that my concern is entirely more frivolous. It's about..." His voice faltered. He was embarrassed. "A woman. She wishes to meet me this evening. I do not know what to think of her."

"But you can't stop thinking of her?" Father Andrew laughed, a deep belly laugh.

"Something like that."

He was bothered by the existence of this woman, bothered by remembering her leaning in close to him, asking him if he were okay. He was afraid, truth be told.

"You are very attracted to her?"

"It overwhelms me."

"And your heart?"

"Over-excited. Yet I don't know her at all. We've barely met. Something, though..."

"Ah, nothing can open your heart like attraction. Like love. This is just your heart gasping for breath after a long submersion in breathlessness. We orphaned ones know this shortness of breath. It is woven into our being. Have you not been in love before, my boy?

Even the Cottage cannot stop this from happening. In fact, it is sometimes the undoing of the procedure entirely..."

Wallace admitted, "I don't think I've truly been in love. I have had a relationship, within the monastery. It was not *this*, however."

"Well." Father Andrew patted the younger man's knee. "I can assure you there is nothing more wonderful or more terrible. What we know, what mystics such as yourself have long known about the heart, and what science itself confirms, is that the heart is a powerful energetic center, and when we open it through love, we become far more connected to the field of Infinity. So whatever is happening here, it can only assist the cause."

W<small>HATEVER THE TRUTH</small> of Father Andrew's words, and whether due to his mentor's suggestion or not, Wallace's heart center was buzzing long before Justicia arrived. The spectacular light fountain in the middle of the square where he waited poured a waterfall of light both downwards into a multi-colored swirling pool, and then upwards several meters where it exploded into the sky. This fountain was the only modern and maintained structure in the Village, and no one could ever explain why—except that it was a landmark, the default meeting place of locals. The square itself was lifeless, grey concrete, weed-cracked and slick with damp clumps of leaves. It was only dusk now; the lights were faint, muted. Justicia rounded the corner through a shimmering, pale pink shaft of light. He'd always been seated in her presence, and, although used to being six foot four and thus taller than many, he was surprised at how much he towered above her.

She was wearing a simple black dress. It was loose and long. Her hair was upswept. Her lips were pale and her mouth closed tight, jaw hard. She was nervous. She barely reached his chest, and stood close enough to him that she had to lift her chin to look up at him.

He could not stop himself from saying, "We could get in trouble by meeting here. Someone could find out what we are working on."

"I will get into trouble, not you," she said. "Officially, I am not here, you might have guessed. I am attending your sessions for Lucio's sake. For the slim possibility this foolishness works. Anyway, this—" She paused to indicate this here, right now—"is personal."

"Personal," Wallace repeated. He took a shallow breath.

"Walk with me around to the trees, where we are more hidden," she said.

The trees at the edge, not long ago saplings, were more a hedge than anything else, but there was sufficient height to conceal their faces.

Before she could begin, words spilled out of Wallace's mouth. "You should know, my parents were part of the founding group of the Ibiza Experiment. They were killed in the bombing when I was five years old. My brother and sister, too."

He was entirely taken aback by his sudden confession, but he also instantly knew why he'd confessed with such temerity. Given her family line, he wanted her to know *how* he'd been orphaned, to know that they were cut from the same cloth, both children of revolutionaries, despite their divergent paths.

Justicia frowned. "I'm sorry to hear that. It is especially cruel to lose loved ones to violence when so many are cancered."

"I no longer have the emotion of those events, since my initiation as a monk."

"The infamous Cottage."

"Yes."

"Cruelty, I believe."

"You might be right. I *have* wondered. My experience was... different."

"I've heard," she said.

They stood in silence. Wallace held onto his robes and attempted to keep a polite distance; still, he verged towards her, leaning in, as if she were downhill.

"I am surprised that you chose the life you did, as a spiritualist," she said.

"Why? Many choose it. I am not more or less special."

"Ah, but you are."

"Much less so before this project."

"I mean, you were raised with a *mission*, and chose a path of surrender."

"You mean to say *chose a path of defeat*, don't you?"

"Well..." She laughed. "I am entitled to my bias."

"As are we all." He smiled, too. "Anyway, I felt I already had a mission, one way or another. I simply desired a quiet life and I enjoyed the promise of solitude. I never imagined how such a mission as this would emerge from a monastic life."

Justicia squinted. He recognized this mannerism already—she was choosing her words.

Finally, "Do you think... if you don't mind me asking something personal...".

"Not at all." His heart buzzed again.

She crinkled her nose and squinted more intently.

"Do you believe that Finley is your past life? Or simply a resonance in the soup of consciousness, as it were, an inexplicable connection."

"Is that why you asked to meet me?" he asked.

She did not respond, but cleared her throat.

He said, "Anyway, yes, I do believe our connection is more personal. Like his soul is mine. I feel myself to be him in a way I cannot put words to."

"That is why you have such a sense of mission, I suppose, because he had such a mission with the cross, too. Maybe also because your parents had a mission, though perhaps you chose them for that exact reason, chicken or the egg, I guess. Though I don't presume to understand how souls choose a path... or if they do. I'm afraid I'm on controversial grounds here."

Flustered, she wrung her hands.

"It's okay. Many do believe it, of course. It's not as controversial as you might think. It's not belief that is the issue so much as it is behavior. Some fear that those who focus on the transmigration of souls are distracting themselves from the task of transcendence."

"Indeed, the Monastery's mission is to focus exclusively on

helping adepts merge with Bliss now, to go beyond. They are all about grasping at the eternal." She swung her arm in a wide arc, as if to demonstrate grasping at something ungraspable.

"You mean to say, *blah, blah, blah*, don't you?" Wallace laughed.

"Oh, you *laugh*." Justicia smiled. "I thought they meditated laughter out of you adepts—as a rite of passage."

"They do try. I'm not so easy to mold."

They both looked out past the buildings of the Monastery into the Quarter Fields, into the waist high grasses, as if to look away from one another in this vulnerable moment.

"Wallace, I need to confess. I did not meet to have this conversation."

He wanted to confess his attraction then and there, but those unarticulated longings caught in his throat. They had to tread carefully here. It was unfamiliar. Their project was secret. There were too many factors to consider, and his mind was a mess of confusion.

Justicia now stared at him. He attempted to look back, though it was too intense, so his eyes wandered to the grasses, to the darkening sky and the ever-brightening explosion of fountain lights, and then back again to her burning stare. His face was hot, his hands clammy. *Why would she say nothing?* he wondered.

At last he broke her improbable silence. "Why did you wish to meet, then?"

She froze, then in a rush breathed out the words, "I feel an attraction to you, which I believe is reciprocated. So I thought it best to be direct, and explore if there is anything to explore."

Justicia stepped forward, and went onto her toes, face tilted up towards his face. He leant down towards her, feeling the heat of his skin, lips brushing lips.

"Okay," he murmured, awkward.

"Okay," she replied.

They came apart, though their energies were intertwined. He had no hope of resisting this woman. He was desperately curious too, and desperately worried about the project.

"You should know something first. My husband is in the penultimate stage. He has been asking me to take a lover, but I resisted, until we met."

Wallace sighed. He felt as if he were suddenly coming up for air, and the world clarified a bit. *Husband. Last stages.*

"I'm sorry for your circumstances, Justicia."

"Don't be. It is the way of the world."

"I despise polyamory. But I understand it is necessary."

"It's vital that we get to know each other on a foundation of truth."

"Yes, I agree," he said.

He searched her face for the grief that surely troubled her. His heart seemed to thump loudly in his chest as he realized: it was there, it had been there all along. Her pale skin shone in the fountain lights and she wrapped her arms around herself to hold her elbows, as if she felt chilled, which couldn't be. It was so warm. There was resignation in her, a quiet fatalism even, lying beneath a stormy surface.

So many endings in this life, Wallace thought. No one was untouched. He couldn't recall a time when one was unfamiliar with a dying body, with family collapse, or with the days and weeks and years that passed after, along with the unremitting reinvention of self and community. It was a constant shifting of human puzzle pieces to fill the gaps, a neverending drive towards wholeness.

Justicia took his hand. "Never mind that now. Let's meet soon. Adepts are allowed weekends out of residential living, correct?"

He nodded, pulled towards her with a force he'd never quite experienced, while another part of him sat back. The sitting back part saw the choice before him. The certain uncertainty of her, of this, of this entire life and planet. The tantalizing possibility that she was the puzzle piece missing all this time for him, and the knowing that any piece was as easily given as taken away.

She squeezed his hand,
he shut his eyes
and allowed all of it.

14

JIA LI & THE HEALING—REPRISED

JUNE, 2019

HONG KONG

The morning Jia Li found her mother collapsed on the couch, she rang Sam without thinking. He came over straight away to help, all the time whispering into her ears about retribution. She told him to back off—their normal trope.

His insistence on the matter still annoyed her.

Her reaction still bruised his boyish pride.

She still secretly liked how he leapt to her defense.

"You let me know when you've figured it out," he snapped. His eyes softened only enough to remove the worst sting of his impatience.

"I'll let you know," she told him, not unkindly. "Thanks for coming over. I need to take my mother to the hospital. You can go now. We'll be okay." She fought the urge, for a moment, to ask him more about his recent healing, but deep down she knew he didn't have any answers. He was only the lab rat in this equation, that much was clear.

"Okay." He kissed her, a bit rough, obviously grumpy at being dismissed. He closed the door behind him as if he'd meant to slam it, but caught it midway so that in the end it barely clicked shut.

Jia Li rushed her mum to the hospital for extensive testing that same evening, claiming Mary had been listless for some weeks. Given the sickly pallor of the older woman's skin, the doctor immediately ordered tests. A lot of tests. The initial tests led immediately to more, highly specialized tests. In the meantime, Jia Li delivered Michael a blood sample from her mother, in case he had answers—or at the very least *hypotheses*—that mainstream medicine *did not*. She was still waiting for any information he had about Sam's arm.

Near the end of the second week of testing, Jia Li and Mary received a panicked phone call from the oncologist, who didn't even wait for an in-person appointment to announce that there was cancer in Mary's liver, lungs, and elsewhere, so thoroughly metastasized that she *had* to have been sick for months, years even. The oncologist, a stern-sounding woman, insisted that Mary should start chemo and radiation right away. But Jia Li stalled. Mary, too. It had only been a couple of weeks in the three to four month 'deadline'. Jia Li had no information to give her mother's attackers anyway, so why put her through more pain if there truly was no hope? From the way the doctors and nurses whispered in hushed tones whenever Mary was near, it was difficult not to believe that treatment was pointless. Jia Li knew they needed Sam's miracle cure, if only she could access whatever had caused it, and make it happen again.

OVER THE WEEK following the attack, Jia made small excuses to see Sam, to meet for a drink, to bring him dinner and stay the night, anything so that she could watch him carefully, to work out if there were any negative side effects of his healing experience while she waited for Michael to give her answers.

Sam did seem more energetic than usual—at once brighter and more wound up. Only, it was difficult to assess properly. He was sulking so much, too. He even brushed her off several times, like he had more important things to do. Terse conversation was punctuated by long silences that grew between them like weeds in the cracks. He made desperate love to her the three nights she stayed over, as if each time were the very last time, then rolled over, unconscious and snoring.

The first such morning she rolled toward him when he woke and asked, "What's bothering you, babe?"

He shook his head. "Nothing. Everything's fine."

But in actual fact, *nothing* had been the same between them since the healing, except for her deepening apathy.

By the start of the second week post healing, he'd stopped offering to get the thugs from her show off her back, or to do anything for her mother, and she wondered if it had to do with that *healing object*, or if he unconsciously recoiled from her psychic energy—a kind of constant surveillance with even less emotional availability than usual. She couldn't be sure, since he no longer talked about anything with her as he used to, not his feelings, and certainly not work.

"I don't know what's going on, Sam, but you're different since that healing. This miracle of yours may be doing more harm than good."

Jia Li named it on her way out, the third and final morning after she'd stayed the night. A parting shot as she stood at the door clutching her handbag, while he lay in bed pointedly *not* walking to the door.

"You're out of reach," she said quietly.

"Feels that way." He frowned at her across the room.

She spent the rest of her morning at Marks and Spencer, where she pocketed a silver bracelet and a pair of sunglasses, both of which she threw in a bin the moment she left, berating herself for petty theft. "You don't need this," she told herself, pushing back against the powerlessness that goaded her. It was all beyond her control. Sam's distance ached. Her mother's sickness gnawed at her. In her room that afternoon she cried for an hour, and then prepared a homemade dinner for her mother, who was in bed most of the time now.

FINALLY, after two weeks of anticipation, two weeks since the attack on her mother and since Sam's healing, Michael told her to come over.

No sooner had she entered his tiny apartment than he double-checked that his door was securely locked. Without his lab coat and safety goggles or glasses he was endearing somehow, this short Asian man with a baby face who shushed her the moment she arrived. At once protective and nerdy, he was rare in his ability to accept Jia Li completely, neither judging her life choices nor watering down his intellectual acuity. He treated her like a scientist first, even if she rebelled with her performance art. She felt safe with him in a way that she had only felt with her father,

and especially *now*, when everything seemed to be falling apart.

Michael had already pulled down all the blinds. He put a finger to his mouth again, *shhh*, and beckoned Jia Li, *there,* he mouthed, and pointed towards the soft glow in the far corner of the room. His microscope sat on a table. She went and leaned over, then peered inside.

Dancing shadows and light, a burst of multiplying cells, blossoming like a field of flowers in timelapse. Jia Li felt the truth of it in her heart before her scientific mind made sense of it.

This was how Sam's arm had healed.

This was the strangeness, the magic, the inexplicable transformation from a centimeters-deep wound to barely a scar in a matter of minutes.

Jia Li was entrained to the life unfolding across the slide. She felt stillness wash over her just like in meditation, from one gentle breath to the next. She did not even ask herself what was happening, or how, so transfixed was she to the incessant movement,

to the rhythm,

like the ocean's current.

Suddenly Michael was tugging her arm until she had to look away. He removed the microscope from the table and locked it in a cupboard, then guided her out of his apartment, locking the door behind them. They got into the lift, took it to the basement, and then left the building by foot. In silence they walked to a bar in SoHo and ordered beers. It was not a place they'd been before, and they chose it for no particular reason, other than its unfamiliarity. They knew to go to different places. Often, one of them would text the other—*grab a beer later*—and they'd meet on a busy street somewhere, then randomly find a bar or restaurant.

It was the only way they could speak openly about whatever was happening in their lab, where Jia Li and Michael worked—where Jia Li's father *used* to work. Just like Jia Li, Michael was sure people were watching him, too, and like her, he blamed HKK Pharmaceutical, the biggest pharmaceutical company in the region—since he and Edward had been contracted to a project for them when Edward had suddenly died. He was sure HKK was doing something unethical. He was convinced his lab was bugged since Edward's death. He'd never told Jia Li what proof he had exactly.

But then, she'd never asked.

Her show was a mirror of that precise rebellion. It was the cross she bore, not from victimhood, but from self-containment. She knew something was deeply amiss, but she had no desire to dedicate her life to uncovering secrets and *proving* anything because it felt so much bigger than her, which was paralysing. Even if she could prove anything, her father was already gone, so what good could it do now?

Michael and Edward had been good friends. In his charming and awkward manner, Michael seemed even *more* protective of Jia Li since her father's death. Always telling her, *Be careful*. Not to ask questions or say anything in public about HKK or her father and especially not to publicly refer to the 'pharma thugs,' as she called them, 'because they might not be guilty of anything, and you definitely don't want to provoke anyone with the power to end your career.' Jia Li was rather touched by his concern, even though she didn't value her career much anyway, even if she felt she didn't need his help.

Until now.

Finally, beers in hand, sitting in a dark corner, Michael exclaimed, "I've never seen anything like it. The fibroblasts and keratinocytes aren't just proliferating, they're in a state of hyper-regeneration! The mitotic rate—it's off the charts. The new cells are perfectly formed, no signs of anaplasia. The extracellular matrix is being deposited at an incredible speed, and we're seeing new collagen bundles forming in real-time. This isn't just healing; it's perfect, instantaneous tissue regeneration." Michael ticked each metric off one by one, a finger at a time, mostly out of sight behind his beer, before fiddling nervously with his bottle, bouncing it back and forth between his hands. "It's insane. It's basically cancer, only the process is rapidly replacing damaged tissue with exceptionally healthy tissue. Even as the new tissue ages, it is being replaced, two weeks later! You saw it yourself, right?"

"The body's healing response is in overdrive," Jia Li said. "I mean, that's obvious."

Michael nodded and leaned forward, as if worried someone might overhear.

"*Over*-overdrive. There was a tissue-repair protein I couldn't identify. Well, which my colleagues couldn't identify. I got a second opinion. Anonymously, of course. But there's more. I'm sorry to say, there's more."

So dramatic, Jia Li thought.

He sat back and sighed into his pause. Maybe he was also gloating a bit. He'd been trying to rope Jia Li into his complex and interconnected *conspiracy* world for some time now.

MICHAEL WAS A SELF-PROCLAIMED 'THEORIST' and he'd been one long before Edward had died under dubious circumstances. Years ago he had set up a lab at home and was always investigating some hidden truth or another, making friends in his secret circles, even (apparently) gaining access to people who seemed to know narratives that were not officially accepted, people who had *proof* of secrets. High level whistleblowers.

Michael always had a story, always had articles to share and hypotheses to espouse. Jia Li had never believed nor disbelieved any of his theories. She didn't really care, or rather she only cared to the extent that it made him a more interesting friend. She didn't want to live in a world in which she had to admit to being a victim of elites, but she admired Michael's commitment and drive, the lengths to which he went to pursue something that mattered to him. Besides, Jia Li found most scientists a little boring, so she had always liked his eccentric take on the world.

Only thing was, these theories didn't make Michael any happier. In fact, he just seemed more and more stressed, especially over the past year as he had watched those men follow Jia Li. And especially since he had started digging closer to home. He was the first to admit to Jia Li that some things just didn't add up about Edward's research at their supposedly independent lab, or about HKK—about the science and its purported uses.

She had outright refused to hear those particular theories, and stopped him every time he began.

He'd regarded her with something like pity.

"I know it's hard to hear," he had told her.

She always changed the subject.

Lately he'd been pushing her a bit. "You don't want to know what is being worked on secretly, in nanotech, in gene therapy, not even as a scientist?"

"Nope."

Especially if it had anything to do with her father.

Now there was this healing thing and Sam's arm. Oh, how the tables had turned! It wasn't lost on Jia Li that she *needed* Michael now, and she squirmed as he readied himself to divulge whatever it was he was playing up by forcing delayed gratification on them both.

"Okay, don't rub it in, Michael," she said. She couldn't take his overexcited, smug vibe a second longer. "I know you've been wanting to tell me stuff for a while. Just tell me."

"You sure you're ready?" he asked.

"Yes, I am ready."

"You're sure? Once I open Pandora's Box…"

"Yes, Michael." She rolled her eyes. "I'm ready now. Please."

He lit up. "Brace yourself."

"I'm bracing, okay? Talk."

Jia Li found his enthusiasm sweet, if somewhat exasperating. Michael was one hundred percent heart and beneath that, cunning. It was easy to overlook him as just another well dressed young professional in his cuffed jeans and brown leather boots. This evening he was wearing a dress shirt with a nice sweater over it. Jia Li wondered how much time he spent getting ready to go out. Jia Li only ever gave clothing a cursory thought when she wasn't in a lab coat or half-naked in ropes. She lived in jeans and t-shirts.

She remembered her beer and began to drink as he began to talk, hoping to take the edge off the conversation, fast.

"I did find trace metals on Sam's clothing. A lot, actually. But I could only identify two, copper and tin, which is bronze. The other metal I found seemed to be an alloy of various metals. It's not my area at all and the test wasn't coming up with anything definitive. So I took it to an old schoolmate who is a chemist and biologist, but he's *also* particularly interested in inexplicable metals, ones that maybe are alien or whatever."

"Alien."

"Yes, but nevermind that. He's a good scientist, and I knew he'd look into it deeply once I told him there were strange things happening at a cellular level. He was able to analyze the faintest traces of the second substance. He determined that it is composed of palladium, silver, copper, with other traces—okay, all common. But it was the structure that was unusual. He says electrons don't follow the normal rules in this alloy, that it's like a superconductor. Look, I don't claim to completely understand what he found, but it makes sense of what I saw in the cells of the tissue sample. I mean, that there is something else going on. Something that doesn't behave according to normal laws of biology, or science in general... something unexplainable."

"Healing."

"Well, that is the *effect* of what is happening, but that's not all that is happening."

He drank. She'd nearly finished her beer.

"What do you mean?"

"I mean that as I don't have an entire body to analyze, I'm slightly restricted in my ability to assess the whole-body effects."

"Sorry, hard to bring you *all* of Sam without him noticing."

"Ha ha."

"I've been watching him. He seems fine so far. Grumpy, but healthy. I mean, you realize before Sam held onto whatever it is he held, he had a gash in his arm. It was a couple of centimeters deep, at least."

"I can guess at the mechanism of healing now from the sample," Michael admitted. "But a guess doesn't mean anything. I can't see his organs, his blood flow, measure his heart rate, anything. Whatever it is has had a real effect, yes. It's impossible to fake what you saw under the microscope. But I just can't say anything else *conclusively* about it. What I do know is that I've been researching things, things I don't fully understand. There's a lot that's *possible* in the world, and some of it's even happening, Jia Li."

"What does that mean?"

"Look. I have no proof. Nothing on paper. But what I do know is this—hang on, is it okay if I tell you now what else I've found out lately?"

"Yes, Michael, *please*. Now's the time. You know those thugs are following me and watching my show. I'm sure they're big pharma. HKK thugs."

"Yes, well. They probably are, since they'd definitely have the resources to follow you—but don't say it too loudly."

"So you keep telling me."

He rolled his eyes at her.

Jia Li knew he was convinced they were following him too, outside the lab, outside his apartment. He suspected that someone had even broken in while he was at work. Jia Li considered Michael a little on the paranoid side when it came to his home lab. He was fastidious about hiding his research. He had built hidden cupboards and had set up all sorts of clever devices to conceal things.

"Edward was working on the HIV project years ago, along with other labs. With another researcher I know who left his lab under some pretty weird circumstances, and anyway, I got in touch with him. We met, actually. I don't want to say his name and put him or you in danger. But he told me the we—all of us combined, with research funded by HKK—found a cure for HIV. I mean, not the medication they have now, that people have to be on for their entire lives. Something that was taken over three to six months and then never again. The participants in the trial who were given the experimental drug *fully recovered*. But the results were quashed. It was totally canceled, like it had never happened. Months later those same trial participants died unexpectedly. Suddenly. From various illnesses. So the results were never published. The drug was blamed. The researchers directly involved also disappeared, maybe paid off, maybe threatened. What was actually a *cure*, he made quotation marks with his hands, 'disappeared.' This researcher who worked with Edward, he said your father made inquiries. Asked questions. I don't know more. But I can guess."

Jia Li could only look down at her hands on the table. She frowned. "I believe he mentioned it once, when I was a kid, when that study was going on, he said to expect great things. He was really excited about it. So everything you say makes perfect sense."

"Do you think he really killed himself?" Michael asked. His tone was tentative. He looked down at the table. "Like maybe he felt he had no choice? To protect you, and your mother?"

Jia Li looked across the room. She felt the urge to shout at him, or cry, but she did neither.

"It never felt like something he'd do. Unless he were really forced to. Anyway—" She quickly changed the subject; tears stung her eyes. "So you think this, the HIV stuff, this is the proof they think I have, the reason they're following me? And for this they want to kill my mother? So they inject her with something? It doesn't add up. That all happened so long ago."

She put her face in her hands.

"No. It doesn't add up," he said, and sighed. "Maybe..."

"What, maybe? Is there something else going on?"

"You want to know more?" He leaned in.

"Fine, yes. More."

"I'm in the early stages of this particular *theory*..." He took his last sip of beer.

"And?" Jia Li actually felt queasy.

"HKK may be up to other things. Um. Significantly more dangerous." His voice shook, as if he were genuinely rattled.

"This doesn't sound good," Jia Li said.

"It's not. It's...." He didn't seem able to grasp the right word. He shook his head. "I can't say more as I don't have sufficient evidence, but it's possible Edward knew about more than just the HIV research."

"But there's no connection to this... this thing that we saw happening under the microscope, and the object that caused it."

"No." Michael's voice was firm. "No, unrelated. At least directly. I mean, it's not related at all as far as I know. But it's probably related to what they injected your mother with. I had a look at her blood. I didn't see anything I recognized, nothing unusual, low hemoglobin and low platelet count as you'd expect with cancer, but nothing inexplicable, even though, trust me, I know her case is inexplicable. Anyway it's not my expertise, so I sent it off to someone else. I haven't gotten it back yet."

Jia Li frowned. Just thinking of her mother's sickness as being *unidentifiable* felt too close to it being *incurable*.

"Anyway, this new thing I'm looking into, I'm calling it Virus X. It may be what HKK has been working on—that we, at the lab, were doing ancillary research for—and we didn't know it. The connection between what we were researching and what they were doing with it —it's been hidden from us. It may be that HKK is actually creating a virus, and... *testing* it. Maybe they're testing it on your mum. It's not good, Jia Li. I don't have any more information I can share yet. I'm sorry."

"Fuck." Jia Li took a deep breath. "Why would they do that? I mean, I can imagine, but..."

"Profit, for one thing, if they're also creating a cure. But beyond that, there could be governments involved. It could be a *much* bigger agenda."

"Fuck." She wiped the tears that had sprung from the corners of her eyes. *Of course.* With Michael there was always a bigger agenda. He clearly believed organizations were far more capable of complex coordination than she did. She believed the sheer enormity of bureaucracy precluded high level hidden agendas, at least the global kind that Michael endorsed.

Still, the possibilities felt unsettling on top of everything else.

"I... can't think about this now too much, Michael. I need to focus. I need to get my hands on whatever healed Sam, for my mother. I just don't know how. Sam's world isn't safe, and if the thing does what it seems to do... then other people would want it, badly, too. Maybe enough to kill for. I'm just, I'm not so sure my special skills are a match for that kind of violence."

He looked puzzled for a moment. *Ah yes*, Jia Li reminded herself, *he doesn't know about my little habit.* Her *former* little habit. Former-*ish*.

"My mother is much worse," she said, changing the subject. "She's had so many tests. All they found was highly advanced, stage four cancer. *Nothing unusual,* they said." Jia Li rolled her eyes as she said the words the doctor had told her.

In fact, it was *extremely* unusual. Mary had declined rapidly. Her color was gone; her glands had swollen; her eyes were bloodshot. She was *exhausted*, and mostly stayed in bed.

"I'm so sorry," Michael said.

"Anyway, I'm planning to ask Sam about the object. I'm just figuring out how. I haven't seen him for a few days."

Her mother had three months, the men had told Mary. Maybe four—if she was healthy, which she had been.

"I'll help you and Mary, somehow," Michael said. "I don't know how yet, but I will. I promise."

AFTER MEETING WITH MICHAEL, Jia Li went home and straight into her bedroom and locked the door behind her. Her childhood room.

Her teenage belongings had been cleared out years before, after she'd first left home, and now it was a spartan space, practical. Its emptiness, its blankness, was precisely what soothed Jia Li, for the same reason she liked Sam's bland and orderly apartment. There was nothing of her past, nothing that sparked a memory. With her blank white walls, her black and white checked bedspread, her near-empty white bookshelves, she just had space to let go of herself.

Sometimes, when she hid in her room after work, she nearly forgot about the thugs following her.

Occasionally she even forgot the grief,
for an hour or two, until it landed in her body,
a stone dropped on her heart.

But she couldn't forget her mother, sick in bed, god-knows-what multiplying and festering inside her.

She sat on her bed and let the consuming fear run through her. Fear for her mother. Fear about talking to Sam. There was no way around it though, and she certainly wasn't going to let it stop her now —so she let her fear be there, and
her hand trembling,
she rang Sam.

It was just a few days since she'd farewelled him in bed, and still two weeks since the attack, since Sam's healing. She didn't want to speak to him about the object. She didn't feel like speaking to him at all.

It rang twice. It was long enough for Jia Li's heart to start racing. She was having difficulty imagining that this could go well.

"Babe, everything okay?" he asked straight away. No *hello*. No *what's up*. He was impatient with her already.

"Listen, I'm going to be straight to the point."

"Okay."

Yet she took a second to gather her thoughts, her courage.

"I'm really busy here, babe," he said after a moment.

"You always say you're prepared to help me. Well I'm asking for help, now. My mother isn't going to get better by any normal means. You saw her. And I *need* her to get better. Whatever healed your arm, that turned your gaping cut into nothing—not even scar tissue—Sam, I need it for my mum."

There was nothingness then, a void between them.

"No." He breathed heavily. "You don't know what kind of trouble you're getting yourself into. You know nothing," he said, and repeated, "You know nothing, remember?"

There was the sound of commotion, men shouting, a door slamming shut.

"I gotta go. There's things happening here you can't understand. It's not safe to be involved. Drop this, babe."

Was that fear in his voice? She didn't give a shit just then.

"Sam, it's for my mother!"

"I know, I'm sorry. I can't help you. I've gotta go."

"Is it still in Hong Kong? With you guys?"

"It's overseas now, okay? So consider it gone. It's not my business, and it's *definitely* not yours."

He hung up.

She was so angry that she would have screamed at him for sure if he'd not hung up. All this time he'd wanted to intervene in her life, and now the one thing she'd asked for, he refused. She howled with gut wrenching sobs, not just because he'd betrayed her with his refusal, but because now she didn't have any kind of plan to help her mother.

JIA LI MADE her mother Lady Grey tea, her favourite, and brought it to her bed on a wooden tray.

"Are you in pain, Mum?"

"Hmmm. My back aches. But I don't feel so terrible."

"You're lying," Jia Li said, and kissed her forehead.

"Maybe," she replied. "Was your phone call okay?"

"How did you know I had a phone call?"

She shrugged. "Good guess. I heard you crying."

"It was fine," Jia Li lied. She'd made herself tea, too, and brought them both cookies, Marks and Spencer favorites. Chocolate chip. American style.

"Now *you're* lying," Mary said.

"Sorry."

"It's okay. You must have a reason. It's not my business. I was just thinking about how you stole the class hamsters because you didn't think they were being fed properly. How old were you? Nine, ten?"

"Something like that. I kidnapped them."

"You must have planned that well."

"I did. I had to wait until after the teacher locked the classroom, and steal her key from the office. It wasn't easy."

"You took them to a pet store, didn't you?"

"We didn't have a cage for them at home. Where else was I going to take them?"

"I was not angry with you. I wondered how you'd become so sneaky."

"You punished me though."

"I had to. I'm your mother."

Mary got a faraway look in her eye. This was her latest thing. She kept referring to random moments from Jia Li's childhood; she was at once nostalgic and whimsical, but often tearful, too. It frightened Jia Li because it seemed like despairing, end-of-life-type behavior.

"You're staring at me again, Mum."

"You're so beautiful. Do you think you'll marry a man or a woman?"

"I love that you ask me that," Jia Li said. She gave the bedside table a wipe with the bottom of her t-shirt, then lined up all the supplement bottles. She wanted everything to be tidy for her mum, it was the only answer she had just then.

"Are we in danger?"

"Why are you asking me that now?" Jia Li said. "I mean, obviously we are."

"We don't have proof of anything though," Mary said.

"No. We do not."

"But they don't know that."

"No, they do not."

Without missing a beat, Mary announced, "I regret that I didn't paint more when you were young. I could have a legacy now."

Jia Li froze, standing there with her hands on her mum's bedspread. She didn't even know what she was doing. What either of them were doing. It was a wonder they weren't panicking more than they were—and then this revelation.

"Mum." She felt her eyes begin to sting. Lately, all she seemed to be doing was crying or trying not to cry. "You do have time. I'll give you time. You can paint till you're 110."

"I'm sick."

"I'll make you better, you wait. I will *not* lose you." She swallowed this uncertainty, this lump in her throat. A tear spilled down her cheek.

"Because there was a man," Mary offered, and fell into a timid, distracted state.

"What are we talking about?" asked Jia Li, wiping her eyes dry. She tugged on the bedspread, smoothing a stray wrinkle. Then pulled the bedsheets and bedspread up higher onto Mary's lap, though this effort clearly wasn't welcome. Her mother pushed the covers away.

"We're talking about why I didn't paint." Her voice was flat.

"Oh, Mum, don't go making confessions now, that worries me. You're going to live, okay?"

"*Jelly.*"

Like her father called her.

"What?"

"I want to share something with you."

Jia Li nodded. "Okay."

She sat on the bed next to her mother, clasped her hands in her lap, and willed herself to focus—when all she could think was *How, exactly, am I going to save her?*

"There was a man, before I met your father, who wanted me to travel and paint, and told me I could be famous. He did not want children. But I wanted a family. So I ended it. Then I met your father."

Another man? Mary looked bereft at the admission.

"You were in love!"

"Yes, but I wanted to forget that. Love isn't everything. We do silly things when we are in love. But listen. There will always be love again. I know that now because I had Edward. And I know you don't really love Sam. It's okay. You'll love someone, one day. You did love someone before him, didn't you?"

Jia Li nodded again, imperceptibly, without meeting her mother's eyes. Her eyes watered again. *Ughh, just get yourself together*, she admonished herself. How dare her mother see so much, know so much, choose this moment, of all moments, to be a mother.

"Anyway, Mum." She faltered. "Well, you know what I'm going to say next."

"No." Mary stared at her hands. She gave a little smile. "You have a habit of surprising me."

"Paint now. Paint *now*! You have time. Do it for love. Do it because you want to. Don't worry about what it looks like. I won't tell."

"Fine."

"Fine?"

"Yes, you're right."

"I am?"

"So, can you bring me my notebook?"

"What notebook?"

"It's a sketchbook," she said. "In my closet. And the pencils."

Jia Li raised an eyebrow. "You had one in there all this time?"

"Of course. But I'm tired of not getting it down. It's worn me out, knowing it's there, and not reaching for it. Also, I'm not tall enough to reach it."

Jia Li went to her mother's closet as requested, and standing on her tip toes, retrieved an A4 size notebook along with a metal box of black and gray watercolor pencils that sat on top of the notebook. The pencil box was sealed shut, as if it had never even been opened.

"Thank you."

"Mum, I really am going to find a way to help you," she told her.

"Okay, but help yourself too, my love."

. . .

But Jia Li couldn't help herself. She was on a downward spiral. At work she was a well-trained zombie without an appetite, especially for conversation, much less for work, even less for food. Michael said nothing when they saw each other there. She had to meet him secretly for anything real.

She told him over dinner what Sam had told her about the object, the healing object, that it was *gone*. Already overseas. How could she possibly find it now? Michael assured her that he would track it down.

So far, he'd found nothing.

For three weeks she'd been watching her mother struggle. Giving her pain relief and supplements and raw juices and heat packs.

It had been three weeks since she'd seen Sam's arm miraculously recover.

And then it was four weeks, and nothing had changed except she'd seen Sam once—only once since she'd spoken to him by phone and he'd refused to help her.

He'd come to her apartment to tell her he would have to travel for work soon, that he'd be in touch. He'd stood shuffling his feet at the door and asked how Mary was. *Horrible*, she told him—*horrible*. He looked down at his feet and mumbled, "I'm sorry." He leaned down to kiss her goodbye. He missed her mouth; his lips landed on her chin. That was it.

Was he breaking up with her?

She searched herself and found nothing. No reaction. Her ambivalence had peaked. Maybe it was just the nature of her connection with Sam, of his recent disengagement after the strange healing. Or maybe it was that her mother needed her more than *she* needed anyone else. For whatever reason, when she shut the door after him, it felt done.

A few more days passed.

Then Nadya rang her in the middle of the night.

. . .

IN RETROSPECT, hadn't she always been expecting this phone call? She knew—*she knew*—that Sam's world was what it was. But still.

When her phone rang and Jia Li saw that it was two a.m., she thought nothing.

Felt nothing.

She saw Nadya's name. Her heart only pounded from the shock of the ring tone rousing her from deep sleep.

Jia Li knew it couldn't be good to get a call from her at this hour, but it was a *knowing* devoid of both emotion and coherent thought. She pressed the green button and held the phone to her ear without saying hello.

"Jia Li? Are you there?"

"Yes."

A pause. Jia Li pulled the blanket up around her chin.

"There's no easy way to say this," Nadya said. She paused again. "Sam's dead."

"*What?*"

Jia Li didn't really grasp Nadya's words. Confusion shook her awake. *Dead.* What does that mean? *Dead?*

"I'm sorry. I wanted to tell you personally. I know that wouldn't make it any better."

Was there a mistake? What did she mean, dead? There were a few moments, seconds piling into minutes, and then a voice.

"Sweetie? Are you there?"

But her ears were ringing, and then, again,

"Jia Li? Are you there?"

"Um, yeah. Hang on…"

and the shock of it slammed into Jia Li, as if she'd been thrown against a wall and had slid down, without realizing it, until she found herself in a fetal position feeling—

What was she feeling?

Shock.

And beneath that?

Where was the sadness, the grief? Maybe it was too soon.

She finally found the words, "What? How?"

"They were shooting. He was just in the middle of everything. It wasn't personal. It was fast, honey."

"Oh, God." Jia Li searched for words. "I've hardly seen him lately. I don't even know what was going on."

"Probably it's better that way. There's a turf war going on now, you haven't heard? Over some powerful... drug or something. I don't know. Anyway, Sam was a good man, you know that. And it's over, so the Sam you knew is at peace now, that's all you need to know. It's over. There's no point thinking about it. Trust me. Just know he's at peace now. I'm so sorry."

Oh my God, *Sam*.

Suddenly, she felt it, shock and terror and a numbing sensation - but not *loss*.

Not like when her father died, which felt like someone had wrenched her heart right out of her chest and she was left gasping for breath.

Not like when her last relationship ended, when she thought she'd never be able to breathe again.

No, now the world faded into mist like when she'd met with Michael earlier and learned all the secrets;

like when she'd found her mother, impotent, accepting what was, just as it was.

She worried that maybe she was broken, maybe she couldn't feel properly anymore.

"But why? He was loyal. I didn't think he was doing anything... controversial?"

Jia Li pulled herself into sitting.

The object.

"No, no I don't think he was either, sweetie. I just think he got caught in the crossfire. It happens. You need to grieve and move on. I'm so sorry. I don't have any advice for you. You just have to keep going."

Nadya's voice faltered on the last bit.

It happens, yes, like to Nadya's husband.

"Okay," Jia Li whispered. "Okay."

"I wanted you to have a friendly voice telling you personally, before you see it in the news or anything. You should forget, you know, that you knew him, that you were involved in any way. Just.... Please. You need to keep a distance. It's not a good life, and you're smart. You have a job. Please. Don't hang around me, or any of us. Just go live your life."

Jia Li nodded, numb, and dropped her phone into her lap without pressing 'end.' Nadya's voice called out, "Jia Li? Are you still there?"

Not really.

She sat in her bed for the next fifteen minutes, knees to her chest, rocking back and forth. Strange that her heart could feel so empty, so without feeling, and yet also be so heavy in her chest.

What now?

She finally roused herself. She *had* to find that object.

Meet me halfway, she bargained with the Universe. She was open to any divine source that existed. *Please, at least help me save my mother. She's innocent in all of this.*

NEAR THE END of the fourth week, she and Michael met at a Korean BBQ. She arrived before him and had finished a beer by the time he stood in the doorway, scanning the room for her. Tipsy, she whispered to him as soon as he sat down, "Sam was killed. Um, I guess a few nights ago."

His eyes downcast, he mumbled, "Jia Li, I'm... so sorry. I saw in the news that there were a few men killed. Some kind of turf war between the Triads and the Russians. I didn't see Sam's name, but... I was hoping it wasn't him. I—I thought it might be."

"Yeah, I don't read the news. I didn't realize it was in there."

He said nothing, as if waiting for her cues. So patient and polite. And loyal.

She burst into tears. Her voice dropped to a whisper. "I think I'm broken. I mean, is it terrible to say that I'm okay? He was my boyfriend, but I don't think I needed him. I hadn't even seen him much the last few weeks."

"No, no it's okay. You weren't in love anymore."

"Can I tell you the truth? I don't think I was ever in love with him."

"That happens all the time, Jia. It's okay."

He wasn't even shocked? *Who am I fooling*, she thought. *Of course he wasn't surprised she hadn't been in love with Sam.* It had probably been obvious. She blinked at Michael through her tears. He cleared his throat and put a hand on her hand. "It's okay," he told her again.

Had Michael even ever *had* a partner? Did he like men or women? Jia Li actually didn't know much about his personal life. But she trusted him and right now, she needed his reassurance.

She got herself together. She dried her face with a napkin and pushed her hair behind her ears. The waiter came around and invited them to go choose dishes at the buffet.

"In a moment, thank you," Jia Li said. "Okay," she said to Michael. "I'm ready. Tell me whatever you know."

"I might have some information that could shine some light on… on the situation." He seemed to wait for her response, as if unsure of her emotional state.

"Yes, go ahead."

"Okay. First, your mother's blood. Nothing obvious so far, but the guy I sent it to is still looking for specific markers. Whatever it is, it's very subtle, despite the obviousness of the effect."

"Okay. What else?"

"I've done a search on the Dark Web, and there are others with similar reports to yours, about an object that heals the body. There's even a Miracle Log, a collection of medical miracles confirmed by doctors—and I think you need to look at this last one. From the United States. It mentions a cross. An antique cross that heals. It says a child was healed from cancer with it, at a hospital in Atlanta."

"A cross? No fucking way!" Jia Li felt energy shift in her core and her heart began to pound as enthusiasm dislodged shock and grief. She brightened and tensed at the same time. There was *hope*.

"Yeah, and the timing is about right. It's dated just a few days ago, so it's possible this object is the same one, just now in America. In

Atlanta. Read for yourself. I printed it for you." He slid a piece of paper across the table.

She read fast. *Child. Leukemia. Cured. Nurse says the child mentioned a cross that she held, that healed her.* Her mind raced.

"I've also found evidence that the war they're talking about in the media, between the Triads and the Russians. Well I didn't want to say it before, but it seems to be about controlling this object, this... cross."

Of course. Jia Li thought. *It was probably the reason Sam got 'caught in the crossfire.' It wasn't a drug like Nadya said. It was that object.*

She tucked the printout into her pocket and disappeared into the womens' toilet. Her hands shook as she splashed cold water on her face, then dried it with a paper towel before she stomped back to the table, still shaking with nervous energy. *God would I kill for ropes right now,* she thought. She wanted to be wrapped so tightly, suspended so high, to keep herself from exploding.

But maybe this was necessary, this energy, this fire.

She sat, and her eyes met Michael's.

"I know what I need to do," she said.

"You're going to Atlanta, aren't you?" he asked.

"This is my opportunity, Michael. The Universe met me halfway."

"Okay. I didn't know you spoke with the Universe."

"Me either."

Michael said, "I don't want to add complexity or danger to your efforts... but I have a wide network and I've seen enough reports and have one particular contact who finally got back to me and..."

"Just say it."

"Okay. So, someone definitely is working on this Virus X, the virus I mentioned before, but I don't know if it's a lab, or HKK Pharma, or what the relationship is. But now I can confirm that whoever it is seems to be simultaneously working on the cure."

"So whoever-they-are can manage the cure, and play God."

"Yes. Everything's about profit. So if this cross actually can cure people, then, you know, they would not be happy about having it out there. Whoever *they* are. I don't know that yet. But if they knew about it—and I don't think they do know, not yet anyway—but if they knew, and they knew you had it, well..."

"It's just *one* object, Michael. It isn't a pharmaceutical solution. No one can *administer* it to everyone."

"Yes, but anything can be replicated, with time and research. I'm just saying if they wanted to create a virus and profit from a cure themselves, they'd do whatever it takes to get the cross right out of the picture, or else use it as a template for themselves to control the cure."

"This is all so dark."

"Yeah, well."

"So dark, Michael."

He shrugged, apologetic. "I'm sorry you have to be involved in it. Anyway, I hope you find it, and I hope it works, and you know, that you find somewhere to hide it or something. Send me names, after you find the nurse who made the report, when you find out who ended up with the object. I can do some digging. Make sure you are dealing with safe people. Please be careful. You're one of my only good friends. I don't trust many people."

Oh, Michael, she thought, tenderness softening her edges.

"Okay, maybe you should work on that, the only good friend thing. It's not healthy," she told him.

"I'll try."

"On second thought, nevermind. It's too dangerous to trust anyone these days. By the way, I'm performing tonight. Come to my show."

"Maybe. Maybe I will."

"You won't, but that's okay."

"It's just awkward, seeing you so naked."

"It's okay. I get it."

THE ROPES WERE ONLY EVER REALLY ABOUT her anyway, so it was easier, actually, without personal acquaintances watching. It was too intimate, the energy she rode, how she communicated it. Easier not to have to explain it—or justify it.

The ropes cured her of carrying too much on her own, whether grief or anger, stress or sadness. There was such relief to be led by movement, to feel moved rather than moving. Such sweet bliss to be hugged tightly, weightless.

The ropes squeezed her free.

As she hung upside down that night, her tempest nicely contained, she looked into the audience and made eye contact, once again, with the two men who were always there. This time, she drew upon all that she had—all she'd not said, all she'd felt since her mother was attacked and Sam was killed.

Not determination, not fear.

It was *rage* she sent through her eyes into theirs, willing it to be like poison inking across the blood brain barrier to cause instant death. As she pulled herself back upright and the blood rushed to her head, she thought for a moment that she was hallucinating Nadya, sitting at a table in the corner. Jia Li stumbled with dizziness as she came back to standing, and the audience cheered, then

Nadya clapped.

Yes, it was indeed Nadya at the table, and she was waiting for Jia Li after her show, in the hallway behind the stage area near the changeroom, well away from the customers and noise of the venue.

The women looked at one another, expressionless, but Jia Li knew that each understood why the other was there, and what each intended. And it wasn't for hugs and sympathy. Nadya leaned into a hip, tottering in her heels, glittering with jewelry and reeking of strong perfume.

"So, you're obviously not here for my show," Jia Li deadpanned.

"It was impressive," Nadya said.

"And?" Jia Li didn't open the door to her changeroom. She stood in front of it, arms crossed.

"Are you planning on leaving town?" Nadya asked her directly.

"Are you spying on me?"

"Listen," Nadya pushed in close, lowering her voice to a hush. "I know what Sam touched—the object. I know about it. I know everyone wants it. I know your mum is sick, and I get how hard this must all be for you. Maybe you're looking for it, too. But please." She was barely audible now. "Please don't get involved, Jia Li. It's dangerous. I'm a friend, but there will be no friends anywhere else, do you understand? No friends to warn you. You just need to forget about it. You don't understand, it's *everyone* who wants it. The Chinese. The Russians. That's why it's dangerous. There is a turf war and you don't want to be in it. You know what happened to Sam."

Jia Li peered behind Nadya—no one was around, fortunately. Still on edge lest those thugs were nearby, she opened her changeroom door and pulled Nadya inside by her arm, then closed the door behind them.

Jia Li kept her voice low too, even though they had some privacy now. "So there was never a big powerful *drug* they were fighting over, was there? Did they kill Sam because of that thing? Because he was trying to get it back, or keep it?"

And was he doing it for me? she wondered with a slight pinch of guilt—but only a pinch. It didn't matter. It wasn't ever about her anyway.

Jia Li knew that Nadya wouldn't have the answer.

"I don't know why he was killed, okay? I really think he was in the wrong place at the wrong time. Anyone involved in that thing is at risk. Others have died, too. All I know is that the Chinese had it, and the Russians wanted it, and then it went overseas, and now those involved with it are all dead and it's *gone*. And that's why I'm here to warn you."

Yes, Jia Li thought, *and now it's impossibly far away, and how the fuck will I get it?*

She fought tears, and spoke more harshly than intended. "Well, for the record, everyone I love is gone except for my mother, and she's dying. So what does it matter what I do now? Or where I go?"

"I'm sorry, Jia Li. I know it's so unfair." Nadya's face, for a moment, revealed her own pain.

"Yes, it's unfair," Jia Li said, softening only slightly. "So you tell me how I can let this go? If you're a friend, you'll understand and you won't say anything to anyone. If you're an enemy, then just go, leave me alone, do your thing. I'm still going."

"Okay, Jia Li. For the record, no one sent me. Sam told me about your mum. He told me you are desperate to make her well. I know you know about the cross. Sam said you wanted it. And you have no more shows coming up, so I thought probably you're going to try to find it... because if I were you, with my mum sick, I'd want it, too. I see, you're really smart. You think you can just ask around quietly and go hunt it down, but please. Be careful. You probably won't ever find it and even if you do, they'll find you first."

Even she knows it's a cross. She knew all along what the 'war' was about and she lied to me.

But she was here. She was here to stop her, to save her, and that didn't come from a bad place, did it?

"Does anyone else know I know about it?"

"No. I swear. I'm here because I don't want to see you hurt. That's the truth." Nadya deflated.

Jia Li felt heat rising in her chest.

"I've already been found. That's what you don't know. I was found some time ago now, and it has nothing to do with you, or Sam, or all this crime bullshit. It has to do with my father, okay? I'm pretty sure he was killed, and there are so many threats now that my life is already fucked. Please say nothing, Nadya, to anyone. Please pretend I know nothing about this... *cross*... and just let me disappear. You don't know what might be at stake here."

Nadya rolled her eyes. "Look, I can't really stop you anyway. So just be careful." Her lower lip trembled. "They're all fuckers, aren't they?"

15

FINLEY, KATE, JIA LI & THE GUTOVNIKS

JUNE 2019

ATLANTA, GEORGIA

Finley arrived at Kate's apartment with a notebook and pen and his copy of *Ikona*. He had prepared carefully—he'd scribbled at least ten pages of notes as he'd scoured the novel for clues. Kate seemed bemused when she saw him sit down at the table and open his notebook.

"Hold on, I just need to ask you one thing," Kate said as she stood with her back to him, preparing them both tea.

Finley put down his pen. "Yes?"

In truth, he'd hoped to avoid both small talk and any more emotional conversation—to stick to logical inquiry, his comfort zone. He felt tension now in his temples.

After what felt like ages, Kate placed two steaming mugs on the table and sat. "I've been wondering what brings on your visions. How do you do it?"

His mind strained with resistance. *Not this, not now.*

"I don't exactly 'do' it. It just happens."

"It's not like a vision, in the traditional sense, is it?" She prodded him.

"Well, erm. It's not a vision, *per se*. It feels more like teleportation, actually. I'm inside his life throughout the experience, or he is in mine. Or both."

The heaviness in his head resolved into a dull ache—*so just thinking about it might trigger another episode*, he reflected.

"I think this could be relevant to what's happening here," she began, taking a breath to continue—but suddenly there was a sharp knock on the door. The same pattern as before. Da da-da. Twice.

"Ughhh. Sorry." Kate rolled her eyes and went to open it. "Good morning, Victoria," she said as she pulled the door towards her, stiffening suddenly, though Finley couldn't see why. He tensed.

"Kate Davies?" He heard a woman's voice, soft but confident.

"And you are?"

The woman leaned forward, only just into Finley's line of sight and lowered her voice. "I've come to talk to you about a cross." He could see now that she was petite, and Asian.

Kate stayed frozen, and there were five seconds or so of pure stalemate during which Finley, too, could barely breathe. He felt he *should* be worried, but this woman appeared harmless—she looked mostly at the floor, for one thing. She held a big black duffle bag that hung to her feet. *Okay, the bag is a little suspicious*, he thought.

"How did you know that knock?" Kate asked.

"I watched," the woman said. "I saw your neighbor at your door yesterday. Please, I just want to talk. *Please*."

The woman wasn't threatening as far as Finley could tell, so he sipped his tea, drumming his fingers on his now quite irrelevant notebook—he was rattled yet curious, an unsteady reconciliation of opposites, as if pulled toward two distinct outcomes, neither of which he could predict.

There was no map where they were headed, he reflected, not any more.

∽

KATE TOOK IN THE VISITOR. Shoulder-length thin, dark brown hair. Jeans, a tight singlet. Nothing unusual about her, aside from the fact that she was there, and asking about the cross. She seemed free of any pretense, her face open, her eyes almost pleading. There was something familiar about her—or maybe it was the urgency that she conveyed.

After all, that was the wavelength she and Finley had been on since they met. First Finley, now this woman, within a few days of each other. Kate felt a sense of momentum, as if time had sped up, and was now in somewhat short supply.

Kate gestured her in, and shut the door behind her—yet they both remained glued to the spot, just barely inside the apartment. *This small, utterly ordinary woman hardly feels threatening,* Kate thought. Although she *did* seem disconcertingly intense and, on top of that, rather nervous, judging by her fidgety inspection of Kate, Finley, and the apartment. But she made no sudden moves, and Kate felt somehow at ease, despite the caution her logical mind insisted upon.

"My name is Jia Li." Her eyes squinted towards Finley. "Who are you?" She squeezed the strap of her bag, her knuckles white with tension.

"He's my friend," Kate snapped. "More importantly, who are you?'

"As long as he's a friend, and not a thug, or the cops." Jia Li stared Finley down.

"You know about the icon too?" Finley asked, then, "And no, I'm none of those things."

Kate glared at him, but he didn't notice, his eyes still focused on their visitor. *Why was he so willing to show his hand? Uggh,* she thought. Now she was pissed off. At the same time, *here they were. There was a cross. This woman knew. It was a thing.* Resigned to this strange new reality, Kate stared at her, close up, wondering what to do next. This woman—Jia Li—knew something they didn't, obviously.

"Icon? I'm not sure what that is. I'm here about a cross." Her eyes narrowed towards Finley. "I know how Kate fits into all this, but not you."

Kate felt suddenly exposed, so she deflected: "An icon is religious artwork. Usually it's a painting. In other cases," here she glared at

Finley again, "it could be an object that's been painted. Anyway, Finley's fine. You're the stranger here."

Finley sat up straighter and leaned forward, as if attempting to look safe. "Exactly," he said. "How do we know *you're* not a thug, or... something?"

Jia Li snorted. "I'm a *scientist*. I work in a lab, I found out about the cross, and I need it. I didn't know it was an icon. Anyway, my mother needs it. She was... she's really sick. She won't survive without it."

Jia Li remained standing beside the door, knuckles still white, still gripping her duffel bag like it was a lifeline.

None of this made sense to Kate. *She came across it in a lab? How? And why did she catch herself when she mentioned her mother?* Kate sensed this woman's ache, in her posture, in how she'd rushed her explanation, and softened, but only slightly.

"Okay. So keep talking, and we'll listen. And then we'll decide if we trust you. Around here, trust is based on gut feelings. There is literally no other way to judge anything in this crazy situation. Finley? Agreed?"

Kate noticed Finley had relaxed somewhat, settling down to work on his tea as it cooled, and she, too, felt the growing calm of surrender.

"Yes, okay," he said. "But I don't claim to be a very good judge of character, and I've only just laid eyes on her."

Kate rolled her eyes.

"Anyway, you might as well sit down." She pointed to the chair near Finley. "Tell us more about how you found a cross in a lab."

"No, those are separate facts," Jia Li shook her head as she moved tentatively toward the chair, slumping into it. She dropped the bag near her feet. She was clearly exhausted. "I work in a lab in Hong Kong, and I found out about the cross. Completely unrelated. But my mum got really sick, so I—I tracked you down, Kate," Jia Li stuttered. "I *had* to."

Finley raised his eyebrows. "We all *had* to."

Kate silenced him with her eyes. There was something more

under the words Jia Li was saying. Her eyes had suddenly filled with tears. More than worry, there was *loss* there.

Jia Li carried on, blinking away the tears. "Look, I know you have it. You healed a little girl with it. I need it for the same thing. My mum has advanced cancer too." She stiffened slightly then. "And there's something else you need to know. If I can track you down, it means other people can too. If bad people get it—and trust me, some really bad ones are looking—it would be very dangerous to be here when they find out it was here."

Kate hardly blinked; she'd said *healed the girl*. She took a sharp breath. "Okay, then you better talk fast." Kate saw Finley's face go blank in the manner of one accustomed to unsettling news; he was, she was beginning to think, easily rattled, but good at masking his reactions.

Jia Li shifted her weight to the front edge of her chair, one foot forward as if ready to leap up at any moment.

"My boyfriend had the cross. He was... he worked with Chinese crime syndicates, or *for* them. The Triads. I'm not sure exactly what he did to be honest. They had a cross they carried around in a padded bag or something. I don't know what the bag was filled with, but I'm certain the effect doesn't work when it's inside the padding, only when it's put against bare skin. Anyway, somehow the Russian mafia got it. The Chinese want it back. There's an underground war starting over it." She hesitated. "And that's only the two groups I know for sure are after it. It's likely there could be more."

Kate twigged at the mention of the padded envelope. Of course. That's why her client had died from the poisoning, and the girl had been cured.

"Please," Kate said, "tell me you're not leading more mafia types to me. I've got enough to worry about."

Jia Li's leg started to bounce under the table. "Trust me, they probably know about you already. There was a listing in an online registry about your daughter's spontaneous recovery from leukaemia. Others would have seen that too."

At the mention of Little Bird as *her daughter,* a pulse shuddered through the fracture that her heart held together with silence. Kate was terrified of destabilising this grief with words, but they poured out nonetheless. "Not my daughter. My neighbor's niece." She clasped one arm around her body. "I've searched my name online a dozen times in the past week. Nothing came up except my website and usual posts. Where was this list?"

"Dark Web," Jia Li said. "A database of medical miracles, and in that recent entry it mentioned the girl's recovery and a cross that heals. Specifically, an antique Russian crucifix. I had an experience with this cross myself, because it healed my boyfriend's arm, before he was—" she took a breath, "*killed.*"

Killed. The word hung in the air. Kate thought of Roman Ivanov, poisoned.

"They say he was killed in a shooting, that it was gang fighting, that it was an accident. But I don't know." Jia Li's voice cracked. "I just know people are being killed for the cross. Anyway, now my mother's sick, so I need to find it, before someone else does."

Finley, gawking, couldn't seem to stop himself from remarking, "Everything is online now, isn't it? I mean absolutely everything. It's just crazy. Is there no such thing as privacy?"

Kate snapped at Finley. "Finley, oh my God. How old *are* you?" To Jia Li, "I used a fake ID and a travel debit card at the hospital. So how in the world did you find me? Was I in the registry?"

Jia Li smiled. It was a cunning smile. "No. But a very religious pediatric nurse posted about a miracle healing on social media. The timing and location tracked with what I found on the Dark Web. Wasn't hard to find her at the hospital. Then I just had to tell her I was making a documentary on medical miracles to prove the existence of God."

"Joleen!" Kate blurted out, remembering how in desperation she'd given the nurse her real number on that scrap of paper.

Jia Li stood and clutched at her duffel bag straps. "So you get it. If I could find you…"

Kate went pale. "Right. If the Russian mafia knows about the cross being here …" She began mentally to tally what she needed to pack.

"Yes, we need to go." Finley's voice shook a little as he gathered his book and notebook and stood.

"Do you have it?" Jia Li moved toward the door.

"Not on me, no." Kate paused at the look on Jia Li's face.

"We *have* to take it with us. I have to get it somewhere safe. It's not just about my mother." Jia Li's voice dropped. "There's something else I haven't told you—about my lab."

There was a collective pause as Finley, Kate, and Jia Li looked at one another.

The weight of fate, Kate thought. She felt that same sentiment reflected in the others' eyes. *They were on the same side, and Truth was the safest path forward.*

Jia Li reached into her duffel bag. After a moment of searching, she pulled out a bit of newspaper and handed it to Kate.

Dr. Macpherson, top independent medical researcher found dead. Questions about top secret research project.

"That article was also posted online and deleted a week later. You can't find it anymore, anywhere. The lab my father and I both worked for was contracted to HKK Pharma for independent research. My friend and I found information that... this is going to sound out there, but we think they're creating a virus, on purpose, and we don't know for sure, but maybe they're doing it so they can also create and then sell the cure." The last sentence tumbled out in a rush, and Kate could see that Jia Li expected them to not believe a word of it.

"My father had started asking questions, and the...." Jia Li's eyes filled again with tears. "The final police report says my father committed suicide. A year ago." Jia Li wiped fiercely at the corners of her eyes. "But he wouldn't do that. Not unless he was forced."

The silence that followed sent a chill through Kate.

"You think he was killed for whatever he knew?" Kate asked.

Jia Li frowned. "I know that whatever trouble he was in, if there were threats to his family, he wouldn't have risked our safety. So either he was coerced or they... or they killed him. If he had proof of the virus, he never shared it with me. But someone is clearly afraid that I have it. I've had thugs following me for the past year."

Finley shook his head slowly, whether in shock, or disbelief, Kate couldn't be sure. But something had changed in his demeanour, and in hers, too.

Kate recognized the hollowness in Jia Li's voice when she spoke of her father,

and felt the space between them fold and soften.

"I'm sorry about your father," she said, her voice nearly a whisper.

"Thanks," Jia Li nodded, wiping her eyes clear of the few tears that lingered. "I don't have any proof that HKK knows about the cross yet. But they will, so we can't leave it here if there's any chance they'll find it. Because I don't trust them. They won't use it for good. They'll make it disappear. And my Mum needs it." Her eyes searched Kate's,

and Kate felt warmth settle softly in her heart, even as it tremored at the daunting reality—

They needed to leave *now*, in case God knows who was on their way in search of the cross—yet the trio froze for a moment, the atmosphere heavy with secrets and dangers. Finley said nothing and stared, stoic, into the middle distance. Jia Li withdrew.

All of a sudden, there was a terrific commotion at the door. It flew open as a group of young men with guns stumbled into Kate's living room.

Four men wearing matching black jeans, white t-shirts, and grey vests stood just inside the doorway with their weapons pointed at the floor. The tallest one—wearing a beanie despite the summer heat—spoke. "We're friendly, don't worry. But we require your help." A statement to which, after a second, he affixed a curt and tentative, "Please?"

Now Kate could hear his Russian accent. *Oh no*, she thought. This is all *too* familiar.

"Who *are* you people?" asked Jia Li. Her incredulous glance encompassed the lot of them, including Kate and Finley.

Finley simply closed his eyes.

"Put down your guns. We'll talk," Kate told them.

The guy with the beanie nodded to the others—he was clearly in charge. Kate relaxed slightly as they lowered their weapons.

"Those aren't real guns, are they?" Kate observed.

Beanie-guy looked sheepish, but quickly pulled a serious, half-disgruntled face. No one responded.

"Seriously?" Finley gasped and spoke as if gravely offended. "They *aren't* real guns. They're *toys* or something. I mean," he pointed, "that one there is maybe even a water gun. What are you? Teenagers?"

"Is this for real?" Kate asked. "Have you burst into my apartment with toy guns from Walmart?"

"We..." Beanie-guy's voice squeaked and he shuffled his feet. "We are here on the behalf of freedom for all! We have no wish to harm anyone!" To Finley. "No we are not *teenagers*, we're *twenties*."

Oh for God's sake, Kate thought, rolling her eyes at his forced bravado, which got him to the end of his pronouncement, but only just. He deflated instantly.

"We have been following you. We want the icon, but not to sell it. We want to use it to lead us to the great author Konstantin Isakevich Gutov, who disappeared more than two decades ago." He pointed, seeing the familiar book on the table near Finley.

Everyone seemed to be holding their breath. The visitors' guns—most definitely toys, judging by the mens' communal drop in confidence—still hung at their sides. Finley and Jia Li cast glances at one another as Kate, strangely calm, muttered a quiet, "Oh, God. Please not now."

"Also, we have questions," Beanie-guy added. "We know who you are, Katya Dmitrieva. We won't hurt you. I am very, very sorry, but you must come to our headquarters."

He nodded at the other three men, who raised their guns again.

Kate snapped, "Put down your toys. You want someone to call the cops?"

"Katya?" Finley said.

"Okay, okay." Beanie-guy gestured. The toys were lowered, tucked more out of sight. "Please come with us, Katya. We can help each other. It's because of your mission. Only *we* can give you the help you need."

"Right," Kate said, sighing. "You're *Gutovniks*, I get it. So what is it? Am I helping you or you're helping me? Oh I forgot—we're a team." She squeezed her eyes shut, her mouth a thin line.

Both Finley and Jia Li looked searchingly at Kate.

"You're Russian?" Finley asked.

"Gutov-whats?" Jia Li asked.

"I'm American," Kate said. "My mother is Russian. I was raised in Ohio."

"*Gutov*-niks," Finley sputtered. "As in, they follow Gutov? The cult you mentioned! Is this for real?"

"Oh for fuck's sake," Jia Li said. "We're wasting time, we *need to go*."

Kate turned to Finley and Jia Li, "It's okay, guys, I can handle this. I'll explain later." To the Gutovniks, "Look, you guys, why are you doing this? Why do you think I have the icon?"

"We know from Russian crime world that it is missing," a short, baby-faced boy-man spoke for the first time.

"And just who do you know in the Russian crime world exactly?" Kate demanded.

"My cousin." Baby-faced boy-man nodded gravely. "He says they are frantic for it, and if it's out there in the world, it means it will end up with you, because *you* are the hero who must use it to lead us. It always finds the hero. So you must have it. And so we must work together, that's always been the mission!"

"Your Russian soul, Katya," Beanie-guy said, and rambled off to her in Russian, and then another one joined in, a man with day-old stubble and curly black hair. Kate nodded, rolled her eyes, and spoke back in Russian, telling them, "Quiet, quiet, no need to be emotional. It's all going to be okay."

∼

JIA LI, still recovering from all that she'd shared earlier, had been making herself as small as possible in order to observe what was taking place. She was hardly comfortable discussing conspiracies and magical events with Michael, much less here with strangers. She was far more at ease standing on stage in sexy undergarments, with a placard, anger cautiously communicated through bitter silence.

But, as she'd spoken to Kate and Finley, as her courage rose, so too did her determination. Her *adrenalin*. Now, as she took in this woman's apparently *Russian* alter ego, she reminded herself of her mission, her intention, and what was at stake. Just how could she get out of this weird situation? What did these young men know, and were they a hindrance or, as she suspected, merely an annoyance?

"They were praising my mother for her... contribution to their cause," Kate translated for Finley and Jia Li.

"English, guys, speak English," she told the Gutovniks.

"You are the one who can lead us, Katya!" said a man with a large nose, like a beak. He stepped forward and implored her in Russian, rambling on. He clasped his hands together in prayer.

"No," she replied in English. "I am NOT Yuk-Or Ba! You guys have got it all wrong. It's not my path. You don't know what you're talking about."

"Yuk-Or-*Who*?" Jia Li asked, shaken from her thoughts by those strange syllables.

"Yuk-Or Ba, the hero of Gutov's books," Finley explained.

"Ah," Jia Li said, not getting it at all. "Of course."

Beanie-guy, now quite obviously their leader, spoke, "Oh, but you are, dear Katya. He is modeled on you, and now you even have *ikona*, therefore you MUST know how to lead us to Shambhala."

"Don't worry. We hurt no one," the short, beaky man said to Finley in a thick Slavic accent. "Is okay!"

"Kostya, of course we hurt no one, why are you even saying that? You are going to freak them out!" The one with the stubble and curly black hair reprimanded him.

Ah, so Kostya was the name of the beaky one, Jia Li thought.

Kate spoke. "Yuk-Or Ba is a fictional character in novels by Gutov, and these guys think that I am the 'real' Yuk-Or Ba, and that like the character, my destiny is to follow the cross to lead humanity to Shambhala. As you can see, it's quite crazy. Welcome to my childhood."

"You've got to be fucking kidding me," Jia Li said.

"Why are you here, really?" Kate spoke directly to the young men. "Just to tell me that you think I'm a fictional character in a novel and therefore it's my job to lead you to Shambhala, is that it?"

"Um, Yes," Beanie-guy said, shuffling his feet. "It's very important." But his voice tapered off.

"How do you know for certain that Shambhala even exists?" Kate challenged him.

"Because!" He spat. "Gutov disappeared—he left a note at the end of his novel saying he was going, and then no one ever heard from him again. And the cross, it exists, *here*, in Atlanta, we *know* this, so you *must* have it, just as Yuk-Or Ba had it. So if it exists in our world—and since Gutov said he was going to Shambhala—and you have it, then all the predictions are *correct*. And *that* means it is also true that YOU, Katya, like Yuk-Or Ba, will be the one to lead us there. See?"

He'd ranted at such a rapid speed that now he wiped spittle from his lips.

"That is a lot of logical connections that don't all add up!" Kate replied. "None of that made any sense!"

"Is true. I have *proof*. We have analyzed the novels and many facts and *you*, Katya."

Beanie-guy rambled on in Russian now, and a tear even came into his eye. Kate spoke back in a soft voice.

Jia Li was transfixed. Kate was at once outspoken, irritable, and also somehow disconcertingly compassionate. Her voice was soothing now, as if she were speaking to very young children—which they kind of were, Jia Li reflected. Absurd children. Possibly insane.

The beaky one, Kostya, interrupted Kate.

"Dimka. *Hurry*."

"Ah, your name is Dimka," Kate said to Beanie-guy. The leader. "So, Dimka." Kate began to speak once more as if mothering them, then with one swift flick of her hair off her shoulder, Kate's tone sharpened with barely contained anger. "Did you consider that Gutov just said that to his fans because he wanted to be left alone? Did you ever consider that it was a lot of pressure for him to deliver the novels and live up to your demands, after years of *hounding him* with petitions, and so on? Sending *me* as an emissary? When I was just a *child*? Did you consider that you drove him *so fucking crazy* that he just disappeared wherever the fuck he wanted, and lied about going to Shambhala?"

Kate's shoulders sunk; her chin dropped to her chest. Jia Li felt a rush of sadness. Warmth enveloped her heart. She leaned over and put a hand on Kate's arm. "You owe them nothing," she told her. To the Gutovniks she said, "I think you should go now."

Kate lifted her chin. Jia Li smiled at her, awkward, aware that empathy had bound them together even earlier, when Kate had said she was sorry about Jia Li's father.

"I agree," Finley said.

"That is *false*!" Kostya screeched. "False! He did not lie! That is what Valeri said, and he nearly brought down our entire operation with his crazy theories. He is now *ex*. It is not true that Gutov lived and hid. He would not do that to us."

Dimka said, wagging a finger, "Valeri was not able to see Truth, that was the danger. If you cannot see, you cannot enter Shambhala."

"What happened to Valeri?" Kate asked.

"He went home to Berlin. Hiding from us like scared little boy. Good riddance," said Kostya.

"But, anyway," Dimka said, "we have a plan to help you find Shambhala. You must come with us, and bring the cross. We have much to share with you. And we are very excited."

Baby-faced boy-child grinned, and the other one, the day-old stubble, said, "Yes, very excited to show you, Katya."

"Um. I just remembered. We cannot go to headquarters exactly *now*, Dimka. We must bring material here," Kostya said.

"That's impossible, Kostya. There is too much to show her."

Kostya tried, and miserably failed, to mumble out of the corner of his mouth, fortunately in English so that Jia Li and Finley could understand. "Yes, but I remember now that my father is home and they have guests for dinner and I won't be able to get her inside."

Finley sighed in exasperation. "Let me guess, the basement of your parents' house, that's your headquarters?"

Kate smirked. Jia Li tittered. Dimka glared at everyone, including his comrades.

"It's okay. We can wait here for you to get the material," Kate spoke softly. Jia Li felt the deceit beneath her saccharine tone, and knew she had a plan. "You go, and come back later," Kate cooed.

"Okay, tie them up then," said day-old stubble with curly black hair.

"That will *not* be necessary," Kate said.

"Is necessary," Dimka nodded. "Tie them up," he repeated, and the Gutovniks surrounded them.

"Who has rope?" Kostya asked.

The young men looked around them searchingly, and baby-faced boy-man finally admitted, "We didn't bring rope."

"I told *you* to bring all the weapons!" Dimka shouted at him.

"I don't think we have rope," day-old stubble with curly black hair said. "I'm sorry."

"Yes. I mean no. No, we don't. Sorry." Baby-faced boy-man looked at his feet.

"I have rope," Jia Li spoke up. Her mind tingled with excitement. "In my bag, here. I'll help. You can put me in last. Honestly, we'll wait here and you can go get your stuff or whatever."

"Seriously?" Finley said. "Are you serious? Why do you have rope?"

"You have rope?" Kostya asked, sneering down his beaky nose. "Why you have rope?"

"Let's just help these guys, okay? So they can help Kate," Jia Li said, and stared hard at Finley, so hard that he had to avert his eyes.

Then, Jia Li unzipped her black duffle bag and peeled back the sides to reveal a pile of red rope. She removed it with reverence. "I am a thief," Jia Li offered the onlookers, who, without exception, appeared mesmerized by her handling of the rope as it pooled in her hands like lava. She knew that quality of watchful curiosity. It spurred her confidence. "I keep my rope in case it's required."

"Great," Dimka said, breaking the spell. "Don't worry, we will come back and free you. Sit in a circle, on the floor, back together. We tie you."

And that was that, no more questions. Kate and Finley sat on the floor back to back. The Gutovniks got to work as Jia Li made herself indispensable, bossing them around. "Hold this, pull there." She guided the boy-men to encircle them, suggesting elaborate ways to do so, tightening it as she went. They seemed grateful, nodding and commenting as the impossibly long rope wound its way around the temporary prisoners, tying each one's legs at the ankles, then arms, pinned to the side, and finally Jia Li sat with her back to the others' sides, and said, "You can just tighten it now. Here, I'll help. Just hand me that bit." She was now entwined with them, and somehow still holding the end. The bumbling Gutovniks thanked her and spoke in Russian and then finally patted Kate on the head.

Jia Li flooded with relief. Of course she knew *exactly* what she was doing, and now this felt like entertainment, and not just an annoyance to overcome.

Dimka said, "We go now, Katya. You be safe. We won't be long."

They left, slamming the door behind them.

"They're not subtle, are they?" Finley asked.

"Now what do we do?" asked Kate.

"Wait until we hear their cars, so that we know they're gone," Jia Li said. "Then we escape."

"How, exactly?" Finley asked. "I'm losing sensation in my left arm. And as I recall, you assisted them—I'm trying not to assume, but I'm really hoping you have a plan."

"Patience," Jia li said. "I'm good with rope, obviously."

"Yes, but why in the world do you travel with rope?" Finley asked. "Because you're a thief, oh right, you did say that already. Is that in addition to being a scientist? Or is it a side hobby?"

"Finley, take a breath," Kate said. "Everybody is more than they seem. You should know that."

"I was going to an event later, if you must know. It's called Shibari. I thought since I was in town I'd check out the local scene."

"Is that their car leaving?" Kate asked, not even pausing on the word *Shibari*.

"Um, I think so," said Jia Li. "Best to wait a few more minutes just to be sure."

She reached for the rope behind her, twisting to her right and leaning down at an odd angle to reach it.

"You okay there?" Finley asked.

She ignored him.

"Anyway, how *did* you come across the cross?" Jia Li asked Kate. "I am guessing it was an accident, because the last I knew it was definitely in the hands of organized crime, and you definitely *don't* fit the profile."

Kate looked defeated. "If you *must* know, the man who had the icon last died in my apartment, but not officially, okay? I didn't know he was even involved in organized crime, or that he was Russian. He died of poisoning. Nothing to do with me."

"So a man in your home, he left it, by accident," Jia Li said.

"Yep."

"So you knew him?"

"Not for long. It was a... let's call it a one night experience."

"I happen to know that a Russian thug was found in his car, dead. So I'm guessing he's the one who had it. And that you somehow put him there," Jia Li pressed.

"Oh my *God*, Kate. How in the world did you do that..." Finley gasped.

Kate closed her eyes as if exhausted by the conversation. "Leave it, both of you. There are bigger problems to solve."

"Hmph," Jia Li shrugged. *So they both liked criminals. Or didn't, perhaps, who knows*, she thought.

She craned her neck towards Finley. "How are you involved anyway?"

"I'm a friend who knows about the icon."

Jia Li still struggled with the rope behind her, but kept talking as if nothing were amiss, not wanting to draw too much attention to herself.

She liked a good show, after all. Now she was half-lying on her side, a piece of rope in her mouth, pulling it towards her. She couldn't manage to keep the rope in her mouth and it dropped to the floor.

"Where's the cross then?" Jia Li asked.

"Somewhere safe," Kate said.

Jia Li was flummoxed. She had no plan beyond this—she'd hoped reason would convince them to bring it out and show her, at which point she could take it and run if need be. Now she realized that it might be more difficult to acquire the cross than she'd first thought.

There was a knock at the door, and a deep voice straightaway.

"Kate? You okay? What's going on? Kate?"

"Get the spare key, Victoria, I'm okay! I just can't open the door!"

"Oh, thank God," Finley said.

"Great, it will be easier with help, actually," Jia Li said. "I wasn't going to say it, but it's actually much more difficult to extricate oneself on one's own."

Finley rolled his eyes. "That was obvious."

After several agonizing moments, a very tall and imposing woman, apparently *Victoria*, burst in.

"What the actual fuck?" she said.

She took a step forward, sideways, clearly unsure where to go and what to do—and began to pant.

"We're fine, Victoria, just breathe," Kate told her.

"I told you not to get involved Kate, honestly."

"If you don't mind grabbing this end bit of the rope here." Jia Li indicated with her chin.

Ah, she felt it: a glow that lit her up from the inside. Just as during her performance, *this* was the moment of truth. The great finale. Here, there would be no suspension, but rather, an unravelling. Just the same, she shone. *Knowledge, not proof*, she told herself. She imagined her father silently nodding his approval, and then questioned herself for desiring his approval.

Victoria stepped forward and took the end of the rope.

"It's not what you think, Victoria. It's my childhood, coming for me," Kate said mournfully.

"Now pull, walking backwards slowly," instructed Jia Li. "And keep pulling till you have it all."

"Your childhood in Ohio?" Victoria asked, as if it were unfathomable that anything strange happened in Ohio. She took a few tentative steps and pulled, and as she did so the rope came undone, a river of red flowing softly towards her, until within seconds it was pooled at her feet. Victoria gasped.

Kate laughed. Finley said, "Brilliant, absolutely brilliant. I take back every doubt and suspicion."

"Really?" Jia Li smirked.

"So far," he replied.

Kate pulled herself upright and stepped over the pooled ropes. "So" she said to Victoria, whose eyebrows were raised so high that Jia Li knew there was a confrontation coming.

"Okay, yeah, so there are things I haven't exactly explained to you about my childhood."

Kate caught Victoria up on the improbable autobiographical facts that Jia Li and Finley now knew: her mother was a Russian immigrant, involved in a cult of science fiction fanatics, and she thought Kate was the chosen one. Guys from that cult tied them all up so Kate wouldn't leave without their help. Or without her helping them.

Victoria looked suitably shocked.

"They're harmless and deluded, so don't freak out, okay? But we do have to get out before they come back and bore us to death. But it's not just them. Apparently the Russian mafia will find out I had the cross soon if they haven't already. And maybe a global pharmaceutical company. So it's go time. No one saw you, right?"

"Pharma—what the? No, no one saw." Victoria tucked a lock of slightly matted, curly hair behind her ear and scrunched up her face. "I—I heard a commotion coming out of your place, that was a bunch of guys from a *cult*? And—I will process this all later. Who the fuck *are* you people?"

Kate sighed. She indicated Jia Li. "This is Jia Li, from Hong Kong. She wants to get the cross for her mom, who's sick."

Victoria gave her a wry smile. "The rope bunny. Nice work there."

Jia Li grinned. "Yes!" *Finally. Someone knew Shibari in this circus.*

Victoria's breathing had returned to normal. "Right," she said. She pointed at Finley. "And you? You sure you're just a new *friend...*?"

Kate apologized to Finley and, turning first to Jia Li, then Victoria, said, "Finley has visions of an apocalyptic future. He needs to find out the origins of the cross in the future so they can reverse engineer it and save humanity or something." She winced in Finley's direction. He squeezed his eyes shut as if embarrassed.

Jia Li's jaw dropped. Her eyes lit up. "No way. That's ..."

"Crazy." Victoria finished her thought. "That's just batshit crazy. So y'all are all allies in a special quest." She spoke said with a drawl as dry and tired as Jia Li felt. "Brought together by fate." She made a circle with her hand. "To help each other like, *save the world* or something."

"Well, yes, I guess so," Kate said, meeting Jia Li's eyes.

Jia Li felt something stir inside.

"So you are both searching for the *origins* of the cross?" Jia Li clarified.

"Yes," Kate said. "And you should help us."

In that moment, Jia Li so badly wanted trust to descend upon her, to find her a willing co-conspirator in these peoples' lives, a shared mission. She didn't want to continue alone—

cautious hope welled up in her now and she closed her eyes against the internal pressure.

"Right, Finley?" Kate asked.

∽

FINLEY NODDED. He liked Jia Li, and not just for her rope antics. She was *reassuring* to him; it was no doubt her desperation masked in determination, a familiar experience of late.

Jia Li said, "For the record, this icon thing? It's not magic. It's not about God or anything. It's science. It's this amalgam—rare metal elements in a particular formation. My lab partner studied a sample of it that I got from some residue. From my ex's arm. He couldn't even identify all of the elements. It's got some strange alloy that behaves differently to most metals apparently. My point is, how in the world will you find where it's from? How can you find the origins of metals that behave in a way we've never seen before, like *ever*?"

Kate livened up. "Whoa, you were able to analyze it? That's amazing! Okay, well obviously we have to do research then, to find out more."

"Research where? And who would you trust? Scientists? Doctors? I don't know if you're aware of how it works, but they're all in the pockets of pharmaceuticals, and pharmaceuticals have unlimited funds, so they would block anyone they want. But also, they wouldn't share the origins of anything even remotely powerful in this way, *even if* they found it themselves, because they don't *want* a cure. A cure can't make them money. Get it?"

Jia Li had communicated all those facts on fiery autopilot. Meanwhile, she had fully packed up her rope and zipped her bag closed.

"And what exactly are you all going to *do*?" asked Victoria.

"Find Valeri," Kate said.

"The ex-cult guy!" Finley said. "He might know where Gutov really is, if he's really alive, and Gutov might know where the cross came from, since he wrote about it in his book."

"Exactly! So we need to go to Berlin. I met Valeri once on my way to Russia, in his apartment when I was six or seven. I remember it well. It was near an orangish red bridge that had these towers on it, like a castle. I remember always seeing it when we walked to the apartment, and there was a big brass *eight* on the outside of his building. I think I'd recognize it. We'd just need to walk around that neighborhood and knock on a few doors."

"If he's still there, in that same apartment," Jia Li said.

"If Valeri's not in the same apartment, his neighbors might know where he's moved to. Anyway we have to try. Victoria, is the cross safe?"

"*You* have it?" Jia Li exclaimed, staring at Victoria.

"It's as safe as you'd expect in rural Georgia. Don't you worry."

"And your father? Is he okay now?" Kate had begun to rummage around the living room, grabbing keys off a hook on the wall, her phone from the table. She stopped to make eye contact with Victoria.

"Cured, least it seems so. Never even knew I visited. I cut a hole in the bottom of his mattress and stuck the cross right up, near the fabric up top, so he'd be laying right on it. After 3 days I snuck back in, took it out, and hid it somewhere no one would find it. Mama says she's never seen him so energetic and they both think God just spared him."

"Someone will find out he miraculously healed. And someone will come looking," Jia Li said.

"Well you obviously don't know rural Georgia. If my daddy says it was from praying to God then people will believe it's from praying to God. He never even laid eyes on any cross. Besides, he's refused to go back to the hospital since his diagnosis and he sure won't now. He doesn't trust doctors."

"Thank you for keeping it safe, Victoria," Kate said. "Right now, I need to pack. We need to get to the airport, like, *now*, before those weirdos get back and before anyone else who may be looking for me or *it*."

"The only thing... it's my mother." Jia Li hesitated for a second. "What I didn't say was that someone injected her with something. To get to me. They think I have information, proof of something. They told her she's only got a few months and that only they can cure her, but only if I give them what I have, but I don't really have anything. Not yet anyhow. So they won't be saving her. Which means she doesn't have much time. She *needs* that cross. That's why I came. I mean, I want to help you all, and I don't want it to fall into the wrong hands. But I also *really* need to help my mother."

Her face fell.

Kate said, "Oh, God."

"They really are bastards," Finley said. "Kate, we need to help her."

Kate bit her lip. Finley knew she agreed.

"She's where?" Victoria asked.

"In Hong Kong," Jia Li said.

"Honey, if you fly her here to Georgia, I can get her to the cross. Much safer than putting a target on your back and traveling with it to her."

"I've only just met you." Jia Li spoke matter-of-fact, forehead creased.

It was more accusation than observation, and Finley knew this feeling well—that it was all happening so fast, all these improbable connections, people and mysteries alike.

Victoria shrugged. "I know. Up to you. You can stay here with me if you'd rather, and wait for your mom."

Kate interjected. "No. We could use your help in Berlin. We need all the help we can get. You're smart, and you seem to have contacts with access to information, and that could come in handy."

Victoria said to Jia Li, "You can trust me, honey. I'm great with moms."

"You're great with *moms*?" Kate guffawed.

"Not that you'd know. But yes."

"You'd really do that for me?" Jia Li asked. "Meet my mum at the airport and take her to the cross? I can pay for hotels, whatever."

Her eyes were wet.

"Of course, honey. I'll take her and she can stay here with me and then you just tell me where to send her next. Easy. Just look after my girl," she nodded towards Kate. "She's family."

Victoria also had a tear in her eye, and Finley started to wonder what kind of emotional alchemy this quest was stirring in them all. He, too, felt a tremor of something in his heart.

Kate went over and hugged Victoria. "You're so kind. What would I do without you?"

"Stay safe, that's what you do. I'd give you my gun but you'd never make it out of the country with it."

"Plus I don't know how to use it."

"That's true, too."

"One last thing, though," Finley said.

"Nope—I need to pack now," Kate stopped him. "You need to go get your stuff from your hotel and order us a taxi to the airport. We can talk more later."

"Just a question. It could be vital."

His tone suggested an imminent revelation—he knew it, he'd aimed for it—so everyone paused to listen. The briefest fractal of memory appeared then vanished in his mind's eye:

when he was a boy,

the ocean, his collapse.

"Kate, what were you going to say, earlier, about me going into the future? You said it's not the same as *seeing* the future and that this might be relevant."

"Yes."

There was silence, during which Finley returned again, in a flash, to the moment on the beach as a child,

the tessellations in the sand—

ouroboros, or lemniscate,

which one was it that he had drawn?

What had he been doing at that moment when he collapsed? He strained to recall.

"So...?" Finley prodded her.

"Okay, fine. In *Ikona*, Yuk-Or Ba said that a vision represents what *is* right now, he called it *an insight into the field of consciousness that precedes form*. In other words, a vision shows you what's in the process of happening, before the results are there for others to see. Or else it shows you what's happening right now that you'd have no way of knowing. Anyway, it's about the field of consciousness you're in *right now, just taken forward in time*. On the other hand, going into the future is like—like stepping into one of infinite possibilities. Into potential futures. It begs the question. When you go to the future, Finley, why do you experience *that* possibility? Why *that* future?"

Jia Li looked at the ceiling. Victoria leaned into her hip, tapping her foot. Finley brought his hands to his temples and held his forehead, as if in anticipation of pain. All speculation, if anyone had any, remained heavy and unspoken.

"This was not the day I was expecting," Finley said, defeated. "I know I asked you to explain, but honestly I don't even know how to answer that. I feel that I should. And that soon, hopefully, I'll be able to. But I can't now." He yawned, overcome with fatigue.

Kate said, "Don't worry about it now. Maybe the answer is in Berlin. Jia Li, so you're coming with us, right?"

Finley sensed something personal in Kate's hope that Jia Li would come. But since he wanted her there too, he didn't overthink it. The more help, the better—the less pressure on him.

"Yes, I'll come," she pronounced with a quick glance at Kate. And then, more quietly to Victoria she said, "Thank you. For offering to help my mum. I'll fly her here. I've been so worried about her."

"Oh honey," Victoria said, "she's most welcome. I'll take good care of her, don't you worry."

16

VISSARION & THE CRUCIFIX
JANUARY 1909
TUNGUSKA REGION, SIBERIA

For many months Vissarion neglected the dull metal nuggets his brother had given him, a puzzling disregard given Pyotr's rapturous state that day. As a holy servant of God, Vissarion of course gave credence to the miraculous workings of Divinity and did not doubt his brother. Pyotr was, after all, a wandering monk held in high regard. Still, as one who forged crucifixes, Vissarion had protocols, routines, and strict beliefs. It was blasphemous to call something holy when it was neither an icon nor a relic, and metal bits plucked from a riverbed were indeed neither.

As well, being eminently practical, Vissarion had not felt compelled by the mysterious lumps of rock, no matter how much his brother insisted on their miraculous nature, because for these past months he had sufficient metals for his needs—copper, tin, and some zinc. Until, that is, he found his supplies depleted just as he was given his latest commission: to create icons for the *ofenya*'s many pious customers across all the southern and eastern regions of Siberia.

So Vissarion retrieved the small cloth sack his brother had left him and inspected its contents. The metal was unique, no question. He could not identify the alloy, however. It was a silvery color, but without knowing its exact nature, Vissarion could not be certain as to its use. Perhaps it was what he needed, or perhaps not. He wished to venerate the King of Glory in bronze, but he had only copper and too little tin. Hence he held the mystery metal and mulled over his dilemma—to do nothing and wait for more supplies, or take a chance and melt it in hopes of bringing to life what existed yet in his imagination:

A crucifix.

He couldn't decide with his mind, so he fasted to make space for spirit to move through him, to reveal how this holy mission might be accomplished and by which means.

AFTER THREE DAYS of fasting and praying he arrived at a decision, but not because he had seen a holy sign or felt the touch of an angel. Rather, because he was at his wit's end. There was no more metal available nor coming anytime soon, the *ofenya* was on his way, and profit demanded ingenuity.

Vissarion got to work as he again recited prayers and belted out a holy song for good measure. He was happy to see, as he melted the clumps, that they behaved very much like other alloys of tin or zinc, and so he mixed in copper, and prayed and sang some more as the heat rose and rose, until the mixture became like fiery, liquid gold. He knew then that he would be able to create the crucifix, God-willing, an *ikona* to sell with the triptych and panel icons created at the monastery. Just in time for the *ofenya*'s arrival from Irkutsk.

He prepared the cast, and poured the molten alloy into the mold of the Orthodox cross, filling three crossbeams.

The top beam would herald the name of the crucified one—*King of Glory*, with angels bowing, and then

the middle beam was that upon which Jesus lay crucified, and below lay

the crooked line of justice—one side ascending to Heaven, the other descending to Hell, a reminder of man's eternal choice, and also a reference to the thieves who hung on either side of Jesus at the crucifixion.

It took him all day from his dawn start, and into the late afternoon.

When the crucifix was done and cooling, Vissarion lay down for a moment on a blanket on the floor, exhausted. He thought of his brother, far away again, no doubt, and wondered if he remained rapturous, and wondered how a person could maintain such faith in the face of need—for food, shelter, connection to others.

Like his brother, Vissarion was happy in solitude. Indeed the life of an iconographer, even one who cast crucifixes, was like that of a monk—holy, devotional, solitary. Yet he could not fathom leaving behind society or shelter, and traveling without a destination, relying on the good will of others for survival.

His own devotion, if he were honest with himself, waned, which caused him to fear that he was not sufficiently worthy as a servant of God. He could well imagine that if he were a wandering monk, he might easily suffer a crisis of conscience on some lonely, isolated road. And in the terror of a frozen, black night, God might surely abandon him for lack of faith.

He crossed himself at the thought of it, tapping his forehead, his shoulders.

Soft winter light shimmered through the one window of his workshop. It warmed him, if only a touch. Night would fall fast and the temperature would drop faster. He sat. He gently removed the crucifix from its cooling spot, and kissed the hands and feet of Jesus.

Forgive me my doubt, he prayed silently.

His heart softened.

He beheld it. Surely there was something different about this cross.

Just as Pyotr had shone in reverence, so Vissarion, too, suddenly felt the movement of spirit,

as if he were bathed in love,

longing and nostalgia and a promise of bliss.

The crucifix was alight in his mind's eye,

its emanation dazzled.

He put down the crucifix and sat next to it. A part of his mind retracted from the light he perceived with his inner sight, and in the emptiness from where it pulled back, he saw the fear which remained. Fear *of what?* he asked himself. Only children feared being smote from above—but he could not fool even himself. He knew this fear. It was that part of him which catalyzed his every devotional act.

It was his bargain with God.

He offered devotion in exchange for certainty's solace, because if what exists could be made to disappear from the face of the Earth, if death could be so final, what surety did he have of love—even the love of God?

He heard Pyotr's voice,

You have exchanged one god for another, brother. You would have placed your heart at the altar of marriage, in devotion to a wife.

Vissarion picked up the crucifix once more, and love washed through him again. It did not dispel fear, but perhaps if he were to hold it longer, he thought, it might. And so he clutched it to his chest and prayed. After several moments he did feel love like Grace enter him and lift fear up from where it had so burdened him—to where sadness lay beneath.

He saw himself, on that day, broken-hearted.

He sat by her side, and watched her die. His love Olya. She would not return to him.

Vissarion could not bear that pain. Fear was much less worse than grief, which deepened and lengthened inside him like a long shadow that would be ceded unto darkness. Perhaps if he continued to hold onto this object of devotion, the grief would overtake the fear, but then would he have to feel this grief forever?

He knew the truth now. It was love that caused sadness, and through this holy instrument, he had been shown that the depth of his grief was in equal proportion to that of his love.

He knew that if he had the courage to feel the grief, Grace might await. But he could not travel any longer in this sad land, even if the destination were fear's cessation.

This crucifix surely was touched by God.

It was known that God had struck many a crucifix with lightning, imbuing it with miraculous powers, so perhaps that is what had happened to the metal. For already he had made the connection between the lumps his brother gave him, and the palpable power of the cross.

He told himself this crucifix was not for him, but for humanity, as were all icons. So he must include it with the others for the *ofenya* to sell. He told himself this, because he knew it was morally just. He decided to part with it in those few minutes, however, for self-preservation.

Again, he kissed the crucifix.

Again, Grace entered to where sadness lay.

He cried, because he could not even accept this Grace.

He placed the crucifix on the shelf, where once the cloth bag of mysterious metal had lain. He would farewell it the next day.

AFTER THE *OFENYA* came and left with the crucifix on his rounds, his cart piled high with panels and crosses, Vissarion went to visit his friends Yuri Sergasin and Vasili Yakunov at the Monastery.

"No word from your brother?" Yuri asked.

"No, he left months ago after a visit," Vissarion explained, and he shared with his friends Pyotr's visit, his rapturous state, the mysterious metal, and the cross he'd forged. He also described to them the Grace that seemed to emanate from it. He asked them if they thought it was right that he had allowed it to be sold, rather than keep it for the Church.

"It is well and good you allowed the peddler to take it, as we can only learn of its true power once it is out in the world, as it should be," said Vasili.

"Yes, it would be contrary to nature for an iconographer to hoard the works he creates," agreed Yuri.

"If it is truly as you say, a miracle, then we have not heard the end of it," Vasili added.

"As I thought," Vissarion said. "I only sought your counsel to feel certain that I have done what is right, because sometimes I am not certain if I am being led by God or by the other voice within me."

"That is the journey," Yuri replied. "You are wise to ask such questions."

The three friends sat on the steps of the monastery, and they each stared into the sky, as if in anticipation of awe,

beholden to an echo from the past.

The sky was empty that day, but for small, high white clouds. Vissarion thought he saw cranes, but maybe that, too, was a remembrance.

17

FINLEY, KATE & JIA LI: TIME TRAVELLERS AND MIND DESTROYERS

JUNE 2019

BERLIN, GERMANY

The cranes made a perfect v in the bright, blue sky. Finley followed them with his eyes as they blinked out of sight.

Strange, he thought,

But then all of it was strange—

How quickly the trio agreed they *had* to go on this mission, to join forces and fly to Germany the same night that they'd left Kate's apartment, and how quickly he'd paid for everything, from the flights to the hotel. The practicalities had arisen with urgency, like a leaking roof in a storm. Finley had never known this joy of using his *means* in service—not for investment, or personal necessity, or whim. He liked this feeling of *being needed.*

Now he, Kate and Jia Li were in this ridiculous pink hotel on the Spree river. United and yet so different. Like the ripples of a pond when a stone has been thrown,

as this icon had been tossed into their reality,

their allegiance was just a matter of physics, after all, he ruminated.

But that was in those moments when Finley did not question the improbabilities with his logical mind so much, and instead began to interpret their joint adventure as a quest, much like *The Lord of the Rings*.

The plan was simple:

Find the ex-Gutovnik Valeri, and through him, hopefully, Gutov, if he had, indeed, gone into hiding. If they could find the old writer, perhaps he knew more about the actual cross, such as its origins. This might lead to understanding how it had been created.

Finley had done his research. The bridge Kate remembered from childhood could only be the Oberbaumbrücke, which she confirmed once she saw the photos. It was, indeed, near a neighborhood which fit her descriptions for Valeri's apartment building—the Kreuzberg neighborhood. All very good sleuthing, the women agreed.

So it was that the trio launched themselves into a most serious endeavor in a most whimsical fashion from their pink hotel. On their warm and sunny first day, after an ample buffet breakfast, they embarked on their first mission which, over equally ample German dinner fare the previous night, had *sounded* simple and straightforward—find a door marked *eight*, in view of the bridge, per Kate's memory.

In actual fact, after two hours of fruitless wandering, the reality of chasing clues in foreign towns, along with the distinct possibility of danger, all began to wear Finley down, and to bring to the surface all that troubled the women.

Of course, there was the Russian mafia—which surely had the means to find out that the dead man had left his precious object in Kate's apartment. As if that weren't enough to explain her moodiness, after a coffee break mid-wander, she admitted that the police had warned her not to leave the country (meaning the US of course). She worried she'd be pursued internationally if the investigation of the dead Russian man didn't turn up any other suspects.

Jia Li, of course, had already expressed her certainty that she *would* be followed by these, as she called them, *pharma thugs*. And if they had followed the same trail and knew about the cross, they might be after *all* of them.

Now, as they continued to look for the numeral *eight* post coffee break, Kate appeared withdrawn and on edge, and Jia Li was constantly checking her peripheral vision. Finley felt their fear like a subtle and disconcerting vibration.

All this being-pursued tension was intensified by how Kate stared at Jia Li and how Jia Li had begun to stare back. Finley squirmed a bit at their unspoken mutual attraction and began to feel, in turns, like a watchful uncle or an awkward third wheel.

"I'm not sure where exactly the building numbers are," Jia Li said.

"Ah," Finley said, grasping his forehead. "I'm not ready for this."

"Is it a vision?" Jia Li asked. "Is it happening?"

"No." Finley sighed. "It's me being jetlagged, but you sound *way* too excited."

"Just checking. I don't know how it happens."

"You'll *know*," Finley said. "Believe me."

Kate snapped. "Eyes on the buildings."

"My eyes are on many buildings. Jia Li—what do you think about this methodology for finding the right building?" Finley knew full well they had no methodology, and needed one.

"What I think is that we all need to split up and when we find an *eight*, text Kate the image. Finley, you go down those streets, and look here on my map, I'll take these streets." She held up her phone to show them.

Ah good, structure, he thought, appreciating her fierce focus. Once more, he found her energy reassuring. Kate still evoked in him, on the other hand (as much as he'd tried to deny it), a subtle protective instinct.

A half hour later, Finley received a text from Jia Li with an image of a brass *eight*.

"That's the one!" Kate texted them both back. "Meet there."

"Someone is following me," Jia Li texted back. "You guys go there without me. Meet back at the hotel later. Good luck."

Finley increased his pace just as Kate suddenly rounded the corner. He felt her tremor with anticipatory nerves, but he could see that she was determined. Together, without pause or conversation, they followed the map to the location Jia Li had sent them.

. . .

FINLEY AND KATE climbed three flights of speckled stone stairs, passing number after number, until they saw the door with an *eight* on it. They caught their breath as they stood before it in the white hallway.

"I'll handle this," Kate said, confirming Finley's hunch about her determination.

She knocked. He stood just behind her.

Nothing.

She called out, *Katya Dmitreva* and then something in Russian.

Within moments, the door slowly opened to a thin, middle aged woman in a white dressing gown, her gray-brown hair unkempt at her shoulders, her pale grey eyes like saucers. She appeared to have just gotten out of bed, and it was already nearly 11 am. She was the same height as Kate, probably about five foot five, so as the two women stood in the door their eyes were level.

Katya Dmitreva, the woman spat, and let out a wail, throwing the door wide open and taking a step back.

Finley instinctively took a step back, too.

"Shhhh, *Tishe,*" Kate said, and spoke in Russian, which of course Finley understood none of.

"I'm asking if she knows Valeri," Kate told him, continuing in Russian as Finley listened without comprehension.

The woman at the door spewed out her words, messy and punctuated by a pointed finger. Her apparent lunacy disconcerted Finley. She was, upon closer inspection, unwashed, her eyes red and skin sallow. She waved her arms as if both angry and afraid, shouting at Kate and at him. Her feet moved in agitation, forwards then back, then sideways, as if all of her individual parts were attempting to get a firm grasp in reality, or at least in the present moment.

"She is asking if we've come from the future. She's not making sense. Asking if we're *time-travelers* and *mind-destroyers.*"

Finley had nothing to say to that. He scrunched up his face in confusion.

The woman started screaming out to someone inside.

"She's calling out for her father. He must be Valeri. Saying that we're back for her."

He wanted to say, *well she is quite clearly insane,* but that was self-evident, and Kate was now saying the same word quietly over and over again.

"*Tishe, tishe.*"

And then, in a soothing tone, like she had with the Gutovniks, Kate let out a stream of Russian, her intonation rising and falling as she intermittently placed a palm on the woman's arm as if to reassure her. She could only have been telling her they were safe, not mind-destroyers, not out to harm anyone.

Finally, the woman went still, her jaw softened and her eyes stopped roaming. "*Evgenia,*" she said, a hand on her chest to indicate herself. Then something else.

"Yes, she is his daughter," Kate told Finley. "I asked her to tell him we're here to see him"

Finley's own agitation waned the longer it went on. His heart loosened a bit, and he felt compassion. He somehow *knew* her mania.

A man's voice came from behind the young woman.

"*Ya* Valeri."

Kate said to Finley, "That's him."

KATE MADE hasty introductions as the old man ushered them inside quickly. He was tall, at least six foot two, and extremely thin, with a white beard and thinning, white hair.

"Katenka," he said in English, shaking his head. "You are here at last. Here you are."

He led them to the kitchen and sat them down at the small table that was pushed against the wall. They filled the space uneasily, as if —and Kate felt the weight of it—as if their mission were too big for such cramped confines, and their unexplained reasons for being there sat heavy between them. The table was crowded with a teapot and jars of jam, a plate of butter, stale white bread. The room smelled of cabbage and coffee. Valeri said something to his daughter, then in English, "Evgenia will make us tea."

Then, to Kate in Russian, "Katenka. I'm so glad you are here. How is this possible? I have wondered how life took you under her wings, and if you found your own. *Ladno,* you must know that we have little time. The doors are closing." A look of distraction and sadness passed over his face.

"Doors, what doors are closing?" she asked.

She said to Finley in English, "He says the doors are closing."

"What doors?" he asked.

Evgenia busied herself at the kettle, so close Kate could smell her, acrid like vinegar. Kate spoke a bit more in Russian, and to Finley said, "Catching him up on my life." Then Evgenia handed them each a cup of black tea with a slice of lemon. There was a chair in the corner of the kitchen, near the door, and she sat there, meek, drinking her tea and watching them.

"I can speak English," Valeri said.

"I appreciate it," said Finley.

The old man sighed. "I meant that the *portal* is closing soon, the connection, between this world and the future one."

"Oh, I um..." Kate grasped for something to say. Finley put down his tea cup and looked away. Kate thought she heard him breathe out, a slight note of exasperation.

"Humanity is dying. A slow and painful death. There will be many deaths," Valeri said.

"And the portal is to a new world?" Kate clarified.

"Well, yes. Some call it Shambhala, as you know. The time is foretold. The *ikona,* that is what will save us, yes? You are looking for it? To light the way?"

Finley widened his eyes at her. They should have discussed their story beforehand, and Kate knew it. She widened her eyes back at him as if to say, *I'll handle it.* Valeri did not seem to notice their silent communication.

"Nevermind the cross," Kate said. "We're looking for Shambhala, yes, because that's always been my mission, as you know. But we can find it without the cross." She cleared her throat. "We're here because the Gutovniks say you left them because you believe that Gutov lives, and *we* believe that might be true, and that he might help us."

"He does live! And those fools would not believe me." He shook his head.

Evgenia, suddenly shifting out of an unfocused gaze, glared at the visitors.

Valeri spoke. "Gutov is the only one who knows about the cross. No one believed me when I told them that he lived, they were so far gone into their conspiracies."

"So you've spoken to Gutov, that's how you know he lives?" Kate asked.

"No."

"No?" Kate faltered.

"Not in person. He has appeared in my dreams."

Kate's face fell. Of course. *Weren't they all a group of magical thinkers? The lot of them. Ughh. How was that going to help? Finley with his visions and she and Valeri with dreams and Evgenia*—she stole a glance at her—*scowling back.*

Evgenia mumbled in Russian, again about mind-destroyers and time travelers.

Putting aside for a moment the dream of Gutov, Kate asked, "What is she talking about?" Mind-destroyers. Time-travelers."

"Oh, that." Valeri sighed. "Poor girl. She's been through a lot."

"What happened?" Kate asked.

"They got to her. She tried—to be of help. I shouldn't have allowed it. I was desperate." He shook his head. "*Visitors*. They've been coming to see us. Every year, this time of year, summer, for the past five years. They speak of a man, they ask about a man. Vals. Fals. Something, I don't remember."

"Wallace." Finley sat to attention. He gawked.

"Yes. Wallace. Is that you?" Hs face lit up.

"I'm Finley Minor."

"You know him then?"

"I... maybe," Finley said. "I mean, probably there are a lot of Wallaces in the world."

Valeri crinkled his nose like he'd caught a bad smell.

Kate glared at him. Again, they hadn't got their story straight. She didn't want to explain Wallace.

"They say they're from the future. No—not exactly. They say they're speaking *for* the future," Valeri said.

"On behalf of the future," Finley clarified. Valeri didn't seem to notice his clarity on the matter, but Kate widened her eyes at Finley once more.

"Yes. My English is not great."

Kate said, "It's very good. Okay, they're speaking on behalf of the future. And they say the door is closing."

"Yes. They come here and they sit here in my kitchen and smoke. They say that they need Vals. Wallace. Because the door is closing, and they need some information."

"Why you? Why here?"

"I don't know these answers. They say very little. It's a delicate situation. I told them once, go look elsewhere, such person is not here, and they said it was *timing*. They were not good at timing. He would be here, they were sure. I felt scared. And Evgenia, she said she wanted to know more and she said she could help them. They said no many times, but she insisted. She was a clever girl. She read all of Gutov's books and she believed she had the gift to see. She did a remote viewing course online. One day, they agreed. They took her someplace and she came back like this. Now she speaks of mind-destroyers. Now she's not well. It's my fault. I should have protected her. Now, I don't know what to do, if they come back." His head sank into his hands, and a look of despair seeped into the corners of his eyes, which was all that could be seen from the edges of his palms.

Kate said, "I'm sorry, Valeri. I'm sorry they're coming and asking, and that they did something to Evgenia."

Evgenia now began to mumble and rock. She was rambling. The words *death* and *cancer* came out. Then *orphans*, something about being orphaned.

"Her mother is not here?" Kate asked.

"She died a long time ago," Valeri said. "But she was a good girl, an easy girl, a so clever girl, until the visitors."

"Why did you trust them?" Finley asked. "I mean, these strangers appear, and say they are waiting for... for whomever it is they're waiting for... and then Evgenia goes with them. I don't understand."

He put a hand on his forehead and squinted, as if in pain.

Valeri removed his face from his hands and stared at his visitors as if dumbfounded.

Kate could not bring herself to explain. Several seconds passed. Kate said quietly, to herself, to anyone, "It's always been like this. Mystery and secrecy, blind faith that there is a grand plan. Maybe there's no grand plan. Maybe nothing's connected."

"It *is* connected," Valeri said. "The visitors told me that Vals would appear, that he would be looking for something important, something to help humanity, and that I must tell them so they could help. I did not trust them then. Yes, I was afraid. But, I was prepared to be *astounded*! I was prepared for Truth. I did not intend to sacrifice my daughter for it. So maybe you are Vals, or know him, but Katya is here, and Katya leads us to Shambhala, so I must believe that something important is happening."

Evgenia lost color. She stood. She pointed at Finley, suddenly lucid and still. She began to speak in Russian without accusation, without apparent lunacy. Calm. Almost gentle. It was a plea: "You know. *You know*. You must stop it. End it. You must find the source, the location, you know this. Gutov waits for you."

Kate tripped on the words as she tried to translate what Evgenia had said, even as Valeri blanched, sputtering, "She's not well. I'm— I'm sorry. She says crazy things. Sometimes they make sense. I don't know..."

Finley received the communication without reaction, other than to grip his forehead.

"We just need to find Gutov," Kate said after a moment. "But seeing him in a dream doesn't help us."

"He's in Siberia. Near Lake Baikal. Fishing. I also received a postcard." Valeri jumped up and left the room. Evgenia remained, staring at the pair with a look of utter equanimity, fully recovered, it seemed. Valeri returned.

"Here."

The postcard—a brilliant blue lake, a view of a single white rock, the mountains framing it. The image was worn. Valeri turned it over. Kate leaned in to read it.

She translated as she read.

"Valeri. You have received my message? Very well. My apologies for my sudden disappearance. It is truly magical here. There are truths more true than you imagine, and there is also pain and sadness, laughter and joy. The heart is the compass. The way forward is always a letting go of what's passed. Perhaps we will meet again, on this or another plane. Be well, my friend." She looked up. " It's signed, Yours, G."

"That's it?" Finley asked. "Where's it from? When?"

"Irkusk. 1998," Valeri replied.

"That's forever ago."

Kate said, "It's all we've got."

"Not all," Valeri said. "I know that his American editor Frank visited him even just a couple years ago, because he told me so. Frank was also my editor. He told me that if I ever wanted to find Gutov, to go to Lake Baikal. He has a dacha there near Port Baikal. He fishes."

FOR JIA LI, the problem was—and this problem had begun to preoccupy her by the time they were all traipsing around town looking for number *eight*—she believed (rationally, not intuitively) that her only relevance in this trio was to use her contacts to get this magical icon replicated *if* they could determine how it had been made. This present task, to find Gutov and discover the origins, did not require her participation necessarily. But an ineluctable pull to understand Kate did, and she could not ignore it.

Especially since she knew, through Michael, that Kate was a prostitute. *Sex worker, rather, that's what one said these days. What a word, what a concept,* she thought.

Sex worker. Prostitute. Whore.

None of those words fit this woman, with her quiet bookishness, her casual disregard for any clothes other than sweatpants and jeans, or her entire Russian and former cult backstory. Nor, no less, did it fit with Kate's obvious interest in *her*. And Jia Li wasn't mistaken; she knew a woman's attraction when she felt it. The entire existence of Kate Davies confused, confounded, and also—and this baffled her most of all—*soothed* her.

The double life was, after all, Jia Li's most resonant self-expression, a familiar bypass in a world that fucked her and those she loved.

Jia li waited for Kate and Finley at the hotel bar. She was drinking beer and had a large greenish bruise on her left cheek which she hoped was concealed by her hair, but apparently not. Kate startled when she saw it, and was at her side in an instant, Finley catching up behind her.

"Are you okay? What happened?"

"I'm fine. I fell. Someone was following me and..." She shrugged and took a large sip. "Anyway, it's been a long day. Join me. You too," she said to Finley.

"Not me. I'm exhausted. My head is killing me. I'm going to order room service. Kate, you catch her up on our day. You understood much more of it than me anyway."

"Sure" Kate said. "Okay I think I'll have a beer too, then."

"Great idea," Jia Li said. Pieces of hair stuck to her forehead and cheeks; she'd been sweating. She pushed a strand of hair over her left cheek, hoping Kate wouldn't stare at the bruise, but to no avail.

"Looks like a bad bruise," Kate observed. She ordered the same beer as Jia Li. She drank fast.

"Don't worry about it. So tell me about today. About Valeri."

Suddenly, Jia Li felt a little unsettled being alone with this woman, without Finley as a buffer.

Kate began to talk, starting with Valeri appearing at the door, and Evgenia and her strange behaviour. She drank as she talked, and she talked *fast*. They were both quickly onto their second beer. The bar filled and grew louder and louder as Kate shared all the details of her meeting. Jia Li could feel Kate's body relax as she drank and rambled on, and her own as well. The volume of their voices increased to compensate for the noise.

Jia Li only realized, as the alcohol hit her bloodstream, the thrill that lay beneath.

"This is crazy," Jia Li said. "So Valeri says that humanity is dying? These guys were from the future? I mean, I've never been opposed to stuff like this—reincarnation, future premonitions, magic. Just not interested. I mean, my own life has been enough to handle. If you know what I mean."

"I know. But this is my normal. I was raised believing in all this. What's not normal is normal."

"You're kinda fascinating," Jia Li said. Then she worried she'd stared a little too long.

"Um, thank you. I guess."

Jia Li thought, *Kate is too smart, and too attractive. The context is confusing and the timing terrible*, and so Jia Li ordered yet another drink.

"Anyway," Jia Li said. "You need another drink, too." She ordered for them both.

"So... tell me about your day, now," Kate said. She looked pointedly at the bruise on Jia Li's cheek.

"Well, I spoke to my friend Michael today. He's a lab assistant I work with. He's the one who analyzed the residue from the cross, which I got off my... the guy I was with."

"In Hong Kong."

"Yes. He told me he knows someone in Argentina who might be able to help us—a scientist who works with metals. He sounds a bit out there. He has some kind of technology that he's used to create alloys that haven't been seen before. He has weird uses for them apparently. He had a patent for an engine to power space travel, but his patent was revoked and someone attempted to murder him. I'm just sharing what Michael told me. I don't claim to know how true any of this stuff is."

"Oh." Kate sounded excited. She was definitely tipsy. "I hear that happens. I mean if the government doesn't want you to have technology, it's easy to revoke a patent."

Jia Li grinned. "So you're a conspiracy theorist, too. You'd love Michael."

"Well, some conspiracies are just truth not yet fully understood or accepted."

"That's it."

Their eyes met. Jia Li grinned.

"So if we can get the cross to this guy in Argentina somehow, maybe he can do something with it. Or, I don't know, I guess if we find out how it was made, we could tell him and he could find the elements somehow and recreate it. I feel like there are a lot of *somehows* in all this." Jia Li sighed.

Kate laughed. "Times like this it's really helpful to have been raised in a cult where visions are taken at face value, and you just have to *trust*. Trusting would be far easier than having a brain that questions things."

Jia Li snorted mid-sip and beer came out of her nose. "Ha! I'm glad there are some perks of being raised in a cult, then." She cleared her throat. "Listen. Um. Can I ask you something... personal?"

"I guess so."

She whispered, "Did that guy who died. Was he... a client? I know you're a sex worker."

Kate swallowed hard.

"Did Finley tell you?"

"No, Michael did. I asked him to do some digging, you know. Before we left for Berlin. I hadn't really looked too deeply into you before, I mean, just enough to know about the girl, and the hospital, and the likelihood you had the cross. But then when I realized I *trusted* you, and that I wanted to go to Berlin. I just had to be absolutely sure you weren't part of any crime syndicate or secretly working for Big Pharma.

Michael found your website. It just adds up, I guess, how you said you ended up with the cross." She gave Kate a nervous smile. "I'm sorry. I feel bad about asking. I'm just curious. It's none of my business."

Kate seemed to empty herself into the stillness between them. Her body went slack and she stared, unfocused, across the heads of the other patrons.

Jia Li, observing this reaction, felt immediately guilty, all too painfully aware just how much she cared what this woman thought of her.

"Well, I'm not doing it now, at the moment. But yes, that is how I paid my bills."

"Okay," Jia Li said. "It's all good. No need to justify your choices. You're an adult. It's crazy how that work led to you having the icon. Given your past, those weirdo fanatics, Valeri, Gutov. It's a series of coincidences that seems to defy reason."

"Or..." Kate said, "Maybe there are no coincidences. Maybe we just can't see the connections." Kate stared out through the glass doors towards the lobby, withdrawn.

"Is that what you think?" Jia Li asked. "That there are no coincidences?"

"I don't know what I think," Kate said. "I was just speculating."

"Hey." Jia Li leaned in as if she were lassoing in Kate's attention, rescuing her from the crowd, the lobby, her worry, from nothingness.

"I think you *do* know what to think. You think there is some kind of destiny thing happening here, don't you? It's okay. You're allowed to have your own perspective."

"What if I'm working out what my perspective is?" She looked Jia Li in the eyes then blinked and studied her hands, clasped on her lap.

"Anyway, know what I think? I think you're kinda aloof. Yet you clearly have a huge heart."

"You really are direct." Kate squirmed.

"I try to be."

"I'm a little guarded, okay? It's my work, partly. And I know I just don't fit in. And I don't want to." She wrung her clasped hands.

"None of us fit in. There's no value in that anyway."

Kate looked up, but not at Jia Li directly. "But you know who you are. Maybe you don't fit into the mainstream, but you don't fit in in a way that makes you *part* of something. Your job—you have colleagues, right? And your rope stuff! People watch you do it, right? I had to look up what Shibari was. I bet it's an entire community. *I* don't fit in in a way that makes me alone. And lonely, sometimes."

"You mean because of your work?"

"Well, yes. And all that crap from my childhood. I guess I'm still hiding from that. Or just plain hiding that. This is a lot to talk about over beer in the middle of a quest." Kate laughed and unclasped her hands, resting them on her knees.

Jia had been holding herself back, but just as she couldn't help but put a hand on Kate when she'd collapsed into a slump after she'd shouted at the Gutovniks, once more she couldn't stop herself from offering comfort. She reached out a hand and wrapped it around one of Kate's hands, holding her fist in her palm.

"Hey. You belong to *us*. You belong to *this*. This—*quest*— as you called it."

Kate's eyes lifted to look right into Jia Li's. It was obvious to Jia Li that she had a difficult time maintaining eye contact.

It was so intense, Jia li felt it, and she felt that flutter, and then, she pulled back, releasing Kate's hand.

"Okay," Kate said.

"Okay."

"Truth is, I do feel like I belong to something. To Little Bird. The little girl who was cured. She went back to Mexico with her uncle but I feel like she belongs with me and I just can't shake it."

Jia leaned right in. "If you feel that way, why don't you go get her?"

Kate didn't answer straight away and stared into Jia Li's eyes as if pleading— for support, or validation, or something.

"I'm... I wanted to say before that I'm sorry your boyfriend was killed," Kate said.

"Thanks. I mean, we'd kinda broken up. I *think*. I cared for him, but we weren't really..." Jia Li struggled to convey the truth of how his death affected her, that tinge of indifference blended with shock and grief, all in the context of fearing for her mother's life.

"You weren't in love?"

"Exactly. That sounds callous I guess." Now she stared at her hands.

"No. Still, it's traumatic, that he was killed."

In the heavy silence that followed, Jia Li cast her eyes to the floor. "I had a girlfriend who basically left me after a year together. I thought what we had was great, but I guess she didn't. I don't really understand it to be honest. Then my father died, and I met Sam a few months later. I guess I liked Sam because he wanted to protect me, and that felt safe. He could be a little aggressive about it, but still."

Kate lowered her voice even more. "I'm sorry. I know how that hurts. I do know what it feels like when someone you care for can't accept you for who you are, or what you do."

"Actually I just learned today that someone I thought maybe didn't accept me completely actually accepted me more than I realized all along." Jia Li lowered her voice to a whisper and placed a finger on her lips. "My father sent me a letter apparently. *Shhhh.*"

"Sorry to interrupt!" came a loud, English accent. Suddenly Finley was there, standing right next to them.

Kate did a double take. "It was just getting really interesting, Finley—what—you look shaken. Are you okay?"

In fact, he was paler than usual, and slightly sweaty with bulging, red eyes.

"Join us," Jia Li said.

"Look, I don't mean to be a party pooper but... honestly, I just ate my dinner, then my headache got significantly worse, and suddenly I was Wallace again, and ermm. This is rather awkward actually, since we're in a bar...."

"Sit," Kate said.

Jia Li grabbed him a barstool.

"If I'm honest, I'm terrified," he admitted.

He did look more unwell by the minute.

"What happened?" Kate asked. She bit her upper lip.

"Did you time travel? Where did you go? What's happening?" Jia Li sat forward. She was too excited, which she failed to conceal.

Kate said, "It's all good, Finley. Just tell us."

"You know how Valeri said there are people attempting to close this connection?"

"Yes," Kate said.

"No," Jia Li said.

"I think I told you that," Kate said to her.

"Oh yeah."

"Well, so maybe that's what's happening. I mean, it's *been* happening, but today it was much worse. The pain in my head is worse. And it gradually closes the connection between me and Wallace. Today I felt like—like I was going to die. It's so awful. It's not the kind of pain I'm built to handle."

His voice grew louder and he stomped his feet like a child having a tantrum. "I am NOT made for this."

The three people at the bar near them and a handful more sitting at the tables nearby all stared at the trio now.

"The last thing we need is attention," Kate whispered to Jia Li.

Jia Li forced a laugh and put a hand on Finley's arm. "Okay, dear, I think you've had too much this time."

"I think we should go upstairs," she whispered to Kate.

Kate took his other arm. "C'mon my friend. Time to call it a night."

JUST AS FINLEY had known the mania of the crazed woman Evgenia earlier, he knew this decline into self—

it wasn't just the headache,

it was the weight of knowing what begged to be known,

and the pain of being the one to name it.

Still, in this interim, even as others bookended his central role, supporting him in a way he'd not experienced so far in his life, the mission that now took up space in his being trembled and shook, kicking up all that lay like silt at the bottom of his self.

He couldn't talk about it. He just wanted to go unconscious, lest he have to face it.

Kate and Jia Li took Finley to his room and eased him into bed with aspirin and reassurance.

"Whatever is happening, or worsening, we're not going to figure it out tonight," Kate said.

"Probably not," Finley agreed. "I'm sorry I made such a scene."

"It was just your turn," Jia Li said. "That's what my mother used to say to me. Everyone loses it. It was just your turn."

"I like her," Finley said.

Kate smiled. "Yeah, me too."

Kate then made him tea and tucked him in. Jia Li handed him the pack of cookies that room service replenished near the kettle each morning.

Kate suggested finding an American movie. Something to escape reality.

He responded to their ministrations with marginal dignity, slightly embarrassed.

"I'm a sook, aren't I?" he quipped.

No one disagreed.

He pouted somewhat, then berated himself. In his mind, a quest called for bravery, and he could not even muster self-control. Where was the analysis he'd so looked forward to? No more analysing a book. Now he had to live this, moment by moment. In the place of eagerness and the clear, bright sky which had lightened his spirits before,

there was only dread.

Maybe he just wasn't cut out for this mission, he considered, but he was too ashamed to even admit that to himself, much less out loud.

"My head really actually fucking hurts, so you know."

"You've made that clear, Finley," Jia Li said. "Let's all get some rest."

"It's just an intermission," he promised them as they left him. "I will be fine tomorrow."

AS FOR KATE—

while they'd spent their first day walking around the neighbourhood looking for the numeral *eight* on apartment doors, her own spontaneous crush on Jia Li, whilst mired in fascination, had also deepened into a sense of *inevitability*—

As if there were an unspoken place for Jia Li in her story, beyond this icon business. As if she, Kate, had just boarded an overcrowded bus and there was only one seat left, and Jia Li was the person next to that one seat.

And it was going to be a long, *long* trip.

It was terrifying and comfortable, all at once.

Now Kate lay in bed and watched the city lights play on the ceiling of her room, pushing away thoughts of danger and thinking too much about this *woman*.

Her phone buzzed.

There was no caller ID.

She watched it ring several times.

Normally she would never answer a call without a recognizable number. But after five or so rings, Kate answered it. She didn't say hello. She waited for echoing voices, the clack clack of keyboards, background static to confirm a spam call. Only too late she thought it might be the police looking for her, then her heart pounded in fear before she realized she was hearing the faraway white noise of a poor connection.

Then high pitched, heavy breathing.

Like that of a child.

"Kate?" a small voice spoke at last.

Kate's heart caught in her throat. "Little Bird? Is it you? Little Bird?"

"It's me," the girl said, matter-of-fact.

Kate's heart raced. She leapt out of bed and began to pace.

"Oh God, are you okay? Are you in Mexico?"

"Yes, in Mexico. At Tio's house. Not okay. You come, okay? I want to go home with you, Tia. Can you get me now?"

A shout in the background. A rooster crowed.

She got to Mexico somehow. Without a passport. She's there.

"Oh baby, I want to get you. You're with family, right?"

"But I want you and Victoria."

Kate felt a tear coming. She sniffed. What was she meant to do? Wouldn't it be kidnapping if she took her away from her uncle?

But she's not okay.

She was obviously *not* okay.

"You're there at the same address your uncle gave me? Number 43?"

She couldn't make out the street name. She should have asked when Jesús scribbled it down. She could only read the house number and suburb.

"I think so. Umm. I go see."

"Wait! Don't go!" Kate said, too late. The line abruptly disconnected.

"No!" Kate cried, futile though it was. She caught her breath and took the scrap of paper with the address out of her phone case. She looked it up on her phone, on Google Earth. Mexico. Guadalajara. Near a lake, Little Bird had said.

Lake Chalpa.

She cried.

She paced.

She rifled through her carry-on luggage, took out the novel *Ikona*, threw it to the floor, then her Kindle, then a makeup bag, then a folded up bunch of papers.

Little Bird's drawings.

She'd taken a bunch of them, but had been too afraid of her grief to look at them properly again.

She sat on the floor and spread them out.

Stick figure mamas, stick figure little girls holding mama's hand, giant waves with the mama, big, fat tears on little girl figures, and sometimes a stick figure man in the corner.

A few times—a stick figure man in the corner.

The man in the corner.

Kate had never noticed before that he had red eyes. What was he doing in the corner?

The man in the corner and the mama and little girl.

Kate had always thought they were saying goodbye. Or maybe that the girl was trying to save mama from the wave, the hurricane.

But maybe not. Maybe—Kate squinted and bit her lip, that stick figure man in the corner had bigger stick hands then the mama or child. *And those red eyes.*

Her stomach began to clench. Her jaw tightened. She remembered when Jesús had come to get Little Bird—his hand, grabbing the girl's shoulder roughly, taking her by the arm and pulling her towards him.

And how Little Bird shrank in his presence, meek and accommodating.

The clenching in Kate's gut turned to churning.

Maybe she'd interpreted those drawings all wrong. Maybe Little Bird's mother had been taking her away from the uncle. Running away with her. Because he hurt her.

Maybe he'd hurt them both.

Or was hurting Little Bird now.

Kate began to sob.

Why had she let her go?

She didn't know. Her intuition hadn't been switched on to that channel. She'd wasted all her time and attention on someone else's magic and had missed the most important thing.

She took Little Bird's passport out from where she kept it hidden in an inside pocket of her carry on. She looked at the girl's face, a much younger face, searching for her soul, for certainty. Jia Li was right. She had to go to her. There was nothing she could do that night, though, so Kate cried herself to sleep and told Little Bird through the ether, *I will come for you someday soon, baby.*

In Atlanta, the small Asian woman, just over five feet tall, arrived in baggage claim looking for "a giant woman with a large bosom, and she may *appear* to have the physique of a man. And please be polite."

Those were Jia Li's exact words to her mother Mary, who merely raised her eyebrows both at the verbal description, as well as at the sight of the actual person towering over the assembled crowd with an eager, searching look.

Victoria spotted the older lady easily, as aside from being so small (she was hardly the only older Asian lady on the flight from Hong Kong), she was pale with a greenish pallor, shuffling along in obvious discomfort. She had that look—like the life was draining out of her. Victoria knew that look from Little Bird, and from her father, whom she had watched from afar on more than one occasion, in secret, those few times she'd gone south to see her mother.

In fact, Victoria and Mary spotted each other at once, at which point the older lady burst into a life-affirming grin.

"Let's get you home to rest for the night," Victoria said. "What would you like to eat? I have some casseroles you might like. And you must drink plenty of water, as you need to hydrate. Don't worry, you'll be better soon, I promise."

"I'm not hungry at all," Mary replied. "But bed would be most appreciated."

"Well, I'm giving you herbal tea," Victoria said, to which her companion responded with a weak smile, "Very kind. That will be sufficient."

They rode together on the airport trains to baggage claim without saying much else, but Mary felt it: there was a certain understanding between them. Jia Li had told her mother unfathomable things about her upcoming journey ahead in Georgia, which the older lady felt she may as well believe, given the lack of alternatives. Besides, her daughter was trusting her with a friend, albeit a new friend, by the sound of it, and this small window into Jia Li's life filled her with nearly as much hope as the magical cure which supposedly, improbably, awaited her.

As for Victoria, well, seeing as she'd been given access to a miracle, she was going to do whatever she could to do God's work. Not to mention, to help Kate however she could.

So, in companionable silence, Mary and Victoria emerged and exited into the parking lot, trudging towards Victoria's car.

"I know you only want tea. But I did bake some homemade banana bread for your arrival and I think you need to have a piece," Victoria said.

"Okay," Mary said. "By the way, are you a man, or a woman? I don't mind either, I just like to understand things better. My daughter will tell you that I ask a lot of questions. And thank you for getting me. I feel absolutely terrible. I thought maybe I'd just die on the plane and you'd get my body on a stretcher."

"I am so happy you didn't. And I'm so happy to answer all your questions, Mary. But it'll be far more pleasant with tea and banana bread."

So it was that they arrived at Victoria's apartment as improbable confidantes,

and there they were—

eating banana bread with herbal tea,

safe in an alliance which, whilst defying their opposite pasts, tentatively promised a shared destiny.

18

YOUNG KATYA & K.I. GUTOV
APRIL 1996
ST. PETERSBURG, RUSSIA

On this particular day, the bells of St. Isaac's Cathedral welcomed spring's first tourists, and—who knows how these things happen—all the loveliest boulevards and squares shed their inhospitable frozen layers. The cheerful babble of foreign tongues resounded in dusty museums and palaces, whose windows and doors were thrown open for the warmer season. Shoots of grass pressed tenderly towards the sun, and tiny green buds erupted on spindly black branches. Soon the countryside would be filled with the cuckoo's song, a Tarkovskian echo at last finding its source.

And they came, some of them, to Konstantin Isakevich Gutov, a dedicated bachelor at fifty-three, a melancholic and monastic best-selling science fantasy author in the English language market with just two books to his name. Despite his overseas success, in his homeland his reception was lukewarm. He reasoned that perhaps this was due to his dislike for vodka, winter, and caviar—that in effect, he was being divinely punished for betraying his national character. His father had once drawn his thick, wrinkled fingers along dusty Tolstoyan spines as if to invoke an honorable ancestor, emphasizing certain words with outbursts of spittle.

"Your hero, Yuk-Or Ba, seems to be searching for *personal* fulfilment, Kostya, of a very *Western* nature! What is the dialectic? And what of the rubbish on the streets? The graffiti? The price of bread?"

There was no rubbish, graffiti, or bread in Gutov's novels, and there was no dialectic. In point of fact, the novels were set on a planet very much like Middle Earth, only with alien invaders, their mining operations, and some massacres for good measure. Gutov tried to explain this, but as always became flustered under the glare of his father's scrutiny. On this particular occasion, Gutov had knocked his teacup off the coffee table, blood rushing to his cheeks. The floorboards creaked when he bent down to gather the cup's remains, and slivers of china quivered in a pool of caramel-colored tea.

Tolstoy's tomes now lined Gutov's shelves, centimeters below the framed photo of their former owner. His father impassively stared out with eyes that seemed to follow Gutov everywhere.

Despite the scorn lavished on his books domestically, for some inexplicable reason foreign fans with even the tiniest drop of Russian ancestry in their blood were compelled to seek him out. Perhaps, Gutov thought, they were like dogs drawn to other dogs' shit, or perhaps they were convinced that in Gutov's tales their Slavic origins gained some kind of importance or renewed life. They demanded a third book—and he was contractually obligated to produce one—but Gutov could not comply. Indeed, he refused. He had taken his character so far that only a divine revelation would be a fitting conclusion, a spiritual epiphany of sorts, something which had eluded Gutov, and which he therefore could not deliver to his readership. He wished only to write it so that he might abandon this life and begin another: he dreamt of a kind of Thoreauvean exile to a quiet wood, of sitting by a body of water, alone with the vigor of the elements, to await whatever god might appear to him.

But for now, on this late morning in early spring, there were visitors to entertain, and they stood in his doorway. A mother and daughter it would seem, the latter a small girl of six or seven, her head eclipsed by a faux fur hat, nose swollen and red. Her mittened hand inexpertly brought an ice-cream cone to her mouth. Her lips, already sticky sweet, were glazed in milky white.

"Konstantin Isakevich Gutov?" asked the woman.

Gutov nodded. She looked him up and down: his height, his paunch, the white bristle, his black trainers. "Valeri sent us here. We met him in Berlin. We have come from Ohio."

"I know. He told me," Gutov replied.

A FEW MINUTES later Katya Dmitrieva contentedly bounced on the couch. Her eyes flitted around the room then lingered on a photo of three men in military uniform, ascending in height and age from left to right. The tallest one was I.V. Gutov, the writer's father.

"Well, she had a dream," said the mother, Galina. Katya, having had the dream herself, and no doubt having heard her mother talk about it before, did not react. Galina pursed her fleshy lips, painted a garish red, and squashed her generous bosoms flat as she pulled her black woollen cardigan tightly around her. Gutov judged her to be in her mid-thirties; still voluptuous, not yet stout.

"It was memories, it seems. She felt they were memories. She said to me—" Here she looked at her daughter for confirmation. "Mama, we lived along the little river—she means the Moika—and she said, Daddy was writing a book about the great transformation and we had a puppy who wore a pink bow. Yes, she said *pink bow*."

Galina stopped abruptly as if puzzled by this mundane detail.

Gutov allowed his eyes to drift to Katya, whose glare met him head-on.

"We had to leave, you see." The little girl spoke directly to him. Despite her age and size, she had the self-assurance of a much older child.

Gutov cleared his throat. "So...you've returned, then?"

Katya nodded, bouncing more insistently as she did so.

"You came to Russia because of her dream?" he addressed Galina.

"Yes—I mean, no. My family left before the Revolution, in 1916..."

Somehow, she could not continue that particular thought, and smiled wanly.

Gutov nodded in his best imitation of sympathy.

She waved a finger in the direction of the photo, the men in uniform. "You understand the weight of one's history. One of these men was your father?"

"My father is the one on the far right."

"A Soviet hero. Of Jewish ancestry?"

"On the question of his Jewry, he was silent. He defended Leningrad during the siege. He was a doctor, head of a tuberculosis unit."

"To have been raised by such a man... quite a role model."

"He did not raise me," he said. His mind threw up an image of Yuk-Or Ba, orphaned by war, and he drummed his fingertips on his knee.

The elder Gutov's belongings still lay here and there—his winter coat on a peg near the door, his yellow-orange velour armchair brought from the crumbling Khrushevka apartment he'd left, a relic, so tacky in this modern, European-style apartment.

Gutov said, "I have cousins in America, in France. I don't know them, of course. My parents lost touch with their parents decades ago. Have some more tea? Katya, take more *pirozhki*."

Katya took one obediently.

"Where did your family settle?" he asked.

"My great grandparents settled in Berlin, then Paris, when my grandmother was still a teenager. Some of my family moved to America in the 1950s."

"What was their family name? Perhaps I have heard of them."

He said this last purely for the sake of appearing polite and interested, which he was not. So far, this meeting was like so many others.

"I doubt you know of them. They were not people of means or connections, and I'm afraid they all left Russia so long ago. They were prescient."

"I see." Gutov reached for his teacup, the thin-as-eggshell china that had belonged to his mother. For guests only. He recalled a visit by a certain clergyman, a dissident, short and wizened with a gravelly voice. How Gutov's stoic mother trembled, pouring the tea into these same cups, whispering about personal salvation. She had raised him, on her own.

"My great-grandfather was writing a book before the Revolution," Galina continued. "He was very influenced by theosophy. He was a personal acquaintance of Helena Blavatsky, you know, when she was very old. His book was a spiritual-philosophical work on Russia's destiny. It was lost, apparently, during the voyage to Berlin. Or perhaps he destroyed it. My grandmother told me about it. She spoke of how he had become embittered and depressed, and no longer believed Russia would be anything but backwards."

Galina was evidently having difficulty restraining herself. Her eyes sparkled and her cheeks were flushed. She leaned forward and brushed a strand of hair from her cheek.

"My grandmother—oh, she was an extraordinary woman. She was psychic. She told people many things that came true. None of her acquaintances ever lost anything for long, for example—she could locate any object just by asking its owner to hold the missing item in their mind."

Katya yawned and rubbed her eyes.

"She died when I was only fifteen. Shortly before her illness she said that she would be back, reborn in me."

Gutov was, it must be said, used to such confessions. His own fertile imagination evoked that in others, he believed. He dimly registered the knowing, almost smug look which passed between mother and daughter. His thoughts wandered for a moment to the fern on the windowsill. Its small leaves had gone alarmingly yellow, those at the top brittle as crepe paper. He felt such pity for it, the poor plant, suffering in this overheated apartment, suffering as well from the cold draft of the small, opened *fortochki*, the only relief in this place. He would have to remember to water it later. Then he had the inspiration to make full use of this immediate source of sympathy by transferring his concern for the plant to the woman. He concentrated on the plant as he frowned at the woman.

But what had she said? That her grandmother had told her she would be *reborn* in her?

The woman and her child were staring at him. The child. *Ah.* He understood.

"You see?" Galina asked.

"You refer to reincarnation."

"Precisely."

"It is a very interesting concept. Yes, I've actually borrowed a few ideas from Buddhism in some of my novels—more for cosmological coherence, really, than as a plot device."

He struggled to restrain a yawn.

"It's unremarkable," Galina said flatly. "But in this case it has some relevance, because Katya *remembers*. She said that we must come to St. Petersburg. There's more. Katya feels certain that the transformation my great-grandfather was writing about is underway. She feels that someone—a man—is continuing a great work that has been lost. That he is the spiritual heir of the great Nicholas Roerich, the painter and thinker, he who revealed the presence of Shambhala to the modern world! I've read your books, Konstantin Isakevich, and I am a big fan, but truly, I believe that you are not just a novelist of great talent. In *The Planet's Relapse,* you finally approach the truth, drawing on profound intuition, and I would dare to say—on knowledge gained in another life. I quote from memory:

THE ICON WOULD LEAD *the followers to its origin in the deepest reach of mystical Shambhala. That this Kingdom of Heaven exists amongst us is undeniable. It shall be reached only when the destined explorer awakens from his dreams of fantasy, to don the cloak of truth. He will enter pure of heart, his mind freed from all doubts...*

. . .

GALINA HAD SPOKEN PASSIONATELY with a sonorous voice, eyes cast heavenward. Now, she took a deep breath and grasped the wooden armrest of the couch, her face red. She looked like a peeled, fat beetroot. And suddenly, she looked all too familiar. Gutov's stomach stirred unpleasantly, but his mind fogged over and he couldn't place her. He leaned back into his armchair, even felt himself lean his head back involuntarily, to distance himself from her.

She spoke gravely.

"Konstantin Isakevich. I have come to awaken you! You see, when Yuk-or Ba in *The Planet Rises* declares that his homeland has suffered so that a precious hope could grow, and this hope would be like a seed of a new kind of spirituality that would change the world for the better—he was speaking of Russia, of course. And in *The Planet's Relapse* you then express—I mean Yuk-or Ba expresses—despair that he would never live to see that day. He must discover this truth in your next book, the manifest revelation of your own intuitive progression!"

She took a sharp breath and continued. "You must not allow Yuk-or Ba to feel despair, Konstantin Isakevich. Katya comes from a long line of women who divine the future, and her dream is true. It has already begun."

Katya had been sitting sedately, almost drowsily, but now, having had her fill of snacks and evidently unable to continue, she picked up a napkin and began systematically tearing it so that the edges were ragged and comb-like in appearance.

Throughout Galina's speech, Gutov had experienced confusion, interest, annoyance, impatience—they had managed to fuse together into a tasteless lump of discomfort, which he swallowed with difficulty. Galina let go of the armrest and sat back in her chair. There was something beyond irksome and eccentric about her. Again, something was *familiar*—was it her passion and ideological fervor?

She was part foreign and part Russian. A mongrel—was that the source of the familiarity? Frank, the American translator of Gutov's last novel, had told him that immigrants and artists are alike in one thing: they live in two worlds and belong to neither. For the immigrant, there is the remembered world of their homeland, and the real world of exile. For the artist, there is the imagined world of their conjuring, and the real world of day to day existence.

"Artists at least belong to Truth," Frank had said, and Gutov sagely agreed.

Frank occupied two worlds as well. His grandparents were Old Believers, immigrants of two generations ago. He was the only one of all his family members with a passion for his heritage. He had taught himself Russian, and aligned himself with Russian artists.

He was the only kindred spirit Gutov had met in his life's journey so far; the only person who imposed no judgements on Gutov's creative work. As if in counterpoint, he caught a glimpse of his father's bookshelf through an open door, and felt rather than saw the inert presence of his first book, its spine uncreased. He bristled. When Gutov's second book, *The Planet's Relapse*, came out, his father asked, "How is Yuk-Or Ba these days, Kostya? Is he after the key to human existence? Will he apply it to the betterment of his fellow citizens? Or reach for God while the masses starve?"

"I don't know, Papa. He is always evolving."

Gutov had scowled and taken a vigorous gulp of his coffee. He scalded his mouth and winced as tears stung his eyes.

Then his novels began to sell all over the world. After the money from books one and two had afforded the elder Gutov a most comfortable retirement, with every domestic luxury, including a Bosch washing machine and dryer and dishwasher, he asked, "And how is Yuk-Or Ba now? Has he understood yet the concept of the greater good, or does he seek his own spiritual fulfillment, like others mine for diamonds in Africa? You know about the child workers?" He tut-tutted.

"He believes the latter will achieve the former."

"Gmmph," the elder Gutov replied, pulling a face.

Galina-the-mongrel stared at him; the girl stared at him. He would again have to ask Valeri, his former Russian editor who now lived in Germany, exactly how he knew this woman. Apparently, she had *new* money, implying connections to tracksuit-wearing thugs in the streets of New York. Whatever the case, with this new money she funded a popular literary magazine with a spiritual-political orientation, and it was published on both sides of the Atlantic. *Voices of Truth* it was called. The magazine was gaining popularity both in émigré communities and in Petersburg. Now, as he considered the reason for her visit, Gutov's hands became clammy with expectation, and to his surprise he had a vision of his father thumbing through Galina's magazine with a broad grin on his face. He brushed aside the image and studied the dying fern on the windowsill.

"What do you want from me?" he asked, snappish. Then, looking straight at his mongrel guest, he saw *her*. With her coiffed, blond helmet, her tailored dress, neat cardigan, and her wild-eyed ideological passion, Galina looked remarkably like Valentina Filippova, professor of philosophy, expert in historical materialism. The married woman for whom the elder Gutov had left his wife and young son all those decades ago.

The mongrel did not respond. Galina lifted the teapot from the coffee table and poured a drop into her cup. She swirled her cup around and drank, then put it back onto the table. She turned to her daughter and placed a hand on the little girl's knee.

"Katya?" Galina prompted.

The girl replied in her small, little girl voice, "Yes, Mama?" She folded her small hands on her lap and addressed the writer.

"Konstantin Isakevich, you must write a book to tell the world about Russia's spiritual destiny, about our true Shambhala, in order to instruct humanity how to reach it. I saw it in my dream. My great-great-grandpa was handing you *his* book. He says *you* are to write it now."

Gutov could not restrain himself, not even with a child.

"Little girl, do you tell many people to do things because your dreams tell you so?"

"Yes," Katya said. She evaded his intense stare and looked to her mother for support.

"She has a gift," Galina said.

To Galina he asked, "You came to Russia for this reason? To speak to me? For this child to speak to me?"

"I am a great fan of your books."

"Yes, I appreciate that."

Gutov tried to appear appreciative. Now, more than ever, she resembled the busty ideologue who'd stolen his father. Decades later, Valentina Filippova had died not long after his own mother—and so Gutov's father was left a widower, which is how the old man came to him, pleading for reconciliation. He hardly survived on his pension, was unable to look after himself. So Gutov took him in and cared for him for five years until his death. After a lifetime away, the old man reunited with his son just when the money had begun coming in from Gutov's first novel.

The two of them—bilious bachelors, discovering their mutual love of *kotletki* garnished with dill and cream, black coffee for breakfast with a slab of black bread, Wagnerian operas. The father, consumed with anger over the state of robber capitalism. The son, increasingly monkish, doing battle with his muses. As it turned out, they got along remarkably well. Still, there were the old man's final words, as he slurped chicken broth in his hospital bed hours before the fatal heart attack: "Keep writing, Kostya. You're making a good living, and that's what seems to matter most these days."

Gutov shifted in his armchair, agitated, unsure how to repel the knife point of bitterness that had suddenly assaulted him. Why had he not defended himself? He could have told his father the source of his inspiration—that his books might give someone hope. The world might crumble around you, but there was still the search for one's soul, *dusha*. This *dusha* was his Russianness intact, a filament of hope and agony and yearning. A personal journey to a personal end.

"Will you do it?" Galina asked, hesitantly, like a small child promised a special gift, and doubting its imminent manifestation.

"Do what, exactly?" He blinked the room back into focus.

"Why, write this book, of course."

Gutov considered his options in an instant—there were few—the woman was clearly mad, but also influential—so he decided to mollify her, without committing himself. Mustering a semblance of enthusiasm, he replied, "Oh, yes, yes. Certainly I will consider your request with a good intention."

She looked wholly unconvinced, still on the edge of her seat, wide-eyed, her dumpling mouth rubbed free of lipstick, moist with expectation. They stared at one another in stalemate. Finally, he clarified.

"The truth is, my sales and my reviews *here*, in my own country, are so dismal. I am shunned at conferences. I can no longer rouse myself to write. So there you have it. I fear I am unable to comply."

When he realized what he'd said, which he'd never said to anyone else, he instantly regretted it. But Galina seized upon the admission and said, "Well, I had no idea... but of course it makes sense. Your countrymen are desperate for practical solutions to difficult lives, and have forgotten the spiritual legacy that is their birthright! Please, Konstantin Isakevich, you must release the past and move forward. In the scope of history, it is the truth which will be remembered."

He dimly registered how at her suggestion 'to move forward' he had stirred with a sudden energy, then felt himself choke, throttled, thrust back into his familiar role.

"Well, that is why we came." Galina grinned, then stated her intention. "I mean, I would like to serialize your imminent work in my magazine... I mean, your upcoming novel, as you produce it!"

"Oh, I quite see, yes," he said, and then having nothing further to say, fell silent.

Galina took her daughter's hand and held it tightly in her own.

Gutov did the only thing he could do to end this awkward and pointless audience—he stood, excused himself, and went into the bathroom. He sat for some time on the toilet, exasperated to find that he did not need evacuation of any sort. He was irritated at his own narrative instincts, that his stories had attracted this sort of visitor. Did no one understand? The fate of their planet, of Yuk-Or Ba's planet—an ecological disaster! It was a given. But spiritual theories, religion, precepts— none of it would save anyone, that was never the point. Might hope? Personal salvation?

Shambhala, he believed, was an enlightened state of mind, not an actual place. The journey was personal. Yet his fans demanded a literal roadmap.

He stood, stretched, and lay in the bath, contorted, knees to chest, scowling into the overbright white porcelain of his modern 'European' apartment. Then he saw his childhood bathtub, its green enamel the color of overcooked peas. The same hue, he remembered, as the faded diamondesque flourishes on that apartment's peeling wallpaper, as the mold sporing on the wall behind the kitchen basin. He pictured his mother, downtrodden and alone, fingering a small icon hidden in her apron, and himself, so often in the care of his elderly grandmother. And, of course, this green hue was just one shade lighter than the green of his father's Soviet military uniform.

He could escape neither his father, nor his dismal life. All pretenses to literary ambition ultimately devolved into a metaphor of this nature—attempting to think his way out of cramped spaces cast in the past's dull, green-brown tint. Yet, in the midst of his despair, inexplicably he again felt himself roused, lurching inwardly, blindly, towards change.

But he could not change.

"Are you okay, Konstantin Isakevich?" Galina's voice rang out.

"Yes," he replied.

Time did not cooperate. Like him, it was constipated and he cursed.

"Did you say something?" called Galina.

The woman has the hearing of a hound, he thought.

"No!"

Surely a half hour must have passed since he left the living room. Gutov said loudly, "I'm not feeling very well. So sorry! You may let yourself out, and leave me your name and contact details on a piece of paper. I will call you with an answer soon. If you like!"

"Oh, we are in no rush," Galina said. "Do you need help at all?"

"No," he growled.

. . .

WHEN GUTOV HAD last met Frank, on a book tour in the latter's native Oregon, they had gone fly fishing. Frank's idea, of course. Gutov was neither athletic nor outdoorsy; he was slothful and contentedly cerebral. Nevertheless, he trusted Frank's judgment. Within two hours they were deep in primeval forests of birch trees, so reminiscent of Karelia, where Gutov had summered in his youth, that he exclaimed so.

"Well, of course, that's why I've taken you here," replied Frank, adding, "It's a meditation." He released his line in an undulating arc that folded back on itself before it reached out again, beyond where Gutov could properly see, a sliver of light refracted in the still, dark river, gleaming in a haze of summer humidity. The line was beyond all control, Gutov thought as he held onto the rod Frank handed him. He prayed that he could maintain his balance over the slippery rocks as he reeled in whatever might pull against him.

"I was sorry to hear about your father's passing," Frank said as they stood knee-deep, squinting into the mirrored water.

"He was old," Gutov said.

"Did he have a chance to read your second novel before he died? I know you always held out hope."

"I don't think he even read all of my first novel. He did buy that one when it came out, but he preferred realism. When communism collapsed, and there were stories on the news about Stalin, the deportations, the camps, he stopped watching television. He began to drink. He believed the world was ending. His world *did* end, in point of fact."

The line in Gutov's hand jerked.

Frank took his rod. "You reel it in a bit." He did so. "Then let it run." He let the line go and the fish swam away. "It struggles too much to reel in at once. It could break the line. So you allow it to fight. When it wears itself out, then you can bring it home. Today, we will release it."

Gutov had found the cycle of struggle and release captivating, and it distracted him from his thoughts.

Now, in his cramped bathtub, he relived it, mesmerized in memory's grasp, withdrawing into his own private war against the enemy within. How could he never have demanded even one, measly compliment of the father who'd abandoned him? Some bare acknowledgement?

His heart, his very soul, thrashed like the fish at the end of the line. He startled at a vision of his father in full Soviet regalia patiently reeling him in, at a vision of *himself* as the frantic fish. It was *his* rage, *his* fear that he thrashed against, and as the water rushed into his eyes and nose, even as he was given the opportunity to be free again and again, still he found every excuse to fight, until some mysterious energy surfaced in him suddenly,

filling him completely,

and he recognized the futility of his struggle and surged past it.

He saw that the line was a string of light connecting father to son, dancing on the dark surface, pulling him back to their morning coffees, as they bickered like a married couple over the last blob of butter for their bread, as they sat for hours together, just reading. Chuckling together, over some witty opinion piece in the newspaper. His father rapt as the younger Gutov described the modernist performance of the Ring Cycle at Covent Garden. Mutual praise for the perfect meal, eaten in companionable silence.

And then Gutov fell back again into the dark river, where though his rage lingered yet, a new wish began to carry him towards the surface—a wish to stop struggling against the past, against himself, against an enemy who lived no more, who had never truly opposed him.

His freedom lay only in this, the blessed cessation of fighting, in surrender, and he grew fervent in his determination to end all struggle. Then abruptly it happened: his anger and hurt evaporated, mist burnt up by the sun, and his heart rushed forward further than ever before, towards hope.

Gutov unfolded his legs and peered around. He felt the gloom of his brown-green-pea world quietly fall away, to be replaced by the glare of his porcelain bath. He grinned stupidly.

WHEN HE EXITED the bathroom at last, Katya lay sprawled on the couch, the shadowy evening light dancing on her face as she stared at the ceiling and hummed to herself. Galina peered hopefully into Gutov's eyes. She sat unnaturally upright and in a voice laboring under the gravity of her expectations, said, "I am listening, Konstantin Isakevich."

"*Ladno.* I will write it, and you can serialize it," he spoke to Galina.

Then, "Katenka!" He turned to the little girl, who at the sound and tone of his voice sat up quickly.

"Yes Konstantin Isakevich?"

He peered directly into her eyes.

"What do you desire in your life, child? Don't fib."

She looked up and to the right, pensive. Gutov waited. Seconds ticked on. Galina appeared nervous and wrung her hands.

"I desire pizza for dinner. And *Guess* jeans. And I desire to walk along the Fontanka and see if there are ducks, because I like to feed ducks. Also, I desire to go someplace where I can play with children. I like hide and seek. And bedtime stories."

She looked straight into his eyes, as if daring him to deny her any of this.

He smiled gently.

"Good, good. Listen here. Your desires, little girl, are messages from your soul. Only take care to follow the desires which come from your passionate heart, and not from the part of you that sometimes must do what she is told. Freedom is for those who know themselves truly. Can you repeat that, to make an old man happy? *Freedom is for those who know themselves truly.*"

She repeated it back to him and giggled. He patted her on the head.

Very shortly, as daylight made its final descent through black branches, after a fluttering of papers and the exchange of particulars, followed by kisses and a wild embrace (Galina's of course), the visitors departed.

Starting that same night, Gutov wrote in a fever, day after day, so that he had completed the manuscript of *Ikona* within three months. He dedicated the book to his father:

"For the elder Gutov, navigating the streams of eternity, from a humble son, who has been freed."

Then, he boarded a plane for Siberia, bound for Lake Baikal, his own mystical Shambhala.

He did not know if he would ever return.

19

WALLACE & THE SAFE PASSAGE
JUNE 2131 AD
KRASNOYARSK, EASTERN FEDERATION

Justicia lay with her legs across Wallace's abdomen, so that they made a cross. Her head hung over the bed. Through the slatted blinds, muted daylight drew stripes on Justicia's thighs.

"What happens when you go into the past? Is it like a dream? Do you watch it like a movie? You make odd sounds, and you can be gone for mere minutes and then you report on days and weeks of events. Does it feel like you are gone that long?"

"It's not easy to explain," he began, and traced a line on her leg down to her foot. He loved the contrast of his black skin with her white. Such a contrast had once promised a statistical advantage for survivability, before it was confirmed that gene therapy did not work.

We are a perfect match anyway, thought Wallace. He studied her small nose and her faint orange eyebrows, raised now in expectation of a reply. He could not help but stroke her nose and touch her lips with a finger.

"Try to explain, please," she said, and pretended to nibble his finger.

"I'm thinking about how to do so," he assured her, although not wholeheartedly. "It's noisy here. Hard to concentrate."

"Excuses," she teased. But then there was a man shouting from somewhere, and a woman calling back to him. The Council District was high density. The view through her blinds revealed the red brick buildings of the neighboring block.

Justicia was draped like a bird against Wallace's solid thighs. He knew her now, the tiny, pale freckles beneath her eyes, her defenseless way of laughing, as if at any moment she'd be chastised for misbehavior. She was softer with him, so much more vulnerable than he'd expected. Wallace felt a deep need for her to understand and know him completely, and searched for the perfect words, to find an explanation even he had not fully arrived at yet.

"You say *go to the past*, but it's not exactly like that, because I *become* Finley. I am there, in a full life. There is no travelling. It's like I wake up as him, and when I begin to recount it, it is like I am still somewhat Finley waking from a dream. Only then do I realize that I am Wallace, and it wasn't a dream."

"That's... fascinating. But, I don't understand the passage of time," she said, her face pink from being upside down. She took one of his hands in hers and kissed his knuckles.

"There, you mean?"

"No, I mean, it seems you experience him... chronologically. As if you are living parallel lives, only his is in the past and yours is now. I mean, rather than randomly finding yourself at different parts of his timeline."

"I can only describe it like this: we seem locked into—it feels like a loop. As if we are one person, living simultaneously, and on different timelines. It's not as I would expect. It's really impossible to explain. I'm not a scientist, after all."

"It's so fascinating. Not at all like the experiences mediums are said to have. It's more immediate."

"It is the most real thing I have ever felt. Other than this."

He felt into the settled feeling of them, and rested his hands on her warm, bare thighs.

Her head still dangled off the side of the bed. She lifted her head to acknowledge him.

"How do you reach him, Wallace? Is he there, waiting for you? Or do you direct yourself in some way?"

"It used to be accidental. I found myself as him, suddenly. And then, as I became him more and more, and the cross became so... compelling... I figured out a way to reach him at will. To avoid other experiences, other times, other scenes, and go to him."

"Oooh, do tell!"

She slid off the bed and rearranged herself, lying against his shoulder, her hand placed on his chest.

"It's like a tone, like music. That's the only way I can describe it. It's like I am tuning myself into a particular tone. I know the tone that is Finley. I feel it rise up inside me, like a vibration, and there is a match. We are the same tone, and suddenly I am there. I do this in our sessions. And sometimes, but rarely, it happens spontaneously when I am alone. But in those cases I have no one to tell when I awaken, so I lose much of the information I think."

"This is amazing," she said. "You must explain this in more depth at our next session. You've not mentioned this before, that you have this much agency in the process. Lucio needs to know this. Schopel too, no doubt."

Wallace rested his chin on the top of Justicia's head and breathed her in. It was almost too much, like he was drunk or obsessed (he had never been drunk and didn't know the difference, but assumed it was a similar experience of being out of control). He didn't know what to do about this connection, how to love another person, or integrate her into his life.

His mind turned to their project.

"Why are you participating in this project, really, Justicia? You have no obligation. Don't say it's because of me, since you committed to it before us."

She looked up at him from his chest.

"I would like to die having done my best for the future inhabitants of this earth. And personally, I would like my legacy to be a successful project, or at worst, if it fails like the others, no one need know of my involvement, and my legacy remains intact. If it succumbs to scandal, that is a whole other dilemma entirely."

"Ah. A legacy. My path on the other hand is to be unknown, to be in service without reward. Well, there is satisfaction, I suppose."

"Really? Would that be enough?"

"To have played a part in saving humanity from dying out? I mean, yes, of course."

"It's fascinating isn't it? The personal gain from impersonal victory. I'm not doubting you. I'm merely pointing out that if this works, if you discover something of this icon which leads to a cure, and that cure ends up saving us—it might not take place in our lifetime."

She nuzzled her face into his chest, turning away from him.

He said, "I suppose I have been trained away from relying on or even expecting a reward in life."

"I know." Her voice was muffled against him. She turned her head to the side now so she could speak clearly.

"Spiritualists imagine only Heavenly rewards. But whilst we are here on earth, in bodies, you must admit that we are built to be driven for worldly gain. Generally, the ego likes tangible reward, a reward that feeds our separate identity, and enables the body-mind to survive. Such was the long obsession with money. Now it is merely power that egos attempt to capture."

"True. But I suppose I would derive personal satisfaction from having played my part," he replied.

"Unless you're playing the pawn in a bigger game," she said.

"What does that mean?"

"Schopel has hinted at it. She's spoken of factions, but not motivations. Not *agendas*. There are machinations, beyond the scope of our work and beyond what we understand in terms of politics."

Wallace didn't know what to say. Justicia sat with her back up against the wall and pulled the bedcovers up over their legs. She crossed her arms beneath her small, bared breasts.

"I'm not supposed to speak about anything, of course, but it hardly matters anymore. You of all people should know what is happening, as you may well hold the key."

Wallace readied himself. "Am I playing the pawn in a bigger game, then?"

"Look, it's not personal." She met his eyes, then looked away, seeming embarrassed.

"You are special, Wallace. Not all of us are evolved to the same degree. Some people are still tribal in orientation. They are filled with fear, and so they see the world in us versus them and seek power to alleviate the fear. Control. These kinds of factions, though not the majority, do have some power—primarily because they seek it. They put energy into seeking power and thus, over time, have accumulated it. Others like them join, contribute more energy and resources, and it snowballs so to speak."

"This is how a minority can still be a force to reckon with," Wallace said.

"Yes, exactly. And in this case, there are those who seek a cure to serve their own interests. Those who seek a cure with their evolutionary bias."

"In fear."

"Grabbing for power," Justicia nodded.

"To what end?"

"Power is an end in itself. In this case, the game seems to be to use power to maintain the power of those who have it, and to disempower all others."

"So." Wallace pulled the covers up to their waists. "They are seeking a cure to deny it to those of their choosing."

"It's worse than that," Justicia said. "There are those who wish to use genetic research to create a superior race, and also, a lesser race, more pliable humans, easy to manipulate, to serve those who will control. Or at the very least, to not question their agenda. And everyone else will simply be left to perish."

Wallace inhaled sharply. "And you know of this, directly?"

"Dr. Rinella knows more than me, but this is about me. I agreed to observe your project in case it works, and if it does, in order that history remain on the good side. On the *evolved* side. But we are taking risks every day. I only wish to work through existing channels, through the Triumvirate that has been functioning for more than thirty years, more or less successfully, rather than start again—which we have done, and it's a painful process, Wallace. It's not easy to create a new system. Do you remember how it began?"

"The Revolution?"

"Yes. But before that. After the populations realized that so much in our world was harming the human genome. The class action lawsuits against corporations from the 50's. First, the drug companies, then all those that polluted. Then, riots, the end of banks. Capitalism fell. Then Revolution, and finally, nuclear attacks. In that specific order. The order of things is important."

"Yes, yes."

"Well, it's happening again."

"What's happening?"

"The seeds of revolution. The foundation for upheaval. When the major powers are challenged, or broken apart by infighting, and combined with an external crisis, environmental or health, then human society collapses. Now we have Monasteries, the Council's administrative bodies, and the Sciences. It's an uneasy alliance. With depopulation, the Monasteries have acquired the largest percentage of the population, as you know, raising the children. That's the majority, Wallace, and it's only growing! Do you understand? We have a perfectly numb populace, thanks to the Cottage! Trained to disavow all cares for Earthly life. Easy to manipulate."

Wallace took a moment to respond, as he measured her words against the truth he knew from life in the Monastery. "I had never thought of it in exactly that way, but it's true what you say about the children raised in monasteries, indifferent. Numb, I would even say."

"Yes, well, that's how most adepts are—not you, you are unique, obviously. There are always exceptions. It's a perfect recipe for the success of a project that is looking for a population that just obeys. But then once that is discovered, and all ploys are eventually found out, there might be a strong reaction, a revolution even, and we are back where we began."

"So you think there is inevitably a drive towards the good, and people cannot be subjugated for long?" Wallace asked her.

"Yes, I suppose so. I never thought of it in terms of the good. History has shown again and again that humans cannot tolerate indefinite servitude in any form."

"So why do we keep doing it? Why are there those who do not learn from past mistakes?"

"Well." Justicia gave him an indulgent smile. "Of course, many do learn. But there will always be those with a lesser consciousness, with weaker morals, who take power."

"You have given up then, on a utopia of any sort?" He wrapped his arms around her spontaneously, and kissed her neck. She laughed, but pulled back.

"I suppose my hope has always been that with the right administration, lesser evolved forces would not gain the upper hand. I am weary, but I will do what I can, through my channels, until I die."

Wallace recoiled internally at her words. Everything was *until one died*. There was no other measure of time.

"And Schopel?" he asked, forcing his mind away from pessimism. "She's obviously on the side of the good."

"Yes. Hence her desire to protect you and whatever you discover."

"And no one was planning to tell me any of this? Schopel herself left this out of her speech when we met."

"It was not exactly relevant to her work with you, which is for psychic protection."

Justicia's cheeks suddenly flushed. She seemed to be becoming exasperated.

"Dr. Rinella has sworn to tell you everything, okay, but of late he is himself unsettled, and I believe he wished to spare you the stress, in case it should inhibit your visions. But there, I did it, saying more than I ought to have said once more." She lowered her forehead into her hands, but he took her hands and lifted her chin so that they could look into each other's eyes.

"No, Justicia, I should know this. It is my life here. All our lives. There is more at stake than I imagined. Will they succeed in finding a cure before us? This is an unsettling race. One I cannot control, alas."

"Shhh, Wallace. Rest easy. There is no pressure on you right now. We are fully in secret."

She smiled and placed her palm against his chest. He placed a hand on hers and held hers at his heart. Her cool, white hand stirred as if she were straining to extricate herself, though she didn't. Instead, she kissed his hand. He felt her breathing. Suddenly, feeling her presence on him, her weight in his heart, their work seemed more risky.

"We have more to do tomorrow Wallace. You should go, and you should rest so that in session you can do your magic. The bus departs in ten minutes." She glanced at a clock on the bedside table as she said it. Then she slid out of bed and, strolling to the other side of her bedroom, picked up his ochre robe from the floor. It spilled over her bare arms and covered her naked body entirely.

"Ridiculously heavy," she pronounced, and threw it at him. "Now. You will walk straight to the front door, and not be seen."

He dressed quickly. It took an hour on the District's only public bus to get back to the Monastery. If he left now, he could make it by sunset and attend Vespers. No one would know he'd been absent all day. Best not to draw attention to this affair, in case anyone asked for the identity of his lover.

Justicia flung open the bedroom door. Wallace could see there, in the living room, the gray hair of her cancered husband as he lay on the couch facing away.

WALLACE REAWOKE WITH A START, grasping his forehead. He blinked slowly. The room spun and for a moment he could not tell which way was up. Shadowy figures stood nearby, forming a blurry human periphery. He remembered who he was, then, with the same *drop* into being as he had experienced earlier when he dropped into Finley. *Ow, and my head*, he thought. He squeezed his eyes closed to try to lessen the pain.

"Finley is in pain," he told them.

"You too?" asked Dr. Rinella.

Justicia jumped up to grab a glass of water, and rushed to his side.

He still gripped his forehead. "I'm fine," he said, and he took a deep breath, and several gulps of water, all eyes on him.

They waited, Schopel leaning forward in her chair, steady and watchful. Dr. Rinella sitting back straight, rubbing his hands together in agitation. Justicia had returned to her chair, and was at the edge, as if prepared to leap up again at any moment.

Wallace began to recount all that he had just experienced. Berlin. The searing pain. The odd Russian woman, Evgenia, and her strange outburst. The German man, Valeri, and the postcard from Gutov. He felt ill with trepidation as he mentioned *those who spoke on the behalf of the future, who said the doors were closing*. He spoke at length, attempting to detail even the smaller impressions he had, as Finley, of all that had taken place, including the vastness of sky, Kate's rapid-fire Russian and her mood after.

When he stopped, he sank back into the armchair, resting his head onto the back, his body suddenly craving sleep. He semi-dozed in this manner, until the sound of Schopel clearing her throat and pushing back her chair startled him awake.

"You won't like what I'm about to say, and yet I think the time has come, and much sooner than I expected."

Schopel stood from her chair and went to stand at the window, holding her chin and frowning.

"The pain. It's because of the interference, I felt it too," she said. "And I do not have a good feeling about the visitors of which you speak, who supposedly speak on behalf of the future. Whose future? They are not on our side, and it seems they are getting closer to the truth, that Wallace here is onto something, as is Finley. There can be only one outcome in our era, and that is that they find Wallace, and use him to discover the icon, and its origins. So we must go."

"Please explain," Justicia demanded, to which Schopel sighed heavily, shaking her head.

Justicia spoke again. "Please, Eden. I insist you share all that you know."

"I suspect I know where you're going with this," Dr. Rinella said. He sat back with a worried look.

Schopel spoke, "Suffice to say the faction that I left behind, which I attempted to neuter by my voluntary joining of the monastery—well they lack political power without me, that is certain. But I have recently become aware that they have been meeting in secret. They have designs on *control*. If they are aware of Wallace's sessions, they may already know how to find him."

She was sweating at her temples now, looking ever more resolutely out of the window at the gray skies and old buildings.

Dr. Rinella said, "You are implying that it is they who are in Finley's time, or their past selves as it were, acting on behalf of your former colleagues now."

Schopel now turned to face all of them. "What I most fear at this exact moment in time is that this faction may be attempting to stop Wallace's journeys and I am not sure to what lengths they might go in order to achieve it. So he is in danger. He's in danger via his mind—but if they know where his *body* is..." Schopel's voice grew at once quieter and more stern. "Well then they will finish what they started at the Cottage."

"What they started?" Wallace asked. "What do you mean, *what they started at the Cottage*?"

"I think you can guess," Schopel said, now turning towards him. "Or maybe you've always known. That's how this began. They failed then and, in fact, made of you a better conduit than they imagined possible."

"You mean, there are forces even within the Monastery who have been aware of me since the beginning of my life?" Wallace winced. "Forces that have been working with the government— with your faction? But how? For how long?"

Schopel looked up and out, across the buildings and towards the clouds, as if to transport herself there, or her mind anyway, as Wallace, tearing his eyes from her inscrutable face, had a flashback of the Cottage. Being held down. The patches stuck to his shaven head. The pain and terror. Ibiza and ash, the bodies of his parents, then blankness. The light. Searing, like a single point of consciousness blossoming out into inky black. It was the beginning, before time warped, before he began to travel. Stumbling into abilities that were indiscriminate and uncontrolled, without explanation, much less mentorship. He was only twenty. He was barely a man.

Justicia gripped the edge of her chair.

"Those who are blocking me, are they from the past or the present? And the Cottage—they were attempting to close my mind?" Wallace felt something stirring in him. Agitated, he pushed against it, feeling the blood rush to his legs, restraining his urge to leap from his chair and pace. His breath came fast.

Schopel turned to him, her back to the window, her face gentle and still, lined with sadness. "They are possibly from both the past and the present, Wallace, aware that you, and Finley, are the person who may be able to find a cure for the Cancer. I know some of the women and men behind it today. Unfortunately, they have an agenda that I do not share. You are in the way. Your body is the conduit, thus you are in danger. And, yes, they have allies in the Monasteries."

Wallace spoke again, now rubbing his temples, as if Finley's pain remained—it didn't—it was the memory of it that somehow guided his thinking, and his feelings, which rose like flames from his gut to his heart, and then ignited at his temples such that he felt hot. Ah, the pain, like a knife through his temples, he remembered it so well that it almost hurt now. He felt that urge to stand and run, and pushed against it once more, so that it collided with the heat in his body and exploded.

He was angry. For the first time that he could remember since boyhood.

Wallace slammed his hands down onto the armrests.

"Tell me the truth! They want to find the icon's origins in my past, don't they? In Finley's life, and use it selectively, to cure an elite, and to ensure we don't have any ability to access it in this era. They are prepared to let most of humanity die, for power."

Dr. Rinella and Schopel both froze for a moment, slack jawed.

Wallace raised his voice now, as Justicia shrank back in the shadows of his hot glare, aimed in her direction. "I deserve to know the truth!"

"I told him," Justicia said. "He does deserve to know the truth—that he is a pawn in others' games."

Dr. Rinella put his face into his hands. "I hate politics. I have had enough of this government. I am sorry, Wallace. I wanted to protect you from the distraction of these power games."

Wallace could not hold the anger for any longer; he balled up his fists to control it, the energy, the force; it lit him up - he so longed to launch it, to *use* it for good. But as he tensed, slowly, the moment began to pass. He felt the energy leave through the top of his head, and he leaned back into the chair, fighting the tears that suddenly appeared in his eyes for no discernible reason—

so much pressure to find the origin of this cross,

so much at stake,

and no one else could do it.

How could it be, after all of recent history, that still humans yearned for power, for control, for no other reason than to have power and control?

Wallace's attention wandered to the sky outside, the crumbling buildings in view, the glance of the Krasnoyarsk towers of the old city, far beyond.

Humans don't deserve this world, as sick as it is, he thought.

Justicia had tears in her eyes. She did not leap up and yell in his defense, or to attack the faction that opposed them, as Wallace would have expected. Instead, she remained sitting, as if defeated, wiping a tear from her eye as she said, "I agree, Lucio. This is obviously a rescue mission as much as it is a quest for a cure. I had hoped those days of protecting the good people were over."

Schopel said, "The truth, Wallace, once more, is that these factions do not know about the icon. *Yet.* They only know that you are close to finding a cure via a past consciousness. When these people interfere, it is as if they wield psychic knives, piercing you, hurting Finley, but they do not, they cannot, be inside your head, understand? They can only ever be inside their own minds, present and past. They do not see what you see. They see what they see—past and present. But right now..." She gave a great sigh. "Right now, the more important question is, where can we hide you?"

DR. RINNELLA STOOD up with a heavy sigh. "It's time. Follow me, I know a safe passage and a safe room."

"From the Revolution?" Justicia asked.

"Yes." Dr. Rinella began to explain as he moved around his office, collecting various items into a pile on the floor: a carafe of water, glasses, a reading device, a stone from his desk, a large box. "First it was a nuclear fallout shelter—during the times of chaos in the 2060s, after the Adjudicator lawsuits brought down Corporatism. *Wallace* carry that," he pointed to the box on the floor. "Justicia, please put those items in this bag." He handed her a canvas sack he had retrieved from his desk drawer. She began to fill the sack as he continued.

"Over the following twenty years as more violent factions emerged, leading up to and during the Revolution, those factions used a network of underground tunnels to distribute arms and blow up their targets—the government holdouts. The room we are going to was part of that network."

"I've heard rumors that they still exist," Justicia said, "but if you know about them, wouldn't others?"

"They've largely been abandoned. The one I have in mind is hidden in plain sight," Dr. Rinella said, "I have been attempting to look after it, in anticipation."

"You've prepared it in anticipation of this?" Justicia barked. "Lucio? You have been expecting this all this time?" Her neck was drawn and taut. She cradled the sack of items Dr. Rinella had assembled.

He and Schopel exchanged glances—which, Wallace noticed, neither Wallace nor Justicia missed. Schopel was poised at the door, now serene and mutely holding a black bag in one hand, and a container of something in another—*where did those things come from?* Wallace wondered. Dr. Rinella seemed to be tallying the items everyone held, as he pointed and mumbled, then he grabbed a few more things, some food, it looked like, dried pulses and oats, putting them into a large rucksack that he slung over a shoulder—and then, as if on autopilot, with an incongruous burst of affection, he watered his plants with a carafe of water from the windowsill.

Within the half hour, all four had exited Dr. Rinella's office, moving quickly down the dilapidated marble staircase and out the door into the alley. Just a few meters away Dr. Rinella, in the lead, took a sudden right through a smaller alley, and then another sharp right hand turn to a passage with a door-sized grate. He pushed it open and led them into what seemed to be an abandoned basement, smelling of mold and urine. No one spoke. They moved down a passageway until there was a row of arched openings, "where services were connected underground centuries ago," he explained. They went through one of them, which Wallace had the presence of mind to notice was the second to last one on the right. Down stairs then, and then left even further down stairs until they entered a tube-like tunnel that wound its way into cavernous dark. Ahead of them Dr. Rinella held a small lantern whose glow bounced off the round inner walls and lit their way, ten meters at a time. They walked for about thirty minutes and then ascended more stairs. Finally, they came into an open space.

"We are beneath the Monastery grounds," Dr. Rinella said. "These tunnels here and the safe rooms were built before the Monastery existed. Few today even know of their existence. Not to mention, no one would expect us here, so close to home, to your home, Wallace."

OUT OF NOWHERE CAME A DULL, muffled, *whooshing* sound, then a metal thump reverberated from deep within the walls, followed by the sound of a door creaking open, then shutting. There were a few seconds of silence, followed by footsteps. Everyone froze; Dr. Rinella stepped out in front of the others and immediately cut off his light. Suddenly, a larger, brighter light filled the space and within it a man appeared.

It was Alex, his face dull, expressionless. Unmoving, as if dazed; he merely stood, just a few feet away, a lantern dangling in one hand.

Alex—of all people, Wallace thought, and as if moved by some instinctive force, he stepped out from behind Dr. Rinella and said, "Alex! What are you doing down here?"

Alex didn't respond.

Dr. Rinella said, "Why are you here, young man?" but then Schopel silenced him. "Just a moment, Lucio."

Alex frowned, eyes downcast, then he looked up again and said, "I was—" he paused.

"—walking in the dark?" Wallace prompted. He put down the box he'd carried the entire way, and took a step closer to Alex.

Alex squinted. "Is that you, Wallace?"

"Yes. It's me. Why are you here, Alex?"

"I—I must have hit my head at the bottom," he looked around, dazed. "I came out here, somewhere."

"From your tunnel?"

"Ye—I—I mean *yes*," he stuttered, his expression quizzical. "I believe so."

"But the tunnel deposits you outside. You're inside now. Do you know where you are?"

Alex blinked slowly. "I cannot recall, actually."

Wallace began to consider that he should mention Alex's strange appearance at his door that morning, his odd questions—but before he could organize his thoughts, Schopel stepped in front of Wallace, blocking him, dropped her bag to the ground, and spoke directly to Alex as if issuing a command, "Young man!" Then to Dr. Rinella, "Lucio, your lantern please."

Lucio handed her his lantern. Schopel lifted it up to Alex's face and switched it on. "Look at me," she instructed.

He winced and his eyes fluttered as they adjusted to the brightness, but he did as instructed.

"His pupils are dilated," she said, and handed Lucio's lantern back to him.

She took Alex's free hand, the one not holding his lantern, lifted his arm to above his shoulder, then let go. It flopped back to his side. He didn't react.

She pressed a thumb onto Alex's forehead, said something in another language, and as his eyes closed, asked in English. "Who is your handler?"

His voice was monotone. "I have escaped my handler. They are mind-destroyers. I work alone."

"What is your mission?"

"I'm here to keep Wallace safe. To patrol the underground. So no one finds the secret room."

"How did you know where to go? You said you work alone. Who are your allies?"

"Bernhardt helps me. He told me where to go."

Schopel removed her thumb from his forehead. "He's in a trance. And he's safe. I know the one who sent him. He is on our side. Leave him be."

Wallace clicked. *Allies. The secret room, from the note.* Could Alex be involved in that? He wanted to ask immediately, but with so many secrets, he was unsure what was safe to name. Instead, he turned to Alex again, "Do you know where this secret room is?"

"Yes of course, that's why I am here."

Without reacting, now somehow resolved in his prior confusion, as if fully entranced once more, Alex walked a few feet past the others into the passageway that curved around to the left. After a few paces, he slid a hand up the wall and grasped something. He tugged and a low hatch, hinged near the floor, about a square meter in size, opened from its top, about a foot above the ground.

"Go in, Wallace. I will patrol now," Alex said, and moved away.

"Come now," Schopel said, gesturing them through the hatch. She was the last to climb through into the small, empty room, and closed it behind her.

. . .

AT FIRST NO one said a word, then Schopel said, "I have allies in a past life who are Seers, and they have been instructed to send emissaries in time to protect Wallace, without knowing the details, only his importance. I will explain later. Suffice to say, Alex is trustworthy. I know his ally." She placed her bag on the floor. "Now, Wallace, you must just settle in, and we will make you as comfortable as we can."

As usual, her presence alone left no room for discussion, and even Wallace's questions evaporated like mist in the brightness of her authority. Dr. Rinella and Justicia also appeared lost for words. Wallace put down the box he'd been carrying, and the others dropped their bags to the floor in silence.

Dr. Rinella suggested Wallace eat. He promised to return with more supplies after nightfall—bedding, food, and so on. So far, he admitted, he'd only prepared the room by sweeping it and assessing its security and privacy. Schopel left with him. Justicia volunteered to remain behind to keep Wallace company. Lucio rummaged in one of his sacks and retrieved a small lantern, which he turned on and handed to her as he departed, holding his own to light the way out.

Wallace's heart raced and he admitted to himself, for the first time that day, the gravity of the situation. Justicia took his hand, and together they sat on the cold, concrete floor. There was nothing but each other's company for solace. The small, dark room offered only a tentative promise of safety. It felt claustrophobic to Wallace, who already missed the glass walls and expansive views of his room somewhere above. There was just one small opening to the world outside here, a rectangular metal grille the size of two bricks stacked together. It was evidently level with the earth above, and all that passed through was a mild draft and the reassuring tang of earth. Wallace hoped that come morning, there would be some glimpse of the outside, a reprieve from the dark, dank space with its indeterminate quality of fear and danger.

"There's something I need to tell you," she said. "It's absolutely the wrong time, and I really don't want to tell you now, today, but you will find out if I don't. Given my... public position, it will most certainly be in the press, and Lucio will see it and mention it. So I must tell you first."

He wanted to say *no—don't say it*. He knew. It could be nothing else.

"Justicia—" he began.

She put a finger to his lips.

"I am in the early stages, Wallace."

The world went static.

That gave her three years, maybe five.

"Wallace?"

"I—I guess I was hoping, if your husband was sick—"

"That I would be spared, because that's only fair, right?" She took his hand. "We both know better."

"I'm sorry, Justicia." He went cold. The draft, so mild before, seemed to pour through the high opening and chill him.

"You're shivering," she said. She sat closer and grasped his forearm with both hands.

It was as if his heart had doubled in weight, it sat so heavy in his chest, so full of her and all the pain of her sickness. But then, his mind began to race from his current situation to Finley, to the cross, the origin of it, a potential cure, and now agitated, he pulled his attention away from Justicia to the pressure of what lay before him—

The task ahead,

and what was now at stake:

this one person, not just the whole of humanity,

Justicia

and the whole of humanity—

his *love*, whose very existence, whose grace in his life meant more than all of the world's pain.

He knew, despite what little he actually knew about love, that to enter into intimacy was to accept pain, eventually, as an ending was always contained in beginnings. He knew of the rounds of treatments at the Cottage for the broken-hearted. He knew that love, more than anything else, could derail a fruitful communion with the Divine.

Here he faced the wreckage of his life and path, even though he had made no choices, done nothing but fall in love.

Life went gray. He could not reconcile the potency of his love with the certainty of her death.

He plummeted to his depths, but not without the lucid thought that there may be time yet, if there were a cure. This thought was like a rope thrown down a well where he sat in darkness, and he merely gazed upon it; it was there, and out of reach.

"You're gone," she whispered.

"I'm here," he sniffed, squeezing his eyes shut against tears. "I'm just not sure how to go on."

"Have you never loved the cancered before?" she asked. "Really?"

"I have not loved before."

"Oh," she cried, and curled up onto the dirt floor, laying her head in his lap, and rolling herself into his warmth. She made herself small. He rested a hand on her head, and stroked her face, though he could not look down at her just then.

"Falling in love feels like falling to your death," she said. "I know this. I am sorry you are on that side, I feel it is far worse than mine. I do not fear death."

"You don't?" Wallace asked.

"I only fear forgetting. I wonder if I might take my memory with me, so that there is continuity of who I have been, and who I will become. I fear the loss of myself, not of my body."

"That is not fear of death?"

"It's a kind of death, I suppose."

She sat up. He held her. This place contained secrets, and none of it felt light. He felt closed in and studied the high window. He would ask Dr. Rinella to remove the weeds so he might see something of nature.

Justicia suddenly squinted up at him with a puzzled expression.

"Wallace, why have we never asked you from what timeline the icon is from, and who sends the image of it? We've been chasing the past and the future, chasing individuals and consciousness, but not the icon itself..."

Her face stilled. She fell back to his lap, slack. Wallace stroked her hair. *I guess,* he wanted to say, but he could not even complete that sentence in his mind, much less give voice to it. She lay with her eyes closed. He closed his, too. With some effort, he pushed against grief and what felt like claustrophobia—he'd never experienced it before, as if the walls were closing in on him, panic rising in his chest. He summoned an image of the icon: the words, the Jesus, an object so woven into his inner experience that he'd never held it to be separate, or considered it a force unto itself.

It *was.*

And when he focused in on it, imagining that he held it, felt its weight and traced its contours, he sensed buzzing in the pit of his stomach, and vibration move through him and overtake him.

"Wallace, why are you trembling?" Justicia asked him.

He lay down on his side, squeezing his eyes closed, holding onto that vibration

because it was a distraction,

within which he did not need to feel anything, or consider his reality—

the sensations took over, until he shook violently, then lost consciousness.

HE AWOKE NEXT TO A LAKE—SUN shimmering through trees, the intense blue water and an old man walking towards him with a knowing smile, as if expecting him.

There's not much time left. We need to talk about the bridge, he said.

20

FINLEY, KATE & JIA LI: REVELATIONS
JUNE 2019
BERLIN, GERMANY

Kate knew she was dreaming, yet she couldn't pull away or wake up as the icon hovered mid-air before her and, from behind it, a cheerful Gutov peered at her with penetrative brown eyes. He gave a playful laugh and put one hand on his heart. In an instant she felt a hand on her heart. He waved both his hands at her and laughed at this joke; she still felt a hand on her and he knew it.

It's there. His voice was clear, but his lips did not move. He spoke directly into her mind.

An image of the thing is not the thing itself, he said.

The image of the cross changed then, in its place a throbbing red love heart, and then Gutov's face and the heart both disappeared into pink mist.

Next, as if looking through a foggy glass into the past, Kate saw her mother, *a dream within the dream.*

Galina, drinking tea with others, prim and determined. Not a hair out of place, her plan fixed. *Katya shall find the cross. She shall see it in her dreams and lead others to it.* No fun vacations. No trips to the beach with girlfriends, or summer camps. Chicago, San Francisco, then Prague, Berlin, Istanbul, *Gutovniks* everywhere, a bunch of desperate, unhappy, people. No city tours or meandering exploration. The only magical landscape, the only hope, was yet to be found, and until then there were guest rooms in houses or small, dark apartments. The table cluttered not with crayons, but with texts and books. *Clues.*

Cold dinners after hours of travel.

No bedtime story.

Late night plotting, mapping the Urals, the Himalayas, comparing Gutov's tales to Blavatsky's texts. So many important discussions, no joyful trivialities.

Katya trotted out to share her dreams one last time before sleep.

In the next dream sequence, Kate saw her mother, frail as she lay dying. Cancered. The smell of death. There was no more pleading and no more trips and Kate lived elsewhere now. Their dream dialogue was faithful to the real life event:

Are you well, Katenka? Are you happy?

"I'm happy," Kate replied. A lie.

Her eyes. *Her mother's eyes.* There was a glimpse of concern, bare and fragile.

"That's good, Katenka."

Kate hadn't known what to make of it at the time. Her anger left no scope for interpretation.

Nothing made sense.

Within this nested dream the pink mist returned, as well as the hand on her heart, which grew warmer and warmer.

Gutov appeared suddenly at a distance, fly fishing at a body of water, his rod thrown back and then out. *Loosen your grip* he said, and the pink mist rushed in to obscure him now. He vanished, but the hand on Kate's heart remained, steady and pulsing.

THE KNOCK on the door woke her up. She put her hand on her chest, as if her heart might still beat to the dream's rhythm.

What had just happened?

But the dream slipped into shadows and light. Kate blinked. The hotel room with its ordinariness. The smell of last night's dinner. She crinkled her nose.

The knock came again, urgent. Kate reluctantly climbed out of bed to answer the door, all the while struggling to remember:

Gutov and her mother. Hand on her heart.

Letting go.

Jia Li stood there, flushed. "Something's wrong with Finley."

"Just a sec," Kate said, and ran to the bathroom. She hurriedly changed out of her pajamas and they went to his room. Jia Li had his keycard and opened the door for them.

"We were at breakfast and his head started hurting. But it's not normal. He was making weird noises so I got him to bed immediately. He was in a lot of pain. I think it's subsided now."

Finley lay on the bed. He was paler than usual and unshaven now since they'd arrived in Germany. His eyes were closed.

"We can't call any doctor or ambulance or anything," Jia Li said. "They'll lock him up in a hospital bed and test him."

"Finley? What happened?" Kate asked him.

He opened his eyes. "What always happens lately. I had a headache and then I traveled, but it stopped. It felt like I was being blocked. I don't know what to do. I feel like time is running out."

"Time for what?" Kate asked.

"Time to help Wallace, in the future."

"Is this what happens?" Jia Li asked. "You see him and he tells you what you need to do, to save humanity, because it's dying? I got that right, didn't I?"

"I don't *see* exactly." He brought a hand to his head. "Could I have a cold facecloth please?"

Kate said, "I'll get it."

"I know that I haven't said much about it. I find it difficult to share."

"I understand," Jia responded. "Secrets work us hard."

"And they become habit." He sat up a bit.

Kate placed the wet cloth on his forehead. "It's okay, Finley. I told her everything, I think. From our visit with Valeri, too."

"My forehead tingles. I should expect a lightning bolt to appear at any moment." He laughed, then winced. "Ow. It hurts to laugh. But seriously." His face darkened. "It's getting worse. It's—it's like a knife and an electric shock at the same time. As dumb as it sounds, it just never occurred to me not to leave Dr. Gloria and my treatment. Maybe I actually need help with this and I've completely snookered myself by just leaving the country."

Jia Li and Kate sat as statues at the bottom of his bed, and a somber mood descended.

Kate said, "This is bigger than Dr. Gloria. She can't go on the journey *for* you. You were moved by urgency just like we all were. And I hate to say it, but it's *your* mind, Finley, and only you can reach Wallace. Maybe she had some strategies, but at some point you'd have to figure it out yourself anyway."

Finley shrugged. "I think you're right, not that it helps. I just wish I had more insight into how to manage this. So I can do my bit."

Jia Li spoke. "I guess we'd better get onto it then."

"Yes. So, on that note," Finley began, and sat up straighter. "I've decided to visit Valeri again today. I need to ask Evgenia about what she told you, Kate. About the mind-destroyers and time-travelers, because I have a feeling that's why my connection feels like it's being blocked. I don't know. I just really want to know what they are doing to me." He pointed at his head. "It seems to be both my greatest asset and my worst enemy ."

"I'll come with you," Kate said. "I'll message him now to let him know we need to see him again."

"I am meeting an old friend of my father's," Jia Li said. "I'll explain later. I promise. You guys go. Meet you back here."

THIS TIME VALERI came to the door. Evgenia appeared behind him, quiet and defeated.

"I told her to behave like grown-up," Valeri said.

Once more they sat in the kitchen with tea, and this time Evgenia sat with them. Kate had prepared Valeri for their arrival, and evidently he'd prepared Evgenia, so it didn't take long to get to the point.

"These mind-destroyers, who are they? Are they the men who visited you from before? Asking about Wallace?" Finley asked, as Kate translated.

Evgenia nodded.

"And where did they take you?"

Valeri shook his head, as if worried to go down that track, but Kate used her quiet, mothering tone and reassured Evgenia that she could take her time responding.

Evgenia, however, was not at all the crazed woman of the previous day and she answered matter of factly, "They took me to the Cottage. To the Cottage in Siberia. They experimented on me there."

As Kate repeated her words in English, Valeri put his face in his hands. He spoke to Evgenia and Kate translated. "He's saying she had not told him this, and how he feels terrible again that he allowed her to go."

"Was it on the lake?" Finley asked. "On Lake Baikal?"

She shook her head.

Kate placed a hand on Evgenia's hand, softening her voice even further. "Can you tell us more?"

"It was beyond the lake, many hours by train. It was near Krasnoyarsk. I escaped them. I escaped and went on the train to Irkutsk, and then Konstantin Isakevich Gutov appeared."

"What happened in the Cottage?" Finley asked as soon as Kate translated. Evgenia seemed to understand, and answered him without waiting for Kate this time.

"I thought they were good guys. I didn't realize until I was alone with them at the Cottage and they told me they wanted me to *spy on the future*. But I would *not*. They did some things to me there, to my brain, with a machine, and then I was able to be in a future life, a future of death—and these people knew I would be able to go there. They knew I have a gift." She indicated the heavens and gestured to the top of her head, as Kate quickly translated again for Finley.

"Many women in my family have this gift. But I was not good at knowing a person's character. I was young and desperate to be like the witch in Gutov's books. So they used me. They broke my brain. They kept me for two weeks to try. I had no control but to go and look out through my soul's window onto another life. But my soul is good. They could not use me. The future me is still *me*—this they do not understand. So after I left, I sent a warning into the future to give hope. They will not win. *We will win*."

Kate repeated Evgenia's words quietly to Finley in English.

Finley said, "Ah," as if he understood something.

"My poor girl, *devochka*," Valeri said in English. "She has not been the same, you know." His eyes were wet.

"The Cottage," Finley said. "Does she know what they used there? It was a machine? And how does it work? Could it hurt someone's brain, like cause pain or interfere with *spying on the future*, as she described it? Just ask her if she knows any other details."

As Evgenia explained, Kate had to take a breath. She struggled to make sense of it. "She's speculating, but she thinks it suppresses emotion. She's saying that it allows a person to experience more of their own consciousness without the emotional confusion and interference of past trauma. But she says that in the wrong hands it can cause harm. That sometimes the mind is opened too much, too fast, and—the universe rushes in. That's what she said."

"That's what happened to me when I was a child," Finley said, bringing a hand to his temples now.

Evgenia spoke a moment longer. Kate didn't translate immediately as her mind filled with questions—how was it possible, she wondered, and could it be true or was Evgenia just deluded in her inconstant mania? Finley stared at them both. Evgenia fell silent—waiting, it was clear, for the translation.

"Okay," she sighed. "Evgenia is saying that these mind-destroyers have allies in the future who are trying to use their own minds to open a person's mind in the same way, without a machine. To open it and to close it, without using the technology. She said the mind-destroyers with her did not know this, that she learned this when she was looking through the window of her future self. She said there are political factions who use the skills of ancient Shamans to harm and possess, but there are also those who do the same thing to help those with a pure heart. Her words."

Finley frowned. He closed his eyes.

"Okay," he said. "That makes sense. The pain is probably from individuals in the future, then. But the Cottage exists in our time though, already. That's... terrifying."

Valeri furrowed his brow. Kate could tell that he didn't understand what Finley was talking about, the *pain* he referred to, or his seeming familiarity with the Cottage. She hoped he wouldn't ask them any more questions. She didn't want to involve anyone else in their mission, not any more than she needed to.

"One more thing," Finley said. "Can she tell me about meeting Gutov?" He spoke to Evgenia directly in English. " You met Gutov after? How?"

"I called him," she said in English.

"You... called him?" Finley repeated her words.

"Yes," she repeated in English. She drank her tea and continued in Russian, after which Kate spoke for her. "With my mind. I knew he was there. I felt him alive in my heart." She patted her heart.

Kate, too, felt the dream-like echo of a thump against her heart, and placed her hand on her heart, too.

"I am wiser now," Kate repeated Evgenia's words verbatim. "And open. Too much open. It was their fault I knew their bad plan, because once they used the Machine on my brain I could see their truth," she said. "I could see them for their evil, but I also could see many other things, and know much more."

Evgenia grinned like a child. "Konstantin Isakevich and I were like magnets," Kate continued for Evgenia, who now brought the palms of her hands together to illustrate. "We met on the astral plane. He appeared and spoke to me." Her eyes teared. "He is at Baikal. He showed me he was there, but I didn't go there. I could not risk being found again. I had to come home, to here. These same men are still looking for you, Wallace. But they do not know who you are in this time."

Kate cleared her throat and lowered her hand from her heart, defeated. Evgenia knew too much. She knew Finley was Wallace. Kate clarified, "He's *Finley*. Wallace exists only in the future."

Valeri whistled slowly as he released his breath like a balloon deflating. "I see," he said. "It was *you* they were looking for. Why?"

Kate had no intention of explaining; fortunately Evgenia interrupted.

"She says Finley and Wallace are like two beads on a string. That she has spoken to his spirit, the string that connects them," Kate translated.

Evgenia mumbled her next words while staring right at Finley. Her tone had dropped an octave and agitation suddenly coursed through her, so that her hand, the one that held her teacup, shook. Her cup and saucer both rattled on the table.

Kate translated quickly, "She says you know what your job is now, and you know why they are looking for you," Kate said. "That it's your responsibility."

"Okay, great. No big deal." Finley's forehead was suddenly damp with perspiration. He wiped it with the back of his hand and finished his half-full teacup in one gulp.

"This is why we are hoping to speak with Konstantin Isakevich," Kate said in English. "I think he can help Finley with his... job."

Evgenia began to hum and rock in her chair, then suddenly she leapt up and pointed at Kate and began to speak at volume about her friend, the woman, *the other woman*, being in danger. Kate blanched; she pushed her chair back, stood up, and grabbed Finley's hand and said, "Let's go."

"What is she saying?" Finley asked Valeri.

"She says—our friend, the other woman. They found her. She's in danger."

"You mean Jia Li?"

"Yes!" Kate leapt out of her chair. "Evegnia is calling her *the thief*. Evgenia says the thief has information that could cause a... a tidal wave. Of revolution or chaos? I don't understand. But she's saying that they have her right now, near our hotel. Fuck. We have to run."

Kate grabbed Finley's hand and tugged until he stood. "C'mon. Now!"

With barely a goodbye, they fled from Valeri's apartment, running back through Kreuzberg and over the Oberbaumbrücke towards the hotel where, from about a block away, they could see Jia Li.

JIA LI WAS PUSHED up against the wall, her two wrists held in a single fist. She was shouting at the tall white man in a suit who held her.

In fact, Jia Li had been running from that man for the past fifteen minutes, ever since she arrived at the Burgermeister on the Schlesisches Tor to meet with her father's friend Todor, who had given her a letter from her father only the day before.

No sooner had she greeted Todor than the tall thin white man and the short, fat Chinese man—the thugs from her show in Hong Kong—appeared just a few feet away. The tall one said, "Let's talk," but she shouted to him, "Fuck you," and stepped away, though as she did so, he reached out as if to grab her by the wrist, at which point she began to run.

The chase was on. She ran straight down the busy road past cafes and people on bikes, weaving through passersby until at a big intersection Jia Li gained distance, pausing near trees and parked bicycles, where the short fat man unceremoniously tripped on what looked like nothing—a crack in the pavement, and, red-faced, started panting, crouched over, unable stand, whereupon the tall thin one caught sight of Jia Li and continued towards her.

She began to run again, towards the bridge and, as she entered the shadowy underside, wove in and out of the arches, then crouched behind one, lowering herself next to a pram as the mother looked on, initially surprised to see her, then speaking in German, gesticulating, clearly worried about her, before she pushed her pram and walked away. For several seconds, maybe ten or fifteen, Jia Li attempted to remain still, crouching behind the arch so no one would spot her.

Then she saw a man's trousers, and a second later— there he was, her lone pursuer, red-faced and sweating, locking eyes.

Shit.

She maneuvered between the post of the arch and that man, who was definitely angry now, and sprinted away across the rest of the bridge back towards the hotel, where, she reasoned, she might make it to her room in time to lose him completely, or if that didn't work, she could make a fuss and get him stopped at the door.

By now adrenalin had taken over, despite approaching her limit of cardiovascular fitness. As she looked back at the man, she could see that he was also struggling, until fortunately—and she didn't catch the entire act, only the grand finale—he collided into an oncoming man on a bicycle, which landed him legs up on the ground.

With this second's pause, bent over and panting, Jia Li rallied herself to continue to the hotel.

She'd made it halfway between the bridge and the hotel, when the man leapt out of nowhere from her left side and body slammed her into the wall of a building, holding her there with his weight, at the exact moment when Finley and Kate rounded the corner and saw her.

JIA LI HAD NOT HAD a moment to process her friends' sudden appearance at the scene when Kate launched herself at the man, knocking him to the ground. The man was only momentarily stunned, then threw Kate off with one arm and with the other, as Jia Li tried to step away from the wall, grabbed Jia Li's leg, which caused her to fall. He wrapped an arm around her chest and held her to him, her arms pinned down under his, at which point Kate tried to launch herself at him again. She'd only made it to crouching when he kicked her in the head, knocking her hard to the ground.

Finley had barely caught up to them both and danced at the edge, obviously panicked and now panting. Suddenly, he grabbed his own skull with two hands and fell to his knees. Kate was on the ground next to him, her head bleeding near her hairline. Jia Li cried out at the attacker, "I don't have the fucking information you want! Let me go!"

Just at that moment, something flew down out of the sky and hit the man's head. He fell half on top of Jia Li and his eyes rolled back. Jia Li wriggled out from under him and crawled to Kate's side, only barely registering that a drone had smashed into the man's skull. He seemed unconscious.

Jia bent over Kate, wiping blood from her forehead. "Kate! Kate!"

Finley roared, a sound of terror and pain so violent, so loud, that passersby who had before been prepared to walk past the obvious violence as it had unfolded, now stopped still in their tracks, staring.

The sound even roused Kate, who, groggy and still, opened her eyes to slits. Jia Li pushed Kate's blond hair off her bloody forehead, tender and impatient.

"You okay? Kate? Can you understand me?" Her heart raced more insistently than ever.

"It's egg-ketchup man," Kate said.

"Huh?" Jia Li said, trying to make sense of those words. Then, a man appeared, standing over them both. He had scraggly, long hair and a fuzzy face and wore fancy-looking glasses. He was holding drone controls.

"And who are you?" Jia Li asked him.

"We need to get you all out of here before he wakes up," the man replied. To Finley he said, bending down over his huddled form, "Get yourself together and help Kate now. Take three deep breaths. You need to learn how to get yourself out of it as easily as you seem to get into it. It doesn't control you unless you let it."

Finley blinked furiously and looked up. "Aren't you..." he whispered, still in a heap on the ground, "the man from the diner, in Atlanta, that I bumped into in the carpark?"

"He's egg-ketchup man," Kate said. "I've seen him there a few times. Always has lots of ketchup over his eggs." She crinkled her nose in distaste.

"Well observed," the man said as he helped Jia Li get Kate to standing. Finley gingerly released his head from the vice grip of his own hands. His face was red. His hands shook. His eyes rolled back into his head.

"I am in *searing* pain," he whimpered.

"Stop it. *Now.* You can journey later," the man said to Finley. He offered Finley a hand, and pulled him to his feet.

Jia Li noticed this 'egg-ketchup man' had a very slight German accent.

"I'm a friend. You need to trust me. I have vital information to share with you. My car is this way. Follow me. Don't worry about him." He indicated Jia Li's attacker, out cold. "Someone will find him. Not our problem."

The man took Finley by the arm—Finley walked haltingly, but at least he had pulled himself together just enough to do so. Jia Li didn't know why or how she followed along—they all did—like lemmings to this man's small yellow Volkswagen. They climbed into the backseat, where Kate slumped down with her head leaning on Jia Li's small shoulder.

HE DROVE them across the Oberbaum bridge through neighborhoods and sidestreets in some indeterminate direction at speed, as though fleeing, although it didn't seem like anyone followed them.

"Where are we going?" Kate asked. Her head had stopped bleeding, though she still leaned against Jia Li.

"We are just having a moment to chat," the man said, "until what you've left behind is cleared up."

"We have to get out of here, all of us. We can't stay," Jia Li said. "They know I'm here and I'm endangering all of you."

"There's more you need to know," the man said. "I'm trying to help you. All of you."

"Who are you exactly?" Kate asked. "Have you been following us since the diner in Atlanta?"

"My name is Bernhardt. I lead a group of Seers who access future timelines through consciousness."

"Of course. Makes sense," Finley said, with his signature dryness.

"Of course," Jia Li said, "like *he* said."

Kate pushed into Jia Li's side as the car careened around a corner. The pressure of her weight was reassuring, anchoring her into something that did actually make sense. *Just look after Kate*, she told herself.

"You might also know me as the author of a collection of miracles on the Dark Web, where Kate's young ward was referred to as a miracle cure after holding onto what she described as a cross."

"You wrote that? That's how I found Kate!" Jia Li exclaimed. She sat up straighter. *Maybe this all did make sense—but how?*

"But, hang on," she said to Kate. "You saw him in Atlanta, and he wrote the piece that got me to Atlana—" Now she addressed Berhhardt. "Did you *want* us to meet? Are you the reason… or?" Her eyes narrowed.

"You were always going to meet. I was tracking you. Until you reached a critical moment, when you are stable on your correct path, the moment when you need the information I'm about to share. I couldn't know for sure that the moment had arrived until it did. And it has!" He chuckled.

"And you know this because…" Jia Li said.

"My future counterpart and I are in contact with Finley from other timelines."

"Right," Jia Li said.

Kate sat up, noticing Finley half-slumped in the front passenger seat. "Finley, you all right?"

"Never better."

"We're just going to park. I'll explain," Bernhardt said.

No one spoke as he negotiated Berlin traffic for a few more minutes, taking sharp turns until he veered off onto a quiet side street and parked in the long shadows of residential buildings.

"I stop now," he announced.

"You said you are Seers. But—that means that in the future you are *Visionaries!*" Finley exclaimed. "You're part of the same group that exists in the future."

"The originators, actually," Bernhardt said. "I began the group in this time and it continues for the next century. Amazing, right? I didn't realize right away that my project, visioning future timelines, was important, or would even last. But it seems it does!"

Bernhardt grinned into the rearview mirror at the women. Delighted, Jia Li thought, by his own future legacy. He was growing on her. Plus, he'd saved her from that man.

"Thank you for saving me, by the way," Jia Li offered hastily.

"You're quite welcome. Thank *you*."

Jia Li frowned. "Me?"

"All of you, actually."

"This is super weird. Is this super weird?" Jia Li asked.

"No more so than anything else," Kate said, her palm pressed against her forehead, still evidently dazed and confused.

"So you are what—working with the Visionaries of the future to help us ... do what exactly?" Finley asked.

Bernhardt seemed... *eager*, Jia Li thought. What did he mean, *thank you*?

"Why, yes, more or less. I follow various actors in this present play, as it were. And I communicate with my counterpart in the future, who alerted me to the necessity of catching you now, to impress upon you the most relevant facts."

"Your future self," Finley clarified.

"Exactly. Which is how I am aware of Finley and his mission in our unfortunately apocalyptic future."

"Apocalyptic? So you are on a mission now to protect me, or all of us?" Finley asked.

"What do you mean, apocalyptic?" Jia Li asked.

"I am here to protect all of you. In this instance, this young woman, for example." He pointed to Jia Li. "She needs to get home so she can get the information out there. And even better if she steals some of the substance they inject her with."

"What the...!" Jia Li began. "How did you..." but she couldn't finish her sentence. *The substance they inject me with?* She thought. *Would they do that? How did he know... ? Oh. Yeah. The future.* Even though she had no way of knowing that his prediction was true, she felt her inner guidepost shift. Truth—something that existed outside of time and was perceivable by others—now interposed itself in her mission, beyond supposition, beyond a shared quest, beyond even fear.

Yet her mind had not caught up to the visceral realization. "Hang on. You know all of that? And you know about the pharmathugs who injected my Mum? They've been watching my shows ever since my father died. They think my father stole information that links HKK to a coverup and that I have it."

"My dear, they are not *pharmathugs*. They are much worse. They have been sent by representatives of a network of governments working together to ensure manipulation of the gene pool for targeted depopulation. But they are very far behind us in terms of what is possible with visioning. They lack understanding of time-lines. Their future counterparts are not able to reach them easily, so they only have vague clues about the future that is being created. They have a very limited mission, please understand. It's just: *Get the information from Jia Li and stop Wallace*—I mean Finley. So they are desperate. And I mean *desperate!*"

"What does he mean they are from governments?" Jia Li said to Kate, as if Bernhardt were not there, and only Kate could make sense of it all.

Kate put a hand on her arm. "I don't know."

"Are they the same ones who took Evgenia and... and tortured her there?" Kate asked.

"Arghhh... a stupid attempt to spy on the future with underdeveloped technology and a woman with a saint's heart and a Seer's vision. They are trying in our era to construct a machine from the future, and they don't have the science to back it yet—and they won't even have it right by the time Wallace first encounters it. Madness. As for Evgenia, I have helped her since, don't worry. I am in contact with her in the future and in the present." He shook his head.

"And no, the ones who took Evgenia are not the same as the ones after Jia Li. Same organization, different branches. The people who took Evgenia are still looking for you, Finley, they just don't know who you are. They don't have the skills to find Wallace's present-day self. Also, neither then nor now do they have any idea that the *icon* is the thing that could save humankind. What they do know is how to interfere with the connection. To interrupt it with psychic practices, through Wallace's mind. Got it?"

"That's the interference, in my head."

"Yes. I will get to that shortly, Finley. Jia Li—the future forces who are trying to stop Wallace and maintain their power and control, they *do* know how to look through historical records and discover facts, like the information about the virus—hence today's escapades. That is why they have been following you, Jia Li. They know what you will do, and sent that information to their past Seers, who notified governments, and enlisted the help of those thugs. Sorry to spoil it for you."

He sought Jia Li's attention again into the rearview mirror, but she stared at him blankly, dissociating for a moment as this messy and confusing assortment of multiple facts and factors dropped into place.

"I don't know what I will do," she protested after a moment. "Why wouldn't they just kill me then?"

"It's worse if they kill you. When you don't exist, their very political factions cease to exist, so they can't have that. The Visionaries have assessed various timelines in an effort to tweak reality so that it goes their way. Right now, there's no need to know exactly what you will do, Jia Li. But know this, those men will follow you back to Hong Kong, which is what we want, so that Kate and Finley can do their part without interference. Got it?"

She nodded, still attempting to make sense of it all.

"I'm here to protect all of you, as best I can. In truth, as Seers, right now our insight is little. Our ability is limited. We are still learning how to do it. Like Finley here. Not to mention, there are shifting timelines, it's so messy. You cannot imagine. We must be very disciplined. What I can tell you for certain is that it is too late for our era. The Earth is sick. A revolution is coming. Viral cancer will kill us all. We cannot stop it, but we can help by helping the future when the consciousness of the planet is somewhat more advanced."

"Oh, that is so dark," Kate said. "Too late?"

"So why wouldn't you come back earlier then, when it wasn't too late?" Finley asked.

"That sounds good, doesn't it? But we cannot, because earlier in our timeline, when there was a crossroads, an opportunity to avoid this genetic disease—as a collective consciousness there just wasn't enough collective desire to do it. I could have found one person, even a few, but it just was never going to shift it at a global level then. And now, it is better, yes, but it's still too late. That's why we must help Wallace's earth. His timeline. That we can do. All of you. You need to just focus on the work ahead. Who you are becoming is far more vital than who you are now."

He started the engine again.

"Okay, I need to get you back to your hotel. The man who attacked you has left the area now."

"You just *know* that?" Kate asked.

"My colleagues texted me, yes." He gave a bemused smile, but his good humor could no longer mask the wisdom that lay beneath, and Jia Li felt his words echo in her mind, *who you are becoming is far more vital than who you are now.*

Finley grasped his forehead. "It's starting again," he said. "How do I stop them from doing this to me?"

"Ah, yes. I was just getting to that. The pain is *not* the interference of others. It's your consciousness fighting back. It's the fight, Finley. It's your mind fighting fear. It will fight when it senses that those other forces are trying to close the door of communication, and it will fight when you are afraid. Pain is a signal that a part of you is trying to keep you safe."

Bernhardt restarted the engine and pulled out from the shadows. Again he sped through the backstreets, then swerved onto the main road.

"You're saying the pain is my fault." He grasped his forehead in that precise moment and added, "Ow."

"Don't worry, you can get past this," Bernhardt said. "You need to learn how to trigger the opening yourself because the interfering forces won't be able to interfere then. I realize that at the start you relied on a therapist. You outgrew this reliance the moment you realized that you *are* Wallace. You just haven't realized yet how to reach him at will."

"What do you mean, trigger the opening?"

"As I said, to *will* yourself to him. You see, the Visionaries of the future are only able to interfere with *Wallace's* consciousness, as from their point in time, your own is nested within his. They cannot reach it independently from Wallace himself. When you feel like you're spontaneously travelling, it's coming from Wallace's consciousness to yours. You're not the one initiating it. And again, your adversaries are aware only of what *his* consciousness is doing, so if *you* initiate the journey to Wallace's timeline, they won't know about it and thus they cannot interfere. Only beware, if you're contracted in fear, your mind will fight and produce pain. Got it?"

"Okay. So I need to reach him on my own. And not be in fear."

"Exactly. You have to be brave, fearless, and do it yourself."

"No big deal," Finley deadpanned.

Kate reached over Jia Li to put a hand on Finley's shoulder. Jia Li had closed her eyes to block everything out, overwhelmed by what lay ahead, the unknown choices she faced.

"How can he initiate it himself?" Kate asked. "Can you help him?"

"Look, I actually can't tell you how. It's like asking someone to tell them how to swallow. You either do it consciously, in which case it's awkward and weird. Or you trust your body to get on with things, in which case the process is automatic and unconscious, and you could never explain it to anyone else. You have to find your own way."

"If you have it all worked out, then why not do it yourself?" Finley asked. "Why not do this quest yourself and send the information to the future..."

"It's not my path."

Finley rolled his eyes. "I knew you'd say that." He grabbed his head. "Ow," he complained.

"We each have a path, one that naturally aligns with our abilities, interests, and desires."

"You think I desire this?" Finley asked, wincing as he rubbed his temples.

"Of course. Just because you resist it doesn't mean you don't desire it. Fear usually speaks the loudest, but that doesn't make it the most powerful voice. Just the one you're used to listening to. But anyway, enough of that. We're back at your hotel. So you guys get out. Keep up the good work. I will reach out again if I get instructions from the future. Until then, good luck."

The three passengers—all flustered and exhausted, each mumbled *thank you* as they exited his car.

No sooner had Finley's feet hit the pavement than his hands flew to his head. He let out a moan, squeezed his eyes shut, then collapsed and lost consciousness, even as the Volkswagen sped out of sight.

FINLEY CAME to just minutes later, to find Kate and Jia Li sitting with him a street away from their hotel. With an arm around each of them, they stumbled back together, took him to his bed, and continued their by now habitual ministrations: a cold face cloth and reassurance, with tea and cookies on the way. As they tended to Finley, Jia Li also cleaned the cut on Kate's forehead and applied antiseptic cream that she'd gotten from the hotel's front desk.

Finley moaned. "Just when I was getting used to it, now it's like someone's got my head in a vice and is putting screws into my brain. It's horrible. But then when I'm actually there, when I'm Wallace, the pain is gone. And I'm so confident and collected and... strong and wise and... well I've never actually seen him in a mirror, I only see the world through his eyes. But I assume I am much better looking too."

Kate and Jia Li burst out laughing.

"No, but really, he's so collected and cool, and I'm *him*, but I'm so fucking *not* him yet. He rarely even has a headache. Sometimes I feel closer to him than ever, and then more far away. And despite what

Bernhardt said, I'm not sure that I can handle this agony. Which makes me pathetic. The most pathetic hero. One who is incapable of his own path, exactly what Wallace is *not*."

"Tea will make you feel better," Kate said, as the kettle came to a boil and she went to find the teabags and got the milk from the mini-fridge.

Jia Li sat on Finley's bed. "Look, Finley. This is all pretty crazy to me, okay? I don't know anything about visions, but I do know fear. And I do know vulnerability. You have to face fear with intention, as the one driving the bus, rather than the passenger. It's a subtle but powerful mind shift." Jia Li grinned. "I do perform in front of a LOT of people, including those who would threaten my life."

"Good advice," Kate said.

"It sounds excellent. Implementing it is another matter," Finley responded.

"So if I understand correctly," Jia Li said. "These men who've been following me, they are from government agencies, and they are really crap at this visioning business, but they want to make sure the proof isn't leaked as it ... presumably it threatens their power in the far future or something? And others are after Wallace, only they don't really know who Wallace is now... hence they aren't chasing you, Finley..."

"That all makes sense," Finley said. He was trying to make sense of it too.

Kate spoke to Jia Li. "Evegenia knew they were after you today. She saw it when Finley and I were with her."

She handed Finley his tea and went to sit next to Jia Li on the bed. He sighed happily, holding the mug in his cupped hands as if it were a treasure. He wanted this one moment to last, this blessed reprieve, before he came to terms with what must come next.

When Kate spoke next, her tone was measured. "We know someone is working hard to find out who Finley is, so listen. I've been thinking. Maybe *I* should be the one to go to Baikal and find Gutov."

Both Jia Li and Finley sputtered at once, "*What?*"

Finley roused himself, confusion turning to shock, and then, moved by that same insistent need to protect her, he insisted, "You can't. You cannot, okay? I'm just complaining, Kate. I know it's my job. Sorry. My *path*." He rolled his eyes.

Jia Li turned to Kate. "Are you serious?"

"No, both of you listen." She put up a hand. "I've been resisting it my whole life, but maybe I should just go to Gutov. I should ask him about the cross. You could just rest, Fin, and then I will tell you what I discover, and you can then journey into the future later or something. I mean, I have been told my entire life that this was my destiny, and my mother isn't even around anymore and look at what's happening. It's nothing to do with her. It's all to do with me, I guess. Gutov's even in my dreams now. I think it means I just need to go find him."

Finley sighed. "You're wrong."

Jia Li looked cross. "No, Kate, that's not true. It's not your destiny. You don't have to go. You should go to Mexico for the child."

Kate shook her head. "I'll save her later. This might be my last chance to do what I've always been told I should do."

"Just—listen. What does your heart say?" Jia Li asked.

Kate shook her head once more, tears filling the corners of her eyes.

Finley suddenly clicked. "Oh Kate, it's been the girl all along, hasn't it?"

How had he missed this? He chastised himself. Now he wanted to protect her from herself. He could see how hard she fought her own instincts. He softened his voice, "Is that what you want to do? Go to Little Bird? You've already led us here. And found Valeri. It's enough. You did your part. You don't need to do any more."

Kate began to cry. Jia grabbed a fistful of tissues from the bedside table and pressed them into Kate's hand.

"You don't need to do anything else," Jia Li said. "You're the only person not being pursued right now by... forces from the future, or representing the future, or whatever. So I would say you've got a free pass. You don't have to be part of this."

"Well that's just it. They're after you two. I'm nobody to them. So I might escape notice and actually get the information. I speak Russian, it makes sense. There's still the mafia, the police, I guess. But if they haven't found me here, yet, maybe I can just sneak into Russia…"

Finley knew she was right, but that wasn't the point. "It's not your job, Kate. I have to get the truth and send it to Wallace immediately, like the second I know the truth. There might not be time if you were to find it, to get it to me, anyone could find any one of us at *any* moment. Anyway, it just has to be me."

Jia Lia sighed. "The police and the mafia could find you anywhere, Kate. Even if you sneak into Mexico. Every scenario has a risk, so you should at least take that risk doing what you feel most strongly about."

"That's true," Finley said. "Anyway, someone needs to hide the icon. You should go, get the cross from Victoria, get the girl, then hide the cross so that no one ever hears about it. My job is to find its origin and tell Wallace. And I need to figure out how to do this on my own. Without the pain, hopefully."

Jia Li said, "That's very brave, Finley. He's right, Kate. It needs to go to Argentina, to that guy I told you about. The one who knows metals."

Kate sniffed. "Really?"

"Yes," Finley and Jia Li said at once.

Kate wiped her eyes. Finley felt proud of himself at that moment. He had convinced her. Protected her. Stepped up. He could do this. He took a deep breath. "Your heart is elsewhere, and you need to follow it."

Kate brought a hand to her heart.

"He's right," Jia Li chimed in. "You go to the child, Kate, and get the cross and hide it. I have to go to Hong Kong. I may have proof now of HKK coverups. Including about the virus. I need to go home and find it."

Finley and Kate now turned their attention to Jia Li.

"You have *proof*?" Kate asked.

"Or I will soon. I've been in contact with a former colleague of my father's, Todor, that's who I was meeting with today. He reached out to me a few months ago and told me to be in touch when I could, but better in person. He's been in hiding in Bulgaria since he resigned more than ten years ago, because of what he knows. When I told him I was going to Berlin, he came here to meet me. To give me a letter from my father that he was asked to hold onto for a year, so yesterday I went to meet him, only I was being followed, and the bruise on my face—okay I didn't actually fall obviously. The same men who chased me today—they followed me yesterday. I shouted at them and they shoved me against a lamp post but I escaped. I knew I was taking a chance meeting Todor again today, but I thought I was being sensible meeting him in public, and I... I just needed that letter from my father."

"There was more than one man yesterday?" Finley asked.

"Two. The same ones who sit at my show in Hong Kong and stare at me. I think one had an asthma attack yesterday or something." Jia Li grinned. "I feel like these guys haven't really met the fitness requirement for professional hitmen training or something."

Kate smiled.

Jia Li pulled a crumpled paper out of her jeans pocket and unfolded it into her open palms. She handed it to Kate.

"I should have got rid of it. But I just... I *will* get rid of it. Soon." She glanced sideways at Kate. "You can read it, too, Finley."

They crowded around.

MY DEAR JELLY,

I PRAY you never read this. If you do, it means I'm gone and it means you're in danger, the worst of all possible outcomes. I organized to send this at least six months after my possible death (to allow the dust to settle) and *only* if my friend who delivered it was certain that your safety has been compromised.

I have proof, and of far more than you imagine. Proof of a virus that will change the human genome. I kept this proof, and what you do with it is at your discretion. If you want no part in this, or God forbid if something happens to you and you cannot, then I have separately included in this envelope details of a colleague in Hong Kong who may be open to taking it from here. Either way, truth will get out.

I'm writing this as you stand at the door watching me. I feel you keenly in my heart. I will tell you I'm going out to lunch with a friend today. I'm not sure what today will bring, but please know that you are with me now and always.

If you are reading these words, also know that you must be exceptionally brave now. You ARE brave. If you're being followed or harassed, then you are in danger, and there are two choices: continue silently and be threatened indefinitely, or access the documents I hid.

I tried to spare you. I wish I could turn you back into the stubborn toddler you were and take you to the playground and get ice cream together. But I am reminding myself that even then, you were the child who thought nothing of getting in trouble if it meant protecting the weak. You were the child who stole the class hamsters, after all. I must trust that you can handle yourself according to your values.

Protect your mother as best you can. I know she has had concerns that she never voiced. I have silenced her in order to protect her. Perhaps that is why she asks so few questions. Let her have a voice now, please, however much you can.

Know that I've loved every moment with you and I am so proud of who you are, strong, brave, indifferent to what others may expect of you, a true rebel. You are what you need to be in this life. I do believe that character is destiny. Don't try to be anyone else. You're perhaps not a scientist at heart, but I know that you'll figure out who you are, and what your role is as time goes on. Your greatest gift to the world is in simply being yourself. No more, no less.

On that note, please encourage your mother to get back to painting. She loved it so much, even before she loved me.

You know the music I love. My old collection of albums. You will find what you need there.

Love,
Dad

. . .

KATE PUT a hand on Jia Li's hand.

Finley blinked slowly and stared at the ceiling, then closed his eyes, checked in on himself. There was a lot at stake. So much more than he had ever imagined. As all this crucial information and its implications sank in; he could feel his hands go clammy, then an upsurging of fear began at his feet and rose, like an electric current, until his eyes burned and his head began to pang. He wanted so desperately to clutch his temples. He did not. So he froze, struggling against the fear and thus the pain until, blessedly, Kate shifted the focus to Jia Li.

"So, obviously, Jia Li needs to go home and find proof of the creation of this deadly virus," Kate said.

Jia Li nodded. "I know Bernhardt said that it's too late and we're not able to change the course of history in our era. But maybe he's wrong. Maybe there *is* hope. Maybe I can stop them, whoever *they* are, from creating the disease, or at least spreading it. I can go get the proof while you find the origin of the cross, Finley, and I can threaten them back, tell them that I have the documents, so they mustn't release it, or whatever they are planning."

"How, exactly, would you stop them? Just show up with documents and say *look what I've got*? They might just shoot you dead. I mean—" Finley sounded harsher than he intended, but he couldn't stop himself.

"Don't do that, Jia Li, please," Kate said.

"I don't know what I'll do. But I can't live with myself if I don't try."

Finley, who just realized that he had, in fact, managed to halt the pain, even if partly because Kate had distracted him, had the presence of mind to offer help to these women in the most effective way he could. Money.

"So—listen, there are practicalities. Kate, I'm giving you my travel visa card. It's loaded with cash. No name on it. They take it everywhere they take visa, and I can put more money on it and get myself another one here—"

He took his wallet out of his pocket and handed her his card.

Kate stalled. "Um. Really?"

"Please accept my white male privilege. It's something I can rely on much better than my...." He pointed at his head.

"Okay. Thank you, Finley. I really appreciate it."

"Jia Li, I will figure out how to send you help later. Right now, I guess I need to figure out how to get to Port Baikal." He looked up at the ceiling again, narrowing his eyes. "I think I have to go to Irkutsk first and take a bus or ferry from there. Does that sound right? Yes, I think so. Nevermind, you probably have no idea. No one really prepares you for the practical challenges involved in a quest, do they? It seems like a logistical nightmare."

He snuggled down into his bed and muttered to himself about the logistics, cursing this latest hurdle, whilst inwardly he flooded with relief to be navigating logical conundrums rather than metaphysical ones.

"You'll be fine, Finley," said Kate.

"You'll be fine. Just find Gutov, and take it from there," Jia Li said.

"Yes, yes. And then what? I convey my findings to Wallace through my mind, and give myself an aneurism? I think I'm going to close my eyes for a bit, and think about trains and airplanes and what to pack."

"You still have to figure out how to initiate the connection with Wallace," Kate said, "remember?"

But Finley had closed his eyes, pulled the sheets up under his chin and turned onto his side.

Kate and Jia Li left Finley and went to Kate's room to order room service. Kate just had one beer left so they decided to open the bottle of sauvignon blanc from the bar fridge. They demolished burgers and fries and half the bottle of wine and pointedly did not discuss the day's events. Then they sat on the floor, drowsy and full, backs against the bed, with the evening light warm on their legs, and chatted about superficialities until the heaviness of unspoken things began to crack Kate open—

and Jia Li burst out with,

"Do you think he'll work it out? How to get to Baikal and find Gutov? It does seem like a crazy quest. What if Gutov's not there?"

"I'm pretty sure he is," Kate said, unsure if she really wanted to go into her own visions or the certainties of her heart, both of which might confirm that Gutov was there. Still, she searched Jia Li for a sign that she was open to a deeper conversation.

Kate shifted around on the floor, suddenly uncomfortable in her own skin.

"Can I ask you," Jia Li began. "You said you know what it feels like when someone doesn't accept you for who you are."

"Oh." Kate rolled her eyes. "Yeah. My ex didn't like that I was a sex worker. It kinda broke my heart. You know, even Victoria didn't know her. Well, she knew *about* her but it fell apart so fast that they never met. She couldn't cope with my work. So I had to choose. I needed an income and I wanted to do it my way. I wanted the choice about how to live my life."

Kate checked she hadn't lost Jia Li, her attention or her approval. In fact, Jia Li had gone brighter and warmer, and spoke softly—

"I guess I can understand that."

"Me too. But I just wasn't willing to compromise."

"I understand both sides. You needing to live your life on your own terms, and she—not wanting to share you."

"She was never *sharing* me." Kate hadn't meant to snap at her.

Now Jia Li seemed to shrink. "Some people wouldn't see it that way."

"Well, if my heart isn't switched on, there's little that is being shared."

She looked right at Jia Li, daring her to disagree.

"That makes sense." Jia Li cleared her throat. "And are you... over her, do you think?"

Kate's eyes wandered from the stubborn corners of Jia Li's mouth, to the softness of her neck, to rest on her chest, which gently rose with each breath just below the delicate lines of her collarbone.

"Well, yeah. I mean, besides, now I've been thrust into some weird alternate universe where there's mystery and danger, and really good food, and I don't have to worry about rent... so I'm not even... you know."

"You're nobody's. Not sharing."

"No." Kate pushed her hair behind her ear, her hand faintly trembling, then rested her hand on the floor, near Jia Li's knee.

Jia Li put her hand on Kate's fluttering hand and held it down.

Kate felt the understanding and connection flow between them, soft and hesitant.

She closed her eyes for a moment; it was so much to allow,

how safe she felt with her,

how that safety was wrapped in desire and an intense curiosity to *know* her, completely, beyond but including the flesh, all that she was, to know what made her *her*.

Kate felt her self-concept shift away from loneliness, and remembered again the warmth of having an ally in love, a soft place to land, the excitement of connection. She'd almost forgotten that her body offered opportunities for discovery, and wasn't just a vehicle of practicality. She felt all of her being pour itself into her heartspace, and how it opened, vulnerable and raw.

She took a little breath, knowing what came next.

JIA LI, seeing Kate's closed eyes, imagined she was being shy, and held herself back momentarily. She wanted to brush the strand of blond hair from Kate's forehead, but could not imagine this without also imagining running her hand along her shoulder and over the curve of her breasts,

and she wondered,

how could someone be so complex, so crazy in how she lived her life, and yet between them lay the fullness of simplicity,

the kind of uncomplicated fullness of being that simply said yes,

Yes.

When Kate opened her eyes, she smiled at her, and Jia Li smiled back, knowing all the very same heart secrets,

and she leaned over to kiss her.

It was immediate, their resonance, how they came together, how Jia Li took Kate's head in her hand and rested her forehead on her forehead just a second before kissing her again,

then letting her hand rise from her side to her waist, pulling her towards her, and herself away from the transactional pleasure she'd had with Sam, in which her body succumbed, but her heart numbed —not now.

All of her was in on it.

Jia Li felt herself slip as if from a high place, falling from where she'd been perched for some time, as if standing on that cliff over the ocean, falling now into life,

even as she held tight the ravages of heartbreak and loneliness that she'd locked away until *this very moment*,

their togetherness measured in the soft touch of no time,

but all the same urgent, as Jia Li's fingers clasped Kates's, finding each other with deftness, until pleasure peaked and then spilled over into love's quiet revelation.

They lay breast to breast and in stillness their worries unwound, until the moments were untroubled and free.

Against the muted laughter of midnight revelers passing by outside, Jia Li found her way back to connection, with herself and with Kate, and they dozed for a while, until the city lights woke them. Jia Li got up to close the curtains.

SOME TIME LATER, after a midnight snack of potato chips and peanuts, and a fruitless search for a movie on the hotel television, Jia Li became serious. "I need to give you something before I go. Here." Jia Li found her phone on the floor and scrolled. "The scientist in Argentina, the one I told you about. Mateo is his name. You need his address. I've taken this screenshot. Tell me your number. But write it down too, just in case. You must take the cross to him after you've got the girl. Or please tell Victoria to take it? And if you see my mother, please if you see her, tell her to go to Mateo's too. I don't think my mother should go back to Hong Kong. She'll be safer far away. I haven't texted her. I was so afraid they'd find her."

Suddenly, her face twisted with worry. Kate held her hand.

"I'll do what I can, I promise. But what about you? I mean, after you've done whatever it is you have to do in Hong Kong, what will you do?"

"I don't know. I've got so much to figure out. I'll probably have to go to Argentina, too, especially if my mother is there. But listen, one way or another, we *will* see each other again."

"Promise?"

"I promise," Jia Li said.

JIA LI reluctantly returned to her room so she could pack and be ready to get to the airport before dawn. Best to book a flight in person and not leave any online trails, she decided—to delay the inevitable if only somewhat, given that those thugs were going to follow her back to Hong Kong—if Bernhardt's predictions were accurate.

And though her logical faculties continued to canvas the many possibilities that lay ahead, the driving force of her nature no longer questioned either Bernhardt's explanations, or Finley's visions.

If it ever truly had.

As if she'd known it all, all along, even when disbelief or hesitation seemed to mask her inner knowing.

The phone rang around midnight, just when she was trying to settle into sleep.

It was Michael. She could hear him breathing. Jia Li could hear people going by. Children laughing. The sound of cars whooshing past.

"Are you running?" she asked him.

"Walking fast, so no one can hear me. Have you told them to get the cross to South America, to the place I said?"

"Yes, but it's not there yet. You sound panicked. What's up?"

"I have more information about X. I'm now 100% sure that's what they injected your mother with. Somehow they are using DNA methylation to imprint genes with a ticking cancer timebomb. Something to do with endocrine function which alters at middle age. I don't have proof with documents from the inside, but I have enough information from the outside to be certain that there *is* proof, somewhere. I don't know what to do but—they have the means, Jia, to create the worst disease. To spread it through biological warfare. To introduce to whomever they like." He gasped for breath. He was still walking. There were car horns in the background, and the murmur of people around.

"Oh, God." Jia Li shook her head. It was too much.

"Suffice to say, should this get out, should the human genome be *programmed* in this way, there's little we can do. It does seem to be true that right now, Pharma has the cure. Even so, it's playing with fire. The virus will evolve and adapt and mutate and their so-called cure will be like last year's flu vaccine. It won't have efficacy for long. It could doom humanity, Jia. They cannot create a cure for something that *evolves*. They *must* know that. Are you there? Did you hear?"

"Shit." It was exactly what Bernhardt had shared.

"Jia, I have no proof of this, the worst thing, but—"

"*Michael*," she interrupted. "Listen to me. I have the proof. I got a letter from my father, and—"

"Edward sent you a letter?"

"Yes, it's just arrived, a year later. Via a friend who found me in Germany. Nevermind. In the letter he says there's proof and he told me where to find it. More or less."

Heavy breathing. "Really?"

"Just stay put. I'll be on the next flight home. I don't want to talk about it by phone. In case. Better that you not know more until we have a plan—until we know what to do with it. It's safer that way. I want to stop them. If they know, if we threaten them with releasing what we have, we may be able to stop it."

"I don't think so, Jia. I think they have more channels than us. I think there are governments involved."

"I *know* there are. I can't explain how I know, but I do. Still, I have to try. My father would have wanted me to try. Just stay safe."

Jia Li hung up and felt the world tilt; she closed her eyes and allowed the confusion, fear, and impotence to fight through her,

until she was left weak and unfocused.

As she gathered her bags and ordered a taxi to the airport, the most persistent thought finally broke free of confusion, lifted to the surface by an electrical impulse:

And if it's too late to stop this, what then?

With that thought came a ferocity she claimed as her own: she would make sure she did *something*. She was ready for the future, even if she didn't yet know *what* she was ready for.

AT DAWN, Kate got up to pack. Then she called Victoria and told her that she had to get to Mexico, with the object, to get Little Bird and take them both someplace safe. Someplace Jia Li had told her to go.

Victoria, as cheerful as she'd ever sounded, told her that she and Mary were leaving the next day to go to Guatemala for a resort holiday, with the anticipation of drinks by the pool, yoga and spa treatments, so she—Kate— should meet them there, and yes, with *it*. The *it* that had cured Mary completely. Kate had neither the time nor the bandwidth to process that development (or how Victoria would get the icon on the plane and into Guatemala), as Victoria rushed to say, "The police have come looking for you at your apartment. A scary Russian man has come looking for you. So girl, I think you definitely can't go home again, ever, unless you're ready to face the music."

Kate agreed with a single word—*obviously*. They organized to meet in Guatemala City at a resort where Victoria and Mary would stay until they handed the icon over to Kate.

And that was it,

just like when Little Bird left with her uncle:

the in-between moment passed in an instant and with it her old life in its entirety.

Kate removed her SIM card (the one with the number she'd given Little Bird). She mapped out the trip from Guatemala City to the Lake Chalpa region in Mexico, then on to Argentina.

Kate wrote a note to Gutov in Russian to send with Finley.

K*onstantin* I*sakevich*! *I'm sending you Yuk-Or Ba, so that you may assist him in this final part of the journey. And thank you for all that you are and have done. You were right about what you told me when I was a child: Freedom is for those who know themselves truly.*

21

PYOTR & THE METALS
AUGUST 1908
TUNGUSKA REGION, SIBERIA

There were no explanations forthcoming. As if it had never happened, as if the heat had not blasted past them, or the windows exploded. As if the dark night had not lain across the horizon for so many days, the world cast in an orange glow.

There was no one to explain, so no theories abounded, but for Pyotr, the wandering monk, there was no mystery so great that God could not guide him, and so he moved in the direction his heart beckoned, towards the place where he'd seen the fire in the sky.

Where once mosquitoes would have swarmed and consumed him, the air was still, and with the temperatures so warm at day, and cool at night, he slept well from dusk till dawn. For weeks, he wandered deeper into the wilderness. He befriended an Evenk man and alongside his family rode a reindeer for part of the way. They told him that their god Agby, the god of thunder, had blasted them with light and lifted them off the ground and made their reindeers vanish. They would not go to where Agby had lit the ground, but indicated the way, so Pyotr left them past Churgin creek and continued towards the Podkammenaya Tunguska river, until he came into the scorched land.

He could hardly believe what he discovered there. Thousands of flattened trees and others standing upright but stripped of branches. And so many hundreds of dead reindeer laying on their sides, black as if left untouched on a spit. Here the air was so still and the earth so laid waste that he had no words or understanding for what his eyes showed him was true.

He crossed himself and said a prayer.

Whatever had happened, it was a force as mighty as God if not God himself, like the Evenk's God of Thunder, but for what purpose he could not fathom. Whatever the nature of its creator, the act itself was a reminder that there is something grander and more powerful than humans, and thus the event prescribed humility.

Pyotr camped near the river and he prayed to understand what had taken place, and what it meant. He aligned himself with the power that had wrought this force, and asked that in its reflection he understand his place in the Universe.

He praised God, whom he knew as a presence throughout every leaf, every grain of soil, every bird.

He bowed low to the ground, prostrate, though his back did protest as he went down—it had begun to spasm now and again since riding the reindeer. He surrendered to the pain, and willed that he know his own nature. Eyes squinting, he saw something glistening in the afternoon sun, on the banks of the river,

metal chunks, such as he'd not seen before,

and he'd seen a fair share as his brother had learnt the forge, and many times had he watched him bring form to life from liquid alloys. Only surely this specimen was different. Pyotr inspected the few clumps in the palm of his hand; they were smooth, lumpy, a dark silverish—like iron, but anyway he couldn't speculate since he was no expert. But for some reason, he desired to hold them and he continued to pray, bowing low to the ground.

It was not difficult for him to enter into a state of complete devotion, as although he was not without his own pain, his relationship to those feelings was not burdened by fear. So he opened to his inner world deeply, allowing the sharp edges of terror or grief or self-doubt, such that he quickly surged past them.

In the midst of his present heart-softening and heart-opening, he unconsciously worked the nuggets between his fingers. Within moments, he felt himself tilt towards that emanation of dizziness in which rapture overcomes imbalance, and he felt the metal in his hand buzzing.

He sat up. The waters of the Podkammenaya rushed past and the sound set off a vibration in all of his being, so that he knew he had to stay, and sit, pray and praise as energy coursed through him.

It seemed so extraordinary a thing, these random clumps of metal in the stream, on the bank, that they should carry the imprint of Grace and transmit this to him, yet it was happening. Then he began to feel the oddest thing,

a combination of longing and homesickness, and then—bliss,

as if an urge were rising within him with every breath and just as quickly satisfied beyond his imagining,

peace,

such peace,

even joy.

He felt so *well*. He made a fire near the river and sat with the stones. He collected more. He slept with them in his pockets and in his clutched hands, and over the next few days, wandered further, his mind ablaze with nothing.

No thing.

Each thought no sooner formed, resolved itself in understanding, and then dissolved back into no thought.

Emptiness, the most joyful emptiness he could have imagined.

The days continued. He wandered. Physical pain was no longer his bedfellow; his back was as supple as in youth, and with pleasure each day he collected firewood. He bent over and stood, and slept on the hard earth, and awoke each day energized.

Pyotr felt he belonged to all the world, and all the world belonged to him.

. . .

IT TOOK him many weeks of days and nights for Pyotr to wander back to the Ascension Monastery and to the forge of his brother Vissarion. When he did, he embraced his brother as if they'd been separated by war and time, as if he'd returned from death.

"You are rapturous, brother. Did you find God so soon?" Vissarion asked him.

"I have found that there is more to miracles than we know. That nature, herself, is a miracle. God is close to the heart, so close that he is there, should you only have the opportunity to open the door and step inside." He pounded his heart with outstretched fingers.

Vissarion squinted.

"Perhaps because you were not so cold this time, being as Autumn has not yet arrived."

"You misunderstand me."

"No, I hear you."

"You hear with your ears. You should see with your heart."

"Okay, enough. I am busy with my own form of devotion, but we will eat together. Are you leaving again soon? Or will you stay at the monastery before it's too cold to live in nature?"

"I only came to give you this." Pyotr pulled a small cloth sack from his bag. So small that it sat in the palm of his hand.

"What is this?"

"Metal. Nuggets that are miracles. I believe they came from the Heavens."

Vissarion felt the onset of trepidation.

"This sounds like blasphemy. But continue."

"I have long held that Nature and God are in communion, Vissarion. I don't wish to debate. I only know that I found this near the Podkamennaya Tunguska River. I only know that I have had such peace since holding it. I feel more alive than ever. I don't claim to know its mechanism, but it is a miracle, brother. I wish you to have it, as I know your heart is still hurting despite your pledge to the Church and your commitment to God. I know you are still human, and some losses will always cause pain."

Pyotr took the cloth bag and opened it gingerly. He withdrew a small, silvery rock, a globule, misshapen and lumpy. It was cool to the touch. He enjoyed the feeling of it.

"Is this tin? An alloy of zinc and some other metals. Hmmm."

"I don't know. Hold it," said Pyotr.

"I will do so later, but not now. I'm sorry brother, I have tasks and no time for…"

"For presence? I only ask you to hold this."

"I do not even know what it is."

"It matters not! Vissarion, listen here. You mustn't approach this with your mind. You are an artist and a servant of God."

Vissarion shrugged.

"What you don't admit into your heart will haunt you," Pyotr said. "It will grow stronger and be like a scar unto your soul. I know you are afraid. Hold this. You will see."

"Later," Vissarion said. He returned the stone to the others in the small bag and placed it on a shelf amongst his tools.

"When you are ready, please, it is here for you."

"Thank you brother. I know you have my best interests at heart."

"I will go again soon, and I do not know that I will be back. I have found peace, Vissarion, such as you cannot imagine. I desire only to live in this state."

"I know, Pyotr. I know you well."

The brothers embraced. So long had been their journey from the Ukraine as young men on a pilgrimage, each escaping their own pain. Vissarion, the pain of loss. Pyotr, the pain of not knowing how he might join with the spirit which seemed to move through him and yet remain at a distance.

So now, they each had found their path. It was what it was.

Pyotr and Vissarion shared a meal, after which Pyotr slept in the hermitage for several nights before he disappeared, and this time, for good.

22

WALLACE & RESONANCE

JUNE 2131 AD

KRASNOYARSK, EASTERN FEDERATION

As Wallace lay on his cot, woken by the sliver of sunlight through the high metal grille in his room, there came a whispered voice calling him. *Wallace.*

He reached for his robe, draped across the bottom of the cot, and used it to cover his naked body as he went to the hatch. "It's me, Alex," the whisper came again.

"Just a moment," Wallace said, sliding his arms into the robe and tying it at the waist. "Is it trance-Alex or regular-Alex?" he asked as he opened the hatch. Alex climbed in.

"It's just me. I—I don't know how I know you're here. I found myself in the tunnels and.... noticed this hatch. Why are you..." he looked around at the space, obviously confounded by what he saw. Drab, dark grey concrete walls and floor. A highish ceiling. No amenities. The grille was the only source of light and fresh air. There was a collection of folding chairs leaning against the wall in the corner, a couple of small tables, and of course Wallace's simple, low metal cot with its flimsy mattress. Dr. Rinella had a habit of bringing odds and ends with each visit, so after a few days, in addition to furniture, there were plates, mugs, extra blankets, and even a bucket with water and a towel for washing.

"Why are you here Wallace? We met here before, didn't we."

"Yes. You were in rather an odd state though. Here, sit." Wallace retrieved two folding chairs and opened them. They sat across from one another.

"I have a memory of being here. I saw you in the tunnel, with others. I don't recall what came next." His gaze drifted towards the hatch.

"Why are you back, Alex?"

"I don't know." His face drew itself into a frown, forehead creased. He looked down at his hands and wrung them. "I don't know. Wallace. I don't understand."

Wallace could not help but notice his friend's days-old stubble and lackluster skin.

"Have you any idea at all why you were down here in the first place?" Wallace prompted, not yet prepared to remind Alex of his words then, how he was *patrolling the tunnels, to keep him safe.*

"Yes, and no." He didn't look up. His expression shifted from baffled to embarrassed.

"It's odd, isn't it, that I'm not surprised you are in such a... strange place..." His eyes briefly danced around the room. "I've not been myself lately. It started in morning meditation. I just lost track of time and when I finished the meditation, everyone had left. Father Andrew assumed I had fallen into a state of devotion, but I have no memory of anything. Then, the next time I lost track of time, I came to just outside in the Quarter Fields. I was terrified. I didn't know how I got there. And then you ran into me in these tunnels. Again, no memory of how."

Wallace appraised his friend's emotional state, now taking in his fear. "I'm no stranger to altered states," he said by way of reassurance. "I'd say that's what's happening to you."

"Yes, I thought you'd understand." Alex frowned. "People are saying you've been transferred. That's what Father Andrew said. That you left on fellowship South."

"So that's the official story."

Suddenly Alex's entire face contorted in despair, and he began to wring his hands even more vigorously.

"Wallace, I—I think someone is in my head, and I think... I think that *that person*, who wrote you a note—is me. Did you get a message, on paper, beneath your door...?"

"That was you then?" Wallace was incredulous. *Of course.* It all added up. Alex had been at his door. And he had said to Schopel, in his trance, that his mission was to keep him safe.

"So you did get a note?" Alex asked.

"Yes I did. Telling me about forces from the past trying to sabotage me. And allies helping me. And about this room! You wrote it?"

"Yes," he stuttered. "I mean, no. I mean." He gasped for breath. "I remember someone else took over me and I wrote that *for* them. I realize this sounds like possession..."

"It's clearly not, Alex."

Wallace wanted to dissuade Alex from viewing recent events through a harmful lens, that of their training.

"That note was an attempt to help me, or *warn* me... Possession is different entirely. But how did you remember that you wrote it?"

"I... I have been so distressed, Wallace. This isn't like me. I don't want what you have. I just want a normal life."

His jaw trembled. His hands, still reflexively wringing, shook. Wallace knew this state: a body that had been trained out of emotion, unable to manage the currents.

"I know this feeling," Wallace said. "I understand."

Alex seemed to pull himself together and spoke fast. "I had a dream that I was leaving you a note. Only it was a woman telling me what to do, telling me that you needed to know about the danger, and about this room, and I think that's also why I was down here. I don't understand any of this."

"It's okay, Alex. No one really does."

There was a faint tapping at the hatch. Wallace went to open it. Eden Schopel stepped through, and when she saw Alex she sighed and said, "Yes, okay," as if answering a question no one had posed.

"Alex believes he left me a note, the one I told you about —and that a woman is communicating to me through him," Wallace said.

Schopel got another chair from the wall and sat with them. She drew a deep breath, her eyes narrowing. It was as if she were gathering all the energy in the room as she prepared to speak, and when she did, her voice pulled Wallace down to earth. He felt his body relax, his belly soften, and even Alex's agitation dialed down to stillness.

"This is what we are dealing with. A grab for power fought in the murky realm of consciousness. But you, my dear young man, are on the side of good. Whether you recall it or not."

Alex shook his head. "I never wanted to be part of this. I don't understand it And yet—not only am I compelled beyond my ability to control, finding myself in odd places, losing time—I am also compelled to keep it secret, as there is a part of my mind which is stronger than me, which *insists*." Here he threw up his hands.

"Hmm," Schopel's voice soothed. "You resist what might otherwise be a natural integration of those *parts*, as you named them, because your Monasteries have done what all institutions do, and that is to compromise on truth in order to serve an agenda. Believe me, young man, when I say that much was lost when your form of spirituality took over."

Alex withered, mournful. "All of this is beyond my understanding. And I—don't want it."

"And yet, there is a part of you that *does* understand, and that part of you has a counterpart in another life, a *past* life, who wants to reach Wallace through you."

"How, though?" Alex asked.

"That's why I've come today, to help Wallace understand how to reach the past more directly, the correct past."

"The correct past...?" Wallace asked.

"Just as there are multiple potential futures, so there are multiple potential pasts. And this young man is from a past in which our allies saw a future in which you, Wallace, were found here, in these tunnels. Hence him surveilling you. Whether he wants to or not. Is aware or not. And believe me. He is not alone. Others, conscious of their role or not, are acting out of impulses and agendas beyond time."

"I should go," Alex said, trembling. "I don't belong here. I'm sorry if I caused anyone trouble."

"Stay," Schopel commanded.

She leaned over, and as she had done to him before, placed her thumb in between his eyebrows, and spoke in another language. Alex blinked a few times, and his eyes fluttered closed, then his head dropped and he became still.

WALLACE ASKED SCHOPEL, "What have you done?"

"He's fine. I've put his parasympathetic system into a deep rest state. I need to speak with you first. That is why I'm here. I'll deal with your friend shortly. Wallace, you seem worried."

"It's not Alex. It's just—perhaps I don't really understand it at all, and suddenly I have more questions than I have peace. Why can we not know for certain if the origins of the icon were found, if the past is... *passed*? Why can I not go directly to the moment of discovery? Why do I have the sense that I locked into Finley's timeline chronologically, from the point at which we made contact?"

The questions poured out of him and left him quivering; they seemed to confirm the enormity of his responsibility, the sense that he was the only one who could make the needed contribution in their era.

"This particular chronology relates to your shared consciousness, and it would seem that you are journeying in parallel, evolving in your shared consciousness as one, so that you cannot receive a revelation beyond your shared capacity to experience it. As for the past being passed, there may be different alternate pasts, ones in which he finds the icon's origins, ones in which he doesn't. You are connecting with the one that most matches your own resonance, which is why keeping you in the correct state is vital, so that your consciousness connects to the past which is the desired one."

"The future affects the past," Wallace said.

Schopel nodded. "The universe is a cobweb, and you can follow many threads, each its own dimension radiating out from a central beginning. Everything is there. Each thread is valid. Which one shall you follow? That is the task here."

"So," Wallace said, "the past, like the future, is linked to consciousness in the present only by the frequency, or collection of thoughts, or you might say, by the emotional tonality of the present moment. That's what you mean by resonance. In a very real sense, there is no time. There are endless timelines. Endless possibilities. There is connection through time via the internal vibration, the resonance, of the one travelling."

"Yes."

"Like tuning into a musical note," Wallace concluded.

"Indeed, that is an apt description."

"Yes, I have been playing with this myself. My visions, it seems, directly relate to the events, the feelings, the tone of my present moment, and carry me towards a similar-feeling tone in Finley's life."

"Indeed, in the same manner, the probable future is linked only to the individuals involved. The future is also a resonance, with what is at present in the field of the Visionary. We—these very few of us—have made a decision that we must go forward, to the happier outcome. We attempt to embody the resonance that represents the happier outcome. It is our only hope."

"So, what is real then? What past is real, what future is real?"

"That is the ancient question. Only the present exists, this limitless, present resonance, in which all possibility exists."

"So I too must work more consciously with the correct tone. One of certainty, of hope. Will Finley feel this too?"

"Yes, that is why I have come to talk with you today, before our session. To help you find a way to be clear with your resonance."

"And the others, the ones who are interfering, who wish to find the origins of the cross first. Do they know about resonance?"

"Yes, yes. But they operate from a different consciousness entirely. They plan insurrection. They desire chaos as a laboratory experiment. To identify the meek based on their behavior and then tag them genetically. It's barbaric. However, this kind of thing will always exist. The key is to build our own resonance, align with our own timeline. They will have their own, and if we do this well, we will operate on a frequency at which their abilities are less effective."

"I'm beginning to understand," Wallace said. "They may have their own timeline, then?"

"Yes."

"And if we hold to the correct resonance, it's as if… as if our universes split. We venture into another alternate universe."

"You may think of it in those terms, certainly. In any case, it's the reason we must hide you from any possibility of discovery. Because you need the space and freedom to fully align with the correct resonance."

Alex's head had fallen forward and he was drooling. Schopel jumped up and tapped him lightly on the sternum. He didn't stir. She lifted one of his arms and dropped it; it fell to his lap, floppy.

She pulled her chair to sit across from him and leaned forward, placing her thumb between his eyebrows. Her eyes rolled back into her head, as if going into some sort of trance state herself. Wallace watched, transfixed, wondering if he looked like this when he was hypnotized and inside Finley's life.

For several long minutes Schopel sat like this across from Alex as Wallace mutely observed, and then there was a faint tap at the hatch.

It was Dr. Rinella and Justicia. Wallace ushered them in, indicating that they should be quiet, pointing at Schopel and Alex.

Dr. Rinella carried a bag. He lay it on one of the tables, and pulled out food and tea flasks. He passed around the flasks, and Justicia gave Wallace a wrapped meal packet. It was an adept's breakfast, still steaming. Porridge with various herbs and protein flakes. Hardly delicious, but it was the nutrition Wallace needed to function.

No one spoke.

Schopel remained in her odd state as everyone drank tea and Wallace ate.

Then Dr. Rinella jumped up to open the hatch again, and Father Andrew came through. For the first time that Wallace had seen, these two men were together in the flesh, and—although clearly they'd been in communication for the duration of their project—it was obvious they'd not seen each other in person for some time. They clasped arms and hugged. "You've become rather stout, my friend," Dr. Rinella said, patting Father Andrew on his back. "Perhaps we need to revisit the courts, shoot some friendly hoops."

"Aging is not something one is prepared for, in these times." Father Andrew laughed.

Schopel suddenly opened her eyes, removed her thumb, and sat back in her chair. Alex opened his eyes, lifted his head abruptly and then looked around, confused.

"It's good to see you, Alex," Father Andrew said. "Are you okay? I had suspected you were experiencing something odd, and then Lucio messaged me that you were wandering around down here."

Alex wiped his mouth with this sleeve. "What just happened?"

"Eden, you've been journeying with him, haven't you!" Dr. Rinella exclaimed. "Remarkable!"

"I shouldn't be here," Alex said. "Wallace, I'm sorry if I've caused you problems. I only wanted to tell you honestly what I knew…"

"It's fine," Schopel said, her voice soft and reassuring. "You don't owe anyone anything. We trust your discretion."

Alex stood hastily, grasped his robes with both hands and walked to the hatch, head bowed.

"Good luck," he said as he went.

"What was that about?" asked Father Andrew. "He's been behaving oddly lately."

"It's not his fault," Schopel said, sighing. Dr. Rinella handed her a flask of tea, which she gratefully took and drank.

"Part of his consciousness in the past has been attempting to reach him in the present, and his mind has been resisting. Thanks in part to all that he's learnt at the Monastery, I might add."

"I admit it's not perfect," Father Andrew said.

"In this case, it's also complicated by the fact that his past self is not entirely sane. She's had her mind carelessly probed by forces who are looking for what Finley and Wallace know, but the sane part of her has been trying to reach us. I only wanted to help him by telling *her*—his past self—that we received the message, and she can leave him be. He won't remember much of what happened, which is best. He will start to feel more at ease soon. And Andrew—it's not so much the training at the Monasteries, but the death focus that you all have, which teaches a child to distrust anything that feels like expansion. Any hint that we might know our multi-dimensional selves. Honestly." She rolled her eyes. "If only you included the wisdom of other traditions."

"I agree," Father Andrew said. "Somehow Wallace escaped this cultural bias. I have done my best to encourage him beyond the strictures of my training…"

"And you have done well." Schopel softened. "There is hope for all adepts, should you step up more and revise some of the precepts."

"Noted." Father Andrew smiled. "When this is done with, I should very much appreciate your counsel in this matter."

"Agreed." Schopel smiled.

Wallace felt a strange new curiosity about Eden Schopel; she was more complex than he understood, and had esoteric knowledge beyond anything he'd experienced before. He wondered what her story was, her true origins.

He felt Justicia's eyes on him, and turned his head to meet her gaze.

"Have you slept?" she asked him.

"Yes, thank you. Fitfully, but it was sufficient."

They continued to stare at one another.

"We have work to do," Dr. Rinella said, but just as the words left his mouth he appeared to do a double take. "Justicia?"

She wiped tears from her cheek. Wallace resolutely closed his eyes.

"Oh, dear," Dr. Rinella said.

Father Andrew appeared uncomfortable and Schopel placed a hand on Justicia's back.

"Justicia, we know you are cancered. I am so sorry my dear," Schopel said. "But do not give up hope—we may be close to a cure."

She nodded and sniffed, wiping her face. "Thank you, Eden. For myself I can accept hope. But my husband is in hospice now. I was with him overnight. I have said my goodbyes. For him, it is too late."

Hospice is where the cancered were sent for their final days, once the centrally tracked home tests reported inevitable organ failure. An ambulance was sent within the hour. Everyone knew that the quick transfer to hospice was more a policy to dispose of the bodies than to provide compassionate or comfortable end of life care. Justicia's husband would probably not last another night.

Wallace wished he'd not heard this now, not on a day he was meant to travel in consciousness. Knowing how Justicia suffered was painful enough, but his pain was amplified as he knew that he would be the one grieving a loss of this nature in just a matter of time, when she too declined. It was inevitable.

Wallace squeezed his eyes closed against what his heart saw— only pain. He opened his eyes to find Dr. Rinella staring at him.

"Wallace, are you okay?" he asked.

"Yes." But he couldn't stop it; his eyes watered.

Schopel said, "I have spoken to Wallace about using resonance."

Justicia gathered herself. "Wallace and I have already discussed this, too."

"Yes," Wallace spoke, as steady as he could muster. "In fact I told her how I direct myself towards Finley, and Scopel's insights have refined my understanding." He rubbed his eyes with the back of a hand.

Dr. Rinella, puzzled, looked to Justicia, then to Wallace, then back again. His face lit up. "You two are lovers!"

Justicia rolled her eyes. "Yes, Lucio. Have your moment, go on."

"But this is fantastic!" he cried.

Wallace could feel heat rising up his neck—again, he felt that anger from days ago, the gathering storm in his heart. He couldn't stop himself. "But she is cancered, as you know. It is *not* fantastic."

Father Andrew sat on the closest chair and leaned forward using a voice Wallace knew well from their time in study and reflection. "Wallace, remember what I have told you, the mystic's heart is opened…"

"… when there is love," Dr. Rinella finished the sentence.

"It creates an opening," Father Andrew said.

"Like a resonance," Schopel added. "As I have just explained to him."

Justicia was attempting to be professional, Wallace could see it, holding herself with crossed arms, expressionless.

"And the pain? The emotional pain? I am sad and afraid, because she is ill," Wallace cried out. "I don't know how to navigate these *feelings*, so how can I… can I… find the required resonance now? And it's exactly what I need, apparently, in order to maintain the correct connection to Finley, the right timeline, and then to find the origin of the cross."

"Pain is simply love inverted," Father Andrew said. "Pain is only as strong as the love that fuels it."

"Yet it's not the same. Please don't tell me it is the same, with all respect. It is *fear,* it is not love."

His anger tipped into despair even as he tightened his fists reflexively, nostrils flaring. Justicia went to him, sat by him, took his hand.

"Your fear speaks to desire, Wallace, which links back to love. Can't you see?" Father Andrew said.

Dr. Rinella speculated. "Might you use the love in your heart as a wave to ride into the past, and by virtue of that, take us into the future we yearn for?"

Justicia and Wallace looked to one another then away, disconsolate; their love had become a curiosity, an experiment in consciousness. Moreover, Wallace reflected, Justicia's husband was taking his last breaths as they spoke, and here she was enduring a pain whose gravity he had only begun to fathom. How could any of this be happening right now?

Schopel said, "It could work. Focusing on love, then holding to a resonance that feels like ultimate joy, like the full blossoming of a love that cannot end, in a world in which we survive."

"I don't know," Wallace said. "I suppose we could try." He steadied himself by clasping Justicia's hand in his. She gave him a reassuring smile.

"We must try," Dr. Rinella said. "Justicia, remain where you are, holding his hand."

"Give me a few moments to settle my breath," Wallace said.

"Wallace," Schopel spoke. She'd pulled her chair closer and rested a hand on his shoulder, pressing down. He felt himself relax under her touch. "We've been trying to hold you in Finley's life long enough, to push the timeline forward far enough, so that we can get the answer we need. So far, it's not happening fast enough and the interference is only growing. This could be the breakthrough we need. Here." She pressed into the back of his neck, and hummed.

"Breathe," she whispered.

"May as well start," Dr. Rinella said.

Always, it began with this. Filling himself with breath completely, then holding himself full, then emptying himself completely and remaining empty for an equal time. To start, he breathed out for longer, knowing this would settle his mood, refocus his attention, conveying to his human body that he was safe.

"Find a resonance, and hold onto it," Schopel said.

Resonance.

But resonance was a thoughtform that hung over him like a heavy cloud and, grasping onto that image, he willed the cloud to shower him with rain so that he might release the thought of it and have the experience of it instead.

I cannot, he thought, and peeked at Justicia, who seemed distracted now. He felt her limp hand in his and summonsed love, reminding himself of her lips against his, her small form rolled up into his, and at the same time he attempted to imbue the rainclouds with this love, willing once more that they break and submerge him, imagining the relief it might provide.

There was only a minor inner movement, a mist that rose up in him, tingling in his heart—

Finally Dr. Rinella began to speak, his habitual induction—

He counted backwards and walked Wallace into the room of his mind where he gathered stillness, in which comfortable yet solitary confinement there was a door. He always imagined the same door since he'd met Dr. Rinella, a prison door. The bars solid. One hand gripped on each. He came forward until his face felt the cold metal, one on each cheek. Then he grunted and pushed and the door swung open. Eyes squinting, then gradually adjusting to the light, to the scene he was in.

A lake.

An old man walking towards him from the rocky shore, glowing in the morning sun.

The man stopped just in front of him and placed a hand on each of Wallace's shoulders. *On Finley's shoulders.* He smiled with such beatitude, his eyes twinkling, as if knowing that he spoke not just to Finley, but to all of the parts of him which together constituted his entire consciousness.

"The Bridge. You will find an explanation there. I will be that troublesome writer who refers to my own work. But it is easier to read than to sit through my explanation."

He laughed.

The old man's brown eyes were a mirror to the penetrating blue sky. The lines at his eyes deepened as he laughed again. "I know who you are," he said, before Wallace's last remaining sense of self fell away and he simply *was* Finley Minor.

PART III
HOMECOMING

The crossing is the shattering place,
    where the one becomes many.
    ~K.I. Gutov, *Ikona*

Faith is the bird that feels the light
    and sings when the dawn is still dark.
    ~Rabindranath Tagore, *Gitanjali*

The clock indicates the moment—
    but what does eternity indicate?
    ~Walt Whitman, "Song of Myself"

23

JIA LI: KNOWLEDGE NOT PROOF - REPRISED

JUNE 2019

HONG KONG

The fog swept down from the mountain and hid her from the world, only now the bare bones of truth lay there for her to see—this rock at Sai Kung bore the brunt of it.

She cried because probably her father was pushed.

Not *probably*. They killed him. Whether he took the final step on his own, or in company, it was not his choice.

She knew that.

All her sorrowful imagining of what it might be like to succumb to the depths dissolved into anger, which gathered into a storm and rolled over her like the choppy waters lapping at the rocks.

The world spun. She sank to her knees.

She wrapped her arms around herself and glared at the water that took him.

Angry, not just for her father, or for herself fatherless,

but for the whole of humanity—

It seemed too much to believe, yet with all that had happened, Jia Li realized that she had accepted Finley's visions as truth, as if the fabric of this present-future visioning were merely one part of a patchwork that contained her father's legacy,

all of which demanded her reaction, lest inaction eat away at her.

How could there be people who so callously gambled with human life for profit? Her mind lashed out with logic to dim the ache at her chest, the fire in her gut.

There was only so much money could buy,
so what was profit and wealth ultimately but power,
and what was power but greed, and therein lay *fear*.

The fear that drove humans to do anything for power and wealth.

Surely one person's fear was only a mirror to the collective, the combined fear of a thousand individual traumas festering in a wound that
simply
needed
relief,
magnetized back to the individual, for whom greed and power was the salve, the heart-hardening gratification,

that of a heart inured to the thousands and millions who would perish.

Jia Li wept.

How she missed her father's green eyes, so intelligent and kind, so accepting.

How she missed believing that he had made a choice, as painful as it was, but a choice nonetheless. That she had a choice now—she could not take it for granted.

She could choose. They would not choose for her.

Kate.

She pushed Kate away in her mind and tried to still her quickening heart at the thought of Kate alone in Mexico with the child. Had she made it to Mexico? Were they trying to set up home? She missed her smell and her smile, and all that had been silently promised in their one night together.

And Finley? Was he okay?

He and Kate, and Michael, they were her tribe, now. Caught up in this patchwork complexity.

The sun was setting. She gathered herself and walked quickly back to her car as the city's lights transformed the sky into a chaotic beacon.

. . .

WHEN MICHAEL SAW Jia Li enter the sushi restaurant his face lit up. He made a rather clumsy attempt to reciprocate her spontaneous hug from his seated position and dropped his chopsticks, along with the scallop that had dangled from them. With his mouth full, as if they were mid-conversation, he garbled, "Is the cross on the way to Argentina? To Mateo? Like I asked?"

"It will get there. Some other things have to happen first. I will let you know more as I do."

Jia Li waved away the server. She wasn't hungry. She was wired from lack of sleep and nerves. It was only a matter of time before they found her again.

She'd gone back to her apartment to find it had been completely ransacked. Her father's desk was upended, the drawers on the floor, papers scattered, the pillows from the couch torn up, the fluffy insides like cotton candy spewed everywhere.

But her father's record collection was intact. There were his fifty or so albums all neatly lined up inside the TV stand shelf, and Jia Li didn't even hesitate. All during her flight, she'd been thinking about that letter, his last day, how she'd stood at the door watching him and how Jimi Hendrix was playing. So no sooner had she arrived than she'd rifled through the albums until she found the one. Inside, stuck flat next to the record itself with blu tac, was a tiny black USB. She grabbed it, along with some of hers and her mother's clothes, then went to the nearest hotel and checked in under another name. They wanted a credit card to hold against the room and she said it had been stolen and insisted they take a pile of cash she'd withdrawn from a random ATM, using a travel card she'd bought at the airport.

She hadn't slept at all. The USB was now in her jeans pocket, her fingers wrapped around it.

Michael didn't wait for her to ask what he'd discovered. Neither could muster any chit chat. He swallowed his food, and began—

"I think whatever the substance was in the icon, whatever the strange molecular formation, and I've asked others to weigh in—it's possible that it's the result of a high-intensity, high heat event. I need to learn more. But right now I'm at a dead end with that. In the meantime, I don't have very good news."

Jia Li could see by the way his lip curled and his eyes half squeezed shut that it must be very bad.

She held her breath.

"I think it may be too late, Jia. I don't want to believe that's the case, but…"

"Too late? You mean Virus X? What do you mean?"

"Remember what I told you on the phone? Well now I have proof that it's out there. Not just in your mother, Jia Li. A pathologist in my network has seen some abnormalities in recent bloodwork that match the information I discovered. I asked if I could access a sample of DNA from the bloodwork and he sent me images. I could be wrong. I hope I'm wrong."

"Go on."

"There are markers in the blood and changes in the DNA consistent with some of the theories floating around out there indicating a new form of viral cancer is already live, present. All I need is proof from inside HKK to link the two. If so, then I can only conclude—"

"But that's just one person. One sample." She cut him off.

"Unfortunately there are more. I asked around. At least five people that I can confirm have this same marker and they are in different countries, Jia. It's not just local. And it's bigger than HKK. There are governments involved. But nevermind that. I have sources I trust who have some pretty compelling information."

"About that," Jia Li said.

He grabbed a napkin and wiped his face, then his brow. His white dress shirt was unbuttoned, and she could see that his face and neck were pink.

He hadn't heard her in his fervour. "The information on the specific virus and how it presents in the blood and the bloodwork from around the world—it's the same. It's just like your mum's blood, Jia. There is no other explanation."

"So the virus has been what, released? Spread? On purpose? Why?"

She thought of Finley, his future travels—and part of her mind thought,

But this can't be happening, the present confirming the future.

The other part thought simply,

It's happening.

"Depopulation," they both said at once.

He winced. "How did you...?"

"Too much to explain."

"Slow and steady depopulation. I think that's the agenda. Or at least it seems that way. There are too many humans on the planet. Some people think we need fewer so that we are easier to control."

"Whose plan? Whose agenda? And anyway, over how much time, and how..."

"...has it been spread?" Michael finished her sentence.

"Yes."

"I can speculate, but the main thing is that I really think it's begun. If it's out there, and we've found five, there are more. It will spread. Organically. Over time, it will just... spread."

He wiped his forehead again and pushed his plate away.

"There's no way to stop it now?" she asked.

"Only if they start dispensing the cure, now."

She understood.

"Too late," she said.

He folded the napkin on the table in front of him, lost to thought.

Then, for Jia Li, it was as if the voices around them disappeared. As if she'd entered a void; she had the thought, briefly, that this was what Finley must experience before he traveled to the future, his consciousness traversing a great pause,

a solid space of no-time where nothing was anything or meant anything

before truth made itself felt,

and so portentous was that truth that time itself was displaced.

It was all as Finley had seen it.

The future existed because the seed had been planted.

She rallied her senses, engaged her critical mind. She had to tell Michael everything she knew, before she became distracted by deciding on the task ahead.

"Listen, you're right about governments being involved. Those guys who follow me, they're not pharma. They're government, or represent some kind of elite faction tied to governments. I think they want to know what information I have, not because I or anybody else has never been able to stop them—you agree that it's too late—but because they want to manage the fallout. They want to prepare a countermove, to respond to whatever information might be leaked. Do you understand?"

"How... how are you so sure?"

"I just can't explain, Michael. I'm just too tired. Trust me that I have my sources like you have yours. Anyway, it's *all* speculation, isn't it? To some extent? But it makes sense, doesn't it? If you're right, and HKK and whoever they are allied with are already spreading X all over the world, then it can't be stopped. It can *never* be stopped. It can only be *revealed*. So I guess... I guess to some people, the real threat is whatever consequence comes from revealing it."

"So you think that whoever is after you is afraid of what would happen if people knew, because they think you might be a whistleblower?"

"I think so."

"That's the wildcard for sure. How news could spread. Whether or not they could control it. What people will do about it—and—I know the media is managed, and it would be easy to suppress this. And they will. They'll create fake news and ban certain information. But I have to tell you, Jia, there are many in the world who will not tolerate anything but the truth. There is a growing movement in the shadows of those who have grave doubts about corporations, governments..."

"I know. Yes. I mean, I don't know. But I feel that must be true."

Michael was on a roll. He'd pushed away his empty beer bottle, his glass, his chopsticks, and his hands were on the table, clasped. He sat upright, and spoke with passion now. "There are groups, individuals, who are prepared to sacrifice a great deal to save this planet, to rescue humanity from corporatism, from secrets."

"I understand. I think..." She took a breath. "I think I have to be on that side, then."

"Okay," he said, as if that were that. "Okay. Me too, obviously. So—what about this proof you said Edward gave you?"

"Ah yes." She smiled. "You'll never believe it."

She recounted meeting the man from Bulgaria and the letter from her father. She told him about her apartment and that she found the album, and the USB.

"*All along the watchtower.* Jimi Hendrix. He was listening to it that last day."

He frowned. "Your dad and I used to talk about music a lot. He used to say that Hendrix captured all the anger of his generation. Fitting."

"I didn't know you and my father talked about music. Here. I need you to take it."

She pulled the USB out of her pocket, reached over and placed it in Michael's hand, then closed his hand into a fist over it. He flinched a bit. "Oh my God, I can't believe this."

"Believe it. They're after me. I have to think about our next steps. I need you to make copies of everything you find here. Hide some. Take some. Disperse it. Make sure no one is following you. Maybe don't go home. I don't know. Be safe. And I have a show tonight. Meet me later, after I text. The intersection one block north of here."

They stood and walked towards the door.

Michael whispered loudly as they wound through busy tables. "Are you serious? You're basically luring them right to you. What if they kill you? And what am I supposed to do with these copies?"

"Keep a copy? Hide some more. I don't know. You're smart. You'll figure it out. And they don't want to kill me. They want to inject me, like they did to my mother. Because they want to know what I know. It's a final *fuck you*. Anyway, I kinda have to do this. I will be in touch after. If you don't hear from me, then you have to blow the whistle without me. Otherwise, we need a plan, Michael, a strategy. I can't do it without you. You know how these things work. How people find the truth, and what to do if no one believes us."

"People believe what they want to believe. We have to find the right platforms to share this information."

"Exactly. See, you know best. Later."

Jia Li squeezed his forearm, and crossed the road without him.

THE MANAGER at the venue had not rostered her in at all for any upcoming shows since she'd left the country, but Jia Li had rung him from Berlin, begging for a last performance, explaining that she'd be overseas indefinitely and it might be his last chance to feature her. She could draw a crowd, and he knew it, so she wasn't surprised when he affixed her act to the end of the Saturday night lineup. Word spread fast on social media. *Jelly Ropes* was on, and so she expected that the thugs would be in the front row. She assumed they'd made it back from Berlin—possibly injured, possibly furious with her.

Jia Li didn't care.

She picked up the ropes as she prepared backstage and smelled them. Oh how she loved the smell, reassuring and familiar, and how soft they were against her cheek.

She put on the sequin bikini, the tight red dress, the heels.

She stretched.

She double checked the rigging, ensured all the points on the ceiling were secure, and conferred with the stagehand about timing. This guy, barely older than a teenager and a club regular—he had helped her before. He knew the ropes, literally, and she always joked with him, but not today.

"You okay?" he asked. He pushed his long hair out of his face and peered at her. "You seem nervous."

"Nah," she said. "Just preoccupied."

"Be careful," he said.

"Sure. As always."

She stared up at the ceiling behind the curtain. Her mind went elsewhere, cast up into the vast universe. She squeezed her eyes shut, imagining the luminescence of stars, and Kate beneath them, staring up into the same sky.

Is that where my father is now? She wondered, suddenly thinking of him, too—another absence that pressed into her heart.

On autopilot, she stretched again.

Then, a slight tremor.

She knew—*it is too late to stop those thugs, so what other choice is there?*

"We're about to start," the stagehand said.

She nodded and opened her eyes. She wound the pile of ropes around her feet and draped some over her hand. She loved this combination, red dress, red ropes at her feet. In her mind, she was like a candle that had melted, the pooled ropes like red wax sticking her to the stage. So still.

She settled into stillness. Dropped to her center.

The music began, *Sigur ros*. A different choice for tonight.

The curtain opened.

The crowd's murmur settled into a hush. A few muffled voices, that was it. The orchestral opening track grew louder.

Jia Li felt the light stirrings of grief, of anger, but it was nothing like last time.

She shook the rope free in her hand, and began working it, and as it flowed, she wound herself in certainty,

and not even not knowing what exactly her next move was, she felt a new solidity in herself nonetheless;

I need only be this, now.

Carefully, she wound up an arm, then, as she hung at an angle, dangling off that one suspended arm, deftly she slipped off her dress so that it hung next to her off of the bound arm. Then she turned in a circle so that the rope was around her middle, and she constructed a harness. For several moments she swung around, contained, using her bound arm as leverage, undulating; she shook off her heels and spread her legs, pointed her toes, dancing mid-air.

The music poured through the amps.

She felt it—the crowd was rapt.

She could feel their energy, and she could feel that *they* felt *her* energy, that something important was happening today.

She made a hand gesture. A giant pill bottle dropped from the ceiling.

She spun; a centrifugal force had her spinning in circles until she pulled herself up the rope and took the stray bits to create a loop.

The rope was now a noose around her neck, but her chest in the harness took the weight.

She gestured, so the stagehand played his part.

And as she was lifted higher and higher, so too her highest self lifted her sadness, drawing it up from her core, transmuting it into

a raw buzzing that became static and

then a roar inside her, till she saw *them*.

She had the fleeting thought that they could abduct her, kill her, but she felt certain that they'd rather inject her, to cover their tracks, that this was the plan— her plan, *the plan,* how it would be—to let her appear to just get sick, counting on her to fear illness, to fear death.

Everyone dies of cancer these days, right?

But then the roar deafened her inner voice.

Jia Li squeezed her eyes closed and felt only anger, the vibration of it shaking and goading her,

oh, how it energized her,

it was her meaning and it was her path.

Again to the stagehand she nodded. Now.

Her placard dropped. It said: *Knowledge not proof.*

Knowledge not was now crossed through with a heavy line, so that it only said,

proof.

THERE WAS THAT VOID AGAIN, as if she were suspended in time and all sound and movement ceased; there was nothing, not even the soft swish of feet, or the clink of beer bottles and glasses, not a word spoken. Jia Li didn't know if she were in a shared reality, or if she had somehow entered her own, in between ticking time.

She felt her body soften, lighten, become insubstantial.

Into this temporal void dropped a hushed thought, the birth of intention—

revolution

Then there arose the sound of slow clapping, hesitant at first, and finally the low, rolling thunder of applause punctuated by a few whistles and cheers. The curtain fell.

Jia Li unwound herself and gathered her ropes. There would be no final bow tonight. She heard commotion and the manager on stage thanking everyone, stalling for her, but she told the stagehand to tell him she wasn't feeling well, and left for the dressing room in the back.

THEY WERE ALREADY THERE, waiting. The tall skinny white man and the short Chinese man. She pushed past them casting the most cursory glance—they stood just inside the door—she grabbed jeans and a t-shirt from the floor and put them on over her bikini. It was a small and dark room, with a table and chair and an old gray fabric couch that was stained and smelled. The men were so close to her now —she could see them, their every nuance, though their faces were inscrutable. Both in jeans with short-sleeved button-up shirts, like any other patrons. Remarkably clean. The tall one had a huge bandage across his forehead, where the drone had hit him.

Jia Li went to sit on the couch, and sank her arm into the crack between the cushions. She took a deep breath. The men stared at her for a moment then moved towards her. Maybe there was a look they exchanged, of mild disbelief, or confusion—that it could be so easy, after their chase in Berlin.

The Chinese one was at her side in an instant, arms around her chest, pinning her arms to her side. She didn't resist. The other one had removed a needle from a small white plastic case in his pocket, and now injected her.

It stung. She screamed loudly, and used that as an opportunity to grab the hand holding the vial and pry it out. He lost his grip, but got it back. All it took was a second.

The arms around her released, and she lay down in a fetal position. She rolled onto her front and pushed herself into the space between the cushions, moaning.

She closed her eyes and remembered Sam's cells under the microscope, the dancing shadows and light, life blossoming like flowers in time lapse. *Let them go*, she thought. She heard their feet shuffling and the door click open. A gruff voice called, "Three months, maybe less. Tell us what you know, swear not to talk and we can help you. Otherwise you'll die from cancer, nothing out of the ordinary. Not even suspicious."

The tall one threw her a business card. It landed on the floor in front of her. He said, "No one will believe you, a grieving daughter. An artist. Doing her angry act on stage with hardly any clothes on. They will shoot the messenger. That's just how life is. The world will kill you for destroying their fantasies, so you may as well give it to us, and live."

And then the short Chinese one added, "Don't bother trying to analyze the cancer under a microscope. You'll get nothing. It's just cancer. Everyone gets cancer. But you know that, already. So it's up to you."

They shut the door behind them.

She didn't need to analyze the cancer. She had the empty vial from the Chinese man, pink with a mixture of her blood and droplets of whatever it had contained. She'd swapped it with a vial she'd pushed into the back of the couch, holding it through the cushion crack to keep it warm so that as they struggled, lost then regained his grip, he wouldn't notice the difference.

Jia Li rubbed her arm. She opened her eyes and groped for her phone behind the couch cushion. She pulled herself up from the couch and packed a bag.

Now.

She had to leave.

She rang Michael.

"They might be on their way to you next—whatever you've got, the copies from the USB, send it out, send it somewhere safe. Friends, colleagues, wherever. Store it, I don't know, online, keep a copy with you. And pack a bag, fast, do it fast, get out of there fast. Meet me where we said at that intersection, give me twenty minutes to get there."

"What did you do? Why are they on their way to me now? What did you say?"

"They didn't mention you, but they probably know about you. I just want to keep you safe. So move fast."

They hadn't won, not by a long shot.

They didn't know about the icon.

SHE TOOK a taxi and at the agreed upon intersection, found Michael carrying a duffle bag and loitering outside a clothing store. *Great. He'd listened. He was ready to leave town.* She slipped the vial into his pocket without him even noticing as they began to wander Kowloon, vigilant, rushed.

"Michael, it's in your pocket, the needle, the vial they used. Get it analyzed fast. It should have some of whatever they put in it, whatever didn't make it into my body. Send it off to someone who can get answers quickly, but don't wait. Just leave. They'll find you, eventually. So you'll have to get to the cross now or later to heal you, so please. Go to Argentina too. Meet me there."

His voice shook. "They injected you. Fuck. You think they're on their way to me right now? I've seen them outside my apartment. It's only a matter of time, shit. Okay. I need to go somewhere, but I barely packed. I—I don't even know where to go. I have to get the vial to someone I can trust, first. I have a friend in Harbin. Maybe I'll go there. I don't know about Argentina. It's so far."

"Did you make copies of what was on the USB?" she asked him.

He nodded.

"Okay. Get the vial analyzed fast. And wherever you go—just leave. Hide. You can't be safe in this world if you know the truth."

He glanced at her; dejected, resigned. "What if they, I mean, will they kill me, do you think?"

"No. I don't think so. They didn't kill me, obviously. We're no good dead unless they're certain they have everything off you and they know what they're dealing with."

"So they'll make me sick, like you and your mum."

"Exactly. Just, please, they must not know about the icon, or else they'd be after that rather than us, right?"

"Of course. Got it."

"Is there anything at all out there, about how it heals? Proof I mean, not the miracle registry."

"I've written nothing down about that substance, on Sam's skin. No notes. No recordings. Only what I've shared with you. But I have saved digital copies of all the information I found on X—speaking of —What are you planning, Jelly?"

He stopped, which stopped her. Frozen, his face twisted in panic now.

"It needs to be in the public domain," she told him.

"You really want me to leak it. The proof. You're sure?"

"Yes. We both must do it. Once we're out of here. Once we're safe. I've got to go. Thank you for your help, Michael."

She picked up speed and left him behind. He ran through the crowd to catch up to her. "Wait!" He pushed through people, saying nothing. He looked terrified as he caught up to her, silently pleading with his eyes.

She stopped and grabbed him by the shoulders. "Don't panic. Focus. First get that vial analysed. Then get yourself out of here."

"Okay. I'll try. I know you have to go," he said. For a moment he looked pained. "I—I don't have much here. I mean, I have a job. But not for long. I just. I never thought it would come to this. I've never lived anywhere else. I've not even really travelled."

She dropped her hands from his shoulders.

"I know you're scared. I know it's intense. I'm not saying you won't be able to come back. I don't know. What I'm saying is I *need* you. We need each other. Once we are there at Mateo's in Argentina, we still have work to do. I'm not sure what, but I feel like this is the only mission I have now."

"Okay. I get it. I'll go." His voice quavered.

They walked side by side, fast.

The enormity of it all suddenly hit her. She'd not be back here. She couldn't. Ever. She had to disappear. To let them think she'd died. She'd never see her home again. The apartment with her father's desk, the photos, the memories. Tears streamed down her face.

"What if they follow me, Jelly? And what if I struggle and—what if I don't make it to you?" Michael asked in a small voice.

"There's a risk. But you have to try."

"Okay. I'm ready, Jia Li. I'll do whatever I can."

They stopped at a crossing, waiting for the light. Pedestrians flowed around them. They were like rocks in a river. Jia Li took his hand and squeezed it hard, then she crossed the road without him and she didn't look back.

24

KATE & LITTLE BIRD - REPRISED
JUNE 2019
GUATEMALA & MEXICO

Some knots, Kate knew, cannot be unraveled, or if they can, it's by the serendipitous tugging of a single tangled bit, which by appearances is nothing special, and therefore cannot be planned or predicted. Yet this undifferentiated bit, once pulled free, loosens all the rest. Kate knew this from experience, since she'd lived with a central knot for as long as she could remember, unable to extricate it from her being. And she knew of those moments, too, in which a stronger force freed her heart, if only a little.

This loosening began at a lodge in Idaho at Christmastime. Men and women sang folk songs and dreamed aloud of enlightenment as they sat around a fireplace. Katya, only eleven at the time, suddenly filled with anger, as if it had just blown into her with the smoke that billowed in her direction. She squeezed shut her eyes and held her breath, lest she cough or scream. When she opened her eyes again, the smoke was gone, but not her anger, and now the flames licked the air and the fire spat embers. Her mother said, "Move away, you'll get burned," but she refused, and her thoughts began to crackle in perfect resonance with the fire.

She was minding a young girl just then. They sat off to the side of the fireplace, on the floor. She blocked the girl from the embers, and herself from her own rage.

She was angry to be there, to have her intuition probed, to tell the people about her vision, of *Shambhala*, so fantastical a place and yet so boring too, seeing as her own land of hope was in Ohio, in the sixth grade. She fantasized about being at a sleepover, gossiping, watching TV, laughing, baking cookies, trying on clothes, sharing her thoughts and feelings and true dreams. Getting in trouble for staying up too late. Making pancakes in the morning. Going for bicycle rides or roller skating.

But here she was, with a child of about five or seven or so years old, waiting to be called to sit before the adults. In adulthood Kate could never recall the child's name, but she recalled her crayons dancing around the page with complete indifference to whatever it was she drew.

The child chirped, "I want to have three kids when I'm older. And a dog."

"Me too. Or maybe just two kids," Kate said. She was trying her best to be a good babysitter.

The girl continued her chaotic drawing. "But you will be too busy leading everyone to Shambhala, you can't be a mom. You have very important work. Everyone says so."

The fire in Kate's heart lit again with fury and hissed angry words at her until her ears buzzed.

"I *can*," Kate said. A tear rolled down her face. "It *is* important work. If you do it well."

"Anyway, you can't," the girl said.

"Katya! It is time." Her mother had broken away from the chorus of adult chattering and stood over them. "Sit with us. Share your latest revelation. We're waiting."

"I can't." Kate was crying.

"What do you mean you can't?" her mother asked. "What on earth is wrong?"

"Not tonight. I don't feel well. My stomach hurts."

"You're probably getting your period. You're at that age." She leaned into one hip and waved her hand dismissively. "Get yourself up. Go lie down and take an Advil. I will come get you in a half hour or forty-five minutes."

Kate ran to the room she shared with her mother. She grabbed her winter coat, snow boots, scarf, hat, gloves, and put everything on. Then she ran through the hallway, to the back door of their rented house. She crunched through the snow—she sank with every step up to her shins. She made it up a hill to the gazebo where she sat on a wooden bench, beyond the lights of the footpath. It was completely dark, and she sobbed,

her chest heaving,

snot pouring out of her nose.

Kate cried until there were no tears and she could breathe freely. Then she sniffed and looked up, mesmerized by a sky that flickered as if a fire shone through a thousand holes in a wall of darkness. She'd never seen the night sky like this before, not home, not overseas, not anywhere like in this country lodge on a winter's night, moonless, the creamy swath of the Milky Way smeared across the black.

A shooting star flashed past and blinked out.

She was so small, and at once at the very center of everything.

She could be a mother, she decided. She could if she wanted to.

She noticed that tight knot in her chest loosen, a knot she'd lived with for so long that she'd forgotten what it felt like for a dream to free itself. She remembered the words Gutov had made her recite: *Freedom is for those who know themselves truly.*

Since their fated meeting, they had a rapport. And since his disappearance, Gutov spoke to her in her mind, and he was always correct, even his slight predictions of the odd world event, presidential elections, weather and so on.

So therefore, he was correct when he assured her that Shambhala would be found,

and so she assured everyone else,

until the Idaho nightscape found that serendipitous thread, and pulled it free.

She would only speak on her terms thereafter.

She would leave her mother and her people, eventually.

Kate awoke from her memory with the realization that she was on a plane, flying from Berlin to Guatemala. This felt like the culmination, the point at which her actions could finally, and fully, free the threads of her wound-tight longing, since she had a mission with Little Bird.

Since, through her, she knew herself as never before.

AFTER GETTING off the airport shuttle, Kate purchased a new SIM card at a convenience store, texted Victoria, and made her way through a blur of buildings and crowded city roads, into an imposing hotel lobby, up the elevator, and down a dark corridor. When the door opened, Kate saw Mary first—a small, sixty-ish Asian woman wrapped in a yellow sarong up to her armpits. She was reclining in an armchair next to floor to ceiling windows as she sketched something on a big drawing pad. From the tenth floor room Kate could see the mountains and Guatemala City spread out below. Victoria appeared from around the back of the door and embraced her, then formally introduced her to Jia Li's mother.

But Victoria didn't waste time after introductions. She let loose with a barrage of ominous information. About the police at Kate's apartment in Atlanta the night before Victoria and Mary left. How they'd entered her apartment and searched it. About the really angry looking, very big mustachioed man on his phone speaking Russian near their building the next morning, just as they left for the airport.

"The only people I haven't seen snooping around your apartment were those nerdy little weirdos," Victoria said.

"They probably assumed I'm on my way to find Shambhala," Kate quipped.

"Ooh, Shambhala, what is that? Tell me more!" Mary looked up from her sketch pad.

Victoria replied to Mary with indulgence, "Later, I will tell you everything I know. Just give us a moment."

Kate had already accepted that her Atlanta life was over, so she wasn't too rattled by Victoria's disclosure, even when she went on to inform her, with perfect equanimity, that if the police at any point decided Kate was a suspect, they could issue alerts at airport customs. They might be tracking her into and out of any country already. But flying, Victoria rushed to say, was still the safest way to travel, because driving across the Mexican border was notoriously dangerous, kidnapping and assault being common. "You'll just have to fly," Victoria said, "and pray it works out."

She didn't even break a sweat with all that catastrophizing. And she didn't seem overtly worried, either. Just telling it like it was.

Boy she'd come a long way since the dead body in the Supreme Donuts parking lot, Kate reflected.

"You're not an expert in international law, Victoria. I'm pretty sure they'd have to get other governments on board. I think I'd have to be extradited. It doesn't seem likely. The Russians might be more dangerous, but I haven't seen any following me *yet*. Anyway, I still have my Russian name on my passport. But when the police spoke to me, I said I was Kate Davies. Which is what my driver's license says. Maybe that's good. Maybe they haven't figured it out yet. Maybe they're looking for Kate Davies, not Katya Konkova."

Victoria shook her head. "Probably that sort of thing would come up in their database or something. I don't know. Or it may buy you time. We just have to pray it buys you time, at least long enough to get Little Bird. You just need to move fast, hun, before things escalate."

Kate realized she'd been standing all throughout this exchange and finally dropped her bag and fell to the couch. "I just need to get on with it. No time to worry." She called out to Mary, "Oh, Jia Li's fine, so you know. She's just arrived in Hong Kong."

She'd no sooner said it then it hit her—*Jia Li was across the world... would they even see each other again?* Kate couldn't stop the sudden eruption of a lone tear, and a lump in her throat. Since she'd left the hotel in Berlin, Jia Li was with her in every moment, with every breath, and in all the voids between. At least she could confirm that Jia Li was safe—since she'd landed in Guatemala she had texts to prove it, short communications ending with *xx*; the buzz from those *xx* electrified her whenever she thought of it.

"She is a warrior, like her father was," said Mary without looking up from her drawing. "My worry is only average."

Victoria laughed. "Mary, you have a way with words. *Average.* Ha. Okay, honey—Kate, it'll be okay. Don't cry." She came to sit next to her and put an arm around her shoulder.

"I'm fine. Honestly, it's been a long week. I'm just exhausted. I have a long road ahead."

Kate then told Victoria about the man in Argentina that Jia Li had told her about, and her plan to get Little Bird, then take the icon to him, to this Mateo. She didn't want to mention her suspicion—that the girl was being harmed, that maybe she'd been abused all along before her mother died trying to save her. It was too much to admit out loud, and it was just one more suspicion without hard evidence.

Right now, more than anything else, she needed to drop right into her heart and be moved by instinct,

not fear, not logic.

She didn't have control over anything else.

"You just have to trust. Goodness will prevail," Victoria said, like she'd been reading her mind and had her own opinions of it.

"What? *Goodness will prevail?* For real?"

Victoria shrugged.

"I don't know how you know that, Victoria, but I sure hope you're right."

"I think that cross changed me. I held it, Kate. I felt... *something*. And I'm different now. I'm not even drinking."

Kate didn't know what to say to that. That cross hadn't changed *her*, had it? And she'd slept with it all night next to Little Bird. Mary looked up from her drawing and smiled at the world through the window, like it held something good for her and she was grateful.

Maybe it was Mary who'd changed Victoria.

"What's going on, Vic? You two seem cozy. I mean, it's sweet."

"I don't know. We just get along. She asks me a lot of questions. No one has ever asked me so many questions. And she really wants to know my answers. She doesn't always understand, but she keeps asking. It's endearing. Plus we laugh all the time. She's hilarious. The poor woman was really sick until she held that cross, and now she's got her entire life back and she wants to have some fun. And Lord knows I need fun. So why not enjoy ourselves? Kate, I would go for you. I know no one's after me. I miss that child with every fiber of my being, and if for some reason you can't get to her, I will go. But you know I'd be a target. Plus I can't leave Mary."

"I never thought you'd go for me Vic. This is my path. I promised Jia Li I'd get the icon to Argentina, and I told her I'd give her mother the address and tell her to go there too, so you both need to go. When you're ready. Please. I'm leaving the address with you. Jia Li will try to come, too. Anyway, first things first. Little Bird probably needs the icon now. And part of me thinks that it wouldn't be my path if it weren't going to work. So maybe goodness *will* prevail. It's so much bigger than me though. I should tell you everything else now, about Finley and Jia Li and the icon. It's gonna sound crazy."

"I do crazy well," Victoria said.

KATE WAS GONE BEFORE first light, out of the Guatemalan hotel by five a.m. and at the airport by six waiting for the flight to Guadalajara Airport in Mexico that she'd just purchased with Finley's travel card. She'd wrapped the icon in an old towel and had stuffed it into her carry on. She estimated that she'd make it to Lake Chalpa by nightfall if she didn't get lost, kidnapped or arrested. She figured anyone would just think she was religious if they saw the cross light up in the airport xray scanners.

At check in, she imagined for a moment that they looked extra closely at her passport. *Katya*, said the dark-haired woman with a tight bun and bright red lips, like she was feeling for the name's meaning. *Katya Konkova*. She conferred with her colleague about something in Spanish; Kate held her breath. She clutched her bag to her chest, imagining the cross might support even this mad dash to Mexico, might protect her from interference.

The woman printed her ticket and waved her through.

In the end, no one even seemed to notice the cross.

As a child, Kate knew travel as freedom. But freedom lay in the movement between two destinations, the heady, high sensation of being transported beyond the set points where all troubles began. If she'd had it her way, she'd always be moving in the in-between spaces.

But such freedom came at a cost. Kate exchanged friendship for long drives. Soulless pop music and sleepovers for her iPod and headphones, losing herself to Led Zeppelin and Pink Floyd, Jimi Hendrix and Fleetwood Mac. Two or so close friends gave her a chance, but in the end were unsure. She could count in advance their final attempts to include her as they grew impatient with her secrecy, or impatient that she didn't invite them over (she wasn't allowed to).

Instead, she was driven to Idaho, California, Georgia, Florida; flown to England, Germany, Croatia. On the road, in the sky, in life rushing past, she found the center of her own being: in-between spaces,

such as beneath the stars on that wintry Idaho night.

And now, in Mexico, despite whoever might be after her, whatever might happen, right now her freedom was all hers to relish. She hooked up her phone and blasted a 70s mix. Speeding down the highway from the Guadalajara airport in a rental car with all this freedom was exhilarating, with the wind buffering the music and the sun pouring through the opened windows. Whenever worries arose, she managed them like wayward children, corralling them towards safety, love, and commitment to the task at hand. When she thought of Jia Li and Little Bird her heart burst wide open, and like a transmitter with a thousand different frequencies,

    she shone gratitude for the clear, blue sky,

    for the hawk that flew high above her, and

    the brown grass and patchwork fields, the silence,

    the mountains in the not so far distance.

Gratitude for Jia Li and Little Bird, for Finley and Victoria and Mary.

Her heart was bare to all of it, this life.

She headed towards the lake, following the map to the address in Buenavista in Jalisco, past fields and horses and hills.

After forty-five minutes, she turned off onto a dusty residential road. She paused the music and searched for the number 43. There were no street numbers. The houses were brick with gates all down the road. Sometimes fences and just dirt for lawns. The houses appeared half-built, half-abandoned, and then sometimes, as if someone just wanted to prove a point, there was a luminous green lawn behind a fancier gate, or a cheerful yellow facade next to lifeless gray cement.

Mostly, it was dead and dusty, although there were trees now and again, sometimes with a burst of pink flowers. Some children played in the road. Kate rolled down her window and pointed to the piece of paper she had. Forty-three Calle J-, she couldn't make it out. They chatted amongst themselves. She referred to Little Bird's first name from her passport, and told them she needed to find her. *Necesito encontrar a una chica llamada Luisa. Pajarita. Su tío es Jesús.*

Thank goodness for Google translate.

A boy who looked about ten beckoned Kate to follow. He had a bicycle leaning against a white wall and he hopped on it and started to cycle off. Kate drove slowly behind him, down three, four streets, left, right, and right. He stopped finally and pointed at a fence. *Cuarenta y tres*, he said. 43. Kate stopped as close to the house as she could, still half in the road, and turned off the car. Her heart beat too fast. She closed her eyes to find courage, and when she opened them the boy had vanished, and she sat in the car alone in front of a small, white house.

SHE GOT out of the car and stood on the pavement. There was a dog barking, and the sound of a plate breaking, then crying. A baby. Before she could make it to the front door a youngish man came out and headed to his truck. Kate watched him leave. Twenty-something. Maybe it was the wrong house. Then she heard a familiar voice calling in the background.

Kate stood at the fence and called out. *Hola!* A woman of indeterminate age opened the door. She was shriveled and dirty and her face was deeply lined.

"Pajarita?" Kate said it hopefully. She heard small footsteps running, and then she was there, arms all around her. "Tia, Tia!"

"Oh baby." Kate fell to her knees. "Are you okay?"

The girl was bruised on the right side of her face—an ugly black and purple mark—and her hair was matted, like she'd not bathed for days. As Kate scanned her, she saw bruises on her left arm, too. The woman began to prattle away at Kate in Spanish, agitated, maybe angry, then she suddenly turned on her heel and marched off.

"Little Bird, are they hurting you?" Kate asked her then. Little Bird froze. Of course they were. Why did she even need to ask? She got to her knees and took the girl by the shoulders and looked into her eyes and asked,

"Baby, did your mama take you away to keep you safe?"

Little Bird nodded.

"Your mama, she knew that your uncle was not a good man. You tried to tell me, didn't you?"

The girl disappeared into her own shadow then, as if turning herself inside out, and hid her face from Kate.

"I want to go with you, *Tia*. Please?"

Kate didn't understand why the girl was so quiet in this moment, so restrained, but as she told herself, she also didn't understand what kind of threat there was, or how the girl's fear accommodated itself within her strong spirit. Who knew how her body contained it, or what kind of compensatory behaviors she'd had to cultivate in order to survive? From the other side of the house, the older woman let out a stream of Spanish, and Little Bird's eyes screwed up and she clenched her jaw like she was trying to hold in a scream.

It was enough for Kate.

"Come, come with me, we are leaving now."

The girl understood. They understood each other.

Then the woman reappeared.

Little Bird took Kate's hand. Kate stood and made eye contact with the woman, who started screaming and grabbed the girl by the arm, yanking her so hard she fell over. Little Bird cried out, scrambled to her feet, and Kate grabbed her. Kate tried to push past the fence again but it was locked somehow, or stuck. She ran around the side of the house, the back, trying to find a way out, and Little Bird ran inside through a side door and was out in a second with her same little pink backpack. She grabbed Kate's hand, and pulled her away.

"Run, Tia," she said.

Just then a man burst out. It was the Uncle. Jesús. He had a gun. Kate shoved Little Bird behind her, her back to the car.

"Why you want little Mexican girl? What is wrong with you?"

"Please, no. I will take care of her. Here's some money." Kate took cash from her jeans pocket and laid it on the ground. It was about two hundred dollars.

"I need more than that if you steal my family," he said.

Kate couldn't tell if he were desperate or angry. How could anyone be willing to part with a child for cash? She didn't have any more cash, but she pretended to search her pockets.

"I don't have more cash on me. Why did you come all the way to Georgia to get her if you are happy to sell her?" Kate snapped.

"She is my sister's daughter. Here, she helps. She has always helped. You give me more money, and we will see. If not you, someone will give me good money for her. She is a pretty young girl, you know what I mean. Some people pay well for that."

Money for her? Kate paused on his vacant eyes, and decided that whatever humanity had been there was long gone. She didn't want to stay another moment and negotiate with someone who could even suggest *selling* a child.

"In the car," she told him. "I have more money in my car, let me get it."

But she didn't have any more cash there, either. He raised the gun and stared her down. Kate saw an opening next to the fence then, between the neighboring property's brick wall, and she turned and scooped up the girl; she squeezed through and lunged for the car. He must have seen through her ruse and decided to stop them. It happened so fast, though: the gun had gone off, and Kate felt the ground fall away from her.

"You have money or no?" he called. "She doesn't even have a passport! You'll be back with her soon enough! You give me more money, and I get her papers. Travel papers."

"Fuck you!" Kate screamed.

"Tia, Tia!" the girl cried. Kate felt searing pain in her left buttock, but her body knew what to do. She opened the back door and pushed the girl into the backseat, and taking a deep breath, pulled herself into the driver's seat even as her leg gave way and the blood soaked her jeans. A wave of nausea washed through her, and with it, dizziness. For a few seconds she forgot why she was there and what she was doing. Then the gun went off again, and she jerked to attention.

Where did the bullet land? She hadn't heard or felt any impact. Little Bird was low in the backseat. Kate pulled out, veering all over the place, her vision blurred. Her fingers tingled. *Oh God no, don't pass out now,* she willed herself. Little Bird started to simper. Jesús was shouting at them as they drove off.

Kate kept telling herself to stay lucid, *focus!* Fear was lifeblood now. *We are getting the fuck out of here.* She had made it about five miles down the highway when she had to pull over to do something about the pain and the blood. The uncle hadn't followed them, not that she could see. She pulled off into a dirt road behind some trees and, moving her seat back, pulled down her jeans right in the car.

"Shit, shit, shit," she cried, and felt around the fleshy bit of her wounded buttock. She let out a scream as she palpated it, and muttered under her breath, "Okay, no bullet, not that I can feel. But it has to be there somewhere. Or else how...?"

Little Bird crawled into the front seat and lay her head on Kate's shoulder.

"You have to help me baby," Kate said. "Go to the trunk. There's a towel, the cross is in the towel. Bring it to me fast."

Little Bird leapt up and shouted from back behind the car, "I can't open it! I can't open it Tia!"

Kate fumbled around the dashboard pulling every lever she could see. The hood popped open, but not the trunk. She took a deep breath to rally herself but paused when a rush of dizziness overcame her. She closed her eyes. It felt pleasant, somehow, this swimming, rocking sensation. *Just a few seconds to rest*, Kate told herself.

"I got it!" shouted the little girl. A moment later she was back on Kate's lap, pulling the icon out of the wrapped towel. She shoved it behind Kate's back, pushed it down to the seat behind her. Little Bird started to cry hard now, heaving sobs, her nose running.

"You okay, Tia?" Her eyes were so big. They held so much pain and so much worry. Kate kissed her forehead.

"It's okay, baby. I know it's a lot of blood, but I will heal fast because of the cross. Remember how it helped you?"

Little Bird exclaimed about *La Cruz* and wrapped both arms around Kate, kissing her neck and chest, and Kate promised her, never again, never again would she be apart from her, not ever for as long as she lived.

After a few more minutes, Kate managed to stand up and get her bag out of the trunk. She changed clothes, wiped blood off the seat, and drove back to the airport with the cross behind her back as the pain lessened minute by minute until it was gone within another half hour. When she returned the rental car she whispered to the female at the desk that she was sorry about getting her period as she was driving. Then she bought tickets to Buenos Aires, praying no one would mention their different passports, and no one did; maybe no one saw anything other than a girl on her hip, hugging her neck. Maybe it was the icon, after all, healing in all ways a miracle could heal, giving them not just life and love's survival, but also safe passage.

In the several hours they had to wait for the flight, Kate fed Little Bird and washed her hair in the bathroom sink, and held her in her lap and kissed her again and again.

Once they were settled and the girl was calm, Kate explained their plans.

"We're going on an airplane on a long flight. To a new country, Little Bird. And then we will drive a car to meet a man who will help us, in a town near a lake. Not your lake. A new lake."

MATEO VARGAS WAS TALL, brown-skinned, with curly black hair and glasses. He held secateurs in one hand, and with the other carried a small, empty basket. Kate had contacted him before they left Mexico so that he'd be expecting them. He'd given her very detailed directions to his property which he said she would not find on any map. But still, she had no idea what to expect, either from him, or this vast, flat and empty landscape. She barely managed a greeting.

She held tightly to Little Bird's sweaty hand. In her other fist, she held onto her duffle bag and her purse and the girl's backpack—all she had left in the world. Kate's arm was rigid and straight. Exhaustion weakened every part of her; she probably had a bullet somewhere in her butt; and all she wanted was a bed and time to rest,

but she couldn't release her grip in either hand and held onto the bags as if for dear life.

"Welcome," Mateo said. He took in Little Bird, who was quiet and clung to Kate. "Do you like to garden, child?"

"I don't know." She shrugged. She leaned her head against Kate's chest.

To Kate he said, 'Well, I don't know what to do with children, as I don't have any. But I need helpers. I have a room downstairs for you both to share. Take your time, rest, have some fruit and coffee—I will leave some outside for you, here." He indicated the outdoor setting, a wooden table and six wooden chairs beneath a terrace. There was a modest spattering of red bougainvillea just beginning to climb the abutting trellis. Kate breathed in deeply. Fresh coffee, damp soil, the air cool and dry.

"Then," he spoke to Little Bird, "I will show you how to look after the garden. You will like it. You can help me pick the ripest tomatoes for our dinner, here, in this basket. I will leave it on the table for you. Call me when you're ready."

    Kate began to cry because he was kind,
    so normal, and this —*haven*, it felt like,
    a safe place for the deliverance of
    this precious child after a long journey.

    Mateo's dark brown eyes met hers, and he said, "One thing you should know about me. I've seen things you wouldn't believe. I've learned the hard way that if something can truly transform the way we do things, it will end up in the wrong hands. I've learned to hide things of value, and that includes people. No one knows about this property but Michael, and there is more to it than meets the eye. You're safe here. And your child, too. And anything else you have to share."

    At last,
    she dropped the bags she clutched tight in her fist,
    and the knot of her being unraveled.

    She planted a mother's heart in this ripe earth, where at last, she knew herself truly,
    and thus was free.

25

FINLEY & YUK-OR BA
JUNE 2019
IRKUTSK TO BAIKAL

After all his fumbling through life without forward motion, Finley felt he had become the current itself, racing towards an unknown destination much as a river has no choice but to rush to the waterfall. On the long flight from Berlin to Irkutsk, on a quest that only he could fulfill, or complete, or whatever it was he was meant to do—he questioned how much agency he actually had, or whether fate merely flowed through him. If his actions did matter, he wondered if he had either the ability or the courage to pull it off. If only it didn't hurt so much, he might feel more confident, he thought. But then again, if he felt more confident, he wouldn't have the pain. It all confounded him.

Just because you resist it doesn't mean you don't desire it. Bernhardt's words echoed in his ears.

Bollocks, he thought.

Okay, maybe it's true.

But wisdom is easy to dispense and difficult to live by.

There it was then, that familiar feeling coming over him at a distinctly awkward moment, as he sat in his business class seat stuck between the window and a large German man—as if his thoughts were coalescing into a pinprick precariously balanced on his worried, self-tortured thoughts, attempting to descend through his brain, threatening to take him through that particular wormhole into another life. *Not here, not now,* he chastised himself, and attempted to find distraction with in-flight entertainment, or reading apps, and eventually even the dog-eared copy of *Ikona* he carried with him everywhere.

He'd already read it twice, with great attention to detail.

Distraction worked to avoid the pain of spontaneous time travelling—it had worked before, in conversation with Kate and Jia Li—but not so much to avoid self-tortured thoughts.

He had nearly fifteen hours to fail to distract himself from those, and it took only four to settle into habitual melancholy,

to mull over his chronic loneliness

faint hopelessness

his fears—

until he settled on feeling inadequate to the task, and then for good measure ruminated some more on his loneliness.

He was quite alone in the world, especially now that he'd flown away from his new allies, those surprising women who had somehow made their way into his heart. His parents had both died within the previous two years. His mother from a heart condition, his father from a stroke. Both in their 80s. He'd not shared those facts with anyone, except for Phil, and of course Clare. But only the facts. He could not have explained (much less did he understand it himself) that he suffered from a painful nostalgia rather than grief as he thought it should be, solemn sadness. Instead he ruminated longingly over certain memories of childhood happiness, the accuracy of which he questioned since he was now the sole living witness to them.

His childhood seemed, in retrospect, as lonely and hollow as his predominant self-concept. So, wasn't it poignant, he thought, that he was orphaned, and at close to fifty years of age, alone both in life and on this trip?

This rumination consumed him mid-flight.

In total self-honesty, he'd always anticipated that he would end up alone, and he was more or less satisfied with how he'd lived so far. He'd survived his rather lonely childhood and had successfully avoided the complexities of feeling so alone in his mystical nature by repressing his abilities. He had acquitted himself well as an investor and employee, living up to all the stereotypes—at least publicly. So, he'd lost his one enduring relationship. Just another necessary rite of passage in the lead up to this solitary finishing lap.

Now he only needed to become the man who was up to the task, a dark realization he arrived at after his fifth hour on the plane.

How in the world could he be up to this task?

Once, in one of his earlier professional roles, he'd been assigned a performance coach, an ultimately futile arrangement since Finley was essentially uncoachable. Anyway, he performed better than most in his job, so it was just a matter of going through the motions to tick boxes. There was only one thing the coach said which landed, the sole remaining memory Finley had retained of being 'coached' by the cheesy, overly enthusiastic man who, Finley decided, had spent far too much time at Tony Robbins events.

He had told Finley that the key to achieving better outcomes was to locate past successes, of any scale or nature, and identify how he'd experienced those successes, then map his *strategies* onto the future.

Of any scale, of any nature.

How did it feel? this man had asked, as Finley stared vacantly at his coach's comb-over, his crisp, baby blue dress shirt, his glow-in-the-dark teeth.

How did it feel, that time you made spaghetti perfectly, when you were ten?

The coach did not comment on the fact that this feat, preparing a meal at age ten, was the only memory that equated to success for Finley in his then three decades of life.

This was despite a mortgage-free apartment, and three hundred thousand dollars in a savings account—it was not an accomplishment, really (he reasoned) when you consider he'd seen certain successful companies in his mind's eye, their tickers glowing in royal blue. That was a gift he never asked for, not a success he'd worked towards.

His conclusion, after fifteen hours of self-torture: there was nothing in his past to suggest he was up for this task—finding Gutov, finding the origin of a healing cross, sending that communication to the future. Just thinking about it gave him a headache, which produced worry, verging on fear—that he would go into a brain-shattering altered state of consciousness and travel to Wallace mid-air, perhaps forcing a landing, once the pilot discovered there was a writhing, groaning, middle-aged mess on aisle three, probably having a stroke.

Finley breathed slowly and deeply as the patchwork fields below gave way to patchwork suburbs. A glistening river appeared and disappeared, and the plane flew lower and lower over buildings and apartment blocks until it finally descended onto the runway of the Irkutsk International Airport.

Once past passport control and customs, Finley bumbled his way to an information desk and inquired how to get to Port Baikal.

"Port Baikal?" the matronly Russian woman asked him in a tone suggesting she'd been asked this fifty times already that day. She smacked her bright pink lips and called out, "Nikolai!"

A thin, pale man in his thirties appeared.

"Port Baikal," she said to him.

"I take you there. Four hours in car. Two hundred dollars. Or you stay in a hotel in city as you've missed the ferry for today."

Finley was absolutely certain this was far too much money, that surely there was another way, but he was tired and defeated by the trip so far, and it was too late in the day to go to a hotel and sleep (or too early to risk sleeping eight hours). So he agreed.

"But I need a room there. A hotel."

"We find."

Most of the way Nikolai chatted in Russian on his phone, which gave Finley plenty of time to admire the green fields, the cute country houses they passed, and the mountains beyond; it all appeared like a countryside from another era, as if he had stepped back into the 19th century.

"American?" Nikolai had suddenly seemed to notice him.

"English, actually."

"Okay." He grinned, but it was not genuine. "You like fishing?"

"My friend does," Finley said.

"You meeting someone in Baikal?"

"Yes," he said, and closed his eyes. "I'm just going to have a short sleep if you don't mind."

"I don't mind," Nikolai said. "You will miss the lake though. See —" He gestured by waving a hand out his open window.

Finley looked. A brilliant blue body of water, as big as an ocean on the horizon, rose up from the land as they cruised downhill. The sun glinted off the water, a flash of white.

"Incredible," Finley said.

He closed his eyes and for a second he could see an imprint of light inside his lids. The warmth was pleasant. Finley kept his eyes closed and his face towards the light. The jetlag weakened his sense of solidity in time and space; identity itself was as thin as crepe paper. He might open his eyes to Wallace's life. He imagined that he could simply will his perspective to shift. Was he not him? Privy to Wallace's life as much as he was privy to this life? Finley would become him in some future life, after all. Or the soul that they shared would take on its next earthly form.

We share something.

This thought descended upon him—it was not conjured: a core truth that was not just forward motion, nor was it fear or bravery. It was the energy of evolution itself. An element of becoming.

Finley felt himself drop into a brief sleep and temporarily let go of his tangled thoughts.

"We are at hotel now in Port Baikal," Nikolai announced, which roused Finley just as the car stopped and his door opened.

It was too dark to judge the exterior of the building. He thought he could vaguely make out the lake, but maybe that was the night's liquid blackness. All Finley took in was the dim reception, where he paid with his credit card and then made his way to a room that looked straight out of the 1970s with olive green bedspreads and yellowing floral wallpaper. It smelled of old porridge, fish and cigarette smoke. He collapsed on one of the single beds and was fast unconscious.

HE AWOKE to the sound of roosters, rubbing sleep from his eyes. He groaned and grabbed *Ikona* from his bedside. He studied the photo of a then much younger Gutov on the back cover.

What was he doing?

Looking for an old man who fishes.

He went down to the hotel restaurant where he had strong tea and forced himself to eat what he could, despite the absence of hunger. The kind young waitress spoke to him in English and asked him what he wanted to see, even as she rattled off a list of favorite tourist sites without waiting for him to answer.

"Fishing. I'd like to do some fishing near here," he said when she took a breath.

Her forehead creased—perhaps she did not think he looked like a fisherman.

"Okay. My cousin fishes. I can call him."

He expected her to ask him for money in order to arrange a tour of some kind, but instead, after feeding him rye bread and caviar with a boiled egg and pouring him more tea, she said. "My cousin is outside. He will take you to fish tour."

THIS NEXT YOUNG man looked like an American college student—again Finley expected a request for payment, but not everyone was as mercenary as Nikolai from Irkutsk. This young man merely said,

"Follow. You fish?"

"Um, I would like to try."

"Okay, there is tour. Not today. You book today. Tour is tomorrow. By the way, I am Nikolai."

"Another Nikolai."

"There are many Nikolais." He grinned.

Nikolai #2 helped Finley book the fish tour and refused to take a tip. He said, "These guys will give me bonus later, when it's my fishing day."

So Finley walked back to his hotel, but stopped across the road at the lake's edge. He picked up the rocky sand and rubbed it into his palm.

He mulled over his fear.

He reviewed his plan.

Find Gutov.

Ask him about the origin of the icon he wrote about.

Wait. His brain unexpectedly ignited in a bright burst of reassuring logic. Didn't Gutov have a phone number? Why had he traveled this far to find him in person? There was nobody on earth who didn't have a phone number! He could have contacted his editor—hadn't Valeri said that he'd visited him here?

It was too late for such thoughts now. Finley sighed, exasperated with himself. He didn't have Valeri's phone number, so how would he even find Gutov's editor? He may as well just ask around for an old man who likes to fish. Someone who keeps to himself. Who had arrived in town in what, the late 90s? After *Ikona* was published?

It wasn't much of a description. Finley began to stress over it. He certainly didn't want to alert anyone that Gutov was a famous writer, in case that caused him problems, in case there were Gutovniks in this part of the world. So he must be vague in his description. How might one describe a writer without saying he was a writer? Maybe say *an old fisherman who has a way with words*? Maybe he could say that his speech was poetic!

He laughed at himself out loud.

Maybe it didn't even matter what he said, he would either find him or not.

Finley began to ask around about an old man who fished, using Google translate as his guide.

He asked the waitress at the cafeteria, and asked her to ask her cousin, Nikolai #2.

He walked back to the tour operators and asked the guys at the fishing tour place.

He asked a couple of old women who looked like locals, because they appeared too downtrodden and hunched over to be tourists.

No one seemed to know anyone that fit his description.

He found some markets and wandered for a while, somewhat taking in the touristy trinkets and postcards, the fat old toothless stall holders and their buckets of local fish. The inescapable cheesy folk music playing from somewhere vaguely grated on him, as did the low, guttural tones of the Russian language all around him. He bought some local fish for lunch. He sat under a tree and enjoyed the feeling of sun on his pale skin.

At some point, Finley noticed there was a man watching him.

Who seemed, Finley had to admit to himself, *to be trailing him*.

He was familiar looking. He wasn't the man who'd attacked Jia Li in Hong Kong, but in theory others *were* looking for Wallace's past self, as crazy as it seemed. Finley didn't panic as, in some ways, it all felt as unreal as a dream, but he was uneasy with an edge of vigilance in the knowing that it *could* become a nightmare.

Finley gave up the hunt and went back to his room to wait for the fishing tour in the morning.

THE NEXT MORNING he went to take the ferry to Listvyanka for a day tour that presumably would include fishing. Nothing felt sensible and nothing felt clear. He second-guessed his very presence, the ferry, his choices so far—all of it. In direct counterpoint to the lack of clarity was his diminishing aptitude for logistical or logical *control*. He accepted a certain futility in trying to manage this quest; it seemed unlikely just then that he even be able to find Gutov.

The morning was clear and warm, the lake a dark blue mirror to the sky. This body of water seemed so vast and so empty; *was anyone even out there fishing*? There were fifty or so people mulling around as Finley boarded the ferry, but clearly not all of them were joining the excursion. He sat near the window, mulling over how illogical his plan was (if you could call it a plan). From the corner of his eye, he noticed the man who had been watching him the previous day. Finley did a double take, certain that he knew him, and he felt a flash of fear —a jolt to his skull. *Who had found him? What would they do to him?* Only when the man stood up from where he sat a few rows away and walked towards him did Finley recognize him.

Could it really be? Finley thought—one of the Gutovniks from Atlanta?

Surely not.

Finley didn't know what to do. Was it actually a threat or... shenanigans again?

The man advanced and as he sat down right next to him, so close that their shoulders touched, he pointedly looked down his beaky nose at a knife that he held against Finley's side.

"Sit with me. We go together," he said in his familiar Russian accent.

"I see you've got a real weapon now," Finley quipped, yet humor did nothing to stop his heart racing, or his palms from going sweaty, or his head beginning to pound. He couldn't imagine what this man's intention was, but they were so far from civilization, what did it matter? He could kill him. *But why would he do that?* Finley's mind teetered between fear and rationality.

"Why are you here?" Finley asked.

"I've come to stop you, the false prophet."

"Are you completely mad? Did you follow me all the way from Atlanta?"

The Gutovnik crossed his arms.

"I followed Katya. But at the airport in Berlin she went to Guatemala and you, you came to Russia. So I knew then."

"What did you know?"

"That you are the false prophet."

"From—from the novel?"

"In real life, obviously."

"I'm just a man. I'm not actually the false prophet."

"You're the real prophet?"

"Yes, I am, actually. I am the real prophet, yes."

"You just said you are just a man."

"Yes, I am that too."

"So you're not the real prophet."

"No. I mean, yes. I am. I'm both, okay? I'm a man and I'm the real prophet."

"So that is why I have to stop you. You are stealing the final act. You sent Katya away."

"Oh my God. You're actually very confused. Please put the knife away for God's sake. I'm not resisting you. Yes, I did send Katya away—but to do something she *wanted* to do. Hang on, what do you think *I'm* doing?"

"You know what you are doing."

"Well, yes I do, but do you?"

"You are looking for Shambhala. You sent Katya away to get rid of her, and probably you told her she could join you later in the special place, but you are going to find Shambhala. I don't trust you, so I must steal the cross back and Katya should be the one to tell us where it leads."

"Oh my God." Finley rolled his eyes. "Where do I even begin? I do NOT have the cross. It is not even on this continent."

The man pushed the knife against his side again—not hard, but enough to cause Finley to take a sharp intake of breath and say nothing else. The ferry had not yet departed. People were still boarding.

"Get off ferry. Come."

The beaky Gutovnik held Finley's arm and hurried him to a waiting car. He shoved him into the backseat, where another man grabbed his wrists and tied them behind his back. This man, not one Finley had ever seen before, was middle-aged, with an enormous beer gut, wearing matching red and white striped tracksuit pants and jacket. He snarled at his captive.

Finley recoiled, more from Beer-gut's fishy breath than anything else. Finley's rational mind was starting to catch up though—maybe this wasn't going to be terribly good after all. It was nerve wracking and uncomfortable, but still far better than the searing pain of his resistance-induced visioning headache.

"Do you have an international network of... what are you... Gutovniks?"

"Yes."

"Yes you are Gutovniks or yes you have an international network?"

"Both."

"I'm not here to do what you think. I'm here to find Gutov himself. To talk to him. Just talk to him about his book."

"Impossible. He has ascended."

Finley had nothing to say to that, which was timely as now Beer-gut had a roll of duct tape; he tore off a bit and taped Finley's mouth shut. The beaky one began to drive.

"Kostya," Beer-gut said from the backseat, then a stream of Russian and jarring laughter.

Ah, yes, Kostya. The beaky one.

They drove over unpaved dirt roads through forest for maybe fifteen minutes (during which time Finley mentally tallied the charge left on his phone, which pressed against his left hip inside his pocket, and as well contemplated the likely strength of his phone's signal, and also wondered if he should have consulted Google translate for words of help in Russian).

"Where is the cross? It was not in your hotel room."

Finley said, his mouth duct-taped shut, "I don't know. Somewhere on the other side of the world," but it sounded like a stream of staccato syllables.

Kostya sighed. "Okay, nevermind. You will tell me later. We will keep you with us and then deport you. I have a friend who can do the paperwork. I have your passport from the hotel, too. You will be on the next flight."

Well at least they weren't murderers, Finley reflected, just thieves and kidnappers.

Of course, he couldn't be one hundred percent sure. But he had to remain vigilant and not let fear get the better of him.

The car stopped at a small brown cottage. It appeared uninhabited. Or rather, *uninhabitable*. There were chickens free-ranging outside and a very old, very fat babushka with her head in a scarf. She was sweeping the front steps. Probably Beer-gut's mother.

"Mama," he called, then a slur of Russian, which had the effect of quickening the old woman's sweeping, hastening her around the side and to the back of the house.

It was Beer-gut's mother.

Finley sighed.

Kostya and Beer-gut pulled him out of the car and took him inside straight through a hall to a bedroom with peeling greenish wallpaper and a thin, low single bed covered by an olive green knit throw. It smelled of mold and pickles and booze. Beer-gut pushed him onto the bed, then tied his feet together with the same rope he'd used on his hands. He'd stored it in his pocket, apparently, along with the duct tape. The coarse white rope began to irritate Finley's ankles within seconds, at which point he noticed his wrists were itchy, too.

They left him there, and shut the door.

The air was warm, at least. Siberia wasn't so bad in summer, Finley decided, until the mosquitoes began to descend on him one by one, attacking his face, arms, neck.

Bloody hell, they are enormous. He writhed and contorted himself and eventually used his tied up hands to swat and smash the mozzies against his forehead.

At some point—it felt like hours had passed—Kostya entered the room with tea and brown bread. He sat Finley up and removed the tape from his mouth.

"Mosquitoes!" Finley spat out. "They are going to kill me!"

"Drink," Kostya said, and put the tea to his mouth. Then the bread. "Deportation soon. Maybe a few days."

"A few days!" Finley dribbled tea as he exclaimed. "I'll have no blood left by then!"

"Quiet," Kostya said. "Eat. Volodya's mother made soup for dinner. Even betrayers like you must be forgiven."

"I am NOT a betrayer!"

"Do you need to piss?"

"Yes, please."

"Okay, come." Kostya helped him stand and pulled him forward, but Finley could only hop as his ankles were tied.

"Do you think you might undo these ropes?" he asked.

"No."

He hopped into the toilet. He managed, despite his bound hands, to undo his pants, but that was all.

"Can you please pull down my pants. Just stay behind me. Just pull down. Yes, that's it. And wait—stay, I need you to pull them back up."

Exasperated (rather than embarrassed, since he'd been to an all boys school and had experienced his share of hazing in communal toilets), he hopped back to the sad, small bed in the moldy room, where he was assisted to lie down. He somehow convinced Kostya to close the window to keep out the mosquitoes. Fortunately, Kostya had not put the tape back over his mouth.

By now, Finley had spent so much time reviewing his life on the presumption that he was going to find Gutov and the origins of the cross and that he would send this information via his mind to the future—that he had not for a moment relaxed.

Now, he considered that he might have missed his opportunity to find the origin of the cross altogether. Maybe he would just have to find Gutov from afar?

Maybe it wasn't such a bad thing to be sent home, he thought. Maybe he'd made this entire adventure far more difficult than it needed to be.

His body began to relax.

He could practice controlling his visions from the comfort of his own apartment, and be ready to send the information. Why had he even thought he needed to be here in person?

Funny, he wasn't scared at all anymore. In fact, he felt happily resigned.

Maybe he wasn't a hero after all.

He fell asleep.

At some point, he was woken up and made to eat soup and more brown bread. Kostya then covered him in a sheet and left him in the dark. As the window was closed, the remaining unsatiated mosquitoes in the room spent a bit of time finishing their feast, after which Finley slept, itchy and exhausted, but untroubled at last. His comfortable and comforting reality would soon be returned to him, he realized, just as soon as he was un-kidnapped and sent home.

Only the smallest pinprick of thought pushed the words through to him: *fight back*,

which he ignored.

Relief was an opiate that rendered him quite incapable of any motivation whatsoever.

IN THE EARLY MORNING, Finley was woken by a loud knock which came from what must be the front door. He squinted into sunlit air shimmering with dust.

There was shouting. The bedroom door was thrown open and an old man with a white beard appeared. He winced. "Finley Minor?"

"Yes?"

The old man shouted in Russian to Kostya, and to Finley, "I told him to free you at once!"

Kostya rushed to do so as Beer-gut poked his head out behind him, very much surprised.

"Hello Finley. I am Konstantin Gutov. I believe you are looking for me?"

. . .

Finley tried to sit. In the end, Gutov had to help him.

"How did you know to find me here? Or him? Or—why are you here?" Finley stuttered.

"My editor Frank was contacted by Valeri, who said you'd be coming. You didn't arrive. Then this scoundrel's mother, who also is a neighbor and a gossip, informed me that her son had an Englishman visiting. Which you may understand is quite unusual in this location."

"You have a phone number? I could have just called you? I knew it!" Finley brought his bound wrists to his forehead to punctuate that statement.

"I have a phone number *and* an email. But that's okay. Good we meet in person. Let's get you freed. *Kostya! Volodya!*" he barked in a firm voice, then continued in Russian.

Finley, once cut free, finally stood. They all crowded into the small room together, he and Gutov, Kostya and Beer-gut-Volodya.

Gutov spoke in English to Kostya, in a scathing tone.

"Finley is not the shapeshifter. He is, in fact, Yuk-Or Ba, and you did not see him for who he was, because you cannot see beyond the misleading beliefs of your own insanity. You have read my book wrongly. There is no Shambhala beyond what dream landscape lies within. Yuk-Or Ba's journey is inside him. Like Finley's. Like yours! You are forgiven, because you did not know. Don't you understand that it's a novel? A fictional story? Stories are merely metaphors wrapped in emotions expressed through characters, young man. Now let this man go. You don't have the authority to have him deported. You are not the KGB."

Then, for good measure (it seemed that way to Finley), he launched into a monologue in Russian, ending in English: "All this time, I have practically been a neighbor to your comrade in crime." He pointed to Beer-gut-Volodya.

"He's not a comrade. I only met him a day ago and paid him to help me. He doesn't even know who you are." Kostya looked as if he were about to cry.

"We're leaving now," Gutov announced.

And with that, Finley and Gutov left the squalid house for an old, brown car that appeared to be a Russian make of some sort. The morning's soft dappled sun glinted off the lake and through the trees like dancing light spirits, as if the forest had come alive and celebrated Finley's escape. His mind was a mess of magic and discomfort and confusion. They drove another ten minutes down dirt roads, and all the time Finley either scratched the pink bites that covered him, or tried very hard not to.

GUTOV'S DACHA was a very different kind of home from Beer-gut-Volodya's. He called it a chalet, and indeed it resembled one, with a balcony above and verandah below, built right up next to a hill and surrounded by trees. It was a traditional log house inside, with rather simple beige furniture and not much of it. Gutov took him straight to the kitchen, which looked out to a yard and from which you could glimpse a shimmer of blue water.

The old man, this fabled author and the guide for Finley's onward journey, made him tea, scrambled eggs, one piece of white bread smothered in butter and black caviar, and another with butter and marmalade, and throughout his preparations said very little. In fact, Gutov hummed to himself and quite ignored his guest. Finley visited the bathroom (blessedly alone and without assistance) and stood for a moment alone in the living room, taking it in once again—the pot bellied stove, walls hung with bright Persian-style carpets, three tall bookshelves overflowing with books bearing Russian and English and French titles.

Finley sighed happily.

He remembered that he had to give Gutov the note from Kate, which of course he'd left at the hotel with his other belongings, including his passport which had apparently been stolen. He'd photographed the note on his phone just in case. Of course, his phone was dead. He explained his predicament and charged his phone while he ate.

"I'll get your passport, don't worry. I'll go back to those guys today and demand it. They have it, I'm sure. But I don't believe they know anyone who can deport you. For now, please eat."

Afterwards, Finley held his phone out for Gutov to read Kate's message.

The old man smiled. "But I know this already. This is exactly what I told those guys earlier."

"You know what?" Finley asked.

"I know that I should help you. And all those other things I said to those fools about Yuk-Or Ba. Now, I think you'd better explain why you're here, in your words. Other than because I rescued you."

FINLEY THOUGHT it best to get straight to the point.

"The cross you wrote about in *Ikona*. Kate—Katya, well she found one exactly like it. And it seems to heal. So I, or rather we, Kate and I, were hoping you had based the icon in your novel on a real cross and that you know how the real one was made. How it actually was created, so that we can figure out how it heals. Because we need it in the future."

"Which future are you referring to?"

"The one I go to."

They stared at one another across the four-person table, so close their hands could touch, were it not for butter, caviar, marmalade, and a teapot.

"It's a long explanation," Finley said.

"I can imagine. But there really is no rush here."

"I have this weird ability to travel to the future in my mind. And in the future there is an incurable disease, and humanity is dying. So if we can find the origin of the cross—which in the future they only know about through me—then there is a chance it can be produced, or rather, *mass* produced then. To save humanity."

"I see. You have a big weight on your shoulders."

"Yes. That's why I'm here."

"And what is your role?"

"I'm the one who must communicate to the future."

"The messenger."

"Yes. That would be me."

"And in the future, you are the one who lights the way."

"I suppose, yes."

Gutov looked impressed, but not surprised.

"Decades ago, I heard rumors of a cross that healed, from the Tunguska region at the beginning of last century. One of those Orthodox crosses with the crooked line at the bottom and a hanging Jesus in the middle. It was a good rumor, from a contact I had in the Orthodox Church. It was during the Soviet era when there were many secrets. I trusted that these rumors could be true, and why not? I like a true mystery, like about Rasputin. But, to be honest with you, I never investigated it very deeply. You know, I wrote fiction, so the absolute facts didn't matter so much to me." His eyes twinkled.

"But you can go to the monastery in Tunguska, and ask about the icons there, and ask them how the icons were made. What materials. Don't mention myths of a magical cross or they will tell you nothing, because if it's true, they would be hiding the truth so it doesn't fall into wrong hands. But if you tell them you have relatives who were Old Believers, emigrants who left Russia, and you're doing family research, well then no one cares. In that case, they'd be happy to help you to know more about your Russian Orthodox heritage. Everyone loves history. Russians love descendants of Russians who ended up overseas, so they would easily be persuaded to tell you what they know. Especially if you're paying a tour guide."

"Got it. Thank you. Which monastery, do you know?"

"Of course. Listen. You need to go to Irkutsk and from there travel to Krasnoyarsk. Then, in Krasnoyarsk, hire a tour guide and translator to take you to the Ascension Monastery on the road towards Vanavara. That is the place where the rumored cross came from. Tell the priest that you are researching how icons are made because of your family history, etc. etc.. And yes, I based the *ikona* on that one in my novel. I have never told anybody of this by the way. But Katya sent you, so, you see." He shrugged.

"Thank you," Finley said, and only then realized, as he stared at

Gutov's folded hands on the kitchen table, that this quest was back on. He was un-kidnapped and not going home, so therefore he was once again becoming the current as it sped towards resolution. Happily, he noticed, there was no pounding in his temples. His head was clear, though his mind was weary from lack of sleep.

"Let's walk. It's such a beautiful summer day, don't you think?" Gutov asked.

"Yes, it's quite beautiful here."

"You can stay. You need a proper rest, but you also need your passport to travel. So you stay here until then."

"Thank you, um, Konstantin? Shall I call you that, or...?"

"Gutov is fine. That's what Frank calls me. Here we go."

They left the dacha and walked down from the house to the lake in a matter of minutes, and then they followed the shoreline in silence.

"I know what your quest is. It doesn't matter the name, or the object. It doesn't matter what the future holds or not. It's always the same quest. So I have some advice, if you don't mind."

The old man stopped just in front of him and placed a hand on each of Finley's shoulders. He smiled, at once with humor and grace, and he spoke as if knowing that he reached not just Finley, but all of the parts of him which together constituted his entire consciousness.

"The Bridge. You will find an explanation there. I will be that troublesome writer who refers to my own work. But it's easier to read than to explain in my own words."

He laughed.

"They are your own words, though," Finley said.

"Please, I myself cannot take credit for it. The chapter moved through me. Creativity is a form of channeling. I was only an instrument. I expect that you understand this somehow."

Gutov winked. The lines at his eyes deepened as he laughed again.

"I know who you are," he said to Finley, who at once felt a presence awaken within him.

And as he expanded into the space, a calmer, more determined energy emanated then, within which, unprompted,
love announced itself, as if it were him.
He had the thought, "Who am I? What is this?"
But he was nothing if not practical,
"I have already read the novel twice," he said.
Gutov laughed. "With your heart, or with your head?"
"I don't know," Finley replied, quite helpless.
"Let's sit here for a while on this rock then."
So they sat where the water lapped the shore,
And allowed for Truth to be felt, at last.

26

THE BRIDGE
IKONA

BY K.I. GUTOV

Children clapping and cheering followed Jem as he wound his way back through the camp. His hands were still bloody and he wore a scowl which slowly transformed into a grin as the crowd gathered. He approached the firepit. The people shouted their appreciation for his great feat. No longer were they under threat of the beast, and they had a meal as well.

"But I honour my wise companion, my elder," said Jem, "for his wisdom is truly a salve for a great many tender hearts."

Yuk-Or Ba's wisdom was hardly the matter at hand, but in respect to the holy man, many bowed and curtsied. Only Yuk-Or Ba saw past the pretense to their true gratitude, which derived from the removal of tangible threat, and the subsequent feast they would consume. His earlier discourse on the inner threat - that of hearts turned against one another - had perished with the beast.

As if in resonance with that thought came the cry, "And we praise you again, Jem, for your brave action!"

A short time later, a bearded man approached with a youth; together they held up the spit with the skinned animal.

"Yes, it is action that can save us," said Jem. "Were it not for wisdom, however, what little guidance would we have to know the correct action." And he laughed, not failing in that moment to flex his muscles.

The charm! Yuk-Or Ba thought. *Words whose very action communicated otherwise.*

Yet the old man retained his dignity, seeing only the innocent fool within the caper.

"Let us feast!" sang out another man, riling the crowd to ever greater heights. More joined to hurrah, despite their communal fatigue and deep hunger, and the days of traversing rough terrain. In addition to the beast, the local men had killed a reindeer earlier in the day, so there would be a feast indeed that night.

Over the meal, Jem regaled the crowd with their plans to find the great Shambhala. Yuk-Or Ba merely smiled agreeably at the other's appropriation of his plans. The local chieftain, who had only just joined their mission as soon as he realized there was an escape from inevitable incursion, presented Jem with the largest plate, and brought him two women as well. Yuk-Or Ba declined the company of the one woman offered him, and so Jem spent the night with three local beauties while his companion meditated by starlight, alone in his tent.

At dawn, as Yuk-Or Ba sat with the glowing icon in his lap in prayer, Jem appeared at the entrance to the tent.

"Is there anything else you need or want, Wise One?"

"No."

"You have already created a miracle in getting us this far, with God's own icon, leading us to the Great Gates of Heaven on Earth, *Shambhala*. You are truly God's greatest emissary, and the world's great hope."

Yuk-Or Ba merely watched the object in his lap, noticing how its glow had muted with Jem's entrance. The man's tone contained a caveat; in his very stance lurked some condition, which Yuk-Or Ba sensed in the clenching of his gut. He said nothing, awaiting the inevitable.

But no words were exchanged.

The elder stared at the younger man, his handsome face and square jaw. Up until this very moment, he had not once distrusted him. Jem had saved the old man at El Minero, after all. Yuk-Or Ba lowered his head in respect. They had both suffered.

Yuk-Or Ba felt Jem's eyes on him. He felt, suddenly, something more than mere vanity penetrate. Was it envy? Lust for control?

So, Jem had a raucous ego. Many men traversed that stage on a path to wisdom, but come to think of it, perhaps Jem had remained in that stage too long.

Perhaps, Yuk-Or Ba reflected on himself with some dismay, his faculties were declining in old age. Maria the cook had scolded him just that morning, after one of Jem's rousing speeches, "If you don't mind me saying so, you sometimes see too much the potential in people, Wise One, rather than the present reality. His heart has deeper scars than most."

She was furtive with her words, advice dished out with bitter herbs "to fortify you, for this journey."

Maybe she'd not meant the journey to Heaven's Gate. Maybe she meant the journey he took with Jem, in his heart.

As Jem lingered in the tent, Yuk-Or Ba lifted his head to meet Jem's burning eyes. He felt his heartbeat quicken.

"Oh Wise One, do you sense we are close?" Jem spoke at last.

"We are not far. I believe our destination lies beyond those hills, beyond which the eye can see, but yet without deviating, towards the East."

Jem bowed his head. "Without deviation, we shall arrive then? We cannot miss it?"

"My vision is clear. The icon is a reliable compass. There may be hurdles, but that is the way."

"We must prepare to depart, then."

Yuk-Or Ba nodded, and the younger man bowed as if to go.

"Tell me," Yuk-Or Ba stopped him.

Jem turned to him, but his stance was impatient.

Yuk-Or Ba made him wait for seconds, until Jem said, "With respect, we must prepare for the journey."

"Yes," Yuk-Or Ba agreed. "We must. Yet I recall another journey, when Jal'Qa was invaded."

Jem put a foot sideways; he either braced himself for the traumatic memory or restrained himself from leaving.

"As I recall, the sound of the space trains was almost imperceptible. It was like a bee, at a great distance. Though at the time, of course, we had no way to make sense of it."

Jem scowled. "I do not recall."

"Yes, yes. I understand. Memory is funny that way. I recall the quiet before, which is perhaps why the buzzing got my attention. Many more heard nothing, or they paid it no mind."

Neither spoke, and both men heard the commotion outside as scouts arrived with the horses, and the camp began to wake up.

"I am sorry, Jem, that your wife and son died," Yuk-Or Ba said.

Someone clanged a pot. A child cried for his mother, and Jem's mouth twitched.

"It was many years ago now. We should go, with all respect," Jem said.

"Yes. I just wonder, the price we pay, the loss we must bear. Will our new home ever make up for that? Will our survival not unwittingly harm those who build a new world?"

"How so?" Terse. Jaw hard.

"The pain we carry. Might it transmute into a desire for revenge? Poison the very air we breathe?"

"We have been told that those from other worlds will not be able to find us there. So how, then, revenge?"

"Ah. I don't mean the invaders."

"You mean the operators, who were forced to collaborate."

"Were they forced?"

"I see it that way. Most do."

"Others might not."

"You wish for a philosophical exploration now, Wise One? Or is this a parable? I do respect your insight. However, I am concerned for the timing."

Impatience had crept into Jem's tone, though he evidently fought against the notion of challenging the group's last remaining elder.

"I'm only interested in your own personal opinion, as one who has lost so much," Yuk-Or Ba said.

"We have all lost so much. Your wife, with respect."

Yuk-Or Ba rose to his knees now. "Yes, as did many, she died in the massacre, on invasion day."

"My wife and son were punished for my insurrection," Jem said. His chin quivered almost imperceptibly.

"You have nothing left to lose. I am sorry for that." The old man squinted at him, probing.

"If you're asking me if I think of revenge, the answer is yes, but it is pointless. It is too late. We have left Minero and our captors. We go towards freedom. So now, please, let us go."

Yuk-Or Ba stood, grabbing a small knapsack as he did. "This is all I need. Let us go," he said.

"Very well," Jem sighed, relieved.

"You know, what we carry in our hearts we still carry. But, I am an old man, so I must be more careful about the weight of things. I'm not as strong as I used to be."

He smiled at Jem, who knew him well enough to see the point of his jokes. Jem replied, smiling as well, "Shall I carry the icon then for you? Perhaps you no longer need bear its weight if you are so certain of the way."

"You carried it for your time, did you not? And yet it found its way back to me. It seems that it is the weight I must bear." Yuk-Or Ba patted him on the arm. "I will bear it for you," he laughed.

TWENTY VERSTS they had traveled since dawn. The mountain peaks crowded together and cast long shadows across their path, and the trees which flanked the slopes were denser, and the elevation made people sick as the sun finally set.

Yuk-Or Ba now walked behind Jem, though the younger man occasionally checked in to confirm their direction, and the old man continued to reassure him that there was only one path, and it was East.

Now, as they approached the place where the dense trees clung to rocky slopes, they set up camp. They were close, Yuk-Or Ba assured Jem, and tomorrow they would have to climb over the rocks and through the trees. Shortly beyond, there would be a bridge, and they would arrive at the shattering place, through which they could step into another world entirely.

Jem was curt since the morning conversation with his elder. Yuk-Or Ba sensed annoyance, but he knew that Jem yet grappled with his pain. All of the survivors did. Yuk-Or Ba considered all he'd said at dawn, and Jem's reaction, which led him into his own past once again. He allowed it to play out in his mind over the long hours of solitude as the distance between him and Minero grew further and further, as they traveled deeper and deeper into the wilderness.

Whilst the main cohort waited for Jem's directions with every breath, praising him as they went, Yuk-Or Ba, quiet and self-reflective, attempted to stop looking backwards, and to focus on his mission: to end suffering and escape to a world of peace. Yet his mind kept returning to the past, and with this, judgment arose. Of himself, principally, for his distraction. Also, there remained in him helpless pain, directed at their captors. His mind wished to rationalize that pain as blame, which he fought against. Meanwhile, he chastised himself for his inattention to the group, which had somehow slipped from his influence. He could not find in himself the energy to refocus.

He half-listened to Jem's wild stories and his boasting about past feats.

"I will not let you down," Jem promised the crowd, and he told them to whisper those words to those behind him, two hundred humans deep.

Such eager faces, and oh how they placed their faith in the one who took directions from *him*, the silent old man! While the other pretended to confidence he did not have, and would deny his own pain, this old man knew the direction truly, and yet grappled with his thoughts and feelings. Yuk-Or Ba held the warm icon in the pouch around his neck. If these people had ever really known, then surely they had forgotten: all humans are fallible. It was this holy object which led them, not even the one who spoke wisdom inspired from it, and especially not this young fool.

BY THE TIME they gathered for a meal that night, Yuk-Or Ba was fully immersed in his mind's struggle. He ate but a handful of bread and went to meditate in his tent, but could not even do that. Instead, he sat on the mat, wondering what new torture this was and how he was meant to overcome it in order to fulfill his mission and lead his people to their new Home.

For so long he'd kept his memories of *her*, his beloved, at a great distance, but now of its own will, his mind conjured Rima, as if she were there, superimposed on the landscape. She smiled at him. Those twenty years ago were a hair's breadth away now; his heart reawakened and with it, the terrible pain.

So much healing had been done. So much of his past rested softly in the gentle, giving land of acceptance, and since that time, he had cultivated a garden of joy, for himself, and others. Abundance in every form, yet not in flesh. The beating of Yuk-Or Ba's heart reverberated throughout his body now, and he felt electrical pulses in his fingertips.

The feeling of her pressed against him, and the sweet, reassuring smell of her hair as it tickled his nose.

It was enough, all that time it was enough to rest in acceptance, yet at this critical moment, all vestiges of his longing for her seemed to emerge from who knows where - he had been certain that this feeling had shriveled from inattention, like a plant that had not been watered.

But no - there it was, the desperate, panicked emptiness of grief. The terrible fear once more of annihilation, that his very identity would cease to be - he who had lost a homeland, who had been orphaned as a child by war, as had countless others, who had reinvented himself again after the loss of his wife. Like an injured animal seeking to hide, alone, to heal, he'd endured the cycle of pain and regeneration once too many times.

There she was again.

Rima.

The desire to smell her, to hold her, consumed him. He fell back onto this meditation rug and hugged himself, squeezed his eyes shut. The once-comforting thought that she was there, somewhere, no longer assuaged the pain.

He did not believe it.

She was gone.

Oh, acceptance of what is, bring me peace, he prayed.

There is no loss in the eternal. No loss, only the calm presence of all and everyone, he told himself.

He lay on the mat, twisting from side to side, and physical pain radiated from his heart and throughout, and tears squeezed out of his eyes.

Rima, Rima, he called to her. He could not dispel the image of the moment life slipped from her. Her wound was not visible. Their weapon triggered instant heart failure. It was so bloodless a battlefield. It was as if hundreds of people lay sleeping.

Why now? The thought did come from a place in him that stood apart from the pain - and so he grabbed onto that thought to ride back the wave of no-pain and *see* Truth.

Yes, why now?

The pain was like a blackness that fell expressly to obscure vision. He could only feel its darkness. Its solid edges and its dense, weighty mass, like being pushed against by cold slabs of marble.

It was in the room with him. He stretched out a hand to feel it, closing his wet eyes against the pressure it brought to bear on his forehead, and the cold, marble heaviness of it pushed back against him again, crushing his heart this time. He heard Jem calling out in concern, but rebuffed him.

He succumbed. He felt himself break open as pain engulfed him. Then he fell into the darkness and let it, too, be his guide.

JEM PEERED INTO THE TENT, hidden, and saw his guru writhing in distress. He was ill, he thought, weakened suddenly, fevered perhaps. He watched for some time. He felt giddy with light-headedness.

"Master, are you unwell?" He rushed into the tent.

This was his moment. He caught his breath and remained tentative as the old man moaned.

"Leave me!" Yuk-Or Ba shouted.

"But you are ill, I cannot. I shall fetch the witch."

"Do not. I am fine. Go."

Jem left the tent but stayed out of sight, watching as the old man cried and moaned, as if protesting his condition. After a time, Yuk-Or Ba fell silent and still. Jem checked on him before dawn, and found him unconscious. He searched his body and the tent, but could not find the icon. He knew the way, though, he thought: East. Without deviation.

He whispered to those nearby that the old man needed to stay back with the Witch as he was unwell, and to be quiet lest they awaken him. He instructed them to send those words two hundred humans deep as they packed and departed.

YUK-OR BA AWOKE TO SILENCE. The first thing he noticed was weightlessness, how light-filled was his body, the very cells and energetic pathways cleared and regenerated. He stretched. Memory, once a tiresome knot, had unwound and become a golden thread. Woven from time and no-time, from beauty and pain, happy remembrances cast a shadow of loss, and both pulsed wisdom deep into his being.

The next thing he noticed was that he had been abandoned. He knew it to be true, before he even peered out of his tent. Finally, he saw that Mary was there. She appraised him thoughtfully, and did not press him to speak before he was ready.

"I am well," he said. He teased her. "You have stayed to feed me then?"

"For two days I have only watched you sleep," she said.

"Two days?"

"Yes. Jem told me to stay. I am the Witch, you know, though I'm just an apprentice truly, which is why I am cooking. As I work with herbs, they assumed that I was a mistress of meals. But yes, Jem told me to stay and tend to you. I hid the icon as you slept. I have returned it to your side."

She closed her eyes and performed a small bow.

"You are a lovely and good witch," Yuk-Or Ba said, sitting up to find a bowl of soup waiting for him. "But where has everyone gone? Don't tell me they followed Jem!"

"He was a shapeshifter all right," she said. "But not everyone followed him. Please, Wise One, those of us who stayed with you, please lead us when you feel able. Those who left have forgotten that you are the one with the icon. They were seduced by Jem's words and his confidence, which was false, as it turned out."

Yuk-Or Ba ate, but as he did the word spread that the Wise One was awake, so he left his tent to find at least fifty souls waiting there for him.

"Let us pack and we shall continue," he announced, sounding very much more courageous than he did before.

"Jem continued with a search party, that way, East," said a woman who approached him. "Only already, at least ten people who started with him turned around and are back here with us. They say that more of his party straggle on, but Jem himself has lost hope. He does not know where it is, Wise One. He keeps moving East and not finding it. We are also losing hope. Please can you tell us how we will find this place you have promised us?"

Then a young man, a scar across his face denoting that he was once property of the mine, approached Yuk-Or Ba, his eyes downcast.

"I am sorry to say that I followed Jem, and then turned back when it became clear that he did not know the way. I left my family there, as my child is too young to walk back without rest. Please can we collect them on the way?"

"We will leave nobody behind. We will find Jem's camp, and gather all, and continue to our destination as a group," Yuk-Or Ba announced.

THOSE FIFTY PEOPLE walked together with Yuk-Or Ba, and when they came to the camp that Jem had abandoned, they found another one hundred or more awaiting them. But where was Jem? He had fled further East, it seemed, taking with him a loyal few.

Yuk-Or Ba said a prayer for him, that he may return and join them before it was too late.

They were only an hour from where Jem had disappeared, but already Yuk-Or Ba could feel the presence of wise beings and he could see the light that emanated from the clouds, so he announced to all that they were near the shattering place and the bridge.

"Why did Jem not see it then himself?" Mary asked him in confidence.

"Eyes can only see what they have been trained to see," he told her. "Which is why we must train the heart instead."

The icon glowed through the neck pouch, and felt warm to his touch.

YUK-OR BA STOPPED where the forest thinned out and a great flat place descended into a ravine. The fog was so dense that only the closest ground was visible, and their tired party were like specters come to haunt the land.

"I will speak to you all now, so please gather round. I am preparing you for what lies ahead. Please listen truly with your hearts and not with your minds."

Everyone stopped. They sat on the hard ground and passed around flasks of water and small packets of food to share. Babies settled into sleep on mothers' breasts and toddlers began to run around, freed at last from being carried. There was happy murmuring and even laughter. They felt it too, their nearness. Yuk-Or Ba gave them time to settle. When he cleared his throat, the crowd hushed.

"I am going to tell you now how to cross the bridge. I'm going to tell you how to live in a new world."

Nature itself stilled as the people held their breath. Even the toddlers plopped onto their bottoms, mesmerized by the Wise One's sonorous tone.

"There is a bridge between all that we know and all that we do not know. It straddles these two sides, the known and unknown lands. You can imagine it, the charming wooden slats and the sturdy railing. On our known side it rests on solid stone piers built into the earth. There is a shallow ravine below it with piers along the way. The other end of the bridge rests on piers that we cannot see, due to its distance. But in any case, the bridge appears solid, and the crossing simple, though over rocky ground. You cannot look down, or back, for that might make you dizzy, and you might fall. You must trust that as you can see the bridge all the way across, that it is, in fact, sturdy.

"But the fact remains, we cannot see, from where we are, the foundation at the other end of the bridge. We assume, because our minds are creatures of habit, that it rests on the same sort of foundation. Yet that assumption is incorrect.

"You see, this unknown land which is across the ravine, it is a different world. It operates by different laws. It proposes a new kind of reality, and so the piers of that bridge are of course constructed of different matter. They follow different rules. They suspend the bridge by means of which we cannot see at present.

"The key difference is the weight they are able to bear.

"Listen with your hearts now, and no longer with your mind. Listen with the part of your consciousness that has experienced loss, and which longs for reunion, for peace."

The crowd stirred. Already, tears spilled from Mary's eyes. She sat on the ground closest to him.

"On this side of the bridge, weight is measured in physical increments. The tonnage of our collective humanness, our belongings. The heaviness of flesh and objects. But, in this new world, weight is purely that which sits as a stone upon our hearts which we wish to hurl at the object of our despair.

"Tis not sadness, or grief. It is, rather, the weighty energy of this stone we wish to use for harm. The piers on the other side, the very structure of the bridge itself, cannot withstand this weight. So if, perchance, you harbor this heaviness, then the bridge will collapse. You will not arrive at the other side."

There was a murmur of disappointment. One man cried out, "Then one person can destroy all of our futures, how can that be? How can we be sure that none of us carry this weight?"

Yuk-Or Ba readied himself for his final words, which he knew would be the deciding factor, if they were all to go along with it.

"The crossing is the shattering place, where the one becomes many."

Faint understanding rippled through the crowd like an exhale.

"As you cross the bridge, there will be a moment when either all will fall, or all will cross, but in reality, each of you will choose your path. In the moment of shattering, like a mirror into a thousand pieces, your self will split into many. Choose now, which self will cross that bridge."

One man called out, "Are you saying that we will not know which self we continue being?"

"You know by the choice you make in your heart. By the choice, in this moment, to release the stone of vengeance, to choose to turn your back on the past and move forward into a new life, or not."

The man continued. "But how can we do this, when we have suffered so much at the hands of evil? Are you saying that we should ignore reality, and dishonor those we have lost by looking past wrongdoings?"

"No, sir. You speak the truth, that we have suffered so much at the hands of evil, in ways that have touched, and destroyed, each of our lives in some way. Yet, there is also truth in this, that what is done is done. I do not urge you to dismiss moral judgements. I only speak to the weight of what would be your response to it, the heavy weight of a heart that fights what is, rather than rests in peace."

There were muffled voices in conversation, an angry voice, some tears. Yuk-Or Ba held the space, feeling all they were feeling, yet from a perspective that saw beyond. He waited several minutes, knowing the conversation was not yet done.

A woman holding a young child on her hip spoke. "It is not easy to simply banish such a weight."

"Ah. It's not the doing that accomplishes the feat so much as the intention you hold. Some feats are accomplished through us, by the great Spirit. You only need do your part."

"Wise One," came a quiet voice from the crowd. "If we should fail, or if I should fail, does that mean we all perish?"

"No, as I said, and I realize this is a concept that is entirely new - if you carry this stone, you will cross the bridge regardless, and the world might appear different, but in fact it will be the same world. That is why your intention matters. You will see the fruits of your heart-work only later."

"If we remain in this world, we will die," a young boy called. "They will find us, and enslave us again."

"We need help!" a woman shouted. "You must show us how to hold this intention!"

The crowd murmured in agreement. Yuk-Or Ba felt pride at their determination, and yet also a knowing that not all would be successful, and they would perhaps not realize this for a time. He also knew that most had already made their decision, long ago. Their hearts already resonated with one truth or another. He spoke for the sake of those who remained in the spaces between, those who needed faith.

He instructed them to gather, as the sun set, and hold their intention. He described intention as a musical note, a resonance that you carry within, a song your heart sings even if you can't remember the lyrics.

Yuk-Or Ba also felt tears as he admitted that the hardest path is to accept what has been, when what was torn away was in fact the very fabric of your life. And yet, to surrender to that darkness was the only way to clear the path ahead.

Mary followed his every word closely, and many others appeared resigned, whilst some wept for their losses.

Yuk-Or Ba wondered, because he could not help it, how many would eventually perish in their refusal to truly see?

There was movement in the crowd, and he could see, from the corners of his eyes, that a few people were departing. He heard the name Jem and felt his heart sadden. Some would seek him, he knew and find their own new world, not the sanctuary across the bridge, but one destined for struggle. Yuk-Or Ba felt only compassion. The desire for retribution was an irresistible energy, a craving that defied logic, a dark demon even. And yet its vanquishment lay in the realization that it was only a stone.

So, those who remained sat with him at sunset.

And they held in their heart only an intention.

Do less, Yuk-Or Ba advised, *less and less. Still your thoughts, your form and be.*

Simply be that intention. Allow it to resonate within you, and call you home to your future.

Hope must become intention.

Intention becomes the way.

He removed the icon from its neck pouch and held it. It glowed in his hand. He held it up for all to see. A collective gasp sounded, a ripple of awe. The icon knew only the highest truth - and everyone understood that in a world so divided and broken, this one object alone was consistently pure. It led them to water, to the path, to food, and away from enemies. Its purity was reliable.

Indeed, it had led him here, and would lead them to the bridge. Yes, it had once faithfully led Jem towards this place too, many versts ago, but that was its gift of course. Its wisdom and magic would guide any soul towards Truth.

Only now, however, did he understand why Jem had not been

able to carry it for long. For as much as it communicated the way, with every material signpost, so too appeared an inner sign; a doorway opened in the heart, to what had been lost, and could now be found. The push towards an inner reckoning was too much for many. Only that person who was prepared to arrive at their inner destination fully could hold it for long. So few were, and so Yuk-Or Ba always ended up with it.

Evening light shimmered through the fog, which dispersed before their eyes. Yuk-Or Ba guided the group across the flat place and onto the white rocks and stones that covered the ground, where the earth sloped down into the ravine. There, at the edge, was a bridge held aloft by stone piers.

27

WALLACE & THE COTTAGE - REPRISED

JUNE, 2131 AD

KRASNOYARSK, EASTERN FEDERATION

Wallace stared up at what was, generously speaking, a window, and desperately missed the view of the sky he'd become accustomed to in his room, a reassuring daily backdrop which he had taken for granted.

And now, only this small grille and its glimpse of green, one of dozens of grilles above many basement rooms, storage spaces, cellars —the forgotten underground of the monastery above.

Nothing was visible from his perspective, but for a flash of sunlight now and again if it reached through the branches of whatever it was.

Ten days he'd been here and already he plotted an escape—

anywhere but here

Only he could not. He had to accept this world if he were to be the one to find the icon's origins. There was no escape from this underground, nor from the world above in which his love was cancered.

Even were he to find the origin of the cross, even if there were a possibility for a cure, how long would it take to create it and administer it? Would there be time enough to save her?

After nearly two weeks of a life in hiding—a life even quieter than the monastic life above, he began to fall into a melancholic state, especially as lately he was often alone. Since Justicia's husband had died, she had many obligations to fulfill, and also she said she needed some time to mourn. To honor her husband and their ten years of marriage. Though, as she explained to Wallace, she expected she would continue to mourn him for some time, even in his arms.

He longed to console her in his arms, but as he could not yet, he distracted himself by contemplating the desolate world outside.

Could it actually be possible to save a world that had been hanging on by a thread for centuries, which had lost and found its way and was again at a crossroads? To this thought was affixed a confusing codicil—the world that would be saved would represent an entire different reality. A world of wellness, and longevity, and with it a political landscape that would have to reshape itself. What might that even look like?

He could not imagine it—yet such were his thoughts as he sat on his too-thin single mattress, observing the forced domesticity of the space. Dr. Rinella, though haggard of late with all the to-ing and fro-ing and secret-keeping, still retained his practical faculties, so had ensured that Wallace had all that he needed, that they *all* needed for their sessions. In addition to the initial bits of furnishing, he had brought a small stove, pots and more cereals. Justicia had brought some things from her home as well, cups, bowls and cutlery, and some herbs to take away the odors which sat in the immovable air. So now, when Wallace had his visitors, they sat around his single mattress where he often sat on his own, cross-legged.

And when he didn't have visitors, which was more often the case, he sat in the same manner, contemplating inconsolable things.

BLESSEDLY, Wallace's tedium that day was to be short-lived, as it was time, again, for another foray into the past. This time, there seemed to be even more at stake: Father Andrew drank from his flask of tea and announced that his superiors were launching a search for Wallace.

"They are close," Schopel said, "in consciousness too. Resonance alone is not enough. We need to take it a step further."

"What does that mean?" Justicia asked.

Dr. Rinella frowned, one arm lying across his lap, the other upright as he leaned onto it, resting his chin on his fist.

"I will explain, Eden," Dr. Rinella said. "But please don't interrupt, Justicia. I believe we need to visit the Cottage."

Father Andrew sighed. As Dr. Rinella began to justify his suggestion, Wallace felt his heart race and a prickle of heat travel the length of his torso to his head, where it became droplets of sweat.

"Hear me out. The process at the Cottage relies on the selective activation of neural pathways via the Machine, and deactivation of others relating to memory and trauma."

Dr. Rinella checked that everyone was following him, then directed his words to Wallace.

"For some reason, for you, it opened certain pathways far too much, and then closed others, so that you have these... *abilities* now. I think that if we recreate the initiation which opened your consciousness, we might gain a stronger and more solid connection to Finley. I have studied your files. Thank you, Andrew, for those."

"It was not easy to obtain, Lucio. I fear my inquiries contributed to this current search for Wallace..."

"Nevermind that. We had little time anyway. We need to get him to the Cottage. I have discussed this with Schopel already, and she has some ideas..."

Justicia shook her head. "No, no, that's dangerous, Lucio. His brain could be harmed by this."

"We will be observing at all times," Dr. Rinella said, "and doing it gradually. We can stop at any moment. But that is not all. Eden, please explain."

Schopel sat on her chair in the shadows at the back of the room, inscrutable. Justicia dropped her face into her hands with a silent reproach.

"We know that beyond changing your consciousness, you must attune yourself to a particular resonance. An emotional tonality. It worked to some extent last time, but still, I'm not sure we are aligning with the right timeline. If the resonance were of a higher vibration, stronger, you might be able to merge with the life in which Finley discovered the icon's origin, and faster. It is not easy, I realize, for you to access and maintain this resonance under these stressed conditions, but there is a way. A psychotropic substance can guarantee it. You see where I'm going."

Schopel's voice calmed Wallace. His heart settled. Justicia shook her head. "It's madness, Eden, but it makes sense. I have heard of these substances."

"I have, too," Wallace said. "I have read about their use in the past."

"Where I come from, there are plants we use for this purpose."

Where she comes from, Wallace thought.

"Plant medicine was once very popular, but as with many approaches..." Father Andrew addressed himself to Wallace. "It's perfectly safe, don't worry."

"The Spiritualists are opposed, I know. After the Revolution, it was stopped," Schopel said.

"Let me guess why," Wallace said, checking in with Father Andrew. "The Machine was designed to remove certain memories and traumas so that we might experience a particular form of transcendence. A kind of generic bliss state that we aim for at the Monasteries. In preparation for the afterlife, of course. But plant medicine, as I understand it, is impossible to control. It can create widely divergent states of consciousness and expose a person to all kinds of emotions, entities, different realities..."

"Yes, that's right, Wallace," Father Andrew said. "And that offers too many possibilities. It cannot be controlled. There was a fear that psychotropic substances could replace the Monasteries altogether."

"My people have managed to exist outside this system," Schopel said. "And our medicine has a very specific effect. It strengthens the state you are already in. It locks in your resonance, as it were."

Justicia clapped her hands together. "You come from Hybrid

communities! I thought they no longer existed. I mean, I heard there are a few, hidden in inhabitable regions."

"You're correct," Schopel said.

"It's never been part of your official biography. It must have taken a lot to leave your people and join the Triumverate…" Justicia's eyes narrowed, her forehead furrowed. Wallace, too, was intrigued by Schopel's apparent lineage, but she deflected this line of inquiry.

"My point is that I can access this substance. This medicine. It's powerful. It can create a channel that is impervious to interference. I should have thought of it before."

"This is new territory for all of us," Dr. Rinella said.

Justicia said, "So Lucio, Eden, you think that the combination of the psychotropic substance and the selective activation of neural pathways at the Cottage can expand Wallace's consciousness towards a very specific timeline, is that right?"

"Yes," Eden said.

"Yes, to the timeline in which we are all successful. And the connection should be strong enough to keep our enemies out," Dr. Rinella added.

Wallace, whose nerves were fortunately subdued by curiosity, had to ask, "So it's entirely possible that even had those so-called enemies physically forced me to the Cottage and run the Machine on me themselves, they may not have even been able to stay on the right timeline —the one in which Finley finds the origin of the cross…"

"No. Possibly not," Schopel replied. "Such are their limitations."

"And in the process it may have damaged your brain," Justicia said. "So, how exactly are we certain it will not do so anyway? The psychotropic substance does not have the power to protect those neural pathways, does it?"

"As I've said, we will go slow and steady, and open up those pathways as before, and if you experience pain, we will stop and adjust. There is no other way at this stage." Dr. Rinella lowered his eyes. "I want to impress upon you the significance of what we are dealing with. The hope we can have for humanity if you find the origin of the icon and it leads us to a cure, Wallace."

Wallace knew this, of course; he couldn't refuse the attempt, even if his body failed to cooperate. Justicia's green eyes bore into him. Fearful.

He clarified, "You want me to focus on a particular tonality using this substance, in order to connect the past with the present and future on the timeline or frequency of healing, before you even... take me there."

He felt strangely calm about this. Resigned and willing, though slightly vigilant to the dangers.

"Yes, Wallace," Dr. Rinella said. "We must try. We are running out of time. It may be the only way to get around the barriers and the factions trying to control your consciousness."

Schopel spoke again from her dark corner. "I have some of this plant that I've stored, just for this eventuality. I will prepare it. It will be ready by nightfall. Thank you, Wallace, for your efforts."

She stood and crossed the room quickly, a fleeting shadow that disappeared through the hatch. As when she first entered Dr. Rinella's office, her departure now seemed to cleanse the space, leaving the group resigned, but serene. In the collective silence that followed, everyone retreated to their thoughts.

"I almost forgot. Has it helped, the Bridge, in *Ikona*?" Father Andrew asked a minute or so later.

"Have you read it, too?" Wallace returned from his rumination on Justicia's husband, on having to revisit the Cottage. Dire thoughts. Realistic thoughts.

"We all have, since your last session," Dr. Rinella said. "I had first read it many years ago, but I won't pretend that I understood its relevance then. What did you take from it?"

"I'm not sure." Wallace sighed. "I think it's about resonance, obviously, as we've discussed. It seems to be saying that resonance comes from hope, which requires letting go of anger about the past. I'm not sure how to use this, practically speaking."

"I think it's very practical," Justicia said. "Shambhala, peace, Heaven, Truth, whatever you call it, is only visible to those whose vision is not obscured by vengeance. By unforgiveness. It's quite spiritual, I should think."

Justicia smiled at Wallace, a little smug perhaps, he thought. So she had touched a spiritual truth whilst he stood on the precipice of losing her, his worldview colored accordingly.

"I agree, Justicia," Father Andrew said. "Perhaps it's not so much the literal putting into practice that matters, Wallace, but rather how the concept might alter your attitude, even subconsciously."

Justicia took Wallace's hand. She smiled. "No need to think any more. You've got a lot on your mind, or a lot to get out of your mind."

"Entirely," Dr. Rinella agreed. "Wallace, you just need to do whatever you can now, to get into a resonant state. You have all afternoon, and then we will administer the substance. We will go to the Cottage after nightfall, when no one is there. I have found a passageway to get us there."

"Okay, but I need to be outside," Wallace said. "With her."

"It's a risk," Dr. Rinella said, "but if it's the only way, we will have to make a plan. Prepare to walk."

OVER THE COURSE of the next hour, Dr. Rinella led them through a series of tunnels that emerged finally beyond the Quarter Fields where the Monasteries' cultivated land ended, past where they held Vespers. It was the wilds, where grasses grew four meters tall and so dense that they had to flatten the area as soon as they emerged from underground, just to find space to stand. The trio dared not move even a step past the earthen door from which they'd emerged, for fear they'd never find their way back to it again. The grasses admitted but a glimpse of the highest mountains beyond, and certainly no buildings. The towns were in the other direction from the Monastery entirely. There was nothing here whatsoever to suggest human existence. The only sound was the whistle-and-rush of stalks swishing.

It was as if they were alone on the Earth, with only the sky to keep them company.

Having bashed back the surrounding grass, Wallace and Justicia arranged themselves on a blanket, with a flask of tea to share, and Dr Rinella spoke before departing.

"I know this task is not easy. I know you're both hurting in your own ways. I don't want to tell you to pretend to optimism when you don't feel it, but you must at least take whatever hope you might have and nurture it, turn that into a reality, meditate on it so that it becomes a single point of light. Andrew will fetch you at dusk."

He departed, leaving them alone on the blanket. For several moments neither spoke, nor moved, and Wallace, face to face with the sky at last, closed his eyes and basked, face heavenward.

"We must hope for a world in which we find a cure," Justicia said.

"I know," he replied, and he could not help but conjure Gutov and the Bridge. What vengeance might he, Gutov, have harbored that led him to write the novel? What unforgiveness might he have been carrying, and did he forgive, in the end? He cast a sidelong glance at Justicia.

"I must meditate first," he told her, and prepared himself with breath.

All roads had led him here, he imagined, and now it was his choice which road to take.

He was able to quieten his mind, casting his eyes again towards the sky, and the black line of cranes fading to white. He imagined what hope felt like without any other options. As if hope were simply Truth, unavoidable and imminent, and thus fear and doubt mere fictions, or perhaps momentary lapses of reason.

Because, if one wished to realize a particular outcome, the best possible world, wasn't hope proof of possibility? Could one hope for something that was not possible? After all, he didn't hope for gravity to disappear, or for fire to not be hot, or water not to hydrate. Hope adhered to the laws of the universe, and reflected an infinite realm of possibility.

"The birds," Justicia said, "I've never seen them before."

"I think they are cranes," Wallace responded, "from the past... no." He laughed. "That can't be. I saw them in Germany, Finley's life."

He squinted—they were already gone.

The white sky in the distance shone golden for a few breathless seconds as the clouds shifted across the sunset and the present slipped into a future of health,

of togetherness,

which he felt as a wave passing over them, warm and comforting. Justicia, with rising excitement, stifled her tears, and short of breath said, "I will be saved, I know it. There is a world in which I live to old age."

"I feel it too," he told her.

"I know it in my cells, Wallace. It's there, somewhere, that future."

He didn't want to jinx it with banal words despite what seemed the certainty of his faith. He held her hand and imagined feeling her health.

His eyes rolled back and he fell silent, lips parted.

"Are you okay?" she asked him, peering closely at his still face.

Nothing.

He saw water, flashes of blue sky, and felt tremors. He smelled a dry earth, and felt a pang in his head.

A black shadow slipped across his torso, pulling at him; it chilled him. He lifted his chin and forced himself to smile towards Justicia.

"My love."

"I am here."

There was a world, a parallel world, in which there was no saving, no cure, or a partial cure for only some, and that was okay. He accepted this without emotion. Infinite universes of experience could not concern him. His reality was only this one, this moment with Justicia's pale, limp hand in his, and her face turned half away.

He placed a finger beneath her chin and pulled her face towards his. He breathed in deeply.

"We are together. This is our life to have together."

Minutes, an hour, hours... time passed and her eyes eventually fluttered shut and she came to lay on his lap. The moments unwound like a twisted rope. There was a certain amount of chaos inherent in the unwinding, stray thoughts and fears and alternate happenings that didn't happen were all there, too, but the present stayed the course. Wallace felt Finley's presence, and felt this unwinding reaching into his counterpart, meeting with the resistance of a mind pushed beyond its evolution. A mind that had not quite woken to infinite possibility, yet which had been pulled and spun so much that it could and did eventually admit that which had no precedent, where hope and fear were eternal twins and yet the good triumphed.

Wallace's mind was at rest as the process worked him;

as if in meditation, he only felt the wordless movement of ether, the rising calm of resolution.

The sun set in the Quarter Fields and the cold set in. Father Andrew appeared as the last sliver of orange lit the tall grasses. He brought a blanket, and wrapped them both in it, along with the one they had been sitting on. They tread lightly now, though weary, following the lantern's light through the dark earth tunnel, to their secret room and dinner, where Schopel and Dr. Rinella waited.

No one spoke as they ate, so as not to disturb the feeling Wallace had arrived at. Justicia sat at his side, occasionally stroking his arm, or fussing over his food—offering more, nudging the tea flask towards him. Dr. Rinella had only just suggested he lie down after the meal for a guided meditation, when Schopel returned.

She carried a satchel, and removed a small container from it. Dr. Rinella handed her Wallace's flask, into which she poured liquid from the container.

"When you feel you are in the correct state, drink this. It tastes bitter. You will not vomit."

He closed his eyes, holding onto all that he'd felt and seen in the fields,

only now sated and sleepy.

Eventually, he drank.

Moments later Schopel said, "We shall walk now. It takes about forty-five minutes to take effect, so we should aim to have him activated by then."

. . .

WALLACE DID NOT FEEL TIRED, or unfocused as he had feared—rather, his mind was crisp. Somehow, through time and practice and sheer will, he'd maintained as even a state as he ever had, despite the pressure and circumstances, and this substance enhanced it, so that he continued to feel the unwinding linger in his system, building in strength.

He knew the soft flow of energy from his core to his crown, and now it left him untroubled and for the first time since captivity, not despairing.

Justicia walked behind him, and Dr. Rinella and Father Andrew in front. He had no notion of time or space, and as his robes swished around him, faintly red with the glow of Dr. Rinella's torch up ahead, he had the sensation of flowing through the underground tunnels—

lifeblood spilling through the capillaries within the spiritual world which lived above,

no agency here, just current.

Deep breath in—he and the tunnel were part of the same entity, breathing each other.

Then, a memory arose without judgment, as if he were watching a play in his mind's eye, still walking through warm darkness.

It was a memory of the Cottage, as he was held down, the electrodes patched to his shaven head and the current cutting into him,

all of his childhood extracted by electromagnetic scalpel, his heart-mind-soul ripped open, and the blood of tears and memory bleeding out until he was dessicated,

hollow

numb.

He shuddered as they rounded a corner and then there were stairs, and a grate, into a basement of sorts, and then up the stairs again and they were inside—

the Cottage.

In blackness.

The Machine was silent.

Wallace was made to lie down on the hospital-like bed, which was semi-inclined and hard and narrow, and with Justicia's reassuring words whispered into his mind, her gentle kisses on his cold cheek, the others placed a blanket over him, and this time did not strap him in, but then,

the electrodes were placed onto his head as before.

He could see Dr. Rinella reading through something on his small pad, referring to it as he placed the patches on his head.

Schopel sat at his feet, humming in the way she did.

And the current, a slight tickle of the brain that collapsed his attention inward

like a piece of paper folded into itself,

and folded again,

and again.

"Hold steady," Schopel said.

"Follow my voice," Dr. Rinella said, and he felt it then, the currents, and he saw Finley's hand, lifting towards his own face.

He was him.

WALLACE BEGAN TO SHAKE. Dr. Rinella said, "It's been just ten minutes in, the mapping of his brain is not yet complete."

They waited, Justicia at his side, observing the shuddering, shaking, writhing which rose to a peak then pulled back, slowing until his body came to a still point.

Schopel sat in trance, equally still, her hands now lifted above her lap, index fingers to thumb, arms at a 90 degree angle.

"I can't tell if he's breathing," Dr. Rinella said.

Father Andrew clasped his hands in prayer.

Justicia began to pant, her voice cracked. "Lucio, I can't feel his pulse. Why is he so still? What have you done?"

28

FINLEY & THE RIVER
JUNE 2019

KRASNOYARSK AND THE ASCENSION MONASTERY

Finley spent three nights with Gutov, mostly being fed and taken for contemplative walks at the lake. Neither made conversation, yet within Finley, there was a change happening in the old man's presence. Not once did he feel pain, or have a vision, or sense that he was travelling. It was as if his abilities had fallen into dormancy. He wasn't even worried about the pain when or if he did. He considered that traipsing through the taiga was even more effective than the threat of deportation when it came to tempering the familiar voice of fear. He memorized the path of larch and birch trees that he followed towards the spruce encircling the hill line above the lake. He could spend an hour just observing ducks and gulls diving for their meal, longer if Gutov packed him a flask of tea and bread with cheese and left him alone. On his second day, he watched a gray heron catch three fat fish as gray clouds hurried across the sky. The whispering leaves and birdsong softened his edges. At night, as he lay in the guest room, he listened to the water murmur at the shore and he drifted in thoughts of peace. Gratitude emerged from his depths like a melody he'd forgotten, but whose familiarity became the tempo of his time with Gutov. Every glimpse of sky and lake, every tree, every creature, every morsel of food that passed his lips, all of it comprised the numinous rhythm of a soul awakening.

In the evenings he made a start rereading *Ikona,* from the heart this time.

Finally, Gutov managed to reclaim Finley's passport from the supposed government contact (an apocryphal story, as Gutov had predicted. There was no such contact. It was at Beer-gut-Volodya's uncle's house in Listvyanka). On their fourth morning together, he told Finley he'd arranged a driver to return him to Irkutsk for his onward journey.

And that was that.

"It's been a pleasure meeting you," Gutov said as he dropped Finley in front of the hotel where he'd first stayed.

"Likewise, thank you for your hospitality."

Finley fumbled for the car door handle. He did not expect Gutov to say anything else, since over the past three days they'd only exchanged formalities, praise and gratitude at meal time. So it was no surprise when the old man grabbed a plastic bag from the backseat and said,

"Here. I packed you some berries for the road, and some other small treats I baked. The food on the train is terrible."

"Oh." Finley released the door handle. "Thank you again."

Still, he half-hoped for some last minute advice. Or a cautionary tale about quests, perhaps. But their mutual silence only invited more silence, the perfect gift both conferred and received.

IT HAD ALREADY BEEN DECIDED by Gutov that Finley take the train to Krasnoyarsk, of course, since there was no flight that day from Irkutsk. It suited Finley just fine, as he felt he needed the time. Eighteen hours on the Trans-Siberian Railway would give him far more time to think than a three hour flight, and at least he could see the landscape and pretend, for a moment, that he was on a fun adventure, rather than,

whatever this was,

a *what* he'd begun to accept, the further from the lake he traveled.

The train's faint vibration lulled him into a daze as the landscape zoomed past. In fleeting moments, his mind anticipated his mission's success and sometimes he grew nervous, imagining the pain that might accompany his transmission to Wallace.

Sometimes, instead, he viewed the pain as simply a plot point in his future life, without anticipation or even fear.

Whenever he began to daydream, his mind threw up memories of the English countryside as a reference—until he saw a ramshackle Siberian dacha, or birch trees, or something that jolted him back to the reality of his whereabouts. To his mind, there was no place more fantastical, remote, or wild as Siberia. And yet the tangible reality of it soon became tedious. He consumed Gutov's gifts of food and purchased more snacks on the train. Four cups of tea and three packets of instant noodles later, he began to regret his inability to meditate.

So he stared, attempting a form of meditation as he understood it: noticing his thoughts. However, he soon became annoyed by the utter chaos of his mind.

He hoped Kate was okay and would soon find the girl, or maybe she'd already found her in Mexico.

He hoped that Jia Li was safe in Hong Kong. In a moment of lucidity, he messaged Phil, sent him Jia Li's number, and instructed him to give her access to all his crypto in the event he no longer needed it—the potential reasons for which eventuality he blocked from his consciousness entirely.

Phil exclaimed and protested—he rang five times in a row and was redirected to voicemail each time. Finley sent a raft of last minute documentation and arguments in defense of his decision, then he turned off his phone and buried it at the bottom of his food bag where it remained blessedly silent beneath empty noodle packets.

He rationalized: *She needed help, in case his mission succeeded or in case it didn't—either way, what good to him was money now?*

The smelly middle aged man sitting across from him, dressed all in brown and with days old white bristle, stared at Finley, which was disconcerting and also served as a circuit breaker, especially when the man drooled as he ate.

Gross.

He might take my bag the moment I look away, Finley thought.

He noticed as well the gray, then blue, then white sky and the light rain, then a burst of sun;

and suddenly the foreignness of it all was erased by the nostalgic smell of wet grass,

like an English summer holiday in Devon.

But no (his mind interjected), this was far East Russia, and someone had opened the window in the hall and the door to his cabin was open, too,

and someone was smoking nearby, the smell of fresh wet soil mixed with cigarette smoke,

Finley closed his eyes.

He was sixteen and sitting near the shore in Torquay, bumming a cigarette and avoiding happy family time at the beach. The ocean disconcerted him, but was not entirely off-putting. Sand between the toes must be avoided at all costs. Best to linger near the shops where the boats were moored, a pretty view of a posh life.

Life is best viewed this way, without sand between the toes.

He dozed on and off. Sometimes, the landscape that Finley saw out the window felt so familiar: the brown and green mountains woven into the land and the simple wooden houses arranged in clumps scattered across the green countryside beyond.

Clare. Her face. It was fuzzy now. What did she look like? He could remember her energy, rather, as if seeing her through frosted glass—a dull and foggy aura. She had been cheerful, right?

She'd loved him, right?

Was he the most boring person on the planet?

Had he bored her to death? Or was it his unhappiness that had been so terminal to their relationship?

Oh yes, she'd said that.

Bobbing around like a little boat far out to sea. *Sinking.* Her words.

His mood lifted a notch.

Not anymore! Look at me now! he thought, willing his thought-beams to Clare.

Here I am on the Trans-Siberian Railway, searching for the origins of a healing cross.

He chuckled.

The smelly man across from him stared.

Finley smiled, trying to look agreeable.

There was hardly anything of value in his bag anyway. He had his passport and money on his waist, like a tourist. (Little did anyone know; they couldn't have guessed his mission!)

Well done, really, he thought, *that I got this far.* His self-congratulatory moment was interrupted by a screaming toddler.

Good luck to Kate. Kids are so loud.

Yes, about this mission.

Wallace was a presence that pushed at the back of his mind. The city, the future version of Krasnoyarsk—was his home. There were towers then. Fields, too. A monastery abutting the fields, with surrounding mountains, like the ones he saw now, even as his eyes drooped and he half-dozed his way towards the journey's end.

Finley strained to remember the future—it always felt like Wallace was so near, and also at a great, intangible distance. The details were faint whilst Finley was in his normal life; retrieving them felt like trying to recite the lyrics of a song from your childhood. The song and all its memories were indelible, a body memory, a deep inner programming—but the *exact* wording remained elusive.

The train crossed the Yenisei river and nature gave way to the dense buildings and a mess of railway tracks in Kransoyarsk.

Something gave way inside Finley, a subtle sense of coming home to himself.

Wallace.

He'd never thought of him as a person outside of himself, as a person who could be assessed on his own merits. But now as he contemplated him, there arose deep compassion for the man Wallace was, who delved without complaint into whatever the past had in store for him, whatever his mind held for him to discover.

The middle-aged man across from Finley burped.

Finley awoke from his reverie and turned his thoughts to the practical matter of finding a hotel room and figuring out how he would get himself to the monastery.

AT THE TERMINAL Finley found the tourist information desk, and the Krasnoyarsk counterpart of the bored tourist information lady from Irkutsk. There were two such women here, in fact. He mumbled hello a few times to indicate that he spoke English. The older woman nudged her co-worker.

Finley was tentative. He had decided to do all bookings in person, so as not to have an online history—the same reason he'd paid for the train ticket in cash. "I need a hotel room tonight, somewhere not far from here, and tomorrow I would like to visit a monastery in the Tunguska region."

"Just monastery? We have many places to visit here," said the younger co-worker. In her thirties, maybe. She had perfectly straight blond hair and was chewing gum.

"I want... to find out my family's heritage."

He blinked. He did not enjoy lying.

The woman deadpanned, "Your heritage is at monastery?"

"Yes, my grandmother's grandmother was Russian Orthodox and from this region, and I'm researching her history."

"Pyotr likes monasteries. He will take. Wait." She shouted, "Pyotr!"

The woman returned with a young man in his early twenties wearing jeans and a t-shirt. He was cheerful and said in perfect English, "Call me Peter. So, you want to go to a monastery in Tunguska?"

Finley repeated his explanation about his grandmother, his family history.

"Ah, your grandmother was Russian? From Siberia? She went to Harbin?"

"Um, yes, we think, and um, eventually to England, where I'm from. I would love to speak to someone at the monastery, if that's possible. My family used to... well they attended church there." *Attended church?* Was that what one did at a Russian Orthodox Monastery? Finley inwardly winced at these lies.

Peter inspected him, almost suspicious, but that may just have been Finley's imagination, given his discomfort, and his eagerness to proceed past the questions to the task at hand.

"It's the Ascension Monastery," Finley said.

"I love this place! It's remote. Four hours drive, maybe five. Terrible history during the purges. Beautiful landscape. A place where you feel you are so isolated, you can really touch the Divine."

"You know it that well? Did you grow up here?" Finley asked.

"No, I grew up in Ukraine. But I decided to study at Krasnoyarsk University because I have always had a deep desire to come to Siberia. Like you, perhaps, because of your heritage."

"Um, yes," Finley lied again.

They agreed on a price, and Finley suggested they meet at whatever hotel Peter might arrange for his stay that night. Peter agreed, and got him a taxi to the Ibis hotel two minutes away.

Finley checked in and showered, then felt compelled to go out. To walk.

Maybe it was all those hours on a train, but also—whereas before he'd felt loneliness, now he felt a sense of inner companionship. It was the strangest feeling, and Finley knew what it was—

It was him, it was *Wallace*, who was so near to him here, in this place he would one day live. So Finley left the hotel and began to walk where his gut led him, all the while convincing his mind that he was not being rash or dangerous, that he would be safe on this warm summer's night, where everyone was out walking, scootering, laughing, unaware of the cataclysm that would take place nearby—

What? When? Finley heard himself ask in response to his pure *knowing.*

A few decades, a nuclear blast just close enough, just far enough, and the skies would never see such spectacular sunsets as after.

Wallace's memory trickled through. Finley just allowed, and his thoughts quieted as he recalled the compassion he'd felt earlier,

as well as the utter lack of pain or discomfort in that very moment as memory flowed freely towards him.

Funny how he'd just asked a question, simple as that, like opening a door into a passageway, as easy as swallowing.

Finley navigated through a complex of shops, behind a theater, even past a McDonalds, through residential apartment blocks and across the river—he racked his brain—there was no river that he recalled in the future through Wallace's eyes.

Once across it, he walked through more random streets, moved by instinct.

No one even seemed to notice him, and why would they? Other pedestrians crossed his path now and again. There was nothing different about Finley, aside from his hidden inner compass. The air smelled of wet soil and petrol and then the sweetness of untamed fields, as he found himself suddenly at a wild area of long grasses surrounded by old buildings.

He could peer through it, towards the countryside, where there would be

The Quarter Fields

It was impassable now.

The Cottage—it was nearby, then and now. Evgenia had said it was near Krasnoyarsk, so surely it was out there, somewhere. He looked across the grasses and sad gray buildings towards the hills visible beyond, and wondered where this Cottage could be, with its still *underdeveloped technology*, as Bernhardt had named it. *What groups were trying to create a machine that removed emotional trauma, and what was their end game in this era?*

Nevermind, he cautioned himself. *Focus on your task.*

He breathed in the smell of grass.

His eyes stung

Was it tears?

He didn't care.

He stood on the edge of Krasnoyarsk facing the wilderness, what would be one day a kind of home, a familiar world that represented the culmination of what was now happening all around and through him,

and he felt love,

only love,

so strange and unbidden that Finley had no resources with which to deflect it, to minimize its impact, much less to understand it. Instead, he could only feel love as it filled him, like the sweetest combination of complete longing and complete surrender. He had to sit, so strong was the dizziness that surged through him, turning the forest upside down until he asked a question in his mind,

What is happening in Wallace's experience that is like this? For surely it was *him*.

Finley had not felt such love in his life so far, not even for Clare.

What was this bliss state, he asked of himself, and his mind swam towards his counterpart—until

he felt the pain arriving suddenly,

and a part of him succumbed whilst another part reached towards the feeling of love—as if the ghost of him rose from his body towards the relief of death.

He was with Wallace then, and Justicia, in the Quarter Fields, for the briefest moment, and then just as quickly he felt thrown back.

The pain had lessened, but his head still throbbed. He walked back to the hotel.

Maybe this was part of the solution—to reach *for* something with as much love as he contracted away from the pain.

He considered, for the first time, that he could do this.

PETER ARRIVED AT 9 AM, cheerful and bearing coffee.

"Coffee at the hotel is not so good," he said.

Finley took a sip and feigned gratitude.

"Do you feel close to your Russian heritage here?" his young tour guide asked as he drove. Finley sat next to him in the front passenger seat.

"Very far actually," Finley said. "Tell me about the trees, the forests, what grows here?"

He preferred to identify pine and spruce, to discuss the minus 20 degree winter lows, to learn about the best attractions in the area, especially winter, when you could go skiing and snowboarding. Peter happily offered many relevant facts which Finley consumed even as he reflected that since his previous night's walk, a certain calm blanketed him.

He cared less for things of this world.

"I like this wild nature here. Sometimes I drive here, out of the city. I like to walk in the Spring, and pick wild flowers, and in the Autumn I look for mushrooms. The air is clean. It feeds my soul. I feel that God is Nature, you know. Sometimes, I lose time. I am walking and feeling and then suddenly it is getting dark, and I don't remember how I came. Once I lost my way to my car. Took me five hours to find it. Do you ever lose time?"

Peter turned to face him; his blue eyes were large and clear and sought connection beyond the person that was Finley, as if reaching towards his soul. He turned back to the road.

Did he know this person? Did Wallace know this person?

Through the eyes of Peter shone an ascetic, Finley was certain, in perpetual devotion to this Nature, Divinity by many other names.

Finley mumbled, "Yes, umm, I have."

"Look," Peter said. "We are close."

The Ascension Monastery's onion dome rose into lonely white skies, surrounded by smaller buildings and an intimidating white wall.

PETER HAD CALLED AHEAD the previous evening to notify the head priest of their arrival. At the gated entrance to the property, it was presumably that priest who awaited them in his long, rather ominous black robe. He led them to an office block, which to Finley seemed to be entirely Soviet, with nothing historical to redeem its blandness. It was completely separate from the historic building, and smelled of dusty books and old shoes—like a library, Finley thought, and this somehow comforted him. He felt nostalgic for a memory he could not remember, but was certain existed. The thought momentarily distracted him.

He reminded himself of his mission.

Everyone sat. The priest cleared his throat. He seemed to Finley reluctant, or grumpy, but in any case, imposing. With one hand, he rubbed his enormous black beard, speckled with white like an Easter egg.

"Thank you for seeing us, um, Father, Brother?"

Finley looked at Peter, who clarified, "Father. He is a priest."

The priest nodded.

"Right, yes. *Father.* I have an object that belonged to my... grandmother's family. An icon. Well, a crucifix, in actual fact. Back in England. And I'm curious. A gold crucifix from this region, how might it have been made?"

"God made it."

"Yes, but how?"

Again he responded, "God made it."

"Ask him," Finley said to Peter, "*how,* from what metals, from where?"

The priest began to titter, then burst into loud laughter. "Joke," he said in English, then spoke, after which Peter translated.

"There is a forge. There was once a forge here. Many metals melted in there."

"Okay, but where does the *metal* come from?"

"From everywhere," the priest answered in English. His face lit with humor again. When he smiled, Finley could see his yellow, crooked teeth.

"What do you mean?" Finley asked.

The priest spoke in Russian.

Peter translated. "He is saying that metal comes from earth. The earth in this region is rich with metals. Which era is the cross you speak of?"

"Turn of the century, ermm, so around 1900."

"I see," Peter said and translated.

The priest answered and Peter grabbed a small English-Russian dictionary from his pocket that Finley hadn't noticed before. Peter explained, "A cross for the Russian Orthodox Church would be bronze and enamel, sometimes gold, sometimes other metals from the soil."

"Would a cross made here, in this monastery, have been locally produced?"

He waited for Peter and the priest.

"Very likely, yes, he said. There was gold prospecting along the Podkamennaya Tunguska river. Other metals too. Maybe some other metal came from elsewhere."

Peter then began to engage in an animated conversation with the priest.

"I am reminding him that the Trans-Siberian Railway line was not completed until 1904, so how can he be sure it was made with local metals if it was made after that time, as maybe metals came on the train, to trade here? He says that he is not an icon or crucifix expert, but that the people at the monastery were isolated here and they did have a forge here on site, and traded all along the river. So probably it was local metal..."

"Thank you, tell him thank you."

"We go now?"

"I guess."

They thanked the priest again, who tried to take them on a tour of the church and once more flashed them his crooked yellow teeth as he grinned, but Finley's heart was heavy. He wanted to leave.

Metals from the earth.

Maybe it was just the earth here. Somehow healing.

Maybe there was some kind of—he racked his brain—portal, or magic (but he didn't believe in magic, although... his brain froze. What might magic be anyway, but unexplained phenomena that followed the laws of nature, just as his visions did?)

Or—could it be that the cross had some kind of Divine blessing?

He struggled more with a religious meaning than the concept of magic, although,

since all that had taken place,

who was he to reject the notion of God and blessed relics?

"What do you think?" Finley asked as they got back into Peter's car.

"Why are you so interested in the metals?" Peter asked.

"It just seems like a special crucifix. It kinda—glows. It's just odd, I guess. I wondered how it was made." *What did he have to lose?* he reasoned. Why not mention something closer to the truth, at this late hour? It felt better than telling more lies. He quickly glanced at Peter from the corner of his eye to assess his reaction.

"Mmmm." Peter shrugged. "Maybe..." Eyes glinting. The corner of his mouth turned up in a question.

"Maybe," he said again, and laughed at his thoughts.

"Okay, then. Please share the joke," Finley said.

"There were many metals in the earth after the blast in 1908. Many scientists found strange things. Metals melted together, unknown elements. Maybe there were some in this family crucifix you mention. A mystery." His teasing, glinting eyes cast a sideways glance at Finley, checking he was sucked in.

"The blast?"

"Oh, you do not know our history here?"

"I have a feeling you will tell me."

He grinned. "There was an explosion in the sky in June 1908. It was a ball of fire and it made—like an earthquake and there was a blast of heat, and so much forest was destroyed. Trees were standing with no branches and no leaves, like after an atomic bomb. In other places, thousands of trees were flattened and there were black bodies of dead reindeer. It was called a meteorite but actually there was no hole in the ground ever found, so maybe it wasn't a meteor. Maybe it was asteroids or spaceships. Some people think it was a UFO explosion."

"Spaceships?"

"Come, we go to a nice restaurant outside Krasnoyarsk, and when we have signal again, you read about it on your phone. You will see. Many myths."

"A myth of strange metals found in the soil?" Finley asked.

"Yes, that's why I'm telling you. Now we drive back four hours."

Peter put on some music, and Finley, for once, rested without thoughts.

ONCE THEY REACHED the outer suburbs of town and his signal returned, Finley did some reading about the Tunguska Event online, as suggested. As much as Finley's rational mind desired to learn more about this fantastic explosion whose seismic shock waves were felt as far away as England, producing a fireball which released energy equivalent to 125 Hiroshimas—

in his heart he had heard enough to determine a course of action, since it all added up:

The forge.

Local metals.

A strange explosion leaving even more weird metals.

And a cross.

Ikona.

So, despite the curiosity of all he saw online, photos of flattened trees, testimonies, the findings of the expedition teams and endless indeterminate facts, his online research mostly evoked an ever-deepening conviction, that *this* was the place where the materials for the creation of the cross existed and yet exist, where the soil might retain, into the future, remnants still. Surely so far into the future they would have the technology to retrieve it?

As to what caused the explosion, no one had ever figured it out, despite countless expeditions, multiple theories, and years of analysis. Anyway, that was not Finley's concern, because his own mind could not argue against what his heart felt was Truth,

one he could not prove, but which he must explore.

A door flew open, through which both fear and hope returned as eternal twins.

His mind began to fly towards Wallace, launched by some other force.

And then, the pain.

He grabbed his forehead reflexively.

Peter turned to him, alarmed.

"It's okay, keep driving," Finley said.

As much as it hurt, Finley drew on every part of his will to go with it, to follow the pain and understand its source and how it moved within. Was it his fear driving it, or the interference of others? As he squeezed his eyes shut, focusing on the blackness, he saw something then, as if watching from outside his body: interference descended through his brain like a knife that knew its mark, straight to a spot that, once pierced, would shut everything down for good. But how? *Nevermind that,* he refocused. As his mind pushed back against the pointy end of the knife, the pain ripped through him. He held his breath as he pushed back, and felt his fingertips go tingly.

Finley knew then that Bernhardt was right. The part of him that *could* fight, *was* fighting. He called on this inner strength by name now, finally seeing courage for what it was. He felt himself veer towards the future, the world around him dimming, and he pulled back and down into himself, refusing to budge. He drew every bit of power up from his core to muffle the sound, so whilst he screamed inside at the pain of pulling himself back,

perhaps Peter heard only a sigh.

From Finley's point of view, the moaning had stopped, and so, too, had the pull of the future. He slept for the rest of the drive.

By the time Peter had placed their supper on the table—meat stew, potatoes, cabbage, black bread and strong tea—Finley had arrived at his decision, and had a plan.

"You like?" Peter asked.

"It looks fantastic, thank you. I read about the event, the explosion."

Peter pushed Finley's tea across the table to him.

"You worry about something. It's not your grandmother's cross, no?" Peter asked.

"Not exactly."

"We found some good information today, right?"

"Yes, thank you."

"That is not what you worry about, though. I see. I feel like, like you are afraid. There is fear. Fear is driving you. You were upset in the car."

"You're like a psychologist, aren't you?"

"I study psychology at university, yes!"

"Oh, you literally are... a psychologist." Finley sighed. "Yes, I was... worried about something. But that's okay. That's life. Sometimes you worry, but you get through it."

"Yes, this is true. Sometimes people worry about worrying. It's better just to let life live through you. Everything changes all the time. I like you, Finley."

"I like you too, Peter."

Peter dished out the food. He filled Finley's plate. It was dinner time now. So far, all they'd eaten the entire day, as they'd driven to the middle of nowhere and back, was tea and bread and some fruit. Now they ate ravenously.

"Is there something else I can do for you?" Peter asked. "Something else to see? I feel like there is more." He watched him carefully.

"I've been thinking about it. I think I need to go to where the blast happened. The Tunguska explosion. To the epicenter."

"You serious?" A fork full carrying meat and potato hovered near his half-open mouth.

"I'm afraid I am."

He put down his fork. "This is not about your grandmother's cross, is it? You don't want to tell me why you are here?"

"I just need to be there. In nature. Where it happened. I, I think it's important. I would like to see the soil—it's crazy I know. To see if anything remains. Weird metals."

"This sounds, important to you. Many have looked there many

times. But, why not. Maybe you find something. Maybe it's yours to find. Only, to go there costs a lot. I can find a tour for you to go on."

"I need you there, too. Not just to translate. I just—I like your company. I will pay for us both."

Peter became flustered then. "Are you sure? This is amazing. Thank you. I have been there before. One time. It's my favorite place."

Finley smiled and continued to eat. Somehow it didn't surprise him that Peter had been there. That it was his favorite place. That they would visit together the next day. Everything felt just right.

"Okay, Finley, we will make this happen tomorrow. We fly to Vanavara which is two hours, and then we take a helicopter tour. And we get our hands dirty!" He leaned forward, his blue eyes lit with excitement. "This is fantastic."

FINLEY SLEPT FITFULLY THAT NIGHT, so when he woke up for the fifth time at three a.m., he decided to stop trying. He sat cross legged in his bed and willed that he travel to Wallace. He needed to figure this out, since the next day he would be in the exact right place and, provided his gut confirmed his theory of the cross's origins in the Siberian soil, he intended to communicate the revelation directly to Wallace.

He hoped that the inspiration of the exact moment of discovery would create a natural surge in courage, bolstering his efforts. Or else, if that proved too fearful, that later he might summon the memory of the discovery and send it then. But it might be too late to wait until after, if the attempts from the future to block their connection succeeded—which, given all that Evgenia and Bernhardt had shared, was possible. Time was running out; he needed to plan for the worst. He circled back around to the imperative to send the location of the metals as soon as possible.

He squeezed his eyes shut and imagined sending a giant thought bubble to Wallace. Nothing, except that he felt fear and he felt hope. He had no roadmap for shifting into his future self on his own, so then he tried to imagine what it might *feel* like to succeed.

Resonance, the word leapt into his mind—and he remembered its significance from the future. Though his journeys remained dream-like and disjointed in memory, he felt (rather than knew by logic's dictation) that resonance meant to summon the feeling and thought and be *within* it somehow, as if tuning into a radio station. He remembered, too, 'the Bridge' from Gutov's novel and recognized that he'd already dropped the weight he carried from within,

that on the long journey here, there had been a certain transformation, a reckoning of sorts—its prelude was the love he'd felt as he and Gutov stood by the lake together,

and then later came love's confirmation, when he'd stood at the edge of the city, a love like no other.

He needed to feel that feeling again, to reach Wallace on his own!

Yet recalling a past feeling was not the same as evoking the feeling itself, and just then, in the middle of the night, he could do nothing about it.

After a time, Finley decided to sleep. Before shutting his eyes, he spoke to that part of his mind that had, in the car the day before, successfully fought back against attempts to shut down the connection between him and Wallace.

Please be there for me tomorrow, I need my own strength like never before.

It HAD TAKEN some organization and negotiation, but Peter managed to charter a helicopter to the Tunguska blast area within two hours of their flight arriving, just after two p.m. And, he'd managed to organize that they land not far from the river, so that Peter could show Finley his favorite spot just beyond where the trees had been flattened and the dead reindeer found. There was very little to do in Vanavara while they waited for their ride, but Peter made them a picnic outside the airport, and they shared it in companionable silence.

Finally, they boarded the helicopter and flew.

Finley felt himself unwinding, despite the deafening roar of the helicopter, despite the height, which generally he disliked—but the view, green and lush and so alive, made gratitude come alive within him.

There was such beauty in the world, he thought.

Peter said very little, even when they landed and began walking down the slope to the river. Finley felt as he had with Gutov and the lake, soft and awakened and grateful.

He'd found it—he knew it to be true, that the explosion (whatever it was) had sent shards of strange metals into the earth, found by whom he knew not, but then sold with other metals to the forge where the crucifix had been made,

the crucifix that healed.

It seemed quite improbable in retrospect, and quite simple a journey despite the gravity and urgency and strange interruptions. His path, this journey, his *role,* felt clear as never before and something elusive made sense for him at last: that it was not meant to be difficult. *Ah,* he thought as lucid as ever now, *one's true path unfolds most smoothly when resistance to that path falls away.* He was always meant to re-visit his fear of the ocean, and through that, travel to the future and then, through a most unlikely series of events, meet Peter and be here, next to the small river in Tunguska.

Certainty of his path roused him to courage now, and it also fed his certainty: that here, in an area impacted by an explosion that had flattened 80 million trees, over 2,150 square kilometers, here indeed lay strange, powerful metals, the origins of the icon, the ingredients for a cure!

A formation of cranes flew overhead, an arrowhead piercing the sky. Could they be the same birds he'd seen in Germany? Finley wondered.

"They are shamans," Peter noticed him watching.

"What?"

"The native people, the Yakuts, believe the white cranes are shamans. Anyways, the Siberian cranes have already migrated north this year. They come from China in April and May. So that, what you saw, probably shamans, guiding us."

He winked at Finley and continued, "Why not? The Evenki say

that the celestial event was Agdy, the god of thunder who had wings of steel. Who is to say that any of us know anything."

They were at the riverbed now. There were cliffs here and there, brown rocks and stones along the sides and in the water, and in other places a blanket of grass and bushes up to the river's edge. Peter stepped gingerly across the rocks and placed a hand in the rushing water.

"Cold," he said, then, "We are more or less in the area, no one knows where exactly it exploded. It happened above the earth. There is a big field where there were trees that fell, like you saw in the photos. But here, here is where I feel at peace. But it is your trip. We can leave the river."

"No," Finley said. "I like it here. I will just sit for a moment."

Peter sat at the water's edge, scooping up handfuls of mud, rocks, letting it fall in clumps between his fingers.

"Here," he said. "You can look for your metal."

Finley sat next to him. He plunged his hand into the wet, loose earth where Peter had dug, and worked the soil between his fingers, freeing small pebbles. He rubbed his hands together and shivered with pleasure as the sandpapery sensation traveled up his forearms until the hairs stood up at the nape of his neck.

He smiled.

He used both hands to loosen the compacted topsoil at the bank, and then began to scoop up earth and dig a hole. He scooted back and dug longer, deeper—a trench. Peter helped him. Ten, twenty minutes later perspiration ran down Finley's forehead, blurring his vision now and again, and he squinted against the sun's assault, but they both carried on digging.

"What am I looking for?" he thought to ask Peter, who laughed at him.

"I don't know! Small metal pieces? We may be fools, my friend. But we are here, so we will dig!"

They dug, until the hole was as a child's summer trench at the beach, and their enthusiasm and concentration seemed to unfocus time, such that Finley seemed to be looking at his own failed attempt at building a rocky sandcastle on the pebbly Brighton beach. He was startled when Peter sat back and sighed. "We can't do this all day, I suppose."

"Is this something?" Finley held up a patch of soil in which there were tiny, glinting copperish dots, as if a strong wind had spray-painted this clutch of earth.

"Maybe?" Peter said. "Must be something bigger."

"No it's enough," Finley said, not knowing if sparkling soil were an unremarkable geological feature in this area, or the sun brightening otherwise dull particles, or mysterious, powerful metal. He blinked and looked again into his hand, and this time saw a little blob, bigger than a dot, which, when he tilted his hand to the side so as to loosen it from the soil, looked like a perfectly intact teardrop.

"See, something," he said, holding open his hand to Peter.

"Ah, yes. A small drop from Heaven."

Finley couldn't tell if Peter was being ironic or earnest.

"I just need to sit a moment and think," Finley said.

"Of course."

Finley went and sat halfway up the slope, with his back to the towering rocks and he squeezed his hand closed, and contemplated how,

How might I communicate this location?

He felt the familiar ache. The certain knowing that there was a connection, and someone or *someones* interfering with it.

Was there someone even now? Wallace perhaps, attempting to peer through his eyes, his mind?

Like a boy playing hide and seek, Finley closed his eyes and thought, *You will NOT. Not until I say so.*

What would the resonance be now? He focused his mind.

That humanity would find this cure, these metals, and no more would people die and no more would children be orphaned—so what would that resonance feel like? Like victory? Like peace? Like love?

What did it feel like to save yourself, he wondered, for he would be doing that too, saving his future self. What part of him was doing the saving?

Finley felt a tremor—within or without, he wasn't sure.

Peter looked up; he frowned.

What does he expect will happen? Finley wondered, following Peter's eyes to the clear, blue sky. *Does he think there will be another celestial event?*

The ground faintly rumbled. Then came a roar like a train plowing across the earth.

"Earthquake," Peter said.

Finley closed his eyes and knew only pure energy.

Nature's fierce rebuttal,

the sound of rocks cascading, like shaking a jar of jelly beans

How many jelly beans were inside the jar? he had to guess, at a summer's fair, age seven.

255, and they will crash, and then, he said, *The big one is there inside, and it is coming towards me.*

What an odd thing to say, the woman at the fair said. *Do you want to make an entry in the contest then?*

No need, small Finley replied.

He opened his eyes. His heart pounded. *He'd known.* He'd known this moment always. He'd seen it then.

Finley looked up at the side of the cliff. Where was it now? He felt it near,

spirit of forward motion,

"Come here!" Peter called out.

Finley saw him, ignored him, kept looking up, then his gaze drew towards the river.

The vibration of the earthquake in the water was fascinating, he thought, an explosion of ripples, as if this giant shaking the jelly beans jar laughed at them, and it shook everything, and nowhere was there control.

Ah, yes, he thought next, *I am afraid. I am afraid.* He trembled, and the pain in his temple grew; he doubled over, grasping his forehead. But it was his own fear, as he launched himself towards the future by sheer will alone. He thought of Wallace, sending out the thought, the image, where he was, the location, the intention, the celestial event, so near to where Wallace was in his future,

these metals which surely had created the strange metallic alloy,

which gave the icon its healing power, and so disrupted history.

He connected across time, to Wallace—*here they were, two beads on the same string.*

a hair's breadth away; he felt him in his heart now,

and fear and love,

(How could he hold both? He couldn't even wonder before the wondering slipped into knowing.)

You have to do this *for me*, he told Wallace, becoming the courage the other had.

It was okay, he told himself. He had nothing else to give, nothing else to do, this moment was all it was, fear and love, pain and clarity—

please Wallace, here it is, the answer.

"Come here!" Peter called again. "The rocks, they will fall!"

Finley looked up, his heart pounding now, the headache gaining strength.

Small stones tumbled and crashed around him, dust flying up around his face. And the large one, on the ledge above.

He felt, *at the same moment*, the message go through and Wallace's pang of recognition, of comprehension.

Both selves rode that wave of fear, knowing love too, as well as triumph, such odd bedfellows!

Oh fate, the inglorious collision of skull and rock, exactly on cue.

The entire area was intact; the helicopter was still on the crest. Peter was shocked at the boulder's handiwork.

A fool's injury, a destined meeting between nature and cranium.

So dumb.

So perfect.

Things don't turn out, but they do, Finley thought, but he was no longer in his body, so who was the one doing the thinking?

Peter cried "Finley!" and he ran towards the boulder.

For a nanosecond Finley was still himself, before the world spun to black, and he fell into an onrush of shimmering light.

29

YURI, VASILI, PYOTR, VISSARION & THE EVENT

JUNE 30, 1908

VANAVARA, TUNGUSKA REGION, SIBERIA

At the end of morning prayers, the novice monks Yuri Sergasin, Vasili Yakunov, and Pyotr Ivanov stepped outside and crossed themselves with their fingers, a firm strike against the forehead and shoulders, then bowed and prayed. Vissarion awaited them on the steps outside the Monastery. He'd brought bread to share and his brother, Pyotr, had somehow convinced a servant to sneak them hot tea. Yuri and Vasili were none the wiser, and asked the brothers what the fuss was about.

"We are celebrating and also wishing me farewell," Pyotr said, "as I leave tomorrow. It may be a while until we meet again."

Yuri and Vasili exclaimed over the news, but Vissarion frowned. "Let's not act surprised. We all knew you would become a wandering monk sooner or later, brother. You disappeared into the forest as soon as we arrived here from Ukraine, as if the Siberian reindeer called to you."

"Indeed," Pyotr said. "And *you* always disappeared into books and to the iconostasis."

"You are but nineteen, not old and mad enough to wander," said Yuri, helping himself to the bread that Vissarion had unwrapped and held out to share.

"I agree," said Vasili.

"We are all nineteen, so what. Except him," Pyotr nodded towards his brother. "He is a year and a half older."

"And I am also much wiser," Vissarion deadpanned.

"Your beard is thicker. That is all, brother."

"I have one at least. You have the face of a baby." He grabbed his brother's hairless chin. He poured himself tea.

In fact, of the four men, only Pyotr was hairless. He also towered above them all at nearly 6'3. Vissarion, Yui and Vasili were nearly identical with their traditional beards and in their black robes, and all of average height. Pyotr stood out wherever he went. His friends and brother had once debated whether that boded well for him as a wanderer or not, but they had reached no conclusions.

"But in all seriousness," said Yuri. "Pyotr, I know you wish to wander. No one will stop you. But it is not an easy life."

"What is easy may not be what is best, though. My devotion is not found in these structures," Pyotr said. "Nature reveals to me the face of God."

Yuri only nodded as he drank his tea and bit another chunk of the black bread.

The others also ate and drank greedily, but not Vissarion. Whether it was because he was most conflicted about his brother's departure, or it was due to his quiet nature, even he didn't know.

He looked up and said, "The sky is strange today."

No one commented.

"Pyotr, may you be blessed," Vasili said. He had finished his meal. "Really, it matters not where you worship. For myself, I prefer a warm bed and the comfort of hot food."

"I actually think you are mad," Yuri said. "But that might serve you well. Be careful that you do not succumb to the temptations of the world."

"Because you think behind your high walls you are safe from temptation?" Pyotr asked. "Perhaps there is more temptation for me with routine and comfort, perhaps staying here would be a temptation to *escape* God, who resides in every leaf, in the soft rain on my skin, in the hunger when I go without meals."

"In the winter cold...." Yuri laughed. "When your dick freezes off, you will no longer have temptation."

They all laughed, even Pyotr.

Vissarion said, "Brother, in winter you must find sanctuary here with us."

"Perhaps. Or perhaps I shall return if my back fails me, and only then."

It was known that Pyotr suffered back spasms at times, which he attributed to his height, and to a bad fall he'd had as a young boy.

The air was still this morning, without the hum of insects or the sounds of birds. It was unsettling, but Vissarion had no urge to speak again, so kept the observation to himself. Only when a v-shaped formation of Siberian cranes flew overhead did the others shift their attention outwards, lifting their eyes to the sky.

"You see, glorious nature." Pyotr raised a hand as the birds went past. They were soon but a line, a smudge, then a faint pinprick.

"Indeed, such as we take for granted," Vasili said.

"We do," agreed Yuri.

"It is not right." Vissarion sniffed, voicing his thoughts at last. "Something is not right."

Pyotr frowned and looked up again—maybe he felt some kind of foreboding, Vissarion thought—but he chose to carry on with his thought, and said,

"I respect the rituals and laws, but liturgy aside, orderliness aside, between a single heart and all of the universe there exists such profound communication in every single moment. Direct communication, should you listen."

"Ah, but that is not proper," said Vissarion. The topic goaded him. "There is a fearsomeness in God which makes communication... unclear. Though I have pledged my life to this endeavor, to hear the Holy Spirit, then create from it."

"Always the iconographer," Pyotr smiled. "I respect your pledge.

But you know how devotion softens the heart. Remember how you felt..."

Vissarion raised a hand to stop him.

When you were to marry Olya, his brother would have said.

Neither Yuri nor Vasili knew this history. They only knew each other from the monastery, after the brothers had arrived from the Ukraine. After their long journey to find God in this wilderness.

"Anyway," said Yuri. "I wish you well. Please visit us here again one day."

"Yes, Godspeed," said Vasili. "I wish you a great communion with Holiness."

It was as if a shadow fell across Pyotr's face suddenly. He glanced now and again at his brother. Then suddenly his eyes sparkled, and he addressed himself as if to Vissarion, only.

"In the future, imagine a very distant future, hundreds or thousands of years from now, will this church even exist?" Pyotr asked.

"That is a crazy question," Yuri said. "It would be blasphemous to say no."

"And yet," Pyotr said, "we can hardly imagine what time will bring. We can hardly imagine how life was hundreds of years ago, so how might humans change? Science has already progressed beyond what we thought possible. Perhaps one day people will worship it, rather than God."

"There will still be good and evil, and a balance will be needed, so we will always need God," Vasili said.

"But perhaps not. Perhaps, as in nature, a balance will be found naturally. I have read Kropotkin, his theory of mutual aid. He argues that throughout time species *collaborate* in order to advance. Whilst there is certainly competition, what Darwin missed is cooperation, the reciprocity of giving and receiving support. He saw that we have a natural tendency to form social relationships in community. I would predict that away from hierarchy, we might in time find God in community, in nature, and so... I ask again, how can we predict how our worship will change? Perhaps ultimately we will have to find answers inside ourselves."

"Brother, you have always been the eccentric, it's no wonder you wish to wander."

"Vissarion." Again he addressed his brother directly. "You are a wonderful devotee, your talents are used well in the forging of holy objects—however, I rather think that you work with objects so as to see the holy in form, rather than use your inner sight to see beyond, in personal communion. As I have said before, you have exchanged one god for another, brother. You know the rest."

Vissarion half-rolled his eyes. He was grateful that Vasili and Yuri did not pry into the secrets between brothers.

"You have a lot of thoughts," Vissarion said. "Some of which may be correct. I am happy in my work. I am happy as an obedient servant."

"And you are afraid of God."

"God is fearsome," Vissarion replied.

"Because he gives and takes away," Pyotr said.

"Exactly."

"I admire your devotion to fear," Pyotr said. "Although I do wonder if it will blind you to goodness."

"Pyotr, I think you have too much education," Vasili said. "Or just enough, that remains to be seen."

The young men laughed, except for Vassarion, who worried over the gloom that had lodged itself in his heart. He did not know whether it referenced the past or predicted what was to come.

Not so much later Vasili asked, "What is that?"

The men looked up.

A blueish-white ball of light hurtled across the sky, leaving a trail of light-streaks, so that it seemed as if Heaven itself were being torn asunder.

"Holy God!" Yuri exclaimed.

There was a collective hush, a momentary preternatural stillness before the ball of light exploded and the earth seemed to roar and the ground shook. Then it sounded as if canons were going off one after the other. Somewhere, glass shattered, and then a powerful hot wind blasted all four men off the steps with such force that they landed several meters away.

The sky was on fire.

Then it was black.

Vissarion felt his heart stop, then he went dizzy with confusion, then panic set in. He found his way to sitting, whereupon he felt that his cassock was warm to the touch. He thought to inspect it; he lifted it up and peered behind him where it half splayed out onto the ground. He thought it may have been singed, but no.

It remained dark as night.

Vitali and Pyotr and Yuri lay near him.

"What just happened?" asked Yuri. No one responded, but Pyotr squinted into the black sky and crossed himself.

Vissarion trembled. He gathered his cassock and stumbled to his feet, then went to stand at a short distance from the others. He heard shouting and a cry—a babushka, one of the cooks, shouted, *the window has shattered*. The morning sky, though still as dark as midnight, now began to glow with a strange luminescence, brighter than a full moon on a cloudless night, only there was no visible source of this light.

It was so bright that it might have been possible to read a book.

There was a low rumbling like distant thunder. Vissarion felt fear rise up from his feet, to the pit of his stomach and further up until it grasped his heart and squeezed, and then came—

a memory of Olya
how her parents wept as she lay still and white,
and how his heart froze in time.

He remembered how, afterwards, Pyotr begged that he follow him to Siberia—to pursue—as he described it to Vissarion: *my boyhood fantasy of exploration, to roam the taiga and the forests far from Ukraine*. Even though they both knew Pyotr searched for God in every church, in every forest, in every brook, in every cloud.

Indeed, as they went, they stopped at cathedrals to pray, and devotion redoubled in both of them, a slow uprising of faith from the naivete of childhood habit.

Pyotr grew lighter as Vissarion made of piety a wall around his heart.

And now, Vissarion reflected, there was this celestial event. God had demonstrated once more his power, even to take away the sky. Thus Vissarion concluded that he must be ever more pious and work ever harder.

Pyotr stood next to him now, and put a hand on his shoulder. Yuri and Valeri joined them, both shaken, and speechless.

"Brother, friends," Pyotr spoke. "Now I see that there is more mystery than I previously understood. I would like to discover what has befallen us, and know myself through this darkness."

Pyotr left that day. He walked in the fiery blackness of noon towards where the giant wind had blown, deep into the forest and towards the river,

and no one followed.

30

LUCIO & ANDREW: GOOD VERSUS EVIL - REPRISED

JANUARY 2101

MIRAMAR SCIENTIFIC RESEARCH CENTER

Lucio waited on the deck and checked the arrival time of the ship once more, a habit borne of impatience and suspicion. He did not trust rigid schedules. The science of time-speed distortion, with its exactitude, was the basis of the technological fanaticism that left his department chronically under-resourced. It wasn't easy to convince department heads fixed on precision that there was value in the murky and imprecise realm of the mind. His life's work was inexact science, so he could be forgiven for hoping that the airship somehow be momentarily displaced, enough to make a point. Without delaying his friend's arrival too much, of course.

It was hot outside. The sky was clear and the sun overbright. Lucio wiped his sweaty forehead with the sleeve of his robe. He wondered how his friend would fare in this climate, having grown up in the mountainous region of their youth, a place where Andrew remained to this day. The last time he'd seen Andrew was ten years earlier when they were nineteen, during their final days of residential schooling at the monastery where fate had thrown them together as young orphans.

Lucio watched the approaching ship as it hovered, then landed. To the minute, of course. His stomach fluttered and he couldn't stand still so he paced those interminable minutes as the passengers no doubt gathered their belongings and queued up to exit.

Ten years had passed, but it was twenty since their fates intertwined. It had been only fourteen days since Lucio confirmed the importance of his discovery, since he'd pleaded with his friend to drop everything and come to Miramar immediately. Yet, despite those two weeks of frenzied preparation and tense anticipation, Lucio had never, until these final minutes, reflected on how remarkable it was that they were coming full circle, at last.

Despite the mystical events of the past few days, he was unprepared to accept that perhaps, just perhaps, his work had always been destined to evolve exactly this way, and their friendship, too.

Andrew was nine years old when he arrived at the Bulgarian orphanage.

Lucio, although also nine, had been in residence since the age of six. In those three years, the monastic routines of meditation and mindfulness had tempered the pain of his loss. More to the point, by the time Andrew arrived, for those three years Lucio had also been navigating the quasi-Darwinian environment of boarding school. He had developed his own behavioral strategies.

Young Andrew, bereft and tearful, was taunted off the court at lunchtime basketball. The boys called him fat and inept. Lucio, whose approach to conflict (after all that practice) was stoic but beneath that, calculated, took Andrew aside at lunch one day and told him to meet him after Vespers on the back court. It was locked to students after the school day ended, but Lucio was the precept and had spare keys.

"You have to be good at something," he told this new kid, pointing out that his timid and tearful demeanor made him an appealing target.

"What are *you* good at then?" Andrew asked him.

"I'm good at watching," Lucio replied.

"Watching what?"

"Watching the kids. Sometimes, I just watch them and I know who they are going to be mean to. And I'm good at figuring out how to be invisible. But anyway, I can teach you how to play basketball, that's a start. And I can show you how to be invisible until you can play."

Lucio never forgot the gratitude that shone from Andrew's eyes on their first evening at the court. The grief-stricken and lonely kid was, as it turned out, a quick study. After a month of stolen court time, Andrew never missed a shot from the three point line. After two months, he had handles and fancy footwork. Finally, at the four month mark, Lucio told him to arrive at lunch with a basketball and to start taking shots before the court got crowded.

So successful were Andrew's attempts to remain invisible during this apprenticeship that no one recognized him as the fat kid who used to fumble with the ball. Anyway, by then he'd slimmed down and shot up an inch or so. Before long, Andrew was a regular on the court. He made enduring friendships, even with those who had once taunted him. As a consequence, he came to believe that most people, given a chance, were more or less good-hearted. None more so than Lucio, the most loyal of all.

Thus their friendship was borne in grief and basketball as well as the endless rituals of monastic life. This was before the Machine, before the Cottage procedure became the norm, either when children reached puberty, or when new adult initiates joined the Monasteries. To some degree, even in those pre-Machine days, the endless meditations and ruminations entrained the nervous system. The eternal was locked into the temporal, and within a few years, all the children, even those who'd arrived so raw, even those who once bullied others, had settled into a rhythm of internal contemplation and external cooperation, no matter the intensity they buried within.

And it *was* there, buried within, but it was exactly that which bound Andrew and Lucio together. They continued to play basketball. Their fundamental traits meanwhile took them on different trajectories: Lucio still watched the world as objectively as he could, managing his place in it, whereas Andrew, once safe in his peer group, drew further into himself, and cultivated his inner life.

By the time their schooling neared its end, it came as no surprise to either of them that their professional paths would take them in opposite directions. Andrew had decided to go to the Eastern Federation Academy to pursue monastic studies. Located near Krasnoyarsk, it was the region's spiritual headquarters, with the best facilities and most famous teachers.

Lucio, on the other hand, had decided to study Biology and the Mind in the Southern Federation.

"You wish to study both? Is the study of the Mind a back up career?"

"Nah. I've got a plan."

Andrew rolled his eyes. "Of course you do, Lucio."

Andrew knew him well. So much was shared without words. As Lucio recalled, on that summer's evening during which they'd shared with each other their tertiary plans, they played basketball for a while in the luminescent orange and purple glow of sunset. Then, at some point, Andrew posed the critical question.

"You want to find a cure, don't you, Lucio?"

Lucio simply stated, "Who doesn't?"

"That's why you're studying Biology and the Mind. I knew there was something in it. But you never intend things without deciding on your success. So you will find a cure. That's your plan, isn't it?"

This time, it was a statement.

"It is my intention, yes."

It was nearly dark. There was but a milky glow behind the line of trees, and only a sliver of moon. Lucio started to pack up. Andrew followed, carrying the ball.

"But why study the Mind, too?"

Lucio said, "Ah!" He expected the question. He had prepared his explanation.

"I believe a cure will be found in our lifetime, whether by me or by someone else. More importantly, I believe that the danger of finding it is that it's used for evil rather than to help humanity. I have watched the Sciences Institutes for years and the infighting, the politics, and then I have studied the histories. Innovation in the wrong hands can harm human civilization. Someone in the sciences needs to understand how people are motivated. To understand how the mind, how consciousness, evolves in individuals, in societies. We need to understand not just how to find a cure but also to ensure it's used for good."

Andrew spoke, "As I've heard it said, *Keep your friends close and your enemies closer.* Are you underestimating people, though? After all that humanity has endured?"

"I cannot know for sure until the moment is upon us. But promise me this, Andrew."

Lucio's tone of voice was arresting. Andrew slowed his pace, as did his friend.

"You are the *good*-est person I know. Pure of heart. A true monastic heart. Just promise me. If I ever find a cure, you will advise me on the part of the good, the holy. You will help me protect it."

They reached the living quarters. They stopped at the door, facing one another.

"You are serious," Andrew said.

"Never more. I lack faith in fellow humankind. I need allies in other places, not just the Sciences. You will have a long and great career as a monk. You will touch the Divine, I know it. I am sure you will become important in your profession. Thus, I might require your support one day. As my oldest and dearest friend, I pray you will be there when I need you."

So Andrew had made him the solemn promise, even if as a young man he may have only half-believed he'd be called to uphold it. But the day had arrived. The ship lifted its door, like a spider rearing to attack, and a mass of people poured forth. Lucio spotted Andrew immediately, the tall, black-haired man in orange robes, a beard-like stubble on ruddy cheeks. He appeared robust, lean, and the grin that spread across his face was a clue to his happiness, too. Lucio pulled him into a tight embrace and told him, "You've not aged, only grown stronger, I see."

"More agile, perhaps. It's the new training, a form of moving meditation. And you, Lucio, you look well. Like an eccentric professor, but well."

"You're referring to my beard, which is superior to yours."

"Not only that, but yes." Andrew laughed.

"We have transport to my rooms, where we can talk freely. Thank you for coming, my friend."

"It is wonderful to see you, and I'm of course intrigued, and nervous."

"We mustn't talk now, in case others overhear," Lucio warned him.

Andrew, ever vague when it came to social convention, fell silent. Both men took in the landscape: the salt flats, the barren planar land and the pounding sun. Very quickly, as their transport sped from the landing platform at over 200 km per hour, Lucio saw the looming research center where he spent his days. It was a monolith in a field of green, the only structure in sight.

In Andrew's world, monasteries of this size and import were nestled into hills or mountains, or tucked between outcrops of rock or forest, made to blend into nature. The Scientific Research center at Miramar, however, was the land and landscape itself, an uncompromising blight on what was left of the region's natural resources. Lucio felt him recoil.

"A monstrosity, I know. And no, not all research centers are this soulless."

"It's a world-class facility, I have been told," Andrew said.

"With many accomplishments, though not yet the primary one. Well, not officially, at least."

Andrew raised his eyebrows, but without further commentary they exited the transport at the main door, greeted by staff, a young man who handed them packets ("our meal," explained Lucio), and then hurried through a byzantine labyrinth of white corridors to an unmarked, unremarkable door at the very end of a hallway.

"My quarters," Lucio announced.

Andrew seemed to relax. It was a charming room by any account, with rather old fashioned furnishing (plush couches and upholstered armchairs), as well as a window, floor to ceiling, with an outlook of a small paved courtyard. All around the window, on either side, were small potted plants.

"My experiments," Lucio explained, and hastened to pour his guest some water. "Sit." He indicated the wall to wall couch. "Amenities are through the hallway there, and your bed is in the last room on the right."

"So," Andrew said, dropping a small round bag to the floor and sinking in the couch. "I am here, as you called me. It's wonderful to see you. But I don't know if I can wait to catch up on all the frivolities of our lives—what prompted this, Lucio? We have barely been in touch all these years. And this statement you made, 'not officially' regarding a cure... speak, please!"

"As I said on our call, I am calling in a favor, the one I asked of you on our last day together as students."

"That one day you would need an ally in the Monasteries."

"Yes."

"Lucio." Andrew's jaw dropped. "Could it be possible that you really have found it?"

"The cure? Well, it's more complicated than that. I needed to speak in person, Andrew, because our conversation must be off the network, and more importantly, I needed to see you, to feel your energy again, and try," here Lucio's voice faltered, "to gauge your true feelings about things, because this is bigger than me, and I need to know you support me unconditionally..."

"Lucio, you're spinning out. Have a drink."

Lucio laughed. "Indeed I am." He went to the far side of the room where there was a kitchen area, poured himself a glass of water from the tap and drank. Then he got another glass, filled it, and handed it Andrew, who emptied it quickly.

Andrew placed the glass on the side table near him, sighing. "You'd best just talk. You're not one to become emotional, so I'm intrigued. I will make myself comfortable on these very plush couches. I am a good listener. Go on."

Lucio dragged over one of the upholstered armchairs to sit across from him.

"As you know, about five years ago, as part of my advanced mind training, I did research on how the regular use of psychotropic substances could help decision-making. What you may not know is that I carried out this research *in situ* within a Hybrid group near Beriloche. My research was specifically about how the regular use of local plant medicines could help decision-making in local councils. Over the course of my research, I became quite friendly with the resident Shaman. We were peers. She was a young apprentice thrust prematurely into her role when her mentor died from cancer—very skilled in her peoples' ways, and very compassionate, but a bit out of her depth."

"I had no idea that this was the nature of your research."

"I was not encouraged to reveal the nature of my research, as the Triumvirate prefers not to promote the existence of these Hybrid groups."

"I want to know more about these Hybrid groups, but first, did it help with decision-making?" asked Andrew.

"Yes and no. This is actually relevant, as I will get to shortly. Between you and me, the thesis I produced, which was the basis of my qualification, did not tell the entire story, because the entire story is unresolved. That is to say, there was a stubborn subset of participants who deviated from the overall result, which was that the substance did affect their decision-making positively."

"Positively meaning what? The decisions had positive results?"

"Positive in the sense that the decisions appeared to be in the best interests of the people, the land, their activities, their communication with the Council, positive across a number of metrics that were statistically meaningful. But there was a subset for whom this was not the case, for whom the substance had little to no effect. I speculated, and continue to consider, any number of explanations, some of which have become clearer in the context of recent events."

Andrew became very still. "I have so many questions. But go on."

"To get back to the present—this Shaman, whom I shall not name for hers and your protection, visited me a few weeks ago. Extraordinary in itself, as normally she would not have occasion to journey beyond this region much less to a scientific research facility. Moreover, she had traveled by foot, which is no small trek. She arrived in a state, exhausted as you can imagine, dirty, hungry, and so on. She said she had something to give me that I needed to keep safe, and that was why she'd traveled by foot, as the transport scans would have recorded all carry-ons, and she could not risk discovery. I told her she must eat, cleanse, and rest, first. After a day and a night she finally came to me here, in this very room, and sat where you sit now, and said she was ready to explain. That she had something magical to share, something she needed to entrust with me."

Lucio paused to gather his thoughts. Andrew leaned forward.

"But first, I should explain her people. The Hybrids in Beriloche are comprised of indigenous peoples and revolutionaries from the 21st century. The only remaining Hybrids on the planet are here in the South. Most intermarried. Were you were aware of their existence?"

"I was not," Andrew said. "I am intrigued. I thought the Hybrids had died out by now from the Cancer? Then most who lived were subsumed within the Monasteries, as their fundamental approach was spiritual. Is that not the case?"

"Yes, indeed. Only there were holdouts, and mostly in this part of the world, as it is here where they originated after the class action lawsuits and revolution. In the Andes region, they created shadow governments on a community level and they have remained more or less outside the Triumvirate—peacefully, I should add. Anyway, this is the reason I was able to do effective research. They used their local plants for ceremonial purposes. The people I lived with comprised a community of about 300 souls. Their Shaman served a dual role as spiritual mentor and healer. It's the latter role which occasioned her accidental discovery.

"She told me that there was a family that had a zero mortality rate. Her mentor had dismissed it, but once he died, she became curious as to how, exactly, they were so long-lived and healthy. They lived to old age—*all* of them. And not only that, she had noticed, over the past five years, that they were never injured, or sick, and beyond *that*, they had the same *resplandor* about them. A *glow* that she found difficult to describe. A state beyond health, it would seem. Incidentally, the Bariloche Hybrids have the same mortality rate as the rest of us, so this survival rate was quite obvious. They claimed that they had no explanation, but she was not convinced. So she went to them in ceremony, when all of the group were flying high, as it were, communally, and she said she knew they had a secret, and what was it?"

"Ah," Andrew said. "Fascinating."

"You cannot really lie when you are in an altered state of consciousness." Lucio laughed. "You could never guess what they told her, not in a million years."

"You're teasing me!" Andew said.

"Do you remember as boys when we devoured the books of K.I. Gutov? *Ikona* and the others?"

"Yes."

"Mmm hmmm. Reality is as strange as fiction, as it turns out."

"Are you still teasing me, Lucio?"

"Not at all. She discovered that the family in question used a sacred object, one that, when it was held, resulted in complete healing on all levels—whether from sickness or wounds, broken bones, mental illness, whatever. Then, right here where you sit, the Shaman withdrew the object from a satchel and presented it to me. I thought, *what does this remind me of*? It was strangely familiar. Only later, after it had all passed and she'd left, as I was staring at this object, did I recall Gutov's novels. So I dug out an old digital copy and reread bits of it. Eerily similar."

Andrew's face lit in recognition. "The icon? The cross, from his novels?"

"Yes. She had it, or its exact likeness, and she gave it to me for safekeeping. I will show you momentarily."

"But this cross, are you saying...?"

"It heals. All illness. At the level of DNA, and cells, it simply... the mechanism is not important now. Anyway, so what she said, this Shaman, was that the long-lived family, once pressed, admitted to her that it was in possession of this cross. Handed down since the earliest days of the Hybrids, within one family, and hidden for decades until a rogue cousin discovered his grandfather had it and insisted that they all use it. So the cat was out of the bag, as they say, and then, well..."

Lucio wrung his hands.

"What?" Andrew asked.

"The family had all begun to use it, but more importantly, the cousin had by then begun to boast, and so by the time the Shaman had discovered its existence, others in the community knew about it and were trying to keep it a secret, but in fact a small mythology was growing around it and spreading fast. So, the Shaman held a meeting, and urged them to allow her, as their spiritual leader, to keep it safe, and determine its appropriate use. But some disagreed with her, and the fighting began. What's worse, they expelled her as their Shaman. They figured they didn't need one, given that they had this magical object."

"Oh, no."

"Within three months, their once peaceful people had split into three factions. One was peaceable, the family that had originally had it, and their allies. The other two were fighting and harming one another over it. So, in the middle of the night, the Shaman stole the icon from a warring family and fled. Here. To me."

"No! They couldn't find a way to agree, then!"

"Indeed not. Are you surprised?"

"Well. Not entirely, I suppose. Still, you'd think a good spiritual leader would be able to help her people understand the moral issue. But then, inevitably, word would get out to the wider public, because so many are unwell..."

"Andrew," Lucio interjected. He now sighed. "Do you recall when you were bullied, and I helped you to learn basketball so that you could make a stronger introduction?"

"Vaguely. I mean, yes, I recall those details. Why?"

"Do you recall that you no longer had troubles with our peers after that?" Lucio asked.

"Yes, of course."

"Why do you think that was the case?"

"Well, I suppose they no longer saw me as different, or considered me a threat." Andrew shrugged, but narrowed his eyes as if probing Lucio for the answer.

"Yes," Lucio said. "And what lesson did you take, do you think, from this example of bullies who then become—kind and agreeable? Bearing in mind that we were all trained in contemplation, so this was a unique case, in a way."

"What lesson did I take? I don't follow."

"About inherent goodness. About the human condition." Lucio smiled.

"Ah, our old debate," Andrew said. "I believed that beneath it all, most people are good."

"That humankind evolves towards the good because we *are* good," Lucio nodded.

"And you take the opposite stance, I know."

"Ah, but my stance has evolved, Andrew."

"As has mine, incidentally. I'm not the schoolboy I was, you know." Andrew smiled. "You would be happy to know that I've tested my theory in my romantic life, and I've come to the conclusion that not all people are good."

Lucio chortled. "I see. And I'm glad and not glad, my friend. What's your new view?"

"My view is that the soul itself is good, but inevitably we arrive at good via a path of learning what it is to be *not* good."

"The ego can experience being *not good*, you mean. But as per many spiritual views, the ego must be transcended." Lucio clarified, "Is that what you mean?"

"That's a very old viewpoint, and one that the Monasteries no longer propose, incidentally. I—we—take the view that the ego must learn to be *in service* to the soul. But we also admit that contrast is a very competent teacher."

"Very well. Our views are converging," Lucio said. "When I was doing my research, this Shaman used to say to me that she knew the answer to my research questions, that all of consciousness knew all of the answers, and she used to laugh and say that the scientific method was the slowest way to Truth with a capital 'T.' I believe this to be true, actually, but the method is what convinces others, it's what moves the needle in slow moving establishments like the Sciences Institutes or the Monasteries.

"She also told me then that some people will never make the most beneficial decisions even if their consciousness is expanded through plant medicine such that they can experience the expanse of all reality, because the individual's free will simply interferes. One's free will, or ego as it were, does not always in every case *want* to embody its greatness beyond ego. Sometimes it wants smallness and must evolve through smallness. It's no use showing someone who cannot add or subtract the beauty of calculus. That beauty is meaningless without the foundation. I digress."

"I agree that we're on the same page," Andrew said. "Except for maths. Never my strong suit."

"Very good. Suffice it to say, once the Shaman had stolen the icon, she came to me because she trusted my judgment. More to the point, she knew that I had both the ability and the moral willingness to conceal the object completely. But that's not the only reason she gave it to me to hide. It's just one object, after all, and we have a global population that is dying."

Andrew nodded. "If it actually heals, still it's an impossible task—to share this object around with all of humanity is not feasible."

"Yes, that's it. We both knew it. The Shaman and I understood that we needed to find the origins of the cross. To discover how it was made and attempt to replicate that on a large scale."

Andrew shook his head wordlessly. "Do you actually think it works?"

Lucio said, "I have run some tests, on samples of the metals from which it is constructed, and yes. I do believe it works."

"Incredible."

"The science is incredible, yes."

"So why have you brought me here? You said back then that you would need an ally. But I don't understand how I can help? Help keep it concealed?"

"There is one more part of this story yet to share."

Lucio swallowed. Suddenly, he was aware that he was hot, and that his friend was sweating. The room had a cooling system, but still, it was a much warmer climate than Andrew was accustomed to, and Lucio noticed his friend pulling at his robe to loosen it around his neck.

"It's hot, I know," Lucio offered.

"Yes. And for some reason I'm nervous," Andrew said.

"Don't be, my friend. I am with you."

"I am part of this concealment now. Concealment of potentially the greatest discovery of our time."

"Yes." Lucio leapt up to fill their glasses again. "Drink. Breathe. We have time."

"Do we, though?" Andrew emptied his glass for a second time.

"Not in the grand scheme of things, perhaps."

"So tell me, Lucio."

Suddenly, Lucio's creased brow, his pursed lips. He sat back down.

Andrew blinked his eyes rapidly, as if he'd seen a ghost.

Lucio stared at his friend, and in an instant saw him as an old man, white beard and wrinkles, like Atlas with the world's weight bearing down upon him.

"Your help will be crucial," he said in a hoarse voice.

"Yes?" Andrew spoke at a near-whisper.

"Andrew, the icon comes with a prophecy, from that family which owned it. They told the Shaman this story before the fighting, before she stole it. It partly was what compelled her to seek me."

Andrew blinked. Lucio straightened his posture in the plush armchair, pressing his reclining arms into the armrests as he leaned forward, conspiratorial.

"The Hybrids said that the Great Spirit, which is what they call divine energy or higher consciousness, channeled to them information about this icon. They said that Spirit ensured that healing be put in a cross because that was how humans could best understand it, at the time of its creation. Humans only knew religion and objects, and so they put this substance in the form they knew would be treated as holy. But there is more of what created it, the substance from which it was created. They say that the time has come to discover it in order to save humankind. They said that a man will travel back through his consciousness to when this cross was made, so that its origin can be known, and its creation iterated. So that humanity can be saved. And that this individual will be known as a traveler in time, and hunted down by powers that would keep the cross for the few at the expense of the many."

Andrew seemed visibly relieved. "Okay. A prophecy is not what I expected, but it is a clear path forward."

Lucio's heart pounded. He hoped Andrew felt the truth of it, as had he when the Shaman first shared it. Truth felt solid. *Weighty,* like his mind hitting the hard edge of something that demanded recognition. He felt this kind of Truth sometimes in meditation, a practice he'd not abandoned even when he left the Monasteries for the Sciences Institute.

Lucio stared at Andrew, gauging his response as he spoke softly. "They said that the traveler is a monk. He has just been born. He will be an orphan of war, not the virus, and will come of age in a monastery in the Eastern Federation. Which is your region."

Andrew only closed his eyes, and

Lucio felt that feeling again, the hard edge, and now it morphed into the solidity of something real between them. He said, "I would not normally believe such things, had I not experienced them myself. The sciences are, as you know, rigid in their approach. I've always kept my mind open…"

"I know," Andrew spoke reassuringly.

"The Shaman could not return to her people, as she had stolen a prized possession, and also for herself, she knew far too much, for which reason only she had the power to act on it. An isolated Hybrid community could never act on a prophecy like this! So, after pleading for my assistance, she left for the city. She changed her name. She sees no choice but to seek a future in our world, in the hope she can assist, when the time comes. When this baby is a man. Because as the prophecy said, forces will discover him, and oppose him. It further said that time itself will split, and there will be a future of healing, and others with less happy outcomes. And this woman, this Shaman, she journeys between worlds, sometimes in animal form, or she so claims. Her intention is to protect this traveler, and ensure he discovers the origin of the icon."

Andrew spoke. "This man, who holds the key, he will be a monk, in my region?"

"Yes. So now you know why I have called you here." Lucio rose from the chair as if he'd dropped the heaviness of the past and future alike, and now weightless, floated to the opposite end of the room from the kitchen. He paused at a collection of plant pots just beyond the floor-to-ceiling window. He bent down, pushed some pots out of the way, and dug his fingernails into a small ledge. He tugged a couple of times until there was a click and something loosened. There was an audible *swish* of a heavy thing sliding.

Lucio stood. He held a velvety, black bag. He walked back to Andrew, and lay the bag across his lap.

"See for yourself."

31

REUNION

JULY, 2019

NEAR MAR CHIQUITA LAKE, ARGENTINA

"See for yourself," Kate said, and held up the padded envelope for Mateo. She pulled out the cross. She placed it next to the small cut on his finger, a minor cooking mishap. They watched together, mesmerized, as over a few minutes, the cut closed over and the skin regained a soft sheen. Kate's heart pounded, since even after all she'd been through, all she knew, she now *saw*.

Mateo was impressed—she could tell. But not overwhelmed as she would have expected. He kept nodding, then at last, "Yes, yes, it is remarkable. Just as Michael told me."

That's it? She thought.

She had hidden it for a few weeks, nurturing trust in Mateo, in herself, in the cross, before she felt ready to place it in his care. He never asked. Never exerted any pressure; not even his manner betrayed impatience or curiosity. Instead, he guided her to tend to the land, to the hearth, and Little Bird participated in everything. Her little backpack lay neglected in their shared bedroom. Kate found some children's shows in English for her to watch in the evenings, so that the girl wouldn't forget their shared language. She hadn't so far, even in the days of long silences,

collecting firewood outside,

harvesting in the greenhouse,
feeding the horses,
the Pampero winds flattening the long golden grasses
with a chill that blew through them in this waiting time.

In the mornings, Little Bird wore a woollen beanie pulled down her forehead, her nose pink and cold.

Now Kate assessed Mateo's reaction to the icon.

"So you understand then, why this must be hidden well. It will bring us trouble if anyone knows about it. There are already people looking for me..."

"Yes, I understand the importance. To you, to history, to the future. I promise that I will keep it safe. I have made arrangements. In the event I am no longer able to protect it, another will. If anyone discovers it here, it will be relocated far away, to the Andes, to a community that will protect it. And we will do what we must."

What we must? He gave her a smile. *What did he mean,* Kate wondered. They had discussed so little beyond practicalities. She didn't know what he knew, what Michael had told him. Or Jia Li. Their shared understanding, after a week here in the Argentine countryside, just Mateo and Kate and Little Bird, was that she and the girl would stay—

That they *must* stay, and as Mateo had more than once said, *there will be a lot to do here, together.*

"What exactly is your profession? Your past, if I can ask." Her confidence had caught up to her curiosity. They knew each other now, even after so short a time, and all tucked within a daily rhythm that enfolded simplicity, that implied trust. She continued in the next breath, "What have you experienced that this icon, what it can do, isn't freaking you out, or concerning you, and what is this *a lot that we will be doing*..." She emphasised her words carefully.

"Ah. I know magic." Mateo took the cross, so gently, from Kate's open hand, and returned it to the envelope. He tucked the envelope under his armpit and held it there, watching the horses across a paddock from them, beyond the Algarrobo trees where he had made

Little Bird a picnic lunch earlier that day; he seemed to speak to the distance, the ungraspable, to the just beyond.

"Once, I was determined to create solutions. I quickly learned that if you create something that could give for free what corporations and governments control, what they demand payment for, well it isn't allowed. I, too, created. I was interested in air travel without pollution. I created an engine using rare alloys to power planes. But. My patents were canceled or my research destroyed. My life was threatened. By the time I met our friend Michael online, I had decided that our era was not ready for innovative solutions. We needed education, first. Awareness of the systems of corruption. I guess you could say that my work as a scientist-entrepreneur turned me into an activist. So that is why, now, you are here, and that is why you must stay. I know what is happening. Michael told me everything. And there is no one else who can do anything about it. We have the cure, we have Grace, and so we must be responsible to the future. The world is not ready for answers. It hasn't yet even asked the right questions."

He took in Kate, and she saw something in his eyes, *wetness*. He quickly looked away. She thought of Finley, and Jia Li. A wave of longing and grief washed through her.

"Where is everyone else?" She also looked towards the paddock, noticing now how the Algarrobo savoured the wind, its branches swaying the way a very old person dances, thoughtful and slow.

"We will know soon. If your friends have survived, we can expect them to come here. And we will together ask the right questions."

She could not say, *and if they do not come?*

YET THAT MOMENT DID ARRIVE, and when it did, Kate couldn't believe that it was Jia Li who emerged from the green car at top of the property. It had been weeks, but also a lifetime, and no word, nothing. It was enough to convince them both of one another's death. Kate was unable to move from the window, breath held,

and not just because it was *her*—

something was wrong.

Jia Li was pale and unsteady, and Kate felt sickness radiate from her every pore as she took faltering steps down the driveway, but then Mateo came out and a few words were exchanged and

Kate rushed outside, but stopped short of her, this ravaged woman, her pallor yellow, eyes sunken. She coughed.

Her voice was raspy, weak. "It's okay. You have the icon. I'll be better soon. They got me. But I got them, too." She managed a smile.

"Oh, God," was all Kate could muster, as Mateo took Jia Li's bag. Suddenly the significance of Jia Li's presence, there, of both of them *together* fully landed. She felt their shared note of overwhelm.

It was so much, to be there, safe,

and their momentary held breath contained the consciousness of lifetimes lived waiting for love to arrive.

Suddenly, Little Bird ran outside to where they all stood, the way children do, bringing with her sunshine and sorrow, innocence and the seeds of her small, passionate mission:

"I am staying in this home," she announced to no one in particular and everyone present. And she twirled, pulling out from behind her back a small ripe tomato. "*Invernadero*," she said, mulling over this new word, *greenhouse*. She had been gardening with Mateo all morning. She pronounced, "We grow *all* the vegetables *in the entire world!*"

Kate pulled her close, leaned down and kissed her on her forehead.

Jia Li's eyes filled with tears, and she moved forward—Little Bird squashed between them until she wiggled her way out and ran to Mateo with the tomato—but the women lingered,

pressing into each other's hips, Kate's face nestled into Jia Li's neck, breathing in her acrid smell of sickness, and Jia Li's hand in the small of Kate's back, holding her in place,

as the air buzzed with the pulse between them, of terrified desire and relief's unrestrained tears, all of it on a rollercoaster of longing and magnetism and fear,

and in their embrace spiraled a looping inevitability, not just of bodies finding their way home, but of souls finding their way in a new world without a map,

but with a shared mission.

With this girl, this tomato, this place, all of it a new foundation.

Jia Li said, "We made it," and kissed Kate on the forehead, tentative and self-assured all at once.

Her fierceness was still there, Kate observed, even in her weakness.

***

JIA LI DID NOT WANT to say his name, to voice any concern, and evidently neither did Kate, so instead Finley was a silent, invisible guest at the table, the one whose chair was empty,

but was there with them all the same.

"I am leaking it all," Jia Li said, catching Kate and Mateo up on her discoveries, after she'd had a night with the icon pressed into her side, Kate's arms wrapped around her. Her color was restored, strength returned twofold, her face flushed with passion. "And I won't stop until justice is done. If it takes my entire life. I will do whatever it takes, flood social media, speak out online, whatever, but we, this place, we remain in secret. Mateo has agreed. We must stay, live here, work together. We cannot tell anyone it is here. That we are here. No one here is safe."

Kate took her hand, "We're safe here. As safe as we can be."

The girl was always near Kate, on her lap, at her side; with every short dance away she returned, re-anchored in Kate's presence, her body now the temple where Little Bird remembered safety.

"What are you looking at?" Kate teased Jia Li.

"You. Real you."

"You've changed too," Kate laughed, "you were a thief, you stole the truth—and now you're the rebel, and apparently we have a cause."

"Yes."

Kate took her hand and Jia Li lit up to feel her so solid by her side.

"Anyway, no expectations," Kate said. "Let's take it day by day."

In politics or in love? Jia Li wondered, but both were true.

"What about the icon?" Jia Li asked. "Where can it be hidden?"

"It will rest beneath the pomegranates and the figs," Mateo said, passing by the table with firewood.

Plates clinked as the sink was filled. Little Bird laughed at something Jia Li said. Stars poured through the gauze clouds and Kate got up to step outside and light a fire in the firepit.

"Hey girl," came the most familiar, unfamiliar voice—

Kate grinned—*as if she'd been expecting them!* But of course, Jia Li thought, because she'd made Kate promise to give Mateo's address to Victoria and Mary. And so there they all were.

Jia Li ran to embrace her vibrant mother. Kate yelped in excitement to see her friend—but Victoria hadn't even made it to Kate before Little Bird realized who had arrived, and, jaw dropping, screeched in glee at the top of her lungs. She leapt up into Victoria's arms like a monkey scaling a huge tree, and she hung there in a trembling ball, mutely crying into her shoulder.

DAYS PASSED. Jia Li was in touch with Michael. He had tried to make it to the airport to fly to Mexico, but was being followed, so at the last minute he turned back, hid with a friend for a few days, then fled overland to Harbin where he had an ally. Once there he began to leak what information he had. Jia Li begged him to come to Argentina, but Michael was afraid to draw any attention to himself, and so he committed to gathering more allies in Harbin.

Jia Li missed him with an ache of resignation; the distance between them would be permanent, inescapable, if they each had to remain in hiding on different continents. Still, with Michael's virtual support, she and Kate filled their days creating a strategy,

    teaching Little Bird to read English and, with Mateo, Spanish,

    and the nights wrapped in the comfort of each other, rediscovering joy,

    not taking their time at all,

    because between them there was a portal,

where the softness of a single kiss collapsed time into
endless
nows.

Finley's name may not have been spoken were it not for Kate, who one day suddenly burst into tears—

"Finley, oh I miss him. It's killing me. Not knowing."

"I heard from his friend, Phil, in Australia..." Jia Li trailed off, admitting, "I didn't want to say it until it's definite. But just as I was leaving Hong Kong, literally when I was at the airport, this man texted me. He said he was Finley's friend, and that Finley had instructed him to send me Bitcoin... a lot of it. I didn't believe him at first, but he sent me documents. Anyway, I have a wallet. The coins will be sent soon, apparently, and if they arrive, we have funding. I just need—to find a way to sell it that doesn't lead back to my name."

Mateo, who with Little Bird was emptying a bag of potatoes onto the kitchen table, said, "Easy. I can arrange that."

"What can't you do Mateo? But Finley, oh my God," Kate said. "Typical. That he would send money, but no news." She wiped a tear from her cheek. "Valeri told me that Gutov confirmed he met Finley. Finley *found* him, and he went to wherever Gutov sent him. presumably to find out the origin of the icon... but then, no more news."

"We have what we need," Jia Li said. "We must press on." She took Kate's hand and kissed it. "I miss him too. Whether he succeeded or not, perhaps, with the truth out there, we can still create the future we need. Even if there are rocky times ahead. Perhaps this is the era of effort, not reward."

Kate gave a little sigh.

Yes, Jia Li thought,
arriving at a final truth:
*so it is better to speak,
no matter what.*

AND SO FINLEY returned to mist–
in the midst of busy days and nights.

No confirmation came.
He disappeared,
as if he'd never existed.
His form shape shifted,
from man to myth,
from myth to muse—
and the hours softened
like time that gathers in the stillness of memory,
until it is called again.

32

WALLACE & THE RETURN OF LOVE
JUNE 2131 AD

KRASNOYARSK, EASTERN FEDERATION

Wallace felt the oxygen return to his lungs in a sudden blast, which caused him to gasp, waking him up completely. Blurry faces pooled at the edge of his vision. He tried to sit, and came to his elbows behind him.

"Steady." Dr. Rinella spoke first, his voice dull and far away.

"Oh, thank God," Justicia cried.

Wallace could feel rather than see the final scene he had lived, the muddy ground, the clutch of trees and sky that seemed to come down upon him, the blow to the head, blackout.

"I don't know if I... if Finley... if he made it."

Now there was a hand on his chest, guiding him to lay back down.

"It hasn't worn off," Justicia said. "Just take your time."

"I'm here, it's okay," he reassured her.

"Just be still and take deep breaths," Schopel said. "There is no rush."

Wallace returned to fixed time, his only reference point the hard bed beneath him and the whirring of the Machine in the background. All of the patches had been removed. He wondered how long he'd lain there after returning to the present.

"It is done," he spoke at last, breathing heavily. "I have the coordinates. I have all that we need. It is deep in the earth about a day's travel from here over land. There will need to be an excavation. The soil contains trace remnants that created the alloy that the icon was created from. It will be there. In the earth. In the taiga... we are so close here..." His voice cracked and he trembled.

"Oh dear." Justicia came to his side and grasped his hand. "Whatever you've seen, or felt, you are safe now."

"I don't know the exact details, only what Finley knew. That there was an explosion in the sky in the early twentieth century in that region, a fireball, that no one understood the origin of at the time. Finley went there to tell me. To where the explosion impacted the earth, to where the metals had been found. He went there to show me exactly where, so that I'd know, without a doubt." He took a shallow breath. "I think... I think he sacrificed himself..."

Wallace gulped. His mind could not comprehend what it meant for one part of himself to put himself in harm's way for another part, consciousness divided, yet as one—and was he divided, or was all of him here, all of him safe now? He squeezed his eyes shut against the lingering sensations—the dust in his nose, the smell of damp earth and the rushing river.

"I don't understand if I survived, or he survived, or..."

"*You* survived, Wallace," Justicia said, squeezing his hand. "Now, take a moment, my darling."

Wallace's eyes remained closed as he began to take slow breaths through his nose. Justicia rested a hand on his heart. "Lucio, you must draw up a grant application. I shall make a report and a recommendation for funding. But how do we search in such a large area?"

Dr. Rinella said, "We have earth-moving machines, abandoned, but hopefully in working order." He added, "I will organize the expedition, the first party, in secret, and we will attempt to deliver the equipment shortly thereafter. But if we have discovered this—others may have, too. Or might not be far behind."

"No, Finley told no one." Wallace opened his eyes. "And he somehow blocked interference."

"I can vouch for that," Schopel said. "Our enemies could not join.

They found no way in. It was only Wallace's resonance, and ours, by extension, and their weapons did not work."

"Just in case," Justicia said, "You mustn't say exactly what you're looking for. We must be clever, so as not to tip anyone else off."

"Agreed," Dr. Rinella said. "I am going to get the ball rolling in secret. Meanwhile, I'm going to the Institute at Miramar. It's best if Wallace comes with me, as the dust settles here. Justicia, you come as well."

She tilted her head and squinted at him.

"You want me to come with you? Why, Lucio? What will be the reason? I mean, of course I want to accompany Wallace..."

"I will think of a reason, officially. You will understand once we are there, and be forever grateful. And maybe even a smidge less high strung." Spoken with a twinkle of his eye.

Wallace didn't understand what seemed to be coded communication, and felt slightly uneasy about it—but anyway, he was relieved that if he had to travel, Justicia would be at his side.

Father Andrew lifted his face towards the Cottage's small skylight, somehow beatific in that instant. Dr. Rinella moved away from Justicia and Wallace, around the equipment, and went to stand by his old friend.

Wallace stared. *What were those two up to now?* He wondered.

"And it is done," Dr. Rinella said softly.

"As you'd planned," Father Andrew said.

Schopel moved to join them.

"I will come with you, Lucio. I haven't been home in a very long time. Not since I left to seek your support. We have done it. I need to return to my people now. It's been long enough."

Father Andrew took her in as if anew. "Did you say, *To your people?*"

Wallace was confused. He struggled to take in the conversation.

Father Andrew exclaimed to Schopel, "You were the Shaman. Your identity has been secret but you hinted—you were from a Hybrid community! It was you!"

Schopel merely smiled and gave a small nod.

Andrew's gaze bounced between his two colleagues. Dr. Rinella sighed, his manner awkward and yet innocent, in the way long held secrets admit relief.

"What's going on?" Wallace asked, rousing himself somewhat. Justicia's hand had remained on his heart all this time, and now she moved it gently to settle him, her attention simultaneously fixed to the unfolding conversation.

Father Andrew wiped his eyes, which had begun to leak. He ignored Wallace completely, addressing Schopel. "I should have known. Your visioning skills. Your entire life. *The last thirty years*. All for this moment. And I never knew your identity..."

"I've been in service to something beyond the politics of our era, as you have been *your* last thirty years Andrew," she said.

Dr. Rinella clasped his hands together. "Full circle, friends."

Father Andrew collected himself. "I will make your transfer to the Cordoba Monastery nearby, Eden. And then you may disappear, should you wish. I will make sure there are no questions."

Justicia narrowed her eyes in their direction. "You all realize that you will need to do some explaining, please."

To Wallace, the room went hazy. He needed no explanation now, as something odd was taking shape within him. His scalp tingled. His breath came faster. His closed eyes squeezed out tears, and he took Justicia's hand, still clasped at his heart, into both of his.

"My love, what's happening? Are you okay?" she asked him.

He whispered, *Shhhh*.

Even as the others had been talking about the last thirty years, about going to the Cordoba Monastery, and even as Wallace sensed—without fully comprehending—the secret collaborations that had led them all to this point in time,

he had begun to surrender to the inner process that rose to consume him,

and he fell into it now, knowing not if there were a net to catch him—

His mind replayed earlier memories, childhood memories, which presented themselves as if for the first time, cast out of some dark holding place in his subconscious.

A dam burst within him, rent him open to relief, to grief, to the overwhelm of discovery. His tears flowed, and he softly cried, it seemed to him, for everything and for nothing. Time wound back, back before he'd encountered Finley, to memories the Cottage was supposed to have neutralized, but could no longer, and his mind finally admitted the image of his mother's arm laying bare with her small wristwatch and the rest of her body pinned beneath blackened concrete of the building. And his father, across the rubble, an ash-covered corpse. Through the dry gaze of a young boy, he saw the unseeable, only now his adult self released the tears the boy had withheld,

a quiet but mounting crescendo, as if oceans washed him through, clearing what lay uncleared,

the memory and the ashes,

and he saw the luminous pearl-white center of his being, inside which he felt

the love he'd had for his parents, and still had

burst into glowing, warm, multi-colored memories of boyhood.

He couldn't stop the flood, nor attend to the conversation surrounding him, or Justicia's silent but concerned presence; he couldn't have stopped had he tried, so he didn't, even as sheer, crazy joy rode in on waves of grief-stricken love—

not separate beasts as he'd known all along,

but one and the same.

And then, with one outtake of breath,

time shattered.

Wallace felt the past release him, every second and every point on every timeline and he opened his eyes to see Justicia, her green eyes, and her warm hand stroking his thumb as she said, "Shhh, shhh, I am here. I love you."

He fell into that present moment, into her eyes, as one might fall into deep sleep after a long, exhausting night, his mind aloft and empty, his heart at rest, and he knew himself to be safe at last.

33

THE ICON
2089

NEAR MAR CHIQUITA LAKE, ARGENTINA

Beneath Mateo's orchard, where the earth wept salt, the soil hummed with a power none had felt since the time of the mystic, the monk, the prostitute and the thief, even though the monk had not yet been born, and the others had played their parts so well that even memory could not recall their contributions.

Yet they were the ones who, in the times of collapse, sang softly into the fractures,

to remind the world it still had a voice.

The fig and pomegranate trees clung to the slope, their roots curled to draw moisture from what the Earth remembered.

They survived to bear fruit—

even as cities fell, and across continents, rebel fires burned, populations dwindled, frogs and cranes disappeared, and orphans trembled,

and even though none of the heroes would live to see the healing,

they walked toward the dusk as if dawn already warmed their feet,

and it did,

And it will.

ACKNOWLEDGMENTS

I am so grateful to those who supported my spiritual and creative path even without knowing *IKONA* as a work. I am particularly grateful to the teachers and peers whose unique embodied awakening path helped me uncover the impulse and conviction to finally birth this novel into the world. A special acknowledgement to Rachael S: *your belief in me as an artist was a voice in the dark at a crucial personal and evolutionary threshold.*

I had the input of Tory H when I really needed a copyedit and feedback into various aspects of this enormous story—*thank you for your attention.* Then at the finish line, I was blessed with an editor with a keen eye for continuity and grammar—*thank you Reigh.*

To my children and my parents: *thank you for your love and quiet belief in me across the years.* Daniel, Hannah, and Galen spent much of their childhood watching me write without a book to hold in my hands, so it's satisfying to release this novel as they find their wings in the world as young adults.

To my daughter for encouraging me to publish this, no matter the nature of its birth. *Your devotion to your own path as an artist has given me the courage to walk mine.*

To J, for your support, belief, and insight into my writing across so many years. At some point, I internalized your master wordsmith with its potent intersection of poetic sensibility and the grammarian's precision. *I am deeply grateful for your belief in me as a writer.*

To R, my love, whose devotion and steadiness have never wavered, even in my most uncertain hours. *Thank you for being the one* person, pre-publication, to read IKONA from start to finish, hanging on every word, tearing up for reasons neither of us could name. Your support at every level has been a treasure chest of gold, one I happily rely upon and unfailingly receive.

And to this novel, this strange and beautiful thing that insisted on being born: *thank you for choosing me as your vessel. Writing it was a blessing and an honour.*

Finally, I am an introvert. A quiet therapist, a suburban parent. Unknown to networks, distant to decision-makers. It was daunting to find any industry support for *IKONA*. In the end, I birthed this novel without a publisher, without an agent, without institutional backing. The rejections numbered over two hundred. The encouragements came like whispers. Still, I chose to finish. I chose to trust the work. I chose to walk this through.

In the absence of external permission, I gave it to myself.

For anyone who knows the ache of carrying something that is meant to be shared, and finding the world not yet ready to receive it:

Write it anyway.

Walk it anyway.

The gate does not open.

You become the gate.

And to those who are at last walking through this particular gate and reading *IKONA–*

It is you who make this real.

Not the gatekeepers. Not the systems.

But you who choose to listen,

who open the page,

who walk with the story.

You are the ones who carry it forward.

By reading this, by passing it on,

you are casting a vote for stories

that ask no permission,

but quietly awaken something within,

so that something can shift without.

In a world of noise, you chose to listen.
Thank you.
Thank you.
Thank you.

ABOUT THE AUTHOR

MD Dixon is a somatic therapist with fifteen years of clinical experience, based in Sydney, Australia. Dixon also holds a Ph.D. in the social sciences, specializing in Russia and Ukraine.

A lifelong student of consciousness and the healing arts, Dixon fuses lived and professional experience with visionary fiction to explore the liminal spaces between past and future, science and mysticism, personal trauma and planetary transformation.

Dixon's work spans the written word, therapeutic practice, and a commitment to human and collective evolution. *IKONA* is Dixon's first published novel.

Dixon also hosts *The Shattering Place*, a podcast that presents a multidimensional framework for healing and consciousness—a protocol for being human inspired by the central themes of *IKONA*. The podcast launches in early 2026 on all major platforms.

JOIN THE COMMUNITY

IKONA may have moved something in you—if so, and if you're drawn to themes like resonance, awakening, reincarnation, timelines, and futures seeded in the past—you're warmly invited to join the free online community of readers.

☞ ikonathecommunity.com

INNER CIRCLE MEMBERSHIP INCLUDES:
    Unpublished scenes and bonus passages
    Concept art and character illustrations
    Podcast exclusives and live online events
    Invitations to contribute to a living, co-creative archive
    And more to come with your participation!

THANK YOU

Thank you for entering the world of *IKONA*. If this story touched you in some way, I'd be honoured if you shared your reflections in a brief review on the platform of your choice (perhaps where you purchased it, or else on Goodreads). *Every review helps this work travel further, reader to reader, heart to heart.*